THE

FIRST

BRIGHT

THING

THE
FIRST
BRIGHT
THING

J . R . D A W S O N

TOR

TOR PUBLISHING GROUP • NEW YORK

This is a work of fiction. All of the characters, organizations, and events portrayed in this novel are either products of the author's imagination or are used fictitiously.

THE FIRST BRIGHT THING

A Tor Book
Published by Tom Doherty Associates / Tor Publishing Group
120 Broadway
New York, NY 10271

www.tor-forge.com

Tor® is a registered trademark of Macmillan Publishing Group, LLC.

The Library of Congress Cataloging-in-Publication Data is available upon request.

ISBN 978-1-250-80554-6 (hardcover)
ISBN 978-1-250-80557-7 (ebook)

Our books may be purchased in bulk for promotional, educational, or business use. Please contact your local bookseller or the Macmillan Corporate and Premium Sales Department at 1-800-221-7945, extension 5442, or by email at MacmillanSpecialMarkets@macmillan.com.

First Edition: 2023

Printed in the United States of America

0 9 8 7 6 5 4 3 2 1

This one is for the children masquerading as adults
who recognize the names of these towns,
the warmth of this family,
and the shadows of these villains.

And to J.
This is a love story.

... the misfits, the rebels, the dreamers, the joyous ... find your way to the circus.

—Advertisement bill for Windy Van Hooten's
Circus of the Fantasticals, dated April 1926

THE

FIRST

BRIGHT

THING

1

THE RINGMASTER, 1926

The Spark circus rolled into town on a Tuesday, early in the morning. The well-worn train snuck onto the tracks right outside of town as the birds woke and the dawn broke through the sleepy shadows of trees cloaked in an early mist.

Train spotters didn't notice the train's approach until it was nearly upon them, appearing in a blink and charging into town, the cars red and gold and blue with a name written along the side: WINDY VAN HOOTEN'S CIRCUS OF THE FANTASTICALS. The last two cars were purple and gold with flowers painted on their thick, sturdy wood siding, the windows laced with red curtains.

Today, here in Des Moines, there had been tracks for the train to appear on. On other days, in other towns, the train simply arrived in the middle of a field, with not a railyard around for miles. Like magic.

But no, it was Sparks.

The Circus of the Fantasticals worked on up-front deposits, meticulous yet flexible planning, and well-placed advertisements, like all circuses; but something more than a seasonal schedule also drove this particular train. The Spark Circus always arrived at the right place at the right time, even if it was just for one person who needed to see their show that night.

In a decade where the past was a nightmare and the future was a dream, the present was an unknown sort of way station where everyone seemed a little lost. Some would recall their visit to the Circus of the Fantasticals vividly as a pivot in their lives; others would simply be inspired to do better or think differently, with no catalyst they could quite put their finger on but would likely trace back to that one time they went to see the circus.

Today, June 8, 1926, was Des Moines, Iowa's turn.

By the time the city awoke, the circus was set up in their rented plot near the tracks. Some townsfolk skipped work and most children ran from chores to watch on the plot's outskirts while the Sparks emerged from the train cars to put up the Big Top and make the midway appear. One Spark changed into an animal, another multiplied themself to get things done faster, while another lifted wagons above their head. The townsfolk might have been slightly afraid, but as the day got older and the posters went up all over town, as they watched with growing fascination, they realized this might be their only chance to see something extraordinary, and so they went to the circus.

The midway held the youth of smoky July evenings and the feeling of a young body rushing down a very steep hill. Something in the electric string lights hanging above, the musical chime of carnival games and candy carts, brought back a safe home that everyone seemed to remember but had never been able to find. Until tonight.

There was a squeal and a small stampede of children dragging their mothers to follow them up a little wooden bridge. The bridge led to the sideshow, which was for everyone, not just gentlemen. And it wasn't a cheap exploitation. It may have only been made of plyboard and luminescent paint, but it still held something exciting in the way it invited the audience to run through it, to explore in their own way. Halfway through, giggling children bounced on a rubber bridge with just enough give, and their parents stood in awe inside a tunnel that looked like it spun through outer space. It was technology carved and moved by wooden gears, like something out of Georges Méliès's dreams.

But the Big Top itself—the archetypal main event—was admittedly nothing special. In fact, it looked more beaten down than other passing circuses the townspeople had seen before. The tent was tattered red-and-white canvas and muslin, thriftily yet expertly sewn together. The audience seats were only benches on bleachers set in a circle outside rings of flimsy painted sawdust curbs with areas on the ground level for those who would have trouble climbing up the rickety steps. The floor was dust that was easy to traverse but still coated boots and wheels and nice Sunday shoes all the same. The lights were too sharp, too few, and seemed mostly to spotlight just how dirty and ramshackle the inside of this Big Top was. It seemed to resemble a barn more than a theater, held together by spit and glue rather than nails.

But that was just the preshow.

When the tent went to blackout, when the audience hushed and the spotlight clicked on, there, in the halo of illumination, stood the Ringmaster.

Commanding in a bright red velvet coat, the Ringmaster looked out to the audience from the center of a large ring. Middle-aged and looking every bit a lioness, the Ringmaster had a wild mane of golden-brown hair that frizzed in the heat, didn't dry fast enough in the cold, and was somehow always getting in her white face, which was either sunburned with a thousand freckles or as pale as a ghost in winter. She had black eyes, unheard of, that either glimmered with possibility or dulled with the density of a black hole. Some thought she was beautiful, some thought she was brash, but it was undeniable that she would take them on an adventure.

When she smiled, it seemed to the crowd like she was looking at the world for the first time. As if she had just caught her first glimpse of them, saw the brilliance of their hearts, and had known what great things they'd already done and would do. The smile was a genuine embrace, the first bright thing in this dark, dusty place.

"Welcome," she said, to every single person in the audience. "Welcome home."

The Ringmaster had run this show from spring to fall for the last six years. Its rhythms shifted slightly from season to season, making room for new Spark performers as their family grew, as their tent got more threadbare, and as she learned more and more what she was doing. She had to remember that, didn't she? That she knew what she was doing.

She fixed the cuffs of her jacket and gave a small bow to the audience, her top hat appearing in her hand. The audience sounded with a small wave of surprise, and her smile grew. "We are honored to be with you for this precious hour." To the side, the Ringmaster saw the interpreter repeat her words in sign language. It looked like a confident dance. "Before this, we may have been strangers. After this, we may never see one another again. But what happens tonight, we will hold together in our memory. And so we are family. The acts you will see may seem out of the limits of this world. But I assure you, this circus is as real as you and me. When we dream for something to be beautiful, it can be. When we wish for the impossible, the impossible can find us. If we just want it loud enough."

That was Mr. Calliope's cue. He was a man made of pipes and strings, and now he smashed down on his brass bones, creating wind that rang out in chords and cadences. The sound enveloped the audience in a well-timed crescendo as the spec parade made its way from the wings and into the hippodrome, dancing in time with the music.

Kell swooped above on his wings.

Tina, a menagerie all her own, transformed from one animal to another.

The fire-breathing archer, the tumblers that floated in the air, the clowns that grew and shrank, all of it a dream.

All of it heaving, flying, singing, pounding with the cheers of the audience. The Ringmaster couldn't see their faces beyond the spotlight, but she could feel the energy radiating onto the arena's stage.

It felt like wonder.

The Ringmaster raised her arms, as if wrapping them around the audience. "Tonight, we celebrate us! We celebrate you! And what we can do together!"

Above, on cue, flew Odette, the blond-bobbed trapeze swinger who looked like an ivory doll. From the platform beside Odette came Mauve, her deep umber skin draped in purple silks, singing with a voice as smooth as a maestro playing her violin. She hit each note then glided to the next as Odette soared on silks.

The Ringmaster loved seeing Odette joyful. The trapeze swinger wore happiness like she wore her sequins, bright and shining and refracting light off her curves like she herself was a star bursting to connect with the dark world around them. Odette had a kind and hopeful soul. And the Ringmaster was lucky enough to hold her heart.

The Ringmaster ran to where Odette would soon descend. She took the bottom of the silk and swung it in a circle as Odette danced high above. The spotlight cut through the dust, illuminating them both, their dislodged locks of hair like golden crowns.

The Ringmaster held the silk steady while Odette flew in circles. The spec parade faded away, back offstage, while Mauve still sang above. The Ringmaster knew the others were getting ready for their next cue. This was Odette's moment.

Here, in the shadow of Odette's love, lived the life the Ringmaster had never been promised. As she held tight to the silk, the Ringmaster imagined herself looking back down a mountain to see how far she'd come. When she had started climbing, she couldn't have imagined this view. And she didn't know when she'd gotten here, when she'd grown up and solidified a kindness around her. She didn't yell anymore. She didn't wake up with the world feeling like cardboard scraping against a concrete sidewalk.

In most Midwestern towns, you'd find a broken street full of potholes and dried up weeds. A street with no shade, hot and stagnant, like a boring Sunday afternoon before a stressful Monday. The feeling of not enough water and being too far away to find any. That used to be how the Ringmaster's life felt; a scratchy vest made of Sunday afternoons.

But now she had learned to take joy for granted.

Odette slipped down the silk, lowering herself slowly, almost sensuously, into the Ringmaster's waiting arms.

"You're doing wonderfully, Rin," Odette whispered.

Rin was the name used by those who knew her best, and her wife knew her better than G-d.

Rin held Odette's firm hips, her fingers feeling the rough sequin hems. Odette smiled, sweat beading down her rosy cheeks, and gave a breathy laugh as the audience swelled in cheers. Rin had nearly forgotten there was anyone else in this tent.

"Amazing job," Rin whispered.

"Love you," Odette said, squeezing her hand before bouncing away and waving emphatically at the audience. She bowed. And Rin felt a hook cut into her gut. If Rin had been a boy, or if Odette had been a boy, they could have kissed in front of these people. In fact, the crowd would have positively swooned for the two of them. Roaring into whistles and croons as they'd have held each other closer.

But even with all the love threaded between them, Rin reminded herself that she couldn't hold Odette for too long in the spotlight.

The audience was enchanted by them; their magic, their different-ness. But a kiss would break the spell, and the audience would realize the magic was no show. This was real. And it was all right to be different, until it wasn't.

The same people who cheered for the Sparks in the Big Top could send them to the sanitariums, where all the bright yellow wagons ended up. The same people in the audience who felt warmth in these lights could go home, realize they had previously been taught that these circus Sparks weren't special, they were freaks. And if the freaks weren't gone by the next morning, there may be a mob.

Rin knew there was a line to toe.

But that didn't mean she couldn't smile. So she did. They had made a home here in their circus, despite the world that did not want them to find a home.

But it was about to all get torn away.

As she smiled, as she looked out into the audience, Rin felt a piercing, cold stare among the many eyes watching her from beyond the spotlight. Like ice running down her back. It was unnerving, how quick the fear rolled back into her heart. How easily the past tore into the present.

Rin could only make out faces for a moment as the spotlight ran from her to Mauve, whose set was now beginning. She saw the usual crowd, families with children, young people on dates. Old women staring at the beauty with awe and old men trying not to cry. But there was someone else in there, someone who stood at attention, staring right at her.

A familiar dark brow. Sharp, angry eyes. A dangerous man. The Circus King.

Something in Rin seized. She waited, as the spotlight passed and shadow fell. But when the bright beam swooped once more across that section, he was gone.

He wasn't here. She was allowing him to infiltrate places he would never be. It was a phantom, a trick of the light. It wasn't real.

I'll find you. I'll find you, and I'll ruin you.

The show carried on.

She couldn't let his memory scare her any longer. He would not turn this into his. He was not a part of this life. She had made a new place for herself, far from him and anything he'd ever seen. This was her story. This was her circus, full of bright colored lights like rainbows, sequined costumes that reflected like prisms, and beautiful horses that could shift into beautiful women who could fly as high in the air as a dove.

This was her home.

✳

As the show ended, the Sparks froze and held their final position while Mr. Calliope struck a final triumphant chord. Right on cue, three copies of Maynard shut off all the lights (the spots, the board, and that one pesky ellipsoidal that wouldn't cooperate with the board). The performers on the floor had fifteen seconds of applause and blackout to vamoose, so they rushed out, disappearing as quickly as they had stormed onto the scene.

When the lights came back up, Rin watched as the crowd dispersed and stopped to poke at the props and set pieces, trying to spot any tricks up the circus's sleeves. Some circuses didn't allow audience members on the main floor after the show, but it was part of Rin's nightly ritual; to watch from the wings as the audience spilled onto the floor like the end of a baseball game, intoxicated and invigorated by what they'd just witnessed. Real magic was a strong drink to take in.

But tonight, there was a young woman who didn't look at the set. She stared right past the ring, past the hippodrome, and her eyes connected with Rin, who stood to the side.

The girl was dressed in an ill-fitting red smock. Her eyes were so empty, she could have been a doll. The smock she wore was not hers; it was Rin's. Rin had left it behind long ago, and now here it was, resurrected and worn like an omen. A threat.

Something deep in Rin told her to turn away, to run. If she acknowledged this woman, her worlds would collide. The façade would end.

Which was why she had to step forward.

"Hello?" Rin said. "Are you all right?"

The girl smiled, like a marionette with too many strings pulling at her cheeks, at the corners of her eyes, to make her face look like . . . his.

"There you are," the girl whispered.

It was all real.

The Ringmaster waited for the girl to take out a knife. To attack her. To hurt herself. To do something angry and unpredictable. To explode in a rage.

But she didn't. The girl only turned and walked away.

Before Rin could react, to call out or move to follow, the girl had disappeared into the crowd.

"Wait." Rin heard her own voice as if from far away. "Wait . . ."

It would have been easier if the girl had stabbed at her, or struck her with a fist, or *something*. Rin remembered the familiarity of him standing above her, saying nothing. He'd smile at her, soaking in her fear, as she waited for him to move, to speak. But he'd never had to do anything; he'd always known she was his. And he would make her rot.

She couldn't breathe. She stumbled back, and Odette grabbed her as she started to fall.

"Rin, darling, what is it? What's wrong?"

Rin shook her head, looking frantically at the faces in the crowd. He was here. He was here, in her home. He had been at her circus.

"He knows I'm alive," she said.

*

2

EDWARD, 1916

No one knows why the Spark came. But it came during the war.

Edward actually saw the beginning of the Sparks, because Edward was seventeen years old and stuck in the thick of the war on the Western Front. He didn't know that's what he saw, because he didn't know anything about Sparks. He'd thought he'd known a lot about war before he left London for these trenches. But he had not.

He thought glory waited. He thought he'd be a hero. He'd sat in his step-father's house, speckled with bruises on all the places that could be hidden, and looked out onto the streets full of proud marching boys ready to fight. He thought to himself that it looked like freedom. It looked like power.

They'd told him to go dig up the ground and sit in it, and glory would come.

They'd lied.

Edward had learned men with power created terror; they didn't drown in it. The ground wasn't supposed to be dug up. Boys weren't supposed to be thrown into these holes, waiting to be buried. He stood in a deep, deep trench, not yet dead but cut off from any life he recognized. The fields were silent, until they weren't. Somewhere beyond sight, but creeping closer, he heard the whistling thunderstorm of mortars and machine guns.

He couldn't breathe. He could barely swallow back vomit from the musty smell in the muddy air: a smell of men's blood and sweat, of earth opened and bombed, and of dead rats' flesh melting onto their bones. Gunpowder, tobacco, and piss. Planes above. Shite below.

Somewhere down the trench, Edward heard two boys laughing about a poker game. Or more specifically, they were laughing about him.

It seemed he didn't fit in here. Or anywhere. The first day, on the platform at King's Cross, all of them had someone to say goodbye to. Edward had stood alone. And when they stepped onto the train to pull out for their lie of an adventure, he found no one to say hello to. They had all paired up, old school chums or new mates who had seemingly learned from the same book how to speak and move. Edward felt like an alien, a thousand steps away and invisible.

If only he were still invisible. Now, the other boys knew he was weak, quick to anger, and even quicker to cry.

So it is understandable that all of this weighed heavier on his mind than what was happening . . . as some boy in a mask dug up a new part of the trench and hit something that sparked like a flint hitting a rock. Something small and soft (or was it small and sharp?) glinted like a flash of lightning. Then, as if it was the speck of a ghost rising from an uncovered grave, the light traveled upward and into the air of the world.

This was the Spark. Not that Edward knew that. No one knew that.

"Oi! Eddie!" one of the boys shouted. "Wallace whipped you hard yesterday, did he?"

Edward managed to breathe in and turn from the shoveling. "Don't call me Eddie."

"Oh ho hohhh!" they laughed.

Just wait until they were all back home, he'd make them pay for—

The earth exploded.

The whistle came before the fall. Then boom. Screams. The end of the world.

He heard a crack in his ear. He felt a surge in his body, up through his toes from the earth and into his heart and out his fingertips. The earth flew to the sky, and many things broke that could not be mended.

"GAS!" someone screamed.

Edward fell in the mud. He couldn't feel anything. He checked his limbs. What happened? His body was intact. He could move. Don't think of the danger, think of the next thing that must be done.

But then he saw the canister. It looked like a giant baby's rattle, and it bounced into the trench, thumping against the mud. It thunked into a thick puddle, and smoke hissed out like a serpent. A yellow ghost, come to collect souls. The boys shot upward into the fight, then fell down to the mud, crying and howling, the smoke curling around them, possessing them. They flailed. They were dying. The smoke split them from the inside, a horrific chemical destruction.

Edward screamed, scrambling to his numb feet. Bloody water splashed into his face. He needed his mask. He grabbed it as the gas cloud slithered closer, an apocalyptic avalanche. But when he put the mask over his head, he couldn't feel the suffocating, the foggy eyeglass . . . the hose.

He checked the hose.

It was torn.

"My mask!" he screamed, throwing his mask off and seeing the world again. He ran. "God *dammit* my mask! Give me a mask!"

And in a selfless act Edward didn't have time to comprehend, a boy named Nathan handed him his own mask and respirator.

Edward grabbed it and pulled it on as he started to run from the gathering smoke. Bullets and bodies erupted.

More men scattered, running upward to a fight rather than sitting down here and having their lungs filled with acid and water. But then those men shattered. Like a butcher shop exploded.

The tanks drew closer. The thick smoke curled with German shouts and British twangs begging and beautiful French words out of place and gasping and dying and a girl in a blue dress standing in the middle of it all, wide-eyed and . . .

Wait.

Edward blinked hard from under his mask. He must be hallucinating.

No. There she was, a girl in a blue dress, her hair in braids, white cheeks, and big eyes staring right at him. Her boots stood ankle-deep in the mud, and she seemed entranced . . . or in shock.

"Aide-moi!" he screamed through his mask. But she didn't say anything. Not French? "How'd you get here?!" He collapsed, screaming, drenched in sweat and fear. "Don't just stand there! Help me! Get out! Do something!"

When she heard him, all hesitation or fear vanished from her eyes. The girl shot toward him with the determination of a trained medic. She held out her hand. She touched his shoulder.

Everything disappeared.

A pop, a light.

✳

Edward stood on white sand, the sun setting before him and the girl. The waves crashed in a soothing rhythm on his mud-caked boots. Palm trees swayed above. A jungle crawled over steep mountains behind the girl's head. Up at the top of those mountains, Edward saw waterfalls cascading down into the air, and then dissipating. Like a city of clouds.

Edward's knees buckled, and he collapsed.

"I'm dead," he muttered through the mask.

The girl knelt down beside him. She took his mask off. He held his breath, but then realized how stupid that was. She was alive and breathing, and this wasn't France. It couldn't be France.

"What the *fuck* is going on!" He tried to scramble away from her, but his limbs failed him. He sat there, in the sand, shaking and crying. "Where are we?"

The girl studied his face. She also shook, but her voice was steady. "Where *were* we?" she said. Her accent. It wasn't British. It wasn't French.

"You're an American," he said weakly. "How—"

"Was that war?" she asked.

"Yes?" he said.

Her eyes widened. "I . . . was wondering why I all of a sudden felt different . . . like I'd gone down a hill on a fast bike, but I was just sitting at home. Then . . . I wasn't at home anymore. What happened?"

"What happened? You're asking *me* what happened?" Edward said, exasperated. "What the hell did you do?"

She shook her head, violently, and he realized she was as scared as he was. "I don't know. I was only thinking of somewhere quieter than where we were, just now. I've always wanted to come here."

"So this is a real place?"

"It's an island in Polynesia," she said.

"We're—did you say—in Polynesia?" he gasped, his throat scratchy. "You're a steamboat now, are you?"

"No, no, I . . . I don't know what . . . happened. . . . I've never done this. . . . I've never heard of anyone doing this. . . ." Her eyes slowly fluttered away from the fantastical beach, and sank with worry. "I don't know what to do. My mother . . . I have to get back to her."

"Where's your mother?"

She looked up at a palm tree. Her lip trembled. "New York," she said, exasperated.

They sat on the beach a while longer. None of this made sense. Maybe he *was* dead. Maybe they were both dead. But it didn't seem likely. He still had his muddy boots on. Surely in the afterlife, your boots were at least clean.

"My name is Edward," he said.

"My name is Ruth," she said quietly.

"How old are you?"

"Almost sixteen."

"I'm seventeen," he said. "You're a young fifteen."

"You're an old seventeen."

Then silence again, as the ocean came in and out. The tide rose. No one came to collect them. They were alone. He watched the sunset, and after a while, he realized she was watching it, too.

"You chose me," he finally said as her face danced in the purples and oranges of an ending. "Why did you take me with you?"

She shook her head, in disbelief. But she looked so genuine as she said, "It felt like you needed me to save you." She bit her lip. "This place probably belongs to someone. We need to leave. We should go back to France. We should try and save the others."

They could. But something choked him hard, inside. He knew if he went back, he would freeze. He would disappear. And if the gas got him or the tanks got him, he would die.

He took her hand. "No, please," he said. "No, forget about saving the other boys. We can't go back. It's too dangerous. Take us to New York."

She looked at him. She had such a sweet face. She understood his fear. She didn't say anything, but she clenched her thin fingers around his. She closed her eyes. He closed his. He took a deep breath in as he felt the sun slip away. The wind brushed his hair.

Then the beach was empty.

＊

3

THE RINGMASTER, 1926

The war had been over for many years. Grief had blended into everyday life. So the circuses had returned.

And with those circuses, the Ringmaster had come to be.

She needed to remember this, as she sat in the dark of her caboose, waiting for Odette and Mauve. She needed to remember things were different than they were when she last saw him. Years had passed. She had grown more than her fair share.

She looked at the space between her bed and the wall. She shouldn't reach down there to what she'd hidden. She didn't need to; she was strong enough without it. But why did she have to be?

She pulled the small flask out of its hiding place. She unscrewed the cap. But something stopped her from putting it to her lips. She'd promised Odette she'd try.

It would be a release, to let it go down into her brain and stop the electric worry. Rin had one foot in dark memories and one foot in fear about what was to come, and she tried to straddle sanity here in the today.

To just take one swig, just a little bit, she could breathe. It wasn't the alcohol that called her, but what the alcohol would give her: peace, and the pain she deserved.

But she screwed the cap back on. She stared soberly at the quilt beneath her, her head pressed against the wall behind. Out the window, the landscape moving, far away from Des Moines and now magically coming for Omaha from the west. She'd flown them to Kearney, then let the train speed along the tracks like it was a normal train, a real train, nothing to see here.

It would be all right.

She was no longer someone he knew. In fact, she had very much hoped he thought her dead and buried. Eternally out of his reach.

The past belonged to the war, to the man who had orchestrated her story, for a time. But she had reclaimed herself, built up defenses of love and beauty, until she felt not quite new, but restored. Like a piece of old furniture, unbroken and with new purpose.

But reclaimed and rebuilt or not, she would still take her circus and she would run. They'd shouted out a John Robinson, and the aftershow on the midway and in the Big Top abruptly ended in a sense of urgent danger. But everything had gone like clockwork, just like they'd practiced in drills, Rin preparing her crew for something she had never really thought would happen. The performers had hurried the few lingering members of the audience out the door. Maynard multiplied and hastily packed up the tents, the midway, the wagons, the sideshow, and shoved it all onto the fourteen train cars linked to the 4–8–2 Mountain engine. Mr. Weathers, the trainmaster, worked with Francis the Fire Starter and Yvanna to heat up the coals and get the train rushing. Once everyone was on board, the train shot forward into the night. Once the wheels were turning and they'd built momentum, Rin had tapped into her Spark, forced herself to concentrate long enough to stiffly move the whole train from Des Moines to the tracks west of Lincoln, rushing east to Omaha.

Then there was only the waiting. The uncertainty of the dark, black space beyond and ahead. Wide Nebraska sky above, dead black fields around them too far from the train's light to see.

You think you're so clever. But I was always the clever one. I know you're afraid.

She shoved her aged body off the bed, still holding the flask and gritting her teeth as she situated her trick leg to walk. Her stiff fingers fumbled around its black metal skin.

She'd promised Odette she wouldn't. It had been six years.

Odette and Mauve would be on their way to the caboose, making sure everyone else was comfortable and got food in the pie car since they'd had to vamoose before getting any dinner after the performance. They'd be here any minute, to get to work and plan for Omaha. But Rin felt a thousand years removed from them, and a million miles away.

Mauve and Odette had not known the Circus King. They knew him in name, they had seen his posters. They had heard the stories. But they had never looked him in the eye. Rin had not only known him, but she had loved him.

She felt the weight of the black flask in her palm. Sometimes the Ringmaster thought she was strong, and sometimes she thought she'd be better off disappearing into nothing.

You are *nothing.*

The girl in Rin's red smock, her monotone voice still whispered in Rin's ears. *There you are.*

The Circus King thought she was dead; she had abandoned her name on a grave for him to find. Years ago, in a cemetery in Chicago, she had cauterized the wounds of everything that had come before. As far as the world was concerned, she was dead. She could let go, start over, try again. And although she'd known it might not protect her forever, it had allowed her to sleep at night.

It had worked for a time, but now he knew—he was wrong, and she was very much alive.

"Rin?"

Odette and Mauve stood in the doorway, the vestibule and the dark night behind them. The metal door shut with a loud clang.

Odette spotted the flask. Rin sucked in air. She handed it over. Odette narrowed her eyes.

"I didn't," Rin said.

Rin knew Odette believed her. But Odette still walked back outside to the vestibule, and even though Rin couldn't see her, she knew she was dumping it out onto the passing gravel.

"Rin," Mauve said again. "Are you ready?"

She had to be ready. One show was done, and they had another show tomorrow night. It was past midnight, which meant they'd get into Omaha soon enough, have a little time to plan and sleep, then they'd get up and start unloading the wagons off the flats. It was usually something full of anticipation and excitement, like a perfect blue-skied day.

Rin looked out the back window, off past the caboose's end railing, as if she would see him trailing behind them.

"We knew this would happen someday," Odette said quietly.

"And now it's happened," Rin said.

"He doesn't get to take our joy," Odette said. "This isn't his circus. He doesn't get to scare us."

"He's more powerful now," Rin said.

"Why do you say that?" Odette said.

"Because I'm more powerful," Rin said, looking at Odette. She tried to believe she looked steadfast in the dark, solid and unafraid. "I'm strong enough, even if it's just enough to outrun him."

Odette took Rin's hand, gloves on. Even after all these years, Rin couldn't let Odette's bare hands touch her unless Odette was healing her. Because the only thing separating the Circus King's Spark from Odette's was good intentions.

"We're here, together," Odette said quietly. "You're not in this alone."

That made her feel worse. Because she *shouldn't* have dragged anyone else into this.

"If he comes," Rin said, "I'll handle him. But you two take the circus and run."

Mauve stroked Rin's hair. "If you're not up for our check-in, we can let it go for tonight. Odette and I can handle it."

"No," Rin said. "Let's do it."

My little starling, you lie. You are terrified. And I know it. I'm coming.

"Come on," Rin said.

The three of them sat on the bed, next to one another. Odette, the one who kept them alive and together. And Mauve, the financier and their navigator. Ringmaster, trying her hardest at being some kind of leader.

The last two cars doubled as the owners' living quarters and offices, and this was where the three of them belonged, here in the private caboose. The train was long; flatbeds for the poles and wagons and canvas, sleeper cars for the performers, even that pie car was put in when there was extra money last spring. They'd made it all quite comfy, their fourteen-car house on wheels.

There on Odette and Rin's bed, covered in colorful quilts that told a story of their years together, the three of them sat cross-legged taking deep breaths in and out. Mauve sniffed, clearing out her nose, then stared straight ahead as if a projector had just clicked on behind her eyes. They narrowed like she was searching through an encyclopedia for an entry she needed and couldn't find.

Her appearance was one of a time traveler; her natural hair was styled in a conglomeration of the current day's fashion and what she called a "pageboy" from the future. Her finger-curls framed her soft, brown face. Right now Mauve was not smiling, but when she did it was a big smile, with perfect teeth and a contagious laugh. Her cheeks were round and full. She had warm brown eyes, looking out to the world like she'd just gotten here and loved everything she saw. She hadn't just gotten here; she knew how ugly things could get. But she still kept looking at it like there was something worth watching.

Mauve's Spark was to see all of time like it was a book in front of her. It was so much for one person to hold. Rin sometimes feared Mauve would get lost, remembering the past, present, and future all at once. But perhaps those who are the most liable to float off are those who take the most precautions to tether themselves.

Odette, on the other hand, walked as if she was made of air, but her body was strong and her spirit was sturdy. Rin had learned over time, Odette wasn't holding on just for Odette's sake; she was holding on for Rin, too.

Something deep stirred within Rin; a warmth like a campfire in summer. Odette was beautiful. Even in this scary night, full of danger and darkness, Odette's presence shimmered. She was someone who would keep trying, someone who wasn't afraid, someone who knew how to love. She was Rin's favorite story.

She will leave you. And I will find you.

The cold chill of the love he taught her, replacing the promise of her wife. Rin's brain wanted to tell her that Odette wasn't real, the Circus King was real. Odette was too good to be true. The Circus King was too terrible to be a lie.

"Oh," Mauve said in that voice that swirled New Orleans and the Midwest together. Her childhood, her adulthood. She reached to the side of the bed and grabbed some Cracker Jacks. She stuffed them in her mouth, still staring ahead, as if she were enraptured in a book. "Okay, I see her."

Every night before a show, Mauve saw someone—"the special guest," they called them—someone whose life could be changed, if only they could see the right spark of hope or magic. With Mauve's direction, they would piece together what it was the special guest needed to see, and they would work it into that evening's show. A week ago, it had been a boy named Henry Dodds. Tonight, it had been a man who Rin hoped had still gotten what he needed, even with the Circus King coming in to mess with her head.

He'd named himself that: the Circus King. He had midnight-black tents, bloodred advertisements, and a crew and cast with Sparks under his control. Bad things happened when the black tents came to a town. Worse things would happen to Windy Van Hooten's.

Mauve's eyes flickered, a film reel flipping to the end of a roll. She shook her head and stared now at Rin. Rin stared back. Mauve wasn't far away, but there was a world between them. Rin gripped the bed quilt with clammy hands. Whatever Mauve said next, they could handle it. They'd handled everything before. Together.

"It's dark," Mauve said, hoarsely. "It's bad. It covers her—the guest. There's a dark over her and her brother, and it spans out to us, and further." Her eyes went back to the film reel only she could see, and despite the Nebraska heat, Rin shivered. Their review sessions had a pattern. Mauve would spot the glowing person in the town, she would list off facts about their life and what they needed, Rin would propose specs—acts—to weave the person's thread into different directions, Mauve would look to see if that would work, and Odette would say something about how it was getting late. They'd pick a spec, say goodnight, and crash into sleep.

For Henry Dodds last week, Mauve had pointed out he was alone, he was scared, and his brain had difficulties knowing what was real and not real. They had concocted a plan and then executed it. Henry had needed to remember why he had loved life before the trenches of war, so Mauve had sung a song about a mother and a child in her set, and the clowns did an extra five minutes. Then when Henry had approached the Ringmaster after the show, the three women had offered medical help from the next century. But the script was unfolding differently tonight.

"There's something in the future," Mauve now said, "and it's big. It doesn't just touch one person, but all the people I can see."

Mauve could not see everything, but she could see the dust that attached to her own thread of life, and that power had grown to see the dust on the threads of those she loved. Now, she'd honed her Spark to see their audience, anyone she met, or had met, or would meet. This was a crucial skill when it came to the business of their circus.

But now Mauve looked around the room, as if all the dead of the world surrounded her, her eyes getting larger, her mouth gaping. She was afraid. Rin had never seen Mauve so afraid.

The Circus King was pushed from Rin's mind, only to be replaced by something heavier. Rin had seen the war. She'd seen the plague. She remembered the entire world stopping, going eerily quiet, and even now years later, when she met a stranger with whom she had nothing else in common, they both held the war and the plague in their hands.

Odette gripped Rin's hand. Rin flickered a look in her direction. Odette's eyes were glued to the patterns on the quilt. Her mouth was a firm line. She knew, too. Something was different, something was wrong, something was coming.

"And when," Mauve said, her steady voice carrying on, "I try to look further, at other special guests, for the rest of the season, just a preliminary list, whatever this is keeps popping up, over and over, from all angles." Mauve hesitated, and she studied the air like it spoke to her, like she could see a small hole through time. Rin wished she could see it, too. "Then I look at us. I look at this train, all the people sleeping on it, where their threads lead. It all leads to the same place. A terrible dark place."

"The Circus King?" Rin asked, but Mauve only shook her head.

"I don't know."

"We have to go forward to see this dark thing," Rin said. "We have to know."

"And why?" Odette said. "There's no reason to jump anywhere tonight. This dark future can wait until morning at least, I'm sure."

"I only see it through threads and wisps," Mauve said. "I agree, if we jump, we can get a clearer picture of what exactly is happening."

"No," Odette said, untucking her legs, ready to leave this bed and dispel this dark feeling. "Whatever it is, the circus has weathered the Outside World a thousand times. We're safe here."

"We aren't," Mauve said. "I think we need to go see what it is, because right now no one looks safe from it."

Odette looked as if she'd been hooked to the back of a slow-moving accident and couldn't escape. She met Rin's eyes, like this was the last time they'd see each other on this side of the carnage. Her entire body was rigid. She clearly didn't want to go.

And Rin had the sinking feeling that the threat of the Circus King, all-encompassing just minutes before, would be preferable to whatever the next few moments would bring.

Rin looked away from Odette and back to Mauve. Some people, when using their Spark, would get exhausted. But others, like Mauve, were invigorated. And Rin saw that energy in Mauve's eyes now, like she could stay up all night, like she would stay up for days on end if that was what it took. Mauve wasn't going to let this go. And that's why they got along so well, because Rin wasn't going to let it go, either.

"All right," Rin said, tonight's tiebreaker. It was two to one.

So now they would go. Odette the healer, Mauve the seer, and Rin the jumper. Never alone. Always together.

The three of them had always been enough.

This was not the first time they'd jumped, not by a long shot. Over the years, they had jumped to keep the circus safe and to help the people who came to their circus.

Whenever someone wanted to join the Windy Van Hooten traveling show, Rin would ask, if they could change one thing about their life, would they still want to join the circus? And if there was anything they could do to help that someone, they would do it.

Just one rule to time jumping: no jumping before 1918. The past held a graveyard in Chicago, where Rin had left her name for the Circus King to find. It also held the beginning of the Spark, which they didn't understand but had all agreed was a gift they wouldn't jeopardize.

Rin quietly took a bracelet out of her pocket. She pulled the hemp string tight around her wrist. There was a sliver of hand-carved driftwood attached that read *not today*. She took a deep breath.

The reality they were about to enter was just a rough draft; it was not her home. It was not reality. Not yet. And anything to come could be changed.

They stood there for a moment, and Rin thought they must look like a menagerie of oddities. The Ringmaster with her freckles and her red velvet coat, Odette with her thin sparkling leotard and blond bob and glitter, and Mauve with her favorite shawl and her eyes already searching the map to where they must disappear.

The three were a Fibonacci sequence in a Renaissance painting, the coven of hags as the curtain rises on the Scottish play. They were three silly women in a world much bigger than they.

Playing as if you're important.

Odette rubbed Rin's hand softly. "It will be okay," she said quietly.

"Trust us," Odette had told Rin a long time ago, had told her a year ago, had told her weeks ago, days ago. "Trust yourself."

But right now, the future waited. And the future was much larger than her, or Odette, or Mauve, or all three stitched together.

Rin's mind had to be clear. She had to follow the words Mauve whispered as Mauve touched Rin's shoulder: "To a beach, deep in the years after a night of glass."

Rin's vision peered through the shadows and walls, the light and the carpet. She saw time like a tunnel and threads and she tried to follow those threads. Supposedly, the makings of time and fate looked different to each person, and sometimes even the same person would see it differently at different times.

To Mauve it looked like an invisible book settled between breaths of air, where Mauve could search the pages and scan for the moments and images she sought. Sometimes, though, she'd say it was more like a thousand films playing in one cinema, images overlapping incomprehensively. To Rin, it was usually like standing in the midst of music, seeing and hearing the whole orchestra ahead of and behind her. All made of light and colors.

And tonight, through the tunnel her Spark let her open in time, she could see the beach Mauve mentioned. She could see it glowing at the end of a long trail about twenty years out.

Twenty years! Usually anything they worked with was so small, little glimpses of the future. But this felt bigger than anything any of them were used to. She couldn't show hesitation. She had to stay focused. And as she focused, the tunnel and the light visible at its end turned into a string. It reached out like a rope through time, through the cracks and creases of moments she had not yet known. In her mind, Rin grabbed on to it. And she readied herself to jump.

"Got it," Rin said.

Mauve and Odette held on to her shoulders. She breathed out. Her body felt charged, so full of life. She jumped, letting go of gravity.

She snapped her head forward. She saw the train disappear. She saw a tunnel of fireworks, moments, the backstage of reality. She gave a shout, a battle cry, but it got caught in the wind as they flew. And they really did fly.

The Ringmaster, Odette, and Mauve soared through time.

✳

4

THE RINGMASTER, 1944

Rin furled through narrow streets, wide oceans, deep promises, broken hearts, mornings from nearly seven thousand days to come.

They would land where they were meant to land. Odette and Mauve held tight.

Rin saw the end of the rope ahead, tied to the faraway beach. It rushed at them as if they had fallen out of a plane. With a roar, she shoved her hands forward, her heart forward, her entire body willing them to land on their feet.

The tunnel closed behind them. The magic disappeared.

She gave a crow. "Slick as ice!" she howled, charged and ready. Odette patted her on the back. Mauve laughed, then stumbled in the sand.

"Heels," she grumbled, throwing off her shoes.

Above was a gray sky, and beside them the ocean roared. But Rin saw something off about the hills; there was a bunker on top. On the beach, there were big X-like blocks everywhere, and barbed wire—

Then, everything exploded.

Odette flung her body over both Rin and Mauve.

Gunshots from above, searing *thwip*s shooting into the flying sand.

Rin peered out from under Odette, who held them in a death grip. Men rushed from the ocean, emerging like lost souls that fell off Charon's boat, spewing from the depths, falling, dying, broken, still running. The water drank their bodies and bled out. And the guns relentlessly *t-t-t-t-t-t-t-t*ed above her head.

Another explosion. Heat. Heat that curled inside bones and made it feel like they were cracking. A ringing in her ear. Shock. She couldn't move. The men were falling like flies, crouched behind the X's, hit and punched through with holes and torn apart like hunted rabbits.

There were no trenches to hide in. There was nothing but full-out war in a wide world.

Was the whole world a battlefield?

Then something hit her leg and she screamed. Mauve gripped Rin's hand. Rin looked to her, wet sand caking both their faces. Odette still covered them. And then in pain, Rin pulled them both down. She felt them fall through the sand, through air, falling down down down . . .

She saw another thread, leading from this battle back to someone sleeping in their bunk on the train. Rin could see the train below, the beach above, the black space in between, and the threads leading somewhere all tied together and gleaming golden. It was like a dream. But she'd learned a long time ago this was never a dream.

She reached out for the thread of the train. It was thick and gold and tied around her heart, leading out and beyond this place. She grabbed it. She held on to it as she swung them through time and they landed

somewhere she didn't recognize.

Rin had followed the train, though. They were supposed to be back on the train. So where the hell was it?

They'd landed straight on their backs, surrounded by darkness, crashing into hard concrete that had been shattered into jagged cracks and edges. Rin heard something snap in Odette's body. Odette took in a deep breath through her teeth, then closed her eyes and concentrated. The snapping cracked back into place. Odette hoisted herself up to sit. Rin didn't ask what had broken. It was fixed.

"Emergency, I'm taking my glove off." Odette pulled off her glove and touched Rin's leg. Rin didn't even have time to look at the bullet wound before it was gone.

Odette hissed through the pain she took from Rin. The blood was still wet and warm on Rin's calf. She reached out a hand to touch Odette, comfort her. Odette put her glove back on, and she pulled Rin and Mauve close. "Where the hell are we?"

It was an apartment. Or at least it *had been* an apartment. It was as if an enormous cinder block had been thrown onto a gravel pile and gnawed away by large teeth. Something was on fire outside. But, most hauntingly, a box of cereal and two bowls were set on the kitchen countertop, as if when people started dying, breakfast had only been paused.

This place wasn't somewhere that should have been touched by bullets. It wasn't a trench. It was a home.

Something whistled outside. Then an explosion. The entire world shook again.

Odette pulled Mauve and Rin to their feet and the three of them scrambled to get to a corner. Rin tried to remember to breathe.

"Why are we here?" Mauve asked her, shaken. Rin shook her head.

"I don't know," Rin said. "I . . . I followed a thread wrapped around me, leading back to the circus. . . ." There was nothing but distant screams echoing down the decimated streets, followed by gunshots, underscored by the crackling of fire. It smelled like burnt hair here, and Rin wanted to vomit.

"Who's in there?" a new voice shot from the other room.

Rin knew that voice.

"Maynard," Mauve whispered. "That's Maynard."

"You're right," Rin said, trying to keep her feet under her.

"Rin," Odette started.

But Rin rushed across the room, her boots tripping on pieces of broken concrete, her mouth and nose bombarded by ash that hung in the air like disintegrating cobwebs, her bones aching with exhaustion. She came to the doorframe, her cut-up hands grabbing the chipped wood to steady herself. She peered into the room, the bedframe still intact and the blankets and pillows still set out like someone would sleep there tonight, but there were floorboards and debris covering the duvet's embroidered flowers. Nothing here was safe.

"No," Maynard's voice sounded hoarsely from the farthest, darkest corner.

Rin's heart tugged, as if the thread that was supposed to lead her home now led her to that corner.

There was a huddled platoon, curled into each other, shivering under their gear. And the one that stood to speak to her, the voice, it was Maynard.

He was older, aged around the eyes and his red hair was completely gone. There were scars on his arms and gauze across his cheek. But he was still Maynard, black bruises against his white skin and that stern and careful glare as he studied her, as if she was a ghost.

"It's you," Maynard breathed, like he was years younger, just joined the magical circus that had been gone for longer than it had been here.

With his words, the huddled bodies in the corner raised their heads and she saw their faces. Her heart shot into her throat, and she gave out a small sob of disbelief. There was Mr. Weathers, ancient, one wing tucked behind him and the other wing missing. She saw Tina, her plump, white cheeks gaunt and her eyes cold, changed from her trademark bubbly shine. And there was Wally, Ford, Jess, Ming-Huá, and Esther. Rin could hardly process what she was seeing—this was their circus.

But they weren't the circus anymore. They were a platoon, huddled together in helmets and with guns and uniforms, their eyes big as saucers and their faces blank.

The thread wrapped around her heart had been the people on the train, not the train itself. It had led her somewhere else in the future, not back to the past. Maybe this is what her heart had really wanted to see; what was going to happen.

"No," Rin whispered.

She realized Maynard had his gun poised at the doorframe, pointed at her. She waited for him to lower it so she could come closer, but he didn't. It would be smart of him to think it was a trick—they were very familiar with the power of magic, after all—but she could tell something in him wanted to believe it was really the Ringmaster. "What?" he said. "How . . . Ringmaster, is it really you?"

"Rin?" A woman behind Maynard shot to her feet and came into view. She had black hair, a pale white face, big blue eyes that welled up as she looked at Rin.

Rin did not know this woman, but this woman clearly knew Rin.

"Rin?" she shouted. She rushed toward her, not showing the same hesitation the others had. Her face relaxed into tears, like she'd been holding her breath and now could let it out. "How are you—"

Then something hit the woman square in the chest. She erupted in blue light. Then another hit, to the platoon. Something choked them all. Something was killing them. Something that was not normal.

Rin stumbled forward. "No!" she screamed.

She saw the woman with her eyes big, staring at her, begging her. The woman's face slowly peeled apart and disintegrated as if the blue light cut her into a thousand pieces, set aflame.

Rin had to save her.

But Odette grabbed Rin, pulled her away from the blue carnage.

"We have to go!" Mauve said, grabbing them both. "Get us home!"

"They're dying!" Rin screamed.

Mauve grabbed Rin, taking Rin's face between her hands. "Focus!" Mauve said. "Get us out of here! Now! Or we can't change it!"

Rin remembered the bracelet. She felt it around her wrist. *Not today.*

Rin threw her arms around them both and yanked them back, jumping off the concrete back into the black, back back back

onto their bed. As if the world had opened up all laws of physics and now suddenly made them play by rules again. The magic dissipated.

A loud clack of the rails. The circus train shot through the night, under their bodies and Rin and Odette's bed, whistling and streaking through the curving, dark Nebraska winds. Rin felt her stiff limbs sink into the goose-feathered mattress.

The beach was gone, the concrete rooms were gone, but as Rin slowly set her boots on the wooden floor of the train car, she felt sand under her heel and toes.

She tore the bracelet off her wrist like it was cursed.

She heard herself make some sort of sound, something between a gag and a roar, and she steadied herself. The smell of burning still curled through her nostrils, down her throat, into her guts.

She heard Mauve vomit into the trash bin. They all sat in silence, then. Waiting for someone to say something.

Rin just watched the sun come up through the window. The railyard appeared in the morning light.

They were in Omaha.

"Rin . . ." Mauve said, looking down at Rin's leg. Rin now saw the new blood, a cut of shrapnel to take the healed bullet wound's place.

"Again?" Rin muttered. "You're just a magnet for trouble, tonight, aren't you?" she growled at her leg.

"It's all right, my dears," Odette said. Rin watched her getting herself together. Odette still shook; she took off her gloves. "Taking them off," she announced. "Can I touch you both?"

Odette would take their fear and injuries away, suck them up into herself and dispose of them somewhere deep inside.

That was her Spark. This is what good Odette did, held them when the pain was the worst. The trapeze swinger bore the brunt of it all and burned it down to ash in her insides. All three of them would keep surviving. Because of Odette.

"Don't take the fear," Rin said. "Just fix my leg. I need the fear."

"Rin—"

"Don't Rin me," she snapped. "You heard what I wanted. If you can't do that, you're not touching me at all."

She didn't mean to snap. Or maybe she did. She had just seen, in years beyond, her target. She knew what she needed to do. And she would be damned if someone took this drive from her. She would remember every single detail of that room, of the smell, of what they had to lose.

Is that why you don't want her to take your fear? the slithering memory of a foul man hissed inside her skull. *Or is it that you know somewhere deep down, she could be just like me? How much of you is really you? How much did I take of you? How much did I leave? Maybe you are only made of those things others have allowed you to keep. Maybe you aren't enough to save them, starling.*

She dug her fingernails into her palms, to distract herself. But when Odette reached out her hand to touch Rin and Mauve, Rin stopped. She could hurt herself, but she couldn't hurt Odette more than she already would.

Rin's leg slowly healed, her skin letting go of shrapnel that dissolved. And the shrapnel reappeared in Odette's leg as Odette grimaced. Odette's skin would swallow up any bullet, any shards, any broken wounds.

But she couldn't swallow the memory of that blue light, the death sweeping through the room—

"It was wide," Odette shivered. Then she took another deep breath, and she, too, was healed. "It was so wide and open. It came from everywhere. What was it?"

Rin knew.

It was war.

5

THE RINGMASTER, 1926

The Ringmaster knew what the world looked like when the light gave out.

She'd seen it after the last war. Iron masks on young boys whose faces hadn't even finished growing into their ears. Graves over bodies that had never seen anything of the world other than their mother's home and then a trench.

She'd seen it on the Circus King's snarling, cocky face as he closed in on his prey, getting everything he wanted in the ways bad men always did.

And she'd seen it last night, when they jumped.

The past and the future were both choking her, here in the present. It was as if they were barreling toward her from different directions, down the timeline, about to collide and wipe her off the tracks.

It was too much. The blue light, the woman she didn't recognize but had watched die, the broken apartment, the beach, the Circus King, the red smock—

Not today.

As hard as it was, she couldn't stew in the thought of all her friends dying. It wouldn't help them. So she walked along the length of the train, trying to ground herself in the now. She clenched her fists, she felt her toes in her thick boots, she breathed in the smell of an Omaha spring: honeysuckles, lilacs, smokestacks, the smell of grilling far off somewhere. This city got bad in the winter. Now was the time for celebration. The circus had come to town.

The sun came up over the railyard between Burlington Station and Union Station. The two stations were marble pillars separated by a long fat line of brown dirt and oil-stained train cars. The circus's lot was directly east of Union Station, sandwiched between the rails, the big jungle of warehouses, and the river. They'd performed here before. They knew the landlord pretty well, and they always got good crowds, being this close to the warehouse district. People from all over came through this station, and people of all kinds worked in the district. A weird hodgepodge, just like their little family.

She watched Maynard's multiples unhitch the wagons as Mrs. Davidson, the clown, and Cherry, their lead cook, headed out to set up the cookhouse in the Back Yard. Their home always looked the same, even in different lots, different railyards, different fairgrounds.

No war, no Circus King would touch this. She could do this. She could protect them all. When Odette had met her, years ago, Rin had been nothing but hard armor. She'd tried so hard to let it go, to let them all into her heart, to believe no shadows would follow her. The world had carried on, and now, in 1926, people knew the future would be bright. It had to be. Nothing could be as bad as what had come before.

Were they all fools?

"Morning, Maynard!" she heard Mauve call out behind her. Mauve sidled into view, holding her shawl close around her shoulders. Rin and Mauve met every morning to walk to the edge of the lot and then head out to make sure their special guest knew the circus had arrived.

The two of them stood at the end of their fencing, looking out at Nebraska cobbled together with brick streets and some sort of valley of warehouses and hotels and open markets. It made this downtown an industrial otherworld; one foot in progress and the other in prairie.

"You look like you're about to go into battle," Mauve said. Rin looked to Mauve, her dear friend, the woman who was never afraid and always two steps ahead of everyone else. But this morning, Mauve's hand was shaking. "Good news, I scanned the threads to see if we're going to have any issues with the Circus King tonight, and I believe we're in the clear."

That *was* good news. Temporary good news, but it meant they didn't have to pack up and skip town.

"I don't understand," Rin said, her head buzzing. "We've been to the future before. We've seen the future, and we didn't see *this*?"

"We've seen bits of the future," Mauve said. "Hours here and there. A song playing on a radio in a barber shop, a futuristic circus, little things out of context. And all of those things can change, Rin. You know that. The world is still writing its story."

"Then it *can* change," Rin said. She didn't know if that was a question, or if it was a declaration. Mauve didn't seem to know, either, so Rin added, "We do it when we help people with the circus. It can change."

"I preface this with the fact that I am not the Ghost of Christmas Yet to Come," Mauve said. "You know there's a lot we don't understand. But . . . yes. Events can change. I stayed up most of the night flipping through the pages of the future, trying to see how to fix it. I've got some ideas. I've gotten no sleep, but I've got ideas. So there's at least that."

"Odette finally drifted off to sleep," Rin said softly, studying the archway above them. The light bulbs sat on the plywood, still sleeping and without the color they'd have tonight.

Rin wished she, too, could rest. The trio had even taken themselves back to the beginning of the night, a small five-hour jump, in hopes of recouping some of their sleep. But it had been fruitless. Rin had spent the night staring into space, stroking Odette's soft bobbed hair. The curls had come out of place, and now she looked so tired. When Odette had finally fallen asleep on her lap, Rin had pulled a blanket over them both.

And somehow, with the world's end on the horizon, they still had to get up with the dawn and do their jobs.

At least, right now, Rin's adrenaline outweighed any fear. Her brain screamed for her to do something, fix everything. And the way Mauve clenched her jaw, Rin could tell she felt the same way.

"They were in a battalion," Mauve said, her eyes a thousand miles away. She cleared her throat. She shook her head, like she had water in her ear. "The Sparks will be recruited for the war. All of our threads are stabbed by blood."

Rin nodded. "Makes sense," she said.

"Does it?" Mauve said.

"The Prince Act," Rin said. "Remember, that fella Odette worked for during the pandemic? Dr. Prince. He went to Congress to broker a stalemate."

"Is that what the Act is?" Mauve said. "I know you yell it at people when they come on our property."

"They leave us alone, and we don't kick their ass," Rin said. "We leave them alone, and the mysterious Sparks well paid by our non-Spark government don't come and kill us. A truce, and no one gets hurt." A tightrope of politics Rin and the circus stayed out of. There was the circus and then everything beyond the circus. They were safe in their little corner of the world, but that seemed to be changing.

"What does that have to do with the war?"

"You're the one with the clairvoyance," Rin said, sticking a toothpick in her mouth, a habit she picked up when she'd quit drinking but knew better than to take up cigarettes. Chew on something that *wouldn't* kill her. "Can't you just sort of look through the timeline and figure it out?"

Mauve rolled her eyes. "Yeah, because my Spark involves reading white men's legislation."

"The Sparks can live freely as long as we don't turn the world into our own personal playground, under the condition that if the world needs us again . . ." Rin chewed on her toothpick. "Well, then we'll come to the rescue."

"Guess fighting their wars for them counts under the conditions." Mauve raspberried. "Small price to pay to not end up in a Pappa Pete wagon. Tha-a-a-anks."

"I'm surprised that I am surprised." Rin folded her arms, leaning back on the midway entrance's beam. She stared backward at the tent. The Big Top was erected now. Red and white. Mostly vinyl. Not perfect, but it kept the rain out.

"I'm not surprised that I'm not surprised," Mauve said, picking lint off her shawl and letting it float to the ground. "Not at all."

"You've never gone outside of what we need to know for the circus. We've never done anything this big. I'm worried about you and your head."

Mauve laughed. "Yeah. Me too. Take a number. And I'm also worried about you."

"You know I can't leave what we saw last night alone," Rin said.

Mauve nodded. "Wouldn't expect anything else of you. I'm sure you've already got a Rin Plan rolling around in your noggin."

"Do you think Odette will agree to it?"

"No," Mauve said. "But she'll go for the same reason I'll go."

"Why's that?" Rin said.

Mauve's round eyes looked square at her. Mauve was shorter, but she had a way of growing right in front of Rin when she wore that serious look. "Because," she said, "we both know that if we don't go, you'll still go. And you'll be alone."

"Alright, alright, I'm up!" Bernard's boisterous voice sounded from behind them as he strode into view. "Ready to go?"

"Morning, Dad," Mauve said, giving him a side hug. Bernard looked nothing like Mauve; he was a large, white, bald-headed man. Mauve had had two fathers. One wealthy (Mr. DesChamps), one his butler (Bernard). One by blood, another secretly a part of the family under the guise of employment. One of them had died, the other had run away to the circus with her.

Rin had never gotten to really know her own father; he died when she was so young. But if she had grown up with him watching, she would have hoped he was just like Bernard.

Bernard gave Rin a big front hug, lifting her off the ground like she was still nineteen and scrawny. "Our noble Ringmaster! Where are we off to today?"

Mauve and Rin didn't need to speak to agree they shouldn't tell Bernard about the hellscape of the future, and Rin felt some relief as Mauve said, "Past the hotel, to an alley deep in the warehouse district."

They started off into the city. The Outside World, is what circus folk called it. It was as if there was a protective ward around their circus, and as soon as they stepped off the grounds and out of the arch's shade, Rin felt like a deer in a field.

Above, the sunrise was blotted out by rows of homogenous buildings. Each brick was placed on one another in a weathered, precarious balancing act. The cracked walls and dirty windows rose out of the cobblestone.

Bernard walked behind them, surveying the area. Omaha's downtown wasn't as dangerous for two misfit women as some other places they'd visited. There were some towns where Mauve and Rin were not welcome. Maybe they would be in vogue in Harlem clubs and Greenwich Village dance halls, but this wasn't New York.

But despite the glances on the street, those same folks would settle into the stands at the Big Top tonight. Buying popcorn and breathing in sawdust and falling silent in glorious anticipation when the lights dimmed. Circus people were allowed to exist, as long as they were entertaining. But here, in the warehouses, it was all different kinds of denizens who filed into the arched brick doorways to start their workday. Rin and Mauve fit in, here in this pseudo-city. If she squinted, she could pretend she was back in Chicago. Omaha was a smaller sister, four hundred miles and a universe away, trying to be bigger than it was.

She knew that even though it was a melting pot in this district, even though everyone would come to the circus, the rest of the town the rest of the time was segregated. This was still Nebraska. And so Bernard still came.

After a long bit of walking without talking, they passed the hotel where some travelers paused for breakfast and coffee out on the patio. It smelled brisk and bitter. Delicious.

Mauve quietly pondered aloud, "Can you miss something you've never had?"

Rin crinkled her nose. "I . . . am sure you can. What do you miss?"

"In about five years," she said, "I believe it's five years . . . I discover this wonderful hazelnut coffee. I know it sounds questionable, but man-o'-war I *love* it. We don't have it here yet. It may not even exist yet. And I miss it. What day is it again?"

"Wednesday," Rin said. "I think."

"I don't like Wednesdays," Mauve said. "Let's skip this day altogether."

Rin knew she was joking. They had made a pact to stay grounded and live each day, even if they jumped around. That's why Rin would move the train through geography, but not through time.

There was something humanizing about time.

Rin checked her wrist. No bracelet. This was her reality, then.

"It's June 1926," Rin said, in a daze. "Our favorite song hasn't been written yet."

"Yes," Mauve said. "We have to be as normal as we can be, and say our favorite song is *Always*. Big hit. Although it is not my favorite song overall, throughout my entire life. Perhaps even the last life and the next . . ."

Rin now gripped Mauve's hand. "Our favorite song is *Always*."

Mauve shook her head, like waking herself up and slamming a book closed. "Yeah." She sighed. Mauve clasped Rin's wrist with her fingers. "I'm so ready for *Oz*. How many more years? I can't keep singing it by myself." Then she said, "Odette worries about us. She worries about you." She kept on, as if forgetting Rin could respond in a dialogue. "I wonder which one of us has it worse in our heads. You travel physically, I travel with my mind. You can put your feet on the ground, but both our brains are always up in the air."

"Well, Odette can keep us grounded," Rin said.

Mauve raised her chin, as if seeing a story written in the clouds. "It's a possible day, years from now, a day I see a lot. I'm on a porch, by myself. My husband is dead. Everyone else is dead or gone. And I'm alone. Sitting on this white porch overlooking an ocean or maybe one of the Great Lakes. I'm looking out, thinking about the circus and . . . I'm the last one."

Rin linked arms with Mauve. "That's not for a very long time. And it could still change. It all could change. You just said it could. You've never seen the war before, have you? No. So maybe you won't be alone."

"It would be nice," Mauve said, "to live one day beginning to middle to end. I hear other people don't have the whole of their stories bouncing around in their heads at all times."

A moment of silence passed between them.

"When does your husband show up anyways?" Rin said. "You still haven't met him yet?"

"Nope," Mauve said.

"Want to elaborate?"

"Nope," Mauve said.

"And what if that future doesn't happen?"

"Then it wasn't worth telling anyway." Then suddenly she jumped. "Today is not an unimportant day. At least there's that. Come on now, the special guest just got kicked out of her father's house, and she's running down the alley about three blocks from here. We'll need to get there soon if we're going to see her Spark in action, and you don't want to miss that show, believe me."

The streets clopped with the hooves of horses on cobblestone. The walls were plastered with bills and posters Maynard had slapped up there before dawn, advertising WINDY VAN HOOTEN'S CIRCUS OF THE FANTASTICALS.

Rin ignored the posters. She hated looking at an illustration of herself. She knew what the posters said, she'd helped design them. She didn't need to look at her own face and pick out all the ways the poster was prettier than her, younger than her, or maybe it captured just how old and plain she actually was.

They passed Omaha's chapter of Petersen's Spark Sanitarium, a colorful building painted to look like a children's museum with ice cream trucks outside, although those trucks had no ice cream. They were closer to police wagons, driving up to homes when parents turned their children over to the Spark catchers.

To fix them.

Rin swallowed. "Did Meredith ever tell you what the inside of those sanitariums look like?" she said to Mauve.

Meredith was a young girl who was learning aerials from Odette. She was quiet, but she and Mauve had struck up a few conversations here and there.

"Yes," Mauve said, and did not offer anything else.

"And is it all true? What we've heard?" Rin asked. Mauve said nothing. "Okay, well, they don't kill them right?"

"You don't have to take someone's life to kill them," Mauve said. "It was a private conversation, but I will tell you that Meredith said they try to take the Spark out of you."

How? How could someone cut out a Spark? It wasn't like it was a toe or a fingernail, it was something deep down. No one knew how it got here, how could someone pretend to know how it could go away?

They kept walking. Rin felt her body wanting to be bigger. She wanted to be stronger. She wanted to look away from the sanitarium.

The Prince Act existed, but so did Pappa Pete's. Anyone could voluntarily go there. But could children do anything voluntarily? The one person no one could save a kid from was their parent.

"This girl we're about to meet," Mauve said. "The Pappa Pete wagons are after her. Her name is Josephine Reed. She goes by Jo."

"And what does she need?" Rin said.

"You."

Rin looked to Mauve, but Mauve didn't extrapolate. Mauve looked right back at her, jutting her chin out teasingly. "If I go telling you everything, how is it your choice and not mine? Now go on, the show is about to start."

As if on cue, a choir of screams rang out from an alley ahead.

"We're picking up the pace, Bernard!" Rin shouted over her shoulder.

And with Bernard behind them, Rin and Mauve rushed through the warehouse maze to turn the corner and come face-to-face with a storm.

Rin saw three wagon men dressed in barbershop pinstripes caught in the midst of trying to hold the line as they descended upon a young girl.

She was scrawny, with blanched white skin and stringy black hair violently braided into haphazard pigtails. Her scarecrow frame was swallowed up in a pair of overalls too big for her, a dirty white shirt that very clearly belonged to an adult man. A boy cowered behind her. The girl had put herself between this boy and the wagon men.

There was something familiar in her stance, something that warmed Rin's heart. The way the girl's knees bent, like she was ready to pounce, to fight. Like she shed her façade of a little girl to become these men's worst nightmare.

The girl squeezed her eyes closed as she snapped her skinny fingers. From her dirt-smudged fingertips burst reds and oranges, shooting out in a screech. A firebird? How was she doing this? She was only a kid, her Spark couldn't have grown that much. But they'd all had it the same amount of time; maybe she'd been practicing?

No, there was nothing practiced about this fury. It was pure power, pure rage. She was strong. Talented. But there was no restraint. The firebird screeched toward the men like a dying banshee. Then from under the flaming wings, this child spun a tornado out of Nebraska cobblestone. Her arms rotated, her fingers grazing her elbows like she stirred a cauldron. She conjured up a storm in the air around her, thunder striking, rain like black tar.

Rin ducked, her heart jumping out of her damned ribs.

"None of it is real," Mauve said. "Just illusions."

But this girl didn't seem in control of it, or to even be fully conscious about how she was doing it. No matter what it was or how it got there, it was enough to terrorize the men that had dared to hurt her.

"Fuck you all!" the girl screamed. The wagon men's legs failed them and they collapsed, going right down on their asses on hard brick.

Well. There was that.

This girl, her crass words and her stalky pigtails, demanded her grit have space in this alley. Rin appreciated a firecracker willing to shine in this Outside World. The Outside was so afraid of anyone who was a reminder that they couldn't control everything, that things were still as shaky as they'd felt during the Great War.

But the uncontrolled could also be liberating.

This feral girl brought the shadows from Omaha's tall buildings off of the street below her feet and curled them into the air and strung them like cords around the men's limbs. They cried out, and Rin felt something tug in her. She needed to stop it, they were afraid. This would not end well.

But Rin didn't move. The men were afraid, but they'd cornered this kid. They'd hurt her. She was afraid, too, and sometimes from fear came shadows.

The girl spat at them.

"Try throwing some more rocks, huh!" she howled. "Try it again, you fucking chumps!"

She'd crowed too soon. A fourth wagon man came from the alley behind her. He knocked her down. Her shadows disappeared. He dragged her by the collar toward a waiting Pappa Pete's wagon.

The boy flew at the man then, attacking him. A scrawny kid, the same size as the girl, but with straw blond hair darting around a sharp-nosed face, the doleful eyes of a loyal basset hound. "Get off my sister!"

The man hit him hard. The boy was unfazed. He tugged his sister away, shielding her under him as the man wailed on his back, trying to get to her, trying to take them both.

That's when Rin stepped forward.

But Mauve pulled her back. "Just watch," she said.

The girl screamed, roared, and a dark green shock wave shot out from her body. Rin felt her own breath leave her as she watched the green pierce through all the wagon men. They screamed and dropped the girl and her brother. The children ran.

Then there was silence.

Rin's neck burned, her eyes unable to blink. Holy hell. That was no Spark, that was dynamite.

"The boy will probably decide to come to the circus, as well," Mauve said. "There is someone he needs at the circus. Not you. But that little girl, she's going to need you."

"What is her Spark?" Rin muttered to Mauve.

"Illusions," Mauve said matter-of-factly. "It's really interesting how you're asking me all this. You don't know anything yet."

"Yeah, real interesting," Rin said. "I thought you said she needed me?"

"She does," Mauve said.

"She seems to be fine on her own, but alright," Rin said. She started walking forward again. Mauve blocked her again.

"She has to find the circus on her own terms," Mauve said. "They both do. Like we all do. It's gotta be their decision." And she pulled some advertisement bills from her dress. She scattered them on the ground.

Rin watched the bills land in the mud. This ignited a bright smile in Mauve, and she gave a small bounce of excitement. "They'll find their way to us. Have faith."

Bernard, catching up, rubbed his sweaty bald head. "Is it safe for us non-Sparks now? Everyone safe? Ah. Rin is trying to push people to do what she wants them to do again?"

"Yup," Mauve said.

"Don't do it, kid." Bernard mussed Rin's hair. Which looked silly, because Rin's hair was graying and her body was maybe a year younger than Bernard's. Although she was not one for being called "kid," she let it slide because, coming from Bernard, it was endearing.

"I'm gonna swing by the market on my way back," Bernard said. "Wanna come or are you two jumping back to the grounds?"

"I shouldn't push my knee," Rin said. "It's behaving right now, but gotta preserve its good graces for tonight. I'm going to jump back."

"Me, too," Mauve said.

They didn't belong in the Outside World. Or more so, the Outside World didn't want them to belong.

The girl and the boy poked their heads out of the shadows, cautiously, gathering their bearings. They looked so alone, so lost. Both were barefoot, as if they'd run away in the night.

Rin had been barefoot, too, when she'd run away, all those years ago.

Not from a wagon, but from a man who now hunted her, was sending red-smocked harbingers to her. Maybe she was still running, just like them.

"Trust," Mauve said.

Trust it would all work out. Trust the circus would be safe. Trust that she and Mauve and Odette were enough to *make* it safe.

The girl looked over. Saw her, for a minute. Something was familiar. She was one of those people Rin saw and felt like she'd known her whole life. She'd felt that way about Mauve. About Odette. About . . . him.

He'd been a trick. Nothing more.

But the flash of power in this girl's eye . . . it reminded her of him. A Spark as powerful as this could bring either good or violent ends.

The kid looked away, and Rin took her friend's arm as Mauve released the rest of the bills for the show she'd brought with them. The two vanished, leaving the advertisements to flutter in the wind.

6

EDWARD, 1916

Edward threw the newspaper down on the restaurant table, in front of the two women.

"There, read it," he said. "Here in New York, people call it the Spark, others are talking about the Peculiarities. In the Zulu tribe in the south of Africa, they called it a name translating to the Gift. In Japan, it's translated to the Curse. But it's all the same, all around the world. It's been going on since last summer, even in the countries not wrapped up in the Western Front, and it's still here."

Ruth and Mrs. Dover looked over the paper sitting on the marble table. Their eyes scanned fast, then widened with disbelief.

"This is absolutely screwy," Mrs. Dover said. She was a fierce-looking woman who had successfully portrayed Medea and Goneril. The New York reviews said it seemed she transformed and melted into the characters onstage.

Well, that was literally true. She was a bona fide shapeshifter. And even now, Mrs. Dover's face slowly turned an unnerving shade of gray. She didn't seem to always have control of her Spark, and it made Edward nervous. What if those around them realized she was a Spark? No one seemed to notice . . . yet. "I don't know if I trust human beings with these Sparks," she said. "I've seen my fair share of men with power."

"There are also good men," Edward sniffed. "Lots of us who are trying." Although it was odd to speak of it in the present tense; he was no longer trying. He'd been hiding in New York. He'd been taken for dead back home. "Do you need anything, Mrs. Dover? You look a little gray."

Mrs. Dover's face turned paper white, and then she snapped herself back to her rosy pink.

Ruth looked to Mrs. Dover, and then Edward, and then back to Mrs. Dover. "So both Mother and I have the Spark. But why? It isn't like we're connected to the war."

"Everyone's connected to the war in some way," Edward said. "And I don't have a Spark. I was there." *Was* there.

But he also *was* alive. He *wasn't* dead in a trench. He *was* a coward. Maybe he didn't deserve a Spark.

"Something has unequivocally happened," Mrs. Dover said. "It feels as if everything has shifted and ripped open somehow. I try to think of what I was doing when my face changed the first time . . . I was rehearsing for a play. Ruth, what were you doing?"

Ruth looked to Edward, and then at the table. "I was wondering why I felt off, what was going on in the world that . . . I saw a shift and I followed the thread. . . ."

"But why did it happen to begin with?" Mrs. Dover asked. "If magic could rear its head—"

"It's not magic," Ruth said. She looked to Edward. "Is it?"

Edward shrugged. "Maybe the war threw the world off, so something decided we needed a little hope?"

These two women had welcomed him into their home as soon as he'd asked them. Over the last few months, they'd become a family.

Mrs. Dover excused herself to get more tea. Edward watched Ruth quietly. She still wore her hair back in those braids. She watched him right back.

"What are you thinking?" she said to him.

"Can I ask you something?" he said.

"Anything."

He leaned in, looking over at the severe Mrs. Dover but speaking to Ruth. "Why did you and your mother take me in? It's been half a year, and you've not asked for anything in return."

She looked down at her hands. "Well," she said, "we had an extra bed and . . . the extra money has been helpful. I . . . am concerned that you'll soon tire of us and return to England."

The night after he'd arrived in New York, he'd realized he only had one personal item on him when Ruth had whisked him away from the front. He still wore his uniform when he met Mrs. Dover. He still smelled like toxic fumes and death. He'd asked for a safe place to change, and Mrs. Dover had complied. She gave him the guest room, with a roaring fire.

He'd peeled his uniform from his body in an instant, like shedding a skin, like waking from a bad dream. If only everything that had come before had been a bad dream. Maybe it could be. This was a new chance, a new life. Edward had never stood in such a warm, opulent room full of ornate oak furniture and thick drapes. He ran his cut-up hand along the engravings on the bedpost as he clutched the horrible uniform in his other.

He could change his name, and no one would know.

No, his father had given him his name. He would keep that much.

Edward had felt around in his new trousers. He'd pulled out his father's old pocketknife before he'd set his clothes aflame. There were the initials, the worn wood handle . . . His father had died and been replaced early in Edward's life, but there was a comfort in this pocketknife. Something warm from a cold, creaky home. Something that could have been.

Something he could have now.

He'd flung the uniform into the hearth. He had watched the soiled, dirty brown army cloth curl and burn into nothing. No one would know where he'd come from, and he would never have to see the blood on those sleeves again.

And now, Ruth was sitting before him, so far away from the ghosts of England and France. "There's nothing left for me there," Edward said. His voice got choked up. And Ruth knew what that meant. Six months is enough time to know each other's wounds. So Ruth took his hand and she said:

"You don't have to go back to the war. You also don't have to go back to him."

Edward swallowed. "Tell me it wasn't my fault."

"It wasn't your fault, Ed," Ruth said. "You're a kind man and you deserved nothing he gave you and deserved all the things he didn't." She squeezed his hand. "Hey, look at me." He did. "You and me, we met for a reason, I think. Don't you?"

Out of all the men in the trench, she'd chosen him. *He'd* been saved. Something had drawn her to him, and him to her. They were connected by a long red string tied around each of their fingers.

And he knew neither of them wanted to let that string break.

It sometimes went like this, he supposed. Two strangers meeting in the smoke, instantly recognizing each other in some manner neither could explain.

So maybe he wasn't a coward for not returning to the front. Maybe this was where he was supposed to be.

"How many people do you think have the Spark?" Ruth asked quietly as they walked down New York's streets later that night. Mrs. Dover was in pre-views for *The Importance of Being Earnest* and they were her invited guests. They'd gotten their nicest shoes together for the occasion. Now they looked like two young lovers, their boots tapping cordially on the clean cobblestone. The streetlights hummed above them and all the other couples and families walking through the city. Someone roasted chestnuts at a vendor down the way. How many of them had the Spark? How was the world going to change?

"I don't know," Edward said honestly. He was jealous of those who had the Spark. He wanted something to give him power in a world where he felt so powerless. Sometimes when the night was quiet and an engine would pop, he'd break out in a sweat. Or Mrs. Dover would clatter her kettle and he'd seize up.

Before the war, his stepfather always said he was a coward. And then men mightier than him had torn out his spine and used it to dig those lines across Europe. So now he was just an empty shell, trying to find some sort of hap-piness here in the peace of New York City. As they entered the park, he saw the quiet snow settled along the iced trees. It was peaceful here. He imagined France, where the snow filled up the trenches and . . . No, he must not think about France. He was in New York.

"I wonder," he said, "if there's any strings attached to the Sparks. When you use your Spark, do you run out of energy? Or does it knock off a year of your life? What's the catch?"

"I don't think there's a catch," Ruth said.

"Where does it come from?" Edward said. "When you use the Spark, how does it feel?"

Ruth stopped. She turned to face him. She smiled from under that big fluffy hat. Her smile always looked like a new, shared secret between them. Just for him.

She took off her mittens. And she raised her hands. "Touch them," she said.

He did.

"It comes from somewhere deep in my mind," she said. "It's like I can see a whole map in my head, and I can jump in and out the other end, somewhere else. It's like my imagination mixes with reality, and then I see the way to go and it's golden. So." She smiled. "Where do you want to go, Ed?"

"Hey." A man walking in the opposite direction had stopped and was watching them. Edward immediately tensed, scanning the stranger for weap-ons. Edward could burn his uniform, but he couldn't kill the soldier who still lived inside him.

The man was bald, wearing an old coat over a large paunch. "Hello, mister, sorry, I thought I recognized you. Didn't mean to startle you."

Ruth dropped her hands, still grasping onto him. Edward didn't have time to think before the man took out a gun and pointed it at Edward's stomach.

"Could you spare your purse and coat then, huh?" he growled.

Ruth immediately unwrapped her little purse from her shoulder with shivering hands. "Please don't hurt us," she whispered.

But Edward felt something come over him. Something that had boiled in fury ever since that moment when he'd been dragged into the gunpowder. He grabbed the man's arm and said in a low voice, "You'll have more luck shooting yourself than drawing that gun on me."

In an instant, the man turned the gun on himself.

Ruth stumbled back.

The fury Edward felt shifted swiftly into fear. "Stop it, what the hell are you doing?"

The man stopped, as if he was a statue. He slowly opened his mouth and said, "You told me I'd have more luck shooting myself."

"Are you drunk?" Edward said. "Ruth, go. Run."

Ruth ran.

Edward peered into the face of the man. He was scruffy, a lot older and missing some teeth. He was just a desperate stranger on the street.

Edward watched Ruth run.

Edward looked to the gun, and a memory came to him as sharp as the light from a flash-pot.

Nathan giving him his own mask, Nathan dying in the middle of the toxic smoke unfurling from the muddy walls and ground of a trench. . . .

Edward touched the man's arm and slowly said, "Your name is Leonard now. What is your name?"

"I'm Leonard," he said.

"And you are going to go far away and never bother me again. If you see me, you'll turn around and walk in the opposite direction from now on. No more pulling that gun on anyone. You hear me?"

"I'm Leonard," he said, calm, as if in a trance. Edward pulled his hand away. And the man now named Leonard left him.

Edward couldn't move. All he could do was watch the man disappear. His mind set the puzzle pieces together, clicking everything into place. He was numb as he walked to the theater. It couldn't be real. It couldn't. He didn't know if it was a nightmare or a dream, but it wasn't real.

But what if it *was* real? What if he had the key to the world? What if . . . he was a Spark?

He lost his breath in a laugh. "A Spark," he muttered to himself, in awe. He hadn't been left behind, he wasn't useless. He had power.

Edward finally saw Ruth standing in the doorway of the theater lobby, crying, surrounded by three cops. The girl who was attached to him by a red thread, the reason for his life. And what a life they would live!

She saw Edward and rushed to his arms.

"I thought he'd gotten you," Ruth sobbed. "I'm so sorry I ran and left you there. I don't know why I did it. I'm so sorry."

Edward felt Ruth in his arms, grasping onto him, wanting him.

"Ruth," he said quietly. "Stop crying."

And she did. Immediately. As if he had commanded it. No, it was a coincidence.

"Laugh," he whispered. "You're happy."

And Ruth laughed, as if he'd tickled her. She jumped farther into his arms, joyful and madly in love.

With that, for Edward, the world shattered. He knew why she'd run. He knew why she'd taken him in. And he knew why she'd saved him.

They sat through the play, the whole house laughing except for him.

He had the Spark all right. He was a mighty powerful person.

And it broke his heart.

✳

7

THE RINGMASTER, 1926

Maynard called thirty minutes until curtain.

Rin breathed in deep, stepping out from between the stalls on the midway. It had rained all afternoon, and a circus without an audience would be a depressing thing. But clouds always ran out of rain eventually (and a particular circus Spark named Esther had a knack for clearing the skies).

Day rolled into evening. People arrived, slowly appearing in the wet streets and puddled sidewalks and making their way down the hill to the circus yard.

They funneled between fences and under the arches and banner. Bernard took their tickets with his apprentice, a young man named Wally from Florida who was learning the ropes to eventually be their proper press agent. Maynard couldn't do everything. Then the audience was met by a barker, a man called Ford who could change his voice to sound however he'd like. Tonight, it was loud with a transatlantic accent, a lilt of a song to his baritone.

Rin felt herself smiling at the children who jumped in the deep potholes of these fairgrounds. There were things for the little ones to do outside the Big Top: carnival games and cotton candy and the magical Mr. Calliope.

This moment was a good one. This evening was a peaceful one. She allowed herself to stand in the midst of it all, smelling the cotton candy and the wood chips, basking in the glow of the circus.

It was a dream patched together in the shape of a circus by three girls who had escaped their lives.

And now it was time to go speak to one of those girls.

Rin dipped out of the fairy lights and Edison bulbs of the midway and into the backstage area behind the box office, sideshow, and Big Top. The Back Yard was grittier than the places the audience could see. Sometimes, when

Rin gave tours to schoolchildren, they'd say, "Why's it so dusty back here? No one picks up after themselves!"

"Every piece has a place, even if that place isn't pretty," Rin would say. "We don't have to worry so much about it looking nice in the Back Yard because you're not supposed to see it. It's just for us. That's why it's so special you got to come back here today."

And the kids would *ooh* and *aah,* and she'd lead them through to the cookhouse to get something to eat.

They didn't have much to share, but they had enough. Odette kept them safe. Mauve kept the money coming in. And Rin kept the heart pumping.

The rehearsal tent was past the dressing tent. Both were less extravagant than the Big Top, the dressing tent lined with trunks and mirrors and the rehearsal tent cluttered with old beat-up platforms and bull tubs and balls and ropes. Boom Boom was in there, whose Spark was exploding. Yvanna, the archer, rolled in on her wheels and situated herself at the vanity. She always did such beautiful makeup, like flames coming out of her eyes. Her chair was painted in gold flames to match. And in the center ring later, she would look every bit a fire goddess as she lit her signature trick arrows.

And, as Rin had expected, there in the rehearsal tent, twenty minutes before curtain, high above, on a thin rope tied taut between two scaffoldings, was Odette.

She balanced delicately, narrow feet to narrow string like a sparrow settled on a clothesline. She belonged there in the sky.

The day Rin met Odette had not been a good one. On that first day, Rin had just come from a graveyard and felt so heavy. But even through her grief, she could see that Odette was a light.

The day Rin married Odette had been her favorite one. The sky was clear; they'd gone to the mountains and stood in the midst of the range on a summit, and they held hands surrounded by their family. The family they'd found, the family who wanted them. The law wasn't involved, of course, and it was secret. But it counted in their hearts. Like so many moments of living in the margins of rules, it would not be written down but always remembered by the chosen few who would hear it and see it for themselves. Odette had worn a flower crown, and Rin had worn her velvet jacket.

This day was a tepid one. Odette wasn't glowing in the sun, but Rin still wanted to be around her.

Mauve was in the rehearsal tent as well, wearing a silk wrap and robe but already in makeup. She paced the ground singing her *oooohhhhs* and *aaauh-hhs* and scales to warm up. They'd done this show fifteen hundred times, or at least six times a week April through October for the last five years. Mauve threw popcorn into her mouth as she warmed up, trying to catch it in the air. Rin would never understand how Mauve could eat popcorn before a performance and still sound perfect. Mauve said it was to laugh in the face of a childhood music instructor who told her she couldn't get away with it. But she could. Somehow. Mauve had talent dripping from every note she sang.

"You gonna show off your real Spark tonight?" Rin said.

"No one wants to really hear the future," Mauve said, popping kernels into her mouth as she pivoted on her feet.

"True enough," Rin said.

Mauve did not retort and ask if Rin would show off her Spark tonight. All three of them knew she couldn't. Although now with the Circus King knowing who she was . . . it barely seemed like a precaution Rin needed to take anymore.

"Odette, can we talk?" Rin said.

"No," came a pointed response from above. Mauve snorted and nearly choked on her popcorn.

"Odette, come on."

Odette set her small feet slowly, one in front of the other, always fluid, always steady.

"I'm warming up," Odette said.

Her body didn't need warming up this way, though, and Rin knew it. With a deep breath and a calm moment, Odette could be limber and ready to perform without ever having to stretch. Most aerialists could only pull off a certain amount of grueling tricks in a certain period of time, because the human body has limits. But Odette's body had no limits. Odette could do as many maneuvers as she needed without ever pulling a muscle or wearing herself out. Odette was eternally youthful and light, and Odette could make sure that never changed.

Odette placed another light foot in front of the other. She raised one high; she was made with strong limbs. She turned on her toes, the rope vibrating and shaking. But she was steady.

"Why are you rehearsing right up to curtain?" Rin said. "Are you avoiding us?"

Odette was not silent because she was angry. She was silent because she didn't know what to say. Rin knew that sometimes when things became too much, Odette would take minutes to hours to curate the exact words she wanted to pour out into the world.

"I said I didn't want to talk," Odette said. "And yet you keep on, heedless of the meditation I am doing."

All right, so maybe Odette was angry.

Odette slowly arched her spine backward, like a beautiful animation one would find in a spinning wheel. Her fingers touched down on the rope, the thin line pressing into her palms and keeping her body afloat while she carefully lifted each leg high above her pelvis.

Rin knew Odette's body, inside and out, and yet she did not know how it worked.

"So you *are* doing that thing again," Rin said. Odette would rehearse and rehearse because her body could take it. "You're spiraling into a hole."

"Said the kettle to the pot," Odette muttered, focusing on arching her back into a small *n*, placing her toes back on the wire. Okay, so sometimes Odette didn't curate anything but muttered snipes.

"Except Rin doesn't have the healing," Mauve said.

"She does," Odette said, "she just refuses to let me heal her. Which is why," she pressed her feet on the rope, and somehow, defying gravity, she lifted her chest upward, to stand once again, "she is old. And we are not."

"Darling, we've talked about this," Rin said. "I was given the time I was given."

"And you're going to use it all up trying to stop that supposed war."

Rin said nothing.

Odette stared pointedly at her from her perch on the wire. "That's what you want to talk about, isn't it?"

"You say 'supposed war,'" Mauve said. "It's very clearly a war."

"War is supposed to be over," Odette said, and Rin could hear denial in her voice. Odette knew it wasn't true, but she had to hold on to the lie like a tightrope with no net. "The War to End All Wars ended in 1918. It's never happening again. That's what they all say, remember? No more offensive wars, they keep saying they're gonna sign something and make it official, the president—"

"Or maybe," Mauve interrupted, "it's the same war, and we're in the eye of the storm." She looked around then, as if she could see the hurricane that was the past and future encircling the tent. Rin felt a surge of adrenaline splinter through her aching shoulders.

"So we're gonna stop it," Rin said.

Odette stopped in her routine, and her head lowered as she balanced above them, a weight of dread draped around her. She looked so tired. "Why us?"

"Because we can," Rin said. "We have Sparks. Three really strong Sparks. So if we have a way to do something right in the world, we do it."

"A mitzvah," Mauve muttered.

"Yup," Rin said, trying to exude confidence. A mitzvah. Something that her mother had instilled in her; it was a soul's job to put the broken parts of the world back together. And Rin had a Spark; she had the energy, the hands, the head, the legs, the spirit.

It was her responsibility, especially since she'd once broken so many things.

It was her fault the only pieces of her Judaism she still had all stemmed from a handful of memories of her mother. She didn't have a Magen David, a mezuzah, not even Shabbat candles. Because when someone joins the Circus King, they lose themselves.

"I love it when you two get in cahoots," Odette grumbled. "I know that face, Rin. If this is a guilt-riddled thing, the Circus King is not your fault."

"This isn't about him," Rin lied. It was a lie, wasn't it? Maybe this was about him. Odette understood a lot of things about Rin, including how Rin looked when she was thinking about bad things. But Odette couldn't understand, not really. She'd never met the Circus King. She'd never known Rin when she was with him. She didn't know all the lives that had been ruined, all the pain and hurt. Odette hadn't seen it. She hadn't tasted it. It wasn't real to her.

Too much. This was all too much. Rin turned away from the two women, quietly crossing her arms and letting her brain go numb. When the thoughts and the fears got jumbled up like this, she needed something to quiet it all. But she didn't have that, so she had to stand here and hope one of them would talk to fill her silence.

"As I told Rin," Mauve said to Odette, "we can't wait for others to come forward and fix this."

"Uh huh, and what about our mitzvah here?" Odette said. "What about *our circus* in the now? We can barely go head-to-head with the Circus King. And now he knows you're alive. Did you forget about that? Because I didn't. Last night, I couldn't decide what to lose sleep over: the Circus King or the Return of the Great War."

"You were the only one who got any sleep," Mauve said.

"Not enough!" Odette declared.

The three women were so small. War was so vast.

"We can outrun the Circus King," Rin finally said. "We can't outrun war. If we don't stop the war, then the war will touch every single one of us. And not just that, it will touch everyone in the audience. We can see it coming, and we care, so we can make a difference."

"I'm not talking about our grit or our Sparks," Odette said. "I'm talking about the reality of the situation. Can *anyone* even stop it?"

"We can try," the Ringmaster said. "That's the first step, not leaving it to someone else and being brave enough to try. Odette, we change a life every night; we can make a difference."

"Rin, we have done small things. We have not . . . stopped an entire global war."

"All things are small things," the Ringmaster said confidently. "Small things clump together to make larger things. The three of us have a chance to change this. Mauve, what do you think?"

"We can travel through time," Mauve said. "We can heal. We can see what's coming. We have a chance at least."

"And no one will suspect us," the Ringmaster said. "We're circus travelers. Not politicians, not soldiers."

"No, no, no, no," Odette said. "No, love. We're going to break our backs trying to carry the world. Look at *you*, you barely sleep. Last night, I had to take a flask from you. And stop giving me the stage smile, I'm not your audience, Rin. What happens when we get killed and the circus doesn't have us anymore? Doesn't have *you* anymore?"

Rin felt a dark thing pull down on her stomach. She ground her teeth, trying to keep the bad thoughts out.

"Odette, I'm sorry," Rin said. "I love you. But can we really move forward and live life without doing anything? That's not who you are. Or who *we* are. We can't go be happy while everyone barrels toward what we saw."

Odette's mouth formed a thin line.

"Odette," Mauve offered. "Eight years ago, you helped with the pandemic. It made a difference." Mauve crossed her legs under her dress skirt and robe and pressed her elbows to her knees as she looked up to Odette. "You were one of the hardest workers in Chicago as a healer. And that whole movement started trust in the Sparks, and then what happened? Then at least there was a truce, and we were safe *enough*. That legislation was made because of you and people like you."

Rin felt as tight as Odette's rope.

Odette did not look down. She pranced to the middle of the rope. It was not really a prance. It was a full on, athletic run. But true dancers can make power look like powder.

"You two are still going to go, aren't you?" Odette said. "No matter what I say."

Rin nodded.

Odette reached her arm up, tilting her shoulder blades to grasp the high ribbon above. "Do you love me?"

"Yes."

"Do you love Mauve?"

"Of course she loves me," Mauve said, throwing an unpopped kernel back into her striped cardboard container. "Everyone loves me."

"Do you love yourself, Rin?" Odette plowed on. "Do you not have worth?"

But the Ringmaster quietly gripped the cuffs of her jacket between her fingertips and her palms. "Of course I have worth," she lied, and her words fell off, like she was being forced to read a line.

Odette sighed. It wasn't a sad sigh, or a dismissive sigh. It was the sigh that came after holding one's breath too long. "Then why doesn't your life ever matter?"

"Why does my life matter more?" Rin said. "If we don't do this, our circus is rounded up and . . . Odette, it's not about me. This is about everyone."

Odette seemed caught in these words. She looked like they'd given her a rope burn, cutting through her skin. She wrapped the ribbon around her arm, then her leg, and she slowly floated off the tightrope and slipped like satin down to the ground. Her pointed toe was the first thing to land, and her blond bob of curls was the last to rustle with impact.

"Odette—"

"And I'm guessing you won't let me erase the extra aging this will do to you," Odette said, flexing her toes on the ground. "All the jumping around more than usual?"

Odette had stopped aging years ago. Mauve only held on to the years that she would have lived without all the jumping. But Rin; Rin wore each one of those years in her body.

The Ringmaster turned away, but her lips unfurled, like one of Odette's ribbons, into a deep frown. It had to work.

Mauve always said the future can change.

More like water than thread, Mauve had said.

A performance had a story: a beginning, a middle, and an end. The finale had already been rehearsed and blocked before the audience even entered the tent. The spec parade is the first thing the crowd sees, the whole plot of the spectacle settled in a pretty line, chronologically. An overture. But in real life, the story shifted. The story backtracked. The story sometimes never ended at all.

"I will go with you two," Odette said quietly. "But you gotta promise me when we fail, we're going to tell everyone, give them a chance to prepare. And you will not waste the rest of our time together."

"Sounds fair to me," Mauve said.

Rin nodded. "I promise. But we're going to stop it. Nothing will be as bad as what has come before."

A thousand questions were typed on Odette's face, but she said none of them out loud. Maybe they all jumbled on the inside of her lips, like Manhattan commuters bottlenecking.

But for now, it was showtime.

✳

8

THE RINGMASTER, 1926

The performing arts were magical. But they were only magical because of the professionals behind the curtain rehearsing and perfecting their craft to make it look magical.

Rin had learned this from a young age, when she had a walk-on part in a large Broadway musical revue. ("It's nothing to brag about," she had cut Mauve off the first time she'd told her, "there were about a hundred kids onstage. It was just whoever happened to be available for the summer, and we were in town.")

She remembered being six years old, dressed in a ruffly, uncomfortable costume, looking around at the way the backstage crew worked like something between a ballet dance and a clock. The big plywood cartoon moon was attached to ropes that were attached to the fly system, and the large run-crew man pulled the ropes on the rigging to make the moon appear for the audience. Then a *larger* crew man stood on a high box, grabbed onto the rope that was attached to the harness of the lead actor out center stage, and he jumped. He fell, his rump hitting the dirty wood floor and his big hairy arms grabbing the rope, pulling it down, down, down toward him to pile in his lap like a charmed snake.

Little Rin had looked out past the curtain legs . . . and had seen a human fly. Her mouth fell open. The lead actor, dressed like a fairy, shot upward as the moon shot downward. The audience gasped and clapped.

Magic.

This was before the days of Sparks. This was the first person she ever saw take flight.

Now the Sparks were here, and now Rin was no longer a child ensemble member but the Ringmaster. But there was still that backstage dance, the effort that it took to conjure magic for the six-year-olds in the crowd.

Years ago, Rin and Odette and Mauve had sat around a dingy little diner table in Chicago and drawn a thousand sketches for their production meeting. Then came the hiring, the buying at auctions of liquidated failed circuses, the finding of winter quarters, the rehearsals, the costumes, the sets, and props, more rehearsals and more and more training, and then the road. On the road there was rehearsal, then a show, then spot-checks, then rehearsals, then a show, around and around again until Rin could do the backstage dance backward and forward and with a concussion (which had only happened once). Then preshow, there was fight call, fire call, spot-checking, warm-ups, and House Open. All of this before the crowd settled in.

Maynard's Spark let him split into an entire run crew, light crew, and house management. Once it was thirty minutes to curtain and the house was open, this show was his and out of Rin's hands. House Open meant the Big Top's canvas entrance flaps were hooked open, and the crowd could enter.

Rin had not grown up in the circus like he had. In theatre, once the show was this close to performance, it was the SM, the stage manager, who took over. So, Rin focused on being a performer and paying enough attention to give notes postshow, and trusted Maynard to run everything else.

When she referred to him as the SM, Maynard would laugh and say, "I'm the production manager, in the circus world, you know. Boy, if you ever go working for another circus, they're gonna laugh you off the lot. They'll sniff you out for a First of May easy enough."

"Good thing I'm not planning on working for another circus," Rin would say. She would live and die with this circus.

Maynard shouted, "Five till curtain," and all shouted back, "Thank you five." Inside, Mr. Calliope already played the preshow fanfare. Outside, the performers stood in a circle in the Back Yard, their costumed feet settled between patchy grass and drying mud. In this circle, there were sequins, flashy scarves, Kell and Mr. Weather's gigantic white wings, Tina's red-and-blue leotard, and all the glitter and makeup they could find to splash on their faces. The players were dressed for the light, and it was time.

They held hands. Rin said, "In every theater there is a ghost."

"Of the past, present, and future," everyone joined in. *The future.*

"So we'll make them proud tonight," they finished.

And then with a deep, low hum, the entire cast caught the same note. Even the ones who couldn't sing. They held that note together. They closed their eyes. From all the different places they'd come from, they all found themselves in the same story now. Rin held Odette and Mauve's hands. Then she cheated, opening her eyes to see everyone else still concentrating.

The performers were supposed to focus on shared energy at this point. It was an old exercise that had brought them together in the days when they barely knew each other but had to learn how to flip over and catch one another under a spotlight. The energy ball was something everyone had to imagine in their mind's eye, then shove it forward into the middle of the circle. Of course, it wasn't a real energy ball; it was imaginary. Which is why Rin could pretend to see it. Even though she never had felt it.

"You don't feel the energy ball?" Odette had said one night as she took out her earrings before bed. "And don't crack a wiseass joke, I know what it sounds like."

Rin laughed. "No, it's just a silly exercise I learned from my mother." She was six when she held hands with her mother, humming with the cast of two hundred. Two hundred voices, pushing energy to the middle of a circle. Rin had felt like a part of something. She didn't grow up to deserve it.

She *had* grown up to learn you never keep your eyes closed around others, even if you loved them.

"So you don't connect with us when you're in the circle. What do you do?"

"I just open my eyes and wait for it to be done," Rin said.

Odette bit her lip. "You're supposed to keep your eyes closed. They all trust you to keep your eyes closed."

Rin usually respected Odette's oath to rules, unless it made it more difficult to do what she wanted to do. And what she wanted to do was be aware of what was going on in the circle at all times. She wanted to see that everything was safe, that all went as planned, that nothing would jump out of the shadows and hurt them.

There you are.

Rin told herself to focus, to stay grounded in the circle she stood in right now, right here. Rin looked to Odette, whose eyes were still closed. Odette gripped Rin's hand hard.

They would hold hands tonight when they jumped to the future.

Just give it a try, Rin. Close your eyes, take a deep breath, believe no one would rush out and stab anyone in the face—

"Have a great show everyone, break a leg," Rin said, and everyone opened their eyes with a big breath. Like they all had just taken a beautiful break together.

Odette raised one eyebrow. "You didn't close your eyes again."

"I'm working on it," Rin said. "Sybill, do you have everything you need?" The interpreter, Sybill, waved as she walked out to take her spot. Her Spark was to know every language under the sun, and maybe some beyond.

"I know you're working on it." Odette turned to her. She took Rin's cheeks, pulled her close, and kissed her on the lips. Here in the dark of the backstage, they could do that. Rin held her closer. The past, present, and future. Here in the dark tent, she could pretend there was no future. But it was all connected—

"Hey," Odette said, "Come to Earth, love." She squeezed Rin. No one gave hugs like Odette. Except for maybe Rin's mother, but her mother had been gone for a very long time.

Well, and Bernard, who came up behind her and Odette at that very moment and threw his burly arms around both of them like a grizzly bear. "My girls!" he said, shaking them. "Break those legs!"

Rin gasped for breath, her rib cage crushed. Odette laughed. "Thanks, Bernard," she said.

"Did Mauve make it to her perch?" Bernard asked. "Mauve? Where are you?"

"On my way!" Mauve shouted as she ran by.

"Can't breathe." Rin pulled away and turned to face the large roly-poly of a man dressed in a button-up and jeans. He was the only relic of Mauve's life, the only parent to all three girls who had come along for the adventure. Rin's were dead. Odette's had disavowed her. But Bernard beamed with pride.

"All right," Bernard said. "Maynard says we've got a full house so I'll be heading out there now."

"Two minutes!" Maynard shouted from above.

"Thank you two," came the chorus.

The lights burned bright from their masts, illuminating dust that seemed like it had been here in this tent for thousands of years. But the tent had only been pitched early that morning, and it would be taken down in a few hours. This was a well-oiled machine, a story that had lasted forever.

As soon as everyone was seated and the canvas marquee was shut, the circus began.

There is no giddier place than the darkness of a theater's wings in the last moment before curtain. The same went for circuses, in the darkness behind the portal. No more lights as people whispered a final "break a leg." Suddenly, the outside world faded away and rolled under a wave of the mystical. When the stage lights clicked on, it was as if this performance was connected to another realm, where all the other actors and specs throughout history lived, always in a place of creation.

Odette said it felt like a light clicking on. Rin thought it felt more like diving into a lake; a smooth washing away of who she was and a transformation into who she could be.

The Ringmaster took to the ring.

"Welcome, each and every one of you," she roared, marching into the spotlight. She was no longer just a woman. She was the circus.

"Tonight, you will not see fanciful flights of parlor tricks." She reached into the air and made appear a long whip from nowhere. Or rather, the Portalitator (Paulie McKinley) waiting in the wings behind the audience had hit his cue. He always hit his cue.

The audience didn't cheer. They never cheered at first. Many of them had never seen magic, and many more of them didn't believe in it.

Ringmaster looked over their heads, connecting with every one of them but never looking them in the eyes. She cracked the whip and smoke and lights emerged from the tent, from the seats, from the wires above, and from her very own hat.

This was, of course, all thanks to Boom Boom (or Frank) who was near Paulie somewhere beyond the dark. Even if they couldn't see each other, they had each other's backs.

It was then time for the spec parade.

The music pounded from background noise to a loud, pulsing heartbeat. Tina roared into the ring, followed by the clowns, and the spec parade twirled around the Ringmaster as she laughed and waved her hands. Beautiful music came from Mr. Calliope, who wheeled himself to his small post off to the side. He sounded like a piano gliding through a machine, nails and strings and something deeper striking notes all at the right time in a cacophonous rush.

Then, on cue, Kell, decked out in his costume, shot through the tent's king pole opening and plummeted to the ground like a god. He slammed his fist and his knee into the center ring. His wings unfolded into a large yawn, a line of feathers and dust, bristling and fluttering in the tent's stale light. It was as if the drafted pencil lines of music counts and rehearsed marks were erased and now they felt their parts in their souls, coming as naturally as breathing or laughing.

They all became characters here in the rings. They were now much bigger than who they'd been. They were THE ANGEL, THE TRAPEZE SWINGER, THE MENAGERIE LADY, THE NIGHTINGALE . . . all the words printed in red paint outside on the large ballyhoo banners. They circled the ring as the audience watched from all sides. They waved and danced. The specs kicked up dirt under their shiny boots and lacy heels, but they didn't seem to really touch the earth. Yes, most of them did walk with heel to dirt, but it was as if they were in one of those old films, the kind where the camera had recorded the real backgrounds and then artists painted cutout figures of faeries and aeronauts to paste on the cell frames, something fantastic and illustrated and otherworldly against the set piece of the ordinary.

And in the middle of it all, the crowd saw the character of the Ringmaster. The only thing grander than her booming voice and her waving arms was the red velvet coat that wrapped around her thick body. She was sweating underneath it, the warmth of a workout on her red freckled cheeks. Her thick hair suffocated the back of her neck, but the auburn mane looked more dramatic when left to billow and fall around her face and shoulders. Although she was uncomfortable, it was the sort of uncomfortable that mixed with adrenaline, music, stage lights, the smell of makeup and hair product and popcorn . . . and the joy contained inside one large canvas tent.

She looked out to her friends, her family, circling the ring, smiling and beaming and being the best versions of themselves. They were happy, a clear night sky full of stars that shone as the audience cheered.

Then the music diminuendoed. The spec parade slowly walked along the hippodrome track, in slow motion, like they were dancing underwater.

It was now time to add the pathos to the logos and ethos.

"We are Windy Van Hooten's Circus of the Fantasticals," Rin sang. "Because that term, Windy Van Hooten's"—she put her knee up on the ring curb and leaned in, like she'd never told anyone this secret—"is a special term to us circus folk. It means the most perfect circus, where all are treated with respect and everyone's paid on time. But of course, nothing can be perfect. And in this world"—she looked up at the tightrope above her—"it seems as if so many more things are broken than fixed. But I hope—" and that's when she looked them in the eyes. And she meant it. Because unlike other ringmasters, she did not stand in the center ring for anyone to applaud her or shine a light on her wonder. No. She had no wonder. She was here to shine a light on everyone else in this tent.

And that's why she had the audience by the neck.

They would go home believing in magic and having some sort of magic in their own hearts.

"I hope," she said, "that for the next hour, you will find something spectacular to keep with you, no matter what may happen once you leave our tent. This hour, this perfect evening, is yours."

She looked to the parade, a tornado of sequins and color, to where she knew two incredible women listened. They'd heard something similar to this spiel a thousand times. Every night, there was something new she said. But it all meant the same thing.

Hope.

"Tonight!" she sounded. "Tonight you will see things you never thought you would live to see! You will realize that in this world, there are dreams that are only just out of reach." And the lights clapped off.

The parade stopped.

The entire menagerie of this circus family silently looked up to the heavens, as if in prayer. The spotlight clicked back on, with a snap that echoed through the hushed Big Top.

The Ringmaster stood in its light. And then she, too, looked upward.

"Sometimes," she said, in a whisper that filled all their ears, "we only need to know where to look."

The spotlight softly floated up the king pole, the main mast, of the tent. And it rested on the aerialist. The Trapeze Swinger. The center of gravity in a chaotic world.

Ribbons flew down Odette's legs, which shimmered in her gold tights. She wrapped herself in the two silks, then prepared for a double star drop. Rin remembered Odette muttering to herself during rehearsal: arms behind head, straight torso. But now in performance, it looked as if Odette had been born doing silks. It was as natural as walking for her.

This had been the one rule Odette had broken. They'd promised themselves they wouldn't bring any art into the circus that hadn't yet been invented. No music, no costuming, nothing. But Odette's wife was a time traveler, and they had traveled to a futuristic circus once for Odette's birthday. And in that circus to come, Odette had seen silks. Odette had fallen in love, and her heart had needed them. So they negotiated between themselves—no posters, no written record, nothing would document that the silks had been in a circus sixty years too early.

It was still a risk. It was still hypocritical. But Rin knew anyone could reason away any hypocrisy with enough desire; even someone as sweet as Odette.

Rin now wondered if maybe one of these audience members would see Odette on silks and tell a story to a grandkid down the line, and then the silks would be invented. Maybe the silks curled around themselves in an infinity sign; like the daisy chain Odette knotted them into for storage on the train.

Their circus felt very removed from the world, but they changed the world's shape every night. They were changing it right now.

But something else gnawed at Rin: even traveling to that circus in the future, she'd not heard anything about a war. Was it in a future that didn't exist anymore? Or was it indeed after the war, but everyone was just trying to move along and forget everything that had happened?

Isn't that what they'd all been trying to do since 1918? Would it happen again?

Would her circus be destroyed and then forgotten?

Odette dropped on her illegal silks, spinning around and around, catching in a knot at the end before hitting the ground.

Odette spun around right ways up, then did a figure-eight foot lock with a fan kick, arabesque, fan kick, arabesque, hold as she spun. Then Odette did a Russian climb and somehow even made that look both graceful and difficult. A quick invert, then landing on the platform to begin the tightrope.

She walked across a tightrope, prancing like she wrote the laws of physics. She jumped, grabbed one of her lyras, and balanced with the power of an athlete and the poise of a princess, her thighs and feet and fingers slowly turning and contorting around the circle high in the sky. Rin could feel a part of the crowd was amazed by her beauty. Another part probably wanted to see her fall. And probably some pedantic fella would point out after the show that trapeze swingers and aerialists were two different jobs. But by the end, they'd all love her as much as Rin did.

And then, with nothing around her but a hoop and the air, Odette began to dance.

Sometimes, if Rin was caught up in the music, she found herself believing Odette could fly.

There may have been music, or maybe the music came from Odette's sturdy arms and her pointed toes and her swirling thighs and her neck craning back to curve into half moons. The ring floated to a trapeze bar, and she grabbed the trapeze.

Then she was off, flying between places of safety and through air as if she couldn't fall. Maybe she couldn't.

The tent smelled like a freshly polished floor, new linens. To watch her felt like dipping downward on a particularly smooth swing. Rin's stomach rushed, her shoulders relaxed, and green grass of a childhood summer filled her heart.

The trapeze swinger hooked her legs around her final ring and left the trapeze. She'd nearly finished her triathalon, or was it a quadrathlon? She wasn't even tired.

She leaned backward until she hung upside down, her arms in a perfect arabesque. The Ringmaster reached up to her, gloved hands raised high. They breathed in the ecstasy the whole tent felt.

Odette looked right at Rin, and there was no one else in the tent but the two of them.

The spotlight clicked off, the audience roared in applause, and the spell was broken. Rin helped Odette off her hoop, and Odette went charging across the floor, no longer a dancer but a worker trying to get the hell out of the way.

Three spotlights clicked back on. Jelly the Juggler (known a half an hour ago as Ford, the barker, who was learning how to clown) now played with Mr. and Mrs. Davidson, the clowns, as Boom Boom readied explosives in the wings.

Rin took this moment to step to the side and look out to the audience.

She suddenly saw her, big eyes wide and stringy pigtails hanging around a slacked jaw. This was who Rin had been playing to.

The little girl from the warehouse district, settled next to her brother, gaping at the circus like she had been searching for this place her entire life.

9

EDWARD, 1917

Edward stepped over the homeless bum in front of the jewelry store, holding his nose at the smell. New York had a lot of cleaning up it needed to do. But that was not his burden. He had a mission already.

Edward knew that buying the ring before asking permission was a brave thing to do. Especially since he needed to watch his wording tonight.

He stood in front of the case, lit up by electric lamps above. These cases stretched all the way to the back of the store, like the diamonds and rubies were choice cuts of pork and the silver was long sausage. How odd; to have a general store only full of riches.

He remembered the day his stepfather proposed to his mother. Or actually, he did not remember that day, because he'd been sent away to stay with a family friend for the weekend. But he did remember the day he returned and saw the large ring on his mother's finger. It had looked cheap, fake. Just like his stepfather's smile.

There would be nothing fake about Ruth, about him, about the family they would create. Edward had been a powerless little boy, and now he was a grown man standing before his future.

His mother and stepfather were dead to him. Let them believe he died in the war. Let them grieve or not grieve for the rest of their lives. They deserved it. Let them writhe in the unknowing. He was an orphan.

Or that is, he had been an orphan until Ruth saved him. Ruth was the light in his dark life, and he would hold on to her. He wasn't alone anymore. He would never be alone again.

Someone coughed beside him, and Edward became painfully aware of the other persons in the store. They all were dressed to the nines, and Edward . . .

Edward didn't even have a jacket on. He nervously nodded to a man who made it clear with his eyes that Edward did not belong there.

"May I help you?" the jeweler behind the counter said. He looked like a bloated walrus. Ordinarily, Edward would have found his words a normal, kind gesture of customer service. But now, something was off about all of this. The jeweler thought he was going to steal something, didn't he?

"Yes," Edward said, clearing his throat. His voice was too small. "Yes, I would like to look at engagement rings."

The jeweler's brow raised. "Congratulations then, sir. Perhaps we should begin down here," he waved to the back, "where there may be something more . . . manageable for you."

Edward narrowed his eyes. "I would like to look at this one, right here. The one that is shaped like a heart."

"Sir," the jeweler said, as if to say "boy" and they were only playing pretend, "that one is from our platinum collection. I cannot let it out of its case without discussion of payment."

"I'm not making sense of this," Edward said. Edward now realized the man standing next to him had been listening in. For what? Just in case he needed to be pushed out of the store? "That is," Edward tried again, "to say, how is a customer supposed to know if a ring is *the* ring if they can't even inspect anything closer?"

"It's the rules of our store, sir."

Edward nodded. "Fine. How much then? Go on, how much?"

"Eight hundred dollars."

Edward stared at him. "Pardon?"

"That ring," the jeweler said, "is eight hundred dollars."

Edward felt something deflate inside him. He shook his head. "You must be joking, that ring can't cost that much. Nothing costs that much!"

"I am joking," the jeweler said. "Of course nothing costs that much."

Edward pulled back, like the display case was a hot stove. The jeweler just stared at him, as if Edward had forgotten a line.

He'd not been careful with his words. God, he'd tried. He always tried so hard. But it hadn't mattered. Here he was, in a jewelry store with no eight hundred dollars and a man in a suit breathing down his neck like he was going to rob them all at gunpoint, and the jeweler waiting to hear how much Edward was going to pay for this ring.

Wait.

Edward slowly turned his head to the man who had crowded him. "You're going to leave us alone now," he said

The man nodded and walked away.

Edward turned back to the jeweler. He had been so careful. He should go look at the other rings, the cheap fake rings. He should understand there was a place for him in this world and it was as a man without a suit, a poor husband for poor Ruth with her poor ring.

But how had that man in that suit been handed eight hundred dollars, and Edward had been handed the war?

Because that man hadn't played by the rules. There was no way he had.

Or perhaps the rules had been written with that man in the suit in mind.

Edward nodded. "Actually, I was in here earlier and paid in full for that particular ring, and I am offended it is still sitting in its case. Here, give it to me and we'll forget this entire thing happened."

The jeweler also nodded. "Very good, sir. Sincere apologies, sir."

And the ring was his.

✳

10

THE RINGMASTER, 1926

Rin never went out to the midway after the show, because it broke the magic. The audience needed her to be a part of the circus, not someone milling about for conversation. She would be a real disappointment in person.

So she hid behind the banners, big canvases advertising the different acts.

An alley between the sideshow and the Big Top was covered with the TRA-PEZE SWINGER banner, just like a curtain door cutting her from a stage. Rin soaked in the sound of the night and the laughs from the passing families. Pretending for a moment she was here with her own family, maybe with a kid, or maybe *she* was the kid, strung between her two parents' arms like a swing that could reach the sky.

The midway was still full of people picking up final cotton candies and *ooh*ing and *aah*ing at the posters now that they knew who was who. There were also games, some for the kids and some for the older folks. One of Rin's favorites was the duck pond, because everyone got a prize. Pull a duck out, see what was on the bottom, get a knickknack.

She also had a special place in her heart for the strongman's bell. Their strongwoman, Agnes Gregor, was a knockout Amazonian lady who made Rin look puny. Her chestnut hair cut short in a bob, Agnes's thick arms would flex as she pulled up the hammer and slammed it down on the target. Agnes was a flirt; not with the men, with the women, and it got her in trouble with the men. It also got her customers. Boyfriends and husbands would feel challenged and stay a lot more motivated to best her at the bell game. They'd usually lose, sometimes not. Rin told her that it wasn't fair to charge them after the third turn, and more so, it wasn't safe. Agnes thought Rin was dampening her prowess. But Agnes wasn't stupid, and she was a pro; she never followed through with anything more than good-humored flirting. She wasn't here to get in a fight; it was all for fun.

"Come on now, Babe Ruth!" Agnes now laughed at a man dressed in a baseball uniform like he'd come right from a game. Rin could see him from her hiding place if she looked into the mirrors across the midway, right outside the sideshow. "That the best you can do? With this little lady waiting for a stuffed panda? Hi, I'm Agnes." Rin snorted. Then the *ding ding* of the bell, and Babe Ruth had won. "See, miss? Your Big Bambino is a bona fide bell ringer. Here ya go, kiddos."

Then someone walked in front of her, casting a shadow through the back of the canvas. Braids, scrawny little arms. It was their special guest.

Jo Reed.

Rin quietly looked through the gap between the banner and the tent. There was the girl, milling around with her brother. Kell approached them.

"You waiting for someone?" he asked, all three of them only feet from the banner.

The girl startled, realizing she had nearly backed into the boy with the big wings. Kell was out of his costume and into his nice pair of jean overalls and no shirt. He was more comfortable that way, with his big white feathery wings sprouting out of his deep dark brown shoulder blades. He rustled his wings and folded them against his body as he studied the new boy and girl. Kell was older than them, but not by much. He held himself like he was ancient, but something about his eyes gave him away. When his laissez-faire gaze landed on the new boy, Rin saw that he cared very much. He looked like he was watching the fireplace for Santa on Christmas Eve; an anticipation of something wonderful to come.

"Hi," the boy said. "I'm Charles. This is Jo, my sister. And you were . . . fantastic tonight."

"Thanks," Kell said. He bit into an apple, giving a cool shrug, although his eyes didn't leave Charles. It's how Rin imagined she had looked when she'd first spoken to Odette. She gave a small smile.

Kell pulled his stare to look at Jo for an answer. "So can I help you or something?"

"Yeah," she said. "The lady with the hair in the center of the ring. Is she in charge? I want to talk to her."

"Ringmaster?" he said. "Eh, she's around here somewhere."

Rin took a step back. These were children, she was the Ringmaster, and still she knew as soon as Jo Reed met her, a bit of the magic would be lost. Rin could never live up to who they had seen on stage.

What does she need? Rin had asked.

You, Mauve had said.

"We want to join the circus," the boy named Charles said.

This didn't surprise Rin.

"Ha," Kell said.

"Those wings real?" Jo said.

"Yup." He kept eating the apple. His wings twitched like he had an itch. "Where are your parents?"

"Are you really an angel?" Charles asked him.

"That's a dumb question," Jo said.

"Not really," Kell said. "I've got wings. It's my stage name." He looked to Charles. "So if you wanna call me an angel . . . I . . ." He cleared his throat and evacuated his attempt. "How old are you?"

"We're both twenty," Jo clearly lied.

He smirked. "You can pick your own way in life if you're twenty." He sighed and threw the apple core in the nearby trash tin. "I'm Kell. And you can't give consent to join a company if you're underage. And regardless of what the other circuses do, *this* circus is real strict about consent."

"You're here," Jo said.

"I'm almost seventeen!" he said. "And my pops is here, too. See?" He nodded across the midway to Mr. Weathers, the old trainmaster, his face full of edges and his hands held together with big knuckles and thin skeletal fingers like he'd written longhand every hour of his life. "He runs the train and makes sure all the mechanisms are working. Smartest man I know. His name is Kell, too, but you call him Mr. Weathers. Hey, Pops!" Mr. Weathers looked up, and he waved one lanky arm over his head like he was calling them out at sea. Kell waved back. Then he turned around, and said to Jo, "Look at Pop's shirt and coat. See his wings coming out? There's holes cut out in the back. We're the same."

"Family trait or something?" Jo said.

No, Rin thought. Sparks weren't hereditary. When Kell Senior and Junior joined, the younger Kell had said, "He wanted to feel free, and I wanted to be like him. So we both woke up with wings." Mr. Weathers found freedom in his son. After what he'd seen as part of the Harlem Hellfighters, he said he kept the war away from his brain by looking at Kell's smile. Now, in the midway's light against the late evening's twilight, Kell's smile broke loose. "So, what are your wings, Charles?"

"Spying?" Odette whispered behind her.

Rin jumped. She stopped herself from falling into the banner, and threw her hands over her mouth as she gasped.

Odette grinned with a mischievous snicker. She patted Rin on the back. "Scoot over." She saw Kell and the boy Charles. "Aww, look. It's us."

"So you see it, too," Rin said.

"I see that Kell is trying to act jake, poor bunny." Odette laughed. Rin snorted. "He reminds me of you, all that posturing."

"I didn't posture."

"You postured," Odette said. Her big eyes looked Rin up and down, drinking her all in. As if she'd memorized every single piece of the Ringmaster, but still was seeing her for the first time.

"Speaking of posturing, you shook up your routine again tonight," Rin said.

Odette's mouth curved with a half smile and a wink. "Gotta make sure you keep watching." And she pecked Rin on the cheek. "You still posture, by the way."

"All right, all right." Rin took Odette's gloved hand.

Odette looked at their fingers entwined. "Why are you hiding again? Did *he*—"

"No," Rin said. "He isn't here. And no one approached me." She swallowed. "I want to believe he's going to just leave us alone."

"We should be so lucky," Odette said.

"I'm an old wretch now," Rin said. "He wants something younger, I'm sure." Odette rolled her eyes.

"Look, let me dream that he'll move along," Rin said. "He has his own circus, we both have our own lives. He . . ." She trailed off, because she didn't really believe it. Neither of them did. But the thought that *he* could touch the circus—

That *anything* could touch the circus.

"You're not a wretch," Odette said. She paused for a second. "I think you're beautiful," she said. "And we're the same age. I've been beside you every minute traveled. But if you never let me heal you, even just to counteract those trips in time you take, I'm going to have more minutes than you. Which means I'll have more minutes *without* you. And that feels . . ." She trailed off, like the thought was too dark to complete.

That is selfish, Rin finished internally. Rin bit the inside of her cheek. She nodded, and she looked out to the children beyond the banner. Maybe someday, Odette and Rin would talk of happy things instead of heavy ones.

Odette said, "I get the whole mitzvah concept. I do. And I agree. But does a mitzvah mean you just keep giving and giving until there's nothing left to give? I don't think it does, Rin."

"Odette, we've already decided."

"If you're off saving everyone," Odette charged on, "when do you save yourself? When does anyone get to save you?"

"I don't need saving." *You're not worth saving.*

"Rin, look at me," Odette said. Rin couldn't. Rin felt like a kite on a long string, floating away. Trying not to accidentally fall backward, fall down, feel anything. Odette said, "We should also talk about that drink last night."

"I didn't drink it," Rin said gruffly. And then softer, she said, "I'm sorry. I know I don't just put myself in danger, I took a risk having it anywhere near our grounds."

"That's not what I was worried about—"

"I'm sorry," Rin said. "It was a bad night. I . . . appreciate you stopping me. And I . . . I snuck some tea bags from the cookhouse, for tonight. Chamomile! Your favorite."

Odette squeezed her hand harder, through her white glove. "Please call for me before you start falling down again," she said. "It's not . . . the booze on its own. . . . Well, it is. But I know what it means."

And Rin knew what Odette meant. When Rin got close to a precipice of losing it, her itch wasn't the hooch. Her brain would clamp onto a dark thing deep inside, and she would want to hurt herself, and the hooch made that road easier to travel. It was a way of letting go, hitting a bottom she didn't want to leave.

"I'm safe enough," Rin said, through gritted teeth and a whole lot of embarrassment.

Odette bit her lip. "And it isn't that I don't care about what happens in the future, you know. But I do worry if the present can hold the future's weight."

"I can hold the weight I need to hold," Rin said solidly. Like she'd formed cement bricks along her bones, burying whatever was beneath and fortifying her to move forward.

"After we speak to these two ragamuffins," Rin said, "we'll jump the train. And then we're going to need to use the night to—"

But her words were cut off by a siren. It wailed from behind them, moving past the magic of the tents, past the ticket line, above on the bridge, and then clattering down the stairs from the bridge and onto the ground and . . .

It happened quick. The wagon men rushed through. The men dressed in pin-striped clothes. They had straw boat hats to cover their faces, thick gloves so they didn't have to touch the kids. To passersby who didn't know, they'd look like a very aggravated barbershop quartet. But to any Spark who understood, they looked like monsters.

And in the midway's post-show carnival, it became apparent who was a Spark and who wasn't. Most of the remaining crowd didn't seem very jolted by the hullabaloo, except to turn their heads to find the fire or the accident or the thief or the communist anarchist. But there were others who ran for it, ducked out of sight, tried to blend in . . . maybe some literally blending in. . . .

Beyond the banner, Jo grabbed Charles and started to run, but it was too late. Hands grabbed them both.

"Get off me!" she screamed. Charles cried out.

Gloved hands dragged them away from the boy with the wings.

The ground slapped their faces as they were pulled away from the lights and the music. Charles reached for his sister. She was trying to claw her arms out of the grip of larger, scarier men.

"Get Bernard!" Rin shouted to Odette, erupting from behind the banners. "Agnes!" Agnes rushed to her side. Kell also followed. Which meant Mr. Weathers would be close behind.

Then the midway was silent. Even the kids had stopped screaming. Rin had learned the real scary things were surrounded by silence, not screaming. Screaming meant you still had two brain cells to make a noise. Silence meant petrification. A moment stopped in time.

She ran forward as they dragged the kids past the box office, too close to the threshold for the Outside World. "I am invoking the Prince Act!" Rin shouted.

The men stopped, but they didn't let go of the kids. It was like a wall had sprung up from the ground in front of them.

Little Jo Reed hung from one of the men's grip, her arm nearly out of its socket, suspended an uncomfortable couple of inches from the ground, backward.

There was a tension. Rin could feel the crowd around her. With the stage lights gone, the magic circus was just a pumpkin. The dreamers on the banners were no longer spectacular, but dirty Sparkies. And the Ringmaster was just a loud woman.

But they'd stopped. No one could touch her. Not like this.

"Hello there," Rin said, low, drawing closer. It was a roar, but calm. Steady. Precise. Not at all nervous. Because the Ringmaster was never nervous, regardless of how Rin felt. "Where are you taking my bull girl and her assistant?"

The kids swung their heads around enough to see Rin. She felt Agnes and Kell at her side, Mr. Weathers catching up, and Bernard's big booming voice sounded somewhere behind her, "Where is she?" as he ran to the rescue.

"Your bull girl?" the wagon man said. His voice was scratchy, like he'd not used it since getting old and shitty. It contrasted with his striped barbershop quartet outfit.

"I've hired these two onto my circus," the Ringmaster said. "My employees say you walked into our rented grounds without buying a ticket and are now kidnapping them from under my nose."

"Listen, lady," the wagon man said. "These two are wards of the state now. Their daddy signed them over last night. I've got the papers."

Rin tried not to think about the horrific implications of a man who was alive but made his kids orphans.

"They're both at least twenty," Kell said.

Then the man called Kell a word no good man says. Kell braced himself.

"Are you fucking serious?" Kell said to the man.

"Say it again," Mr. Weathers stepped forward, in front of his son.

"Your words are absolutely not welcome here," the Ringmaster said to the wagon man as he stepped forward, too. Agnes met him. This was going to be a brawl. "I'm asking you to leave this land we've leased for the duration of our show."

"And I'm asking you, you bull-dagger freakshow, to get the fuck out of my way. Those are my kids and I'll be taking them."

"Kids? At the age of twenty," the Ringmaster said, coolly, "they're adults and can only sign themselves over. Unless you're kidnapping them. But their father, regardless of what he thinks, doesn't have any say in their where-abouts."

"I'm just following orders."

"I bet you are," Mr. Weathers retorted.

"I don't really give a damn if you're following Jesus Christ," the Ringmaster said. "You're going to leave these grounds right now. Come back tomorrow after noon, and our rental will be finished, and then I won't care where you are. But until then, this is our land and this is our cast and crew. Goodbye."

"You better watch your mouths," the second wagon man said. "You act tough, bitch, but you're all Sparkies and freaks. One word and the city burns down your freak show and we take all of you in."

"According to the Prince Act of 1921, there will be none of that, unless you are inciting a riot," the Ringmaster said. "We are on our rented land. You are causing unlawful agitation with multiple Sparks. I'm giving you ten seconds to get off this property, or I'll remove you myself."

The men dropped Jo and Charles and ran for the street.

Sparks were afraid of wagon men, but wagon men were more afraid of Sparks.

11

THE RINGMASTER, 1926

The Ringmaster interviewed potential performers in her office, which in reality was just part of the pie car they'd siphoned off, a back area they'd separated with a plyboard wall and painted with everyone's handprints. It had three oak desks—one for each of the three managers, Odette and Mauve and Rin. The office had red carpet and fancy baubles outlining the doorframe to the vestibule outside, with a few odds and ends scattered around that gave it a homey feel.

It wasn't much, just a small area that smelled like typewriter ink and cheap paper with plywood boards for walls. But it was an important place on the train; a place of beginnings.

Mauve and Odette sat at their desks, Mauve counting the alfalfa and fiddling with the lockbox, and Odette taking note of the numbers Mauve told her. Rin sat behind her desk with her hands folded.

Jo and Charles Reed perched on old, hard folding chairs before the Ringmaster, covered in dirt and trying their hardest to clean their faces with some complimentary towels. In front of Rin on her desk was a now-completed incident report with carbon copies for the Weathers and and Agnes and Bernard. Now she and these children sat in their settling adrenaline, staring at each other through a summer night's receding heat.

Jo Reed looked very nervous, though Rin could tell she was the type that would never say so. Energy emanated from her shoulders, her steely ocean-blue eyes . . . she was like a stray puppy. One that desperately wanted a warm embrace but wouldn't be caught dead coming out from under the porch they hid beneath.

Rin's eyes flickered, smiling. Trying not to look imposing. What did this girl need?

You.

Rin didn't think that would be enough, but right now the girl needed someone. "Did you enjoy the show?"

The girl stared at her, dumbfounded. She looked like a shivering Chihuahua but her voice was flat and steady when she blurted out, "Are . . . are you serious?"

The Ringmaster paused. "Yes?"

"Nah, we didn't enjoy a literal magical circus *of course we enjoyed the show.*" Her face animated like a cartoon, her hands flailed.

Mauve snorted. Rin allowed a real grin. She laughed. "Good," she said. She had been right about this kid; there were a thousand volts of electricity in that noggin.

Rin had come to see that every single person was their own song. Some songs were quiet, some songs were reminiscent of others. But some other songs reminded her of the dramatic sound found in her childhood synagogue. Some people pressed into key changes, deep soulful strings clipped with a piano solo.

Jo Reed held a symphony inside her.

"Thanks for saving us," Jo said.

Rin nodded. "The team will be taking down our tents and fitting the train to move on as we speak. Can't be too careful with those types."

"You had them running," Jo said.

The Ringmaster now half smiled, and she looked down at her hands. "Yes, well, unfortunately, they can always switch the direction they're running if enough of them flock together." She looked over her desk to Jo and Charles. "I'm supposing since the wagon men wanted you, you two are a lot like us." The kids didn't know she and Mauve had seen them fighting the wagon men on their own earlier, in town.

Jo nodded. "And so are you. All of you," she directed the not-question to Odette and Mauve. Odette nodded, too.

Charles still hadn't said anything.

"You all right?" the Ringmaster asked him. Charles started.

"Yes, ma'am."

"This is my twin," Jo said. "We're a package deal."

"Are you two really twenty then?" the Ringmaster said. "Because I think you're actually about thirteen."

"Fifteen, but yeah, let's say twenty for the books," Jo said. "We really are twins. We take care of each other. Always have. I'm the brains and he's the muscle, see?"

"We're the youngest. . . ." Charles said. "Well, I mean . . . we're the only now . . . I was too young for the war . . . good for me, too, huh? As a Spark, they'd like to use us in those . . . ways. . . ." He trailed off as Rin's black eyes flicked to look at him. Through him.

To the beach with the barbed wire full of boys, dying in the future—

"The war is over," Rin said quick, shoving it all away and into the back of her skull. "It's been over."

"And the war made us into freaks somehow," Jo said. "That's how this all happened, right? Something got messed up or something? At least that's what I heard."

The Ringmaster pushed her hair out of her face, pulled an elastic from her trousers pocket, and started the makings of a ponytail. "The proper term is Peculiarities, in Britain. In Zulu, it's Isiphiwo. Here in the boonies, we say the Spark. We don't say Freaks."

"Who decided that?" Jo said. "Did y'all hold a meeting and vote?"

The Ringmaster narrowed her eyes, but her mouth curled up. "You're a smartass."

"I'm Jo," Jo said. "This is Charles. We need a ride out of town, and you need some fresh new acts."

"Oho, do I now?"

"Yup." Jo crossed one leg over the other, stretching her arms out lazily, very theatrically. "You got a nice setup here, but you're lacking in the danger, the magic. Trapeze swingers? Ringling Brothers got like five or six of them."

"Huh," Odette said.

"You do know Odette Paris can do much more than all five or six Ringling Brothers aerialists, right?" Rin said. "You putting down other acts isn't going to ingratiate you."

"Then fine, we'll be on *par* with what you got. Your aeri—aero—" She couldn't seem to say it. "The flying lady; we'll be remembered as a shining act like that."

"The flying lady?" Odette shook her head but she didn't laugh.

"The Illusionist and the Unkillable Devil," Jo kept on.

Charles was a cherub-faced baby, too young for anyone to be thinking about how killable he was. Definitely not a devil.

"How are you unkillable, Charles?" the Ringmaster said.

Charles beamed. "Shoot me."

"Yeah, no thank you." She laughed. But Charles was already on his feet.

"It's okay," Jo said. "Go ahead. Do you have a gun?"

"You want me to shoot you."

"Not me," Jo said. "Him."

"Yeah," Charles said. "Make sure it's me. Or you know, just hit me real hard."

"How did you find this out?" the Ringmaster said.

"Well, ma'am," Charles said, "our dad—" Jo shoved her elbow in his scrawny ribs. "Trial and error," he redacted.

They didn't say anything else.

"The same man who sold you to the wagons," the Ringmaster said. She looked them up and down. She'd had an inkling that the Sparks doled out were the Sparks that were needed. If Charles couldn't be hurt, that painted enough of a picture for Rin. She remembered that morning, Charles covering Jo with his body, just like Odette would do. He'd needed the Spark not for himself, but so he could be a shield.

"I see," Rin said.

They had been running for their lives this morning. He was one of many calcified children who had to grow up too fast. And Jo was one of many invisible girls trying to disappear into the cracks of the world.

Luckily for Jo and Charles Reed, that's exactly where the circus traveled.

It's where Rin had disappeared when she needed to, time and time again. And for years, her tent had sheltered many other castaways who'd had to leave their old homes barefoot.

The Ringmaster now stood and pushed past the desk. She pulled off her velvet coat and hung it on the back of her chair. Jo stared at it, like it shone. Rin walked past them, going to the cabinet to grab a couple of Coca-Colas. It was 1926, she had to remind herself by looking at her wrist. Warm would have to do. Refrigeration wasn't a thing Jo or Charles would worry about.

"I'm not going to shoot or hit you," the Ringmaster said, fumbling with the bottle cap. That was one thing she hated about the present. No screw tops. She sighed, returned to her desk, and rifled through a drawer for a bottle opener.

"Oh don't worry," Charles said as she did so. "It doesn't bounce off and hurt anything else, it just sorta drops. And I don't bruise—"

"Yeah, yeah, get on with it, ya chicken," Jo said.

"No," the Ringmaster said. She handed them both the bottles of pop. "I will trust you and take your word."

"So you're in agreement," Jo said, swiping hers, leaning back on her chair and taking a long sip before saying: "We belong."

The Ringmaster granted herself another small grin. "You need a lot more than a Spark to be a part of this circus, kiddos. We don't just entertain, we try to help."

"What, like fundraising or something?" Jo said. "You Salvation Army bell ringers? Or a secret militia of elite crime fighters? Rubber ration collectors?"

The Ringmaster didn't laugh. "No one knows why the Spark showed up in some people," she said. "You must be one of the youngest Sparks out there. I haven't met many who were children at the time. There's Kell and Meredith, but . . . you're babies."

"Well, you're old," Jo retorted.

The Ringmaster wrinkled her nose. "Thanks," she said.

Odette offered, "Guess her age and you get a free gumball."

Rin ignored her. "How old were you when the Spark came?"

"I don't know," Jo said. "After our brother left for the war."

Rin nodded. "I don't know if it's because we all broke or if we all are here to mend, but I prefer to think we are here to make a difference. To change something essential . . ." She looked down at her hands, the ones that grabbed at time itself. "We here at the circus have found this place to be safe enough. We don't have to fight wars, we don't have to get involved in politics and legislation. We've found our place, and we slip through the cracks of the rest of the world's places."

"This circus is a way to hide?" Jo said.

"No," the Ringmaster said calmly. "No, we do much good here. Empires have always underestimated artists. And it works in our favor. It makes us powerful. No one expects us to change the world, and so we do. And I expect you both to change the world if I take you two on. I won't invest in anyone less."

It was now Jo's turn to grin. "I wouldn't invest in anyone who wanted less." Ha.

The Ringmaster cocked a brow and gave a small guffaw. She fixed herself in her chair, rolling her creaky back. "And Charles, what do you think?"

"Oh, ma'am, if you'll have us!" Charles burst into a smile, and Rin realized just because he didn't talk much didn't mean he was quiet inside. "I've been keen on this place since we saw the posters. It's the real McCoy."

"Oh, I thought we weren't the Ringling Brothers," Mauve snorted.

"Well, I think you're a lot better than the brothers," Charles said.

"Thank you." Mauve tipped an invisible hat. "One of you has appreciation."

Rin cleared her throat. "So," she said, putting her fingers together in attention, her elbows on the desk. "Charles is an Unkillable cherub-faced Devil.

But what about Jo. What's your Spark, kid? Illusions? Want to explain to me what it is?"

"I can make pictures," Jo said.

It seemed more than that, but the Ringmaster let her lead. "What was the first picture you made?" she asked. She knew Odette and Mauve were listening, even if they acted like they weren't.

Jo swallowed. "I was cleaning the kitchen floor," she said. "I looked up at the wall and there was a painting of water. I started thinking about waves and the ocean, and then . . ." Jo looked at Charles, and she rolled up her sleeves. "Here. I'll show you."

Jo didn't wait for the Ringmaster to say anything; she just shot to her feet and took a position like a martial artist, up on her toes and her arms braced out in front of her. Maybe she was going to dance?

Jo breathed in. "So I'm thinking of pictures I've seen of other places," she said. "Islands far away from Nebraska. A big open sky. Curvy palm trees. The way you can see fish through clear blue water. And I . . . I can . . ."

And there, from her hands came the white waves rolling, curling in on themselves, an ocean that was both fearsome and tranquil. It was alive. She was alive.

The Ringmaster saw the cool waves fly from her fingertips. Magic seemed to thrust out of her shoulders and heart, into the air ahead of her. The room splashed, slowly simmering into another thing altogether. There was the sound of seagulls, the smell of salt, the bright horizon, the wet, pulling, tugging tide that washed over sand that sank between her toes.

Jo whipped her hands clean of it all.

Then it was silent. Dry. Just an office made of plywood on one half of a hand-me-down pie car. Like nothing miraculous had happened.

Rin felt her mouth gape open. Wow. She couldn't think of a word to say, so she quickly sutured the rip in her composure and just nodded. That's when she realized Odette and Mauve were standing at their desks, respectively disturbed.

It was as she'd seen that morning. But this time, Jo had been in control. It had been beautiful. How had she been so frightening hours ago, and now so wondrous?

That's what Sparks were, though, weren't they? They could be something terrible, or they could be something terribly helpful.

Jo sat again next to Charles in the chairs without being prompted. The three women stared at the two children.

The Ringmaster broke the silence. "Charles, can you eat fire?"

"No, ma'am," he said. "It's only my skin. But I could set myself on fire?"

"That works," the Ringmaster said. "But the moment anything becomes dangerous, you will stop. Do you hear me? You follow my instructions and stay safe."

"All right!" Charles said cheerfully.

"And Jo," she said. "You'll create exactly what I tell you *when* I tell you."

"Why do you get to choose?"

"Because I'm the Ringmaster," she said. "You'll get a full explanation, but we don't discuss anything else until you agree to that."

"Fine," Jo said.

The Ringmaster nodded. "Then we'll need to discuss your contracts."

"Nah nah nah," Jo said. "We don't sign contracts. We're no suckers."

Mauve pulled out two papers from her desk and gave them to the kids. "This contract is more for your protection of rights than it is for us. Hi, I'm Mauve. Producer. Nightingale. Person who will be paying you."

"We get paid for this?!" Jo said.

"Yes," Rin said. "That's what it says in the contract. We treat you as professionals. Now the thing is, you're both young. Which means this is working more as an understanding of what is owed to you, how you will be treated. If at any time you feel as if there was a breach or there is somewhere better for you than here, you are free to leave. You are *always* free to leave."

Jo nodded.

"But I expect you will let me know, if you do," the Ringmaster said. "Because I need to prepare another act. Fair?"

"Fair."

"Now you're going to be paid forty-five dollars a week, every Saturday evening," Mauve said, pointing at the paper from over their shoulder. "This is negotiable for a raise after your first season. We'd like you to stick around for winter quarters for training and rehearsal, but understand if you need to make ends meet with a second job."

"Forty-five dollars a *week*?!" Charles said. "Holy schnickers are you serious?!"

"Forty-five dollars a week per act," Mauve clarified. "You are two acts, so you each will be paid forty-five dollars."

"No, you're pulling my leg!" Charles squeaked.

"You have a right to room and board," Mauve went on, and the Ringmaster smiled as the kids lit up. "You have a right to a safe work environment.

We have a right to you being respectful, mindful, and responsible. Punctual, too."

They were so young. They pored over the contract with Mauve, and Rin knew none of it was binding. But they would be paid, they would be looked after, and when the time came, they would go their own way.

Jo and Charles both signed with pens Mauve handed them. Then it was the Ringmaster's turn.

"Now one more thing," the Ringmaster said. "We ask three very serious questions before it's finalized and we sign your contract on our dotted line."

"Go on," Jo said.

The Ringmaster nodded. "First question. Are you here of your own free will?"

"Yes," Jo said immediately.

"Yes, ma'am," Charles said.

The Ringmaster studied their faces. And continued.

"Do you understand that circus life is hard?"

"Like how?" Charles said.

"Odd hours, always on the road, it's not like home."

"Good riddance, yes," Jo said.

"Yes, ma'am," Charles said.

The Ringmaster then leaned in, her face glowing in the lantern on her desk as if she was going to share a dark and dangerous secret. "I have the ability to make one wish come true," she said quietly. "Anything you could want. Money? Raise the dead? Fame? Love? I will give you one thing to make your life better. But only if you don't come with us." Rin let this hang for a moment. "Now, do you still want to join our circus?"

They weren't ready for that question. The offer was true. She'd decided long ago, when they started this circus, that no one would have to turn to them as a last resort. If Rin could travel through time and space, then Rin could change threads. Just little things. Making sure someone didn't get run over by a car, pushing someone to another era so they could get the medical help they needed. Mauve would check ahead of time to make sure the ways they might change a person's thread wouldn't disrupt anything else.

She remembered the first boy who she'd asked this question to. He and his brother had come in; they were workers at a nearby factory. The boy's older brother had been trying to sell him off, but the boy didn't want to join the circus. When Rin asked him what his wish would be, the boy had answered he'd wish to bring his ma back. Odette had said it was impossible, they'd ruin everything in the whole universe. Mauve had said that's not how all changes worked. Sometimes something would be small to the universe, but the entire universe to one person. They'd saved his mother from the accident. The three women had returned to the factory. No one had heard of either brother. So their work was done.

Now Jo and Charles Reed sat before her. Mauve had checked their threads. She'd given the go. Like the circus, the three women worked behind the scenes, rehearsing, training, planning, to make the present seamless.

"Is that your Spark?" Jo said. "To grant wishes?"

"Answer the question," the Ringmaster said.

"You can make anything happen?" Jo said. "So you could make it so the war never happened?"

This jarred the Ringmaster. Rin couldn't go back beyond the graveyard. She couldn't go back beyond the Spark. And ahead of them, there was a new war waiting. So the Ringmaster was silent.

"Then you can't make *anything* happen," Jo said. "I'm in."

Charles nodded. "Yes, ma'am."

Then you can't make anything happen.

No. Rin swallowed herself back and let the Ringmaster blossom as she forced a smile and outstretched her hands. "Welcome to the circus," she said. Jo took one, and Charles took the other. And the Ringmaster clamped down on their fingers tight like a vice.

"One last thing," she said. "Will you stay away from the Circus King?"

Jo tried to pull away. She couldn't. The Ringmaster was too strong, too serious. The Ringmaster was afraid she was scaring them. But she couldn't let go of their hands.

"Who the hell is the Circus King?" Jo said. "Some kind of competition?"

"Yes," she said. "He runs the other Spark circus. And his Sparks aren't as cuddly as ours. He's never come after us. And we do our best to keep safe. But there was . . ." She stopped herself. She'd told the others in the circus there was a risk. They all knew. It used to be there was a hypothetical risk, but now it was an elevated risk. "There's a growing risk that you should be aware of."

"Oh, we're used to competition clauses, ma'am," Charles said. "We've had a lot of different jobs—"

"I didn't say this part of the discussion was a back-and-forth," the Ringmaster said. "If you see the Circus King or you see his black tents, you get the hell away from them. He's got a Spark and his cronies have Sparks you're not going to be able to go up against. You understand?"

Jo narrowed her eyes. Like she could see the deep crevice cracking open somewhere in the Ringmaster's façade, behind the Ringmaster's eyes and her hands and her heart.

Jo was a smart kid. She could see the hurt in others because she had hurt inside herself. Part of an unspoken covenant between those who had survived something.

"Fine," Jo said.

Charles nodded.

The Ringmaster's mask was put back in place. "Welcome to the circus, kids," she said.

"All right, lovelies." Odette clasped her hands and came forward, nearly dancing on her toes as she maneuvered around the cramped office. "Are we ready to see the LQ?"

"The uh . . ." Charles looked confused. Jo curled her lip. They raised their brows in the same way as they shot each other a questioning look. Maybe it was a twin thing.

"Living Quarters," Odette said. "We're heading out, so we should get you settled!"

Jo and Charles Reed followed Odette out through the vestibule and onto the track's gravel, curbing around to the sleeper cars. "We must G to the LQ so we can S, my dear B," Jo's voice trailed out of earshot.

Mauve looked to Rin as Rin rubbed her face, like rubbing makeup off. Rin relaxed, but tensed again when she saw Mauve waiting expectantly.

"Can I help you?" Rin asked.

"You are either really bad with faces or you're tired or both. You don't recognize her?" Mauve said. "I wasn't sure, but now that we've seen her closer . . . it's definitely her."

Rin narrowed her eyes. "Jo Reed? She's the kid from this morning, our special guest."

Mauve sighed and shook her head. "Oh, Rin."

Not everyone called her Rin. Mauve was one of a few who knew her well enough, under the surface of the Ringmaster's velvet red coat and big smile, to call her—

Mauve's voice faded from Rin's ears. The blue eyes. The black hair. The woman, in the apartment far away, before the blue light of the bomb, the unknown woman had rushed to her: "*Rin*?"

Something crashed over Rin like the waves out of Jo's fingers.

She remembered the tears in the woman's eyes as the cement room exploded. There had been something desperate, hurting . . . grief.

"Jo Reed," Rin said suddenly. "She's the girl we saw in the war. She's going to die in the war. No, that can't be her only future."

"I'm telling you what I see so we can prevent it, not so we can be afraid," Mauve said.

"Can we stop it?" Rin said. "Can we give her something good to have? Or should I send her away? Would that be better for her?"

"I don't know!" Mauve wearily picked up her shawl and threw it on. "With kids, anything is possible. Now," she said, forcing an upbeat tone into her voice, "you've taken up a lot of my time today. I'm gonna go grab some grub before we take off tonight. Lockbox is back in the safe. We netted some good bunce. Which, good, because I cannot keep hemorrhaging my account. Keep the numbers up in Lawrence. G'day ma'am, nice doing business with you."

Mauve took her exit.

And the Ringmaster was left alone looking at the chair where Jo Reed had negotiated her way into their circus.

Those big blue eyes, tearing up, looking at her in the midst of hell itself. "Rin," she'd called her . . . or she *would* call her. Like she'd just seen the one person in the world she'd wanted to see more than anything. The Ringmaster was her title, most people casually called her Ringmaster with no *The* . . . but Rin, Rin was a name that she held behind walls and under false floors. This kid was going to mean something to her, and she was gonna mean something to this kid, which twisted Rin's brain into a pretzel because they'd just met but . . .

Now the future was in the present. Those blue eyes were so alive. This girl was sitting on a precipice and she could fall or she could fly. Maybe Rin could build her a bridge. . . .

There had once been another kid whose Spark shot like lightning into the world.

"No," Rin said. She grabbed her coat and doused her light. "Not gonna think about that." With kids, anything is possible.

✳

12

EDWARD, 1917

Edward nervously stood, perched between Mrs. Dover and the door. The parlor had an air of danger.

Mrs. Dover was wearing her red coat, a beautiful thing. She stood by the candle table, then slowly moved to the hearth in this beautiful home that she could afford thanks to her acting success. She may have already made it to Broadway when Edward met her, but he had made her a star in such little time. They were a family, and that was real. Yes, there had been a few slip-ups, where he'd forgotten to ask or he'd forgotten to say something like "Well, I believe" before a statement, and some of those things had resulted in Mrs. Dover procuring this house, Ruth being happy on rainy days, only good things.

But this question needed to be real. He needed to be more careful with his words. He needed to be careful with Ruth. She had to be his honestly, deep down in her heart; not a mirage, not a trick.

It would be him, not his Spark, that would make Ruth love him.

"I know what you want," Mrs. Dover said. "I've known for a while." Her severe eyes looked to him. Tonight, she looked like a lady King Lear. "So why don't you ask for it?"

"Because I want you to want to give your blessing," he said. It was honest. But Mrs. Dover didn't know how honest it was.

She looked at the mantel. The pictures of her on all the stages she'd ever wanted. Her Spark had been good to her.

His Spark had been good to them. It was nothing to feel guilty for, nothing to regret. They were in a warm, happy home. Sparks were nothing but extensions, weren't they? So that meant if his Spark had done these things, then he had done them. He had made them happen. And he deserved what he had.

"I have taken you in as my own," she said. "With Ruth plucking you from No Man's Land, it came naturally. Perhaps it was one of the most natural things I ever did. And yet, you are not my son. You are not Ruth's brother. That's been clear since the moment you two appeared in my apartment with sand in your muddy boots and a sunburn on your cheeks."

Edward could have cut this short. He didn't have to listen to any more explanations, patronizations from anyone.

But he couldn't stop it. This is how it needed to go.

"And although I know you love her and you mean best," she said, "I can't give you my permission to marry my daughter."

Edward stood. "What?" he said. "Why? Answer me, why!"

She drew her hands back to her stomach, and she looked him up and down like he was a belligerent pet. How dare she. "Quite frankly, Edward, because you are demanding me to answer you as if you own the world."

He did own the world. He could rip everything he'd given her away from her greedy fingers. He could make it hurt.

He took a breath. "I love Ruth. She loves me. Why don't you think that's enough?"

Their eyes locked. She was his now. She would answer.

"Because," she said, her voice calm, perhaps in a trance, "before Ruth found you, she didn't hunch her shoulders. She didn't cower behind you. She did not listen to every word a man said and follow his directions to every letter. She is to be a woman of her own, and I am afraid of you."

I am afraid of you.

The words tore his brain in two. Half of him thought *good, let her be afraid,* but the other half, perhaps the better half, felt as if he'd been swatted across the face. The woman who had treated him like a son was afraid of him.

"I don't understand," Edward said. "How are you afraid of me?"

Mrs. Dover turned from the hearth, turned from Edward. "The things you do when you think no one is watching," she said. "You wear them in the creases of your mouth, like Dorian Gray. You believe in nothing larger than yourself. And regardless of what I think of your lack of kindness toward your fellow man . . . my daughter deserves someone who makes her laugh. And you, Edward, do not make her laugh. You know this. You've *known* this."

That was the end of the conversation. He stormed out and down the hall. He rested in his room for a moment to calm down before opening Ruth's door quietly. Then they lay in bed, holding each other. His eyes locked on the wall, where Ruth had cut pictures of beautiful places around the world from magazines and posters and she'd stuck them to the soft green wallpaper. There was London, Chicago, New York, Iceland, the Rocky Mountains, and a familiar beach where once she'd taken them when they escaped the trench.

It was the safest, most desolate, most beautiful place. It was the day his life began again. In Ruth, he had a chance to be happy. No one else had ever shown him an ocean so blue; no one else had held him so close in her bed.

"She won't let me marry you," he told her.

"You wanted to marry me?" Ruth said.

"I did," he said.

"Then ask me," Ruth said. "I'm the one who matters. Who is she to tell me what to do with my life?"

"I would rather you ask me—" Edward caught himself. "If . . . that's what you want. Only if that's what you want."

Ruth snuggled in deeper to Edward. She said, "What would we do?"

"Well," Edward said. "I have lots of luck." Yes, that was his Spark; just luck, nothing else. "We can do whatever we like. Fly a crop duster? See the Great Wall? Become rich and build ourselves a mansion?"

Ruth nestled her face into his rough dark hair. "Whatever you want," she said. "We'll leave in the morning before Mother wakes up."

"It's not whatever I want," Edward said. "If you come with me, everything we do is because we both want it."

"All right," Ruth said quietly, as if she was in a trance.

"I want to see the world with you," he said, holding her close. He ran his fingers through her hair. Her arms enveloped him. "You are the best thing in my life, Ruth. I love you."

"I love you, too," she said.

"Really? You do?"

"Of course I do," Ruth kissed his chest. "Wake me up in a few hours. I'm a fast packer, just one suitcase."

"I will," Edward said.

With that, Ruth fell asleep. But Edward couldn't find rest. Whatever you want. *Whatever you want.*

She must love him. She'd kept with him all these months, all the times they'd gone out on the street and gone to their favorite shops. That day at the natural history museum, and the visit to Boston Harbor, and the holiday to Maine? Those couldn't all be false, could they?

"Ruth? Do you really love me?" he said again as she slept.

But she was deep under her covers, quietly snoring through her freckled nose. And he could only hold her closer until she woke in the morning.

And in the morning, they packed one suitcase. Ruth had finer things than he did. He packed a few clothes and the engagement ring. Of course, he kept his father's pocketknife in his trousers. But as they tried to quietly stow away through the front door, Mrs. Dover appeared.

"I see you didn't take our conversation to heart last night," she said to Edward.

Edward kept his mouth shut. Then he could look back on this moment and know there was more to this than his words.

"Mother," Ruth said. "I love Edward. And nothing is going to stop us from loving each other."

"Ruth," Mrs. Dover said. "*I* love *you*. Please, you've trusted me all your life and I always try to do the right thing by you. Ruth, you and I need to leave and get you away from here."

"Leave?" Edward said. Mrs. Dover's eyes cut through Edward. It was as if her entire body manifested a cold, dark shadow. Hatred seemed to seep through her fingertips, her teeth, her eyes. It was at this moment he realized he had a knife in his pocket. He could use it.

"Please, Ed, I don't want to leave you," Ruth begged. Edward held Ruth's hand tighter. "Mother, please, please, I love him."

He could use the knife.

"Ruth, he's dangerous," Mrs. Dover said. "His Spark isn't luck." No. No no, please. Don't take Ruth away. "It's—"

"Look at her," Edward cut through her dark words. "She's a monster, Ruth. Do you see it? Look at her!"

She was not a monster. She was only Mrs. Dover. But Ruth fell to the floor, screaming.

Mrs. Dover shuddered into her own coat, and she rushed to Ruth. "Darling . . ." But Edward barked:

"Stop where you are."

She stopped.

He didn't need to wield his knife. He was so much more dangerous than anything that anyone could hold in their hand.

He glared at Mrs. Dover, deep into her. "I clench your heart in my hand," he said, pantomiming. "You're nothing, you pathetic old hag." He clenched his fist. She collapsed to her knees.

Ruth shrieked.

"Stop it, Ruth," Edward snapped. Ruth stopped.

Ruth would never leave him. He wouldn't choke in the dark. He would hold on to this light. He would save himself if no one else would. He would save them both.

"Do you want to be with me?" Edward asked Ruth. Ruth nodded, staring at him wide-eyed and apprehensive like he was made of thorns. "Say it. Say you want to leave with me. Say you love me."

"I want to leave with you. I love you."

"Say it like you mean it," Edward begged her.

"I want to leave with you, I love you," she begged him. And she meant it. They both turned to face Mrs. Dover, Ruth in fear and Edward in absolute hatred. They were together, side by side, a team no one would ever rip apart. They were sewn at the edges with red threads. With invincible red thread. He'd make it so.

Mrs. Dover cowered between the grandfather clock and his boots, writhing on the floor on her beautiful rug with the elephants bordering her plump, ugly body.

"Mrs. Dover," Edward growled. "I am taking your daughter. We love each other and we will have a good life. You will never find us, even if we stand right in front of your nose. You will never recognize us again. But that doesn't mean you will ever stop searching. You will go mad with searching. And it will have no end."

Mrs. Dover howled, her eyes looking through him. And then he turned to Ruth.

"Ruth," he said. "You'll forget this morning and remember what I tell you to remember. Your mother tried to keep us apart. You said you wanted to leave with me. This was your choice, your doing. So Ruth, I'm going to get you away from here."

Ruth nodded, her eyes wide, her mouth slack like she was sleepwalking. She took Edward's hand. Edward put his arm around her shoulders and squeezed her hand.

As they left, Mrs. Dover's screams were so much louder than he thought they'd be. He could hear them through the door. As the rage subsided, he realized how horrible the grief of a mother must feel.

He wondered if his own mother had sounded that way, when she realized he was never coming home.

But that was all in the past. He told Ruth to cheer up. No need to let the past tether them.

They caught the next train out West.

The East never saw them again.

✳

13

THE RINGMASTER, 1926

It was time to jump the train.

Rin sat cross-legged on the tin roof of Mauve's sleeper car. She looked out to the Midwest sailing past, the stars above and the prairie sea below and the half moon's bright shine on her shoulders and possibility beyond.

She was flying.

"You would've really loved this, Ma," Rin whispered to the stars. Once, her mother took her to a park and showed her the helicopter seeds spinning and swirling through the air. Rin asked if humans could fly. Her mother said if there was a way for a girl to fly, Rin would be the one to figure it out.

She had to remember that once, her mother had existed. And now, this train existed, no matter what they found beyond it tonight. She couldn't forget to breathe joy.

Odette and Mauve clambered up the ladder. "We thought we'd find you here," Odette said.

It may have taken the Circus King some time to find her, but from the first day of her new life, Rin had been on the defense. She did not follow a normal route for the circus. She would hop the entire caravan off one track and land it somewhere else. Rin tried to do the jumps late in the evening, when most of the crew could sleep through it. It could be disorienting, like a clock changing on a long steamliner's ride across the ocean. Go to sleep in one place on a Monday night, arrive in the morning three states west.

The Circus King may be powerful, but so was Rin. Regardless of what he believed of her, she could move entire trains with just her hands.

"Alright," Rin said, rolling up her sleeves. Odette and Mauve sat down. Rin got on her knees and closed her eyes.

She raised her hands above her head, feeling the wind whip through her jacket, her hair, like she really was soaring through the air. She smiled.

Rin could feel her Spark radiating through her arms. She was ready for what came next. The anticipation, the adrenaline, the energy that churned from an engine she couldn't see within her own self; it made her feel electric.

Rin remembered sitting with her mother at the synagogue, uncomfortable in the balcony. They rarely went. But that morning, she'd listened intently as the rabbi said, "Why are we here? We are here to help life sing the song it was meant for. We are here to heal the world."

There was more magic in the universe than what the Spark had given them. *They* were the magic.

"Ready," she whispered.

She swung her arms forward in an arc and slammed her palms onto the metal below her.

She opened her eyes then and looked to the horizon. The land dissipated around her. They disappeared into what looked like a rip, a tunnel, and were swallowed whole as they shot forward, forward, into the black dotted with stars made of memories, of things to come and things that had been, things that could still be. It was like jumping from one cliff's edge to another, the feeling of flying, falling, hoping in between. But she wasn't afraid. She knew the way; she always knew the way. She saw her string, strong, like an anchor pulling them forward. Kansas. She roared out into the void, but no one could hear her over the sound of rushing. . . .

She saw the train tracks she was looking for ahead. She thrust herself and the train forward, pushing the locomotive to land perfectly on the tracks with a clack, not a beat missed.

They charged into the new night, the tunnel closing behind them.

Magic.

Odette helped Rin off her old knees to sit beside them. After using her Spark, Odette was often tired. But after the jump, Rin was invigorated. It felt like she'd drank three cups of coffee and would be up all night.

"Slick as ice," she let herself say, like she always said.

The other two knew all this. They were ready for the manic crows she allowed herself in these moments, an unrestrained abandon that would have usually made Rin turn red. But there was nothing to be self-conscious about or anything to explain. Because they'd been here with her for years now, jump after jump, and they were here tonight.

"Your knees aren't gonna always let you do that maneuver," Odette said.

"Well, my Spark is still roaring," Rin said.

Odette nodded.

Mauve sighed. "Just next time you start feeling like we don't need you," Mauve said, "remember I'm not jumping a train and neither is Odette."

"And the Circus King is alone," Odette said. "You are not alone."

But you should be. You're putting them all in danger.

Rin narrowed her eyes. She couldn't think about him tonight, there was too much to do.

They made their way down the ladder and into the caboose. They still had a couple more hours until dawn.

Just enough time to stop a war.

✳

Tonight, they would leave for the future from Mauve's room.

Mauve had built a princess's chambers in a train car. She'd hung a flock of glass birds from fishing line, strung and stuck to the ceiling. The walls were made of mirrors, and Rin was faced with her own velvet jacket, her curved figure, her hard, aged face. She didn't even recognize herself. In her head, she was still a young girl who could fit into much slimmer trousers. But this woman who looked back at her from a thousand angles between glass birds? She was a stranger.

Mauve lay on her pink silk bed and pushed her blankets out of the way. Odette and Rin followed. They sat in a circle on the mattress. They held hands.

"What's the plan?" Odette asked.

"Well." Rin swallowed hard. "There has to be some small piece we can move. Where does the war begin?"

Mauve gave a small snort. "Where does a war begin? In a thousand places. We have to find not where it begins, but where it can be changed. Now I haven't seen this far away from the circus before, so it might take me a second."

"Wait," Odette said. "I didn't know you could do that. Did your Spark grow, too?"

"Too?" Mauve said. "What do you mean 'too?' Did *yours* grow?"

Odette made a face that looked like she was smiling through a wince. "I . . . can take a lot more than I used to."

Rin nodded quietly. "Yeah," was all she said.

"Sounds like it's happening to a lot of Sparks," Mauve said.

"Are you okay, Mauve?" Rin asked.

Mauve laughed. "I'm looking at the war of the worlds through time and you're asking me if I'm okay."

"We don't have to do this—" Odette said.

"Stop," Mauve said. "We already decided."

Mauve closed her eyes, her brow furrowed. She took a deep breath, and when she opened them, her eyes traced the room as if a million ghosts crowded around her. It was only supposed to be one film reel, but this was multiple screens all at the same time, it seemed. Mauve gasped for air and closed her eyes again. Her body jerked, like the train had swerved when it had not, and Rin could tell she was struggling to brace herself.

"Mauve?" Rin said. "Please check in, if you need to step back—"

"It starts so many places," Mauve said, her eyes still closed. "So many threads it's like a loom . . ." She nodded her head, to herself, and opened her eyes again. "Wow." She closed her eyes again. "I wish we could tell Dad."

Bernard had been the one to help Mauve when she was young and the Spark first came. Bernard always told the story of how he used a book to explain that even though she could hold the whole story in her hands, she must focus on one chapter at a time. Bernard also said Mauve was always special, that it doesn't take a Spark to light someone up.

"If you could have a Spark," Mauve had asked him once as they all ate at the cookhouse, "what would it be?"

"I'd take yours," Bernard had said, matter-of-factly, like he'd thought about this before. "So you wouldn't have to do it."

Now, Mauve had her eyes open and fixed on one space in the room. "A lot of it is politics," she said, her jaw set. "A *lot* of talking and lies and promises and deals, and headlines and gestures, and threats . . . I'm trying to find a human in this mess . . . there!" She gave a little jump. "There's a coward," she said. "Ha! It's working! Damn I'm good!"

"Are you sure you're okay?" Rin and Odette both asked, nearly in unison.

"I'm fine, I'm fine, I'm in it now, stop henpecking." Mauve yanked their hands as if to swat them, but she couldn't let go. "Let me focus on this fella. I think he's some higher-up in England, and he's waving a piece of paper in the air. The piece of paper has a promise on it. Now take it away, Rin."

Rin closed her eyes now, and she searched the thread for this image. She saw the space between thoughts, between words, between moments, in that place in the back of her skull, right behind her eyes. She pictured her calendars, the threads sifting between the dates on the timeline.

A day looked like a clock. A week looked like an upside-down protractor. A year looked like a rounded square. A century looked like a long incline of a line. Multiple centuries were lines stacked on top of each other, corresponding. It churned around, surrounded by starlight, floating in her imagination, the threads leading in and out in those staves of music like ... yes ... a loom. Now that Mauve had called it that, she could see the resemblance.

There, in the small space of the 1930s, she saw him. A man with a crown of gray hair around his face, the rest still a shock of black, neatly parted. She peered closer, as if diving into the calendar square on the timeline. She saw him, fuzzy, like a dream. He was happy. The people around him cheered on cue. He liked the cheering. And the paper had two signatures on it.

"I see him," Rin said. "Why's he so happy?"

"He made a deal," Mauve said, "with a devil. The devil said he wouldn't start the war."

"And he just believed him?" Odette said.

Mauve nodded. "The devil's not going to keep his word. Devils never do."

"It's not the literal devil," Rin clarified. "Right?"

"Oh come on, Rin, no," Mauve said. "Sometimes it all comes to me in imagery and metaphor. Although"—Mauve raised one brow—"how bully would that be, if it *was* literal? Heading down to Hell with flaming swords! Anyhoo." Mauve squinted. Mauve was looking further and further, while Rin put a mental bookmark where the happy coward sat on the loom.

"He needs courage," Mauve said. "He needs to know to stand up to a bully. The devil is bluffing. He won't go to war, he's too weak right now. The coward needs to cut off his legs and fight back, before they all appease and the evil can grow and grow and plague everything . . ." She blinked, like turning off the film reel in her head. She looked to Rin, a big smile on her face. "Scottish play," she said. "Macduff, standing up against a bluffing king. It's playing that year. Can you pinpoint it?"

Rin nodded. "Lemme see." She checked the surrounding threads, all the months and weeks close to the image of the man. She tried to find the feeling of her mother's Lady M costume against her cheek, the smell of fake ice and low-budget fog.

She found it. Five months before the paper and the crowd. April, 1938. It was a Tuesday, on the first curve of the protractor, on the first curve of the rounded square. She had her target.

"Got it," she said. "1938." Rin looked to the women beside her, the pillars of her life. "Shall I take us?"

"I can't tell if it's . . . safe but . . ." Mauve checked. "Hopefully safe enough to make a quick appearance at a cocktail party if we stick together."

It was never a certainty they'd be safe. Not if they were outside the circus. But they would be together. They would have their Sparks. It had to be enough.

"Cocktail party?" Rin asked.

"Mrs. Chamberlain is at a cocktail party," Mauve said. "She is looking for a small holiday with her husband. He's the man with the paper, the prime minister. Neville Chamberlain. He's stressed."

"All right then," Rin said. "Let's get this coward to see some theater, huh?"

"This is your plan?" Odette said as Rin leaned in.

Rin smiled. "We've always changed the world with small gestures of lights and shadows, my love. Why would the future be any different?"

She pulled the worn bracelet from her coat pocket. *Not today.*

Rin slid the twine and wood over her fingers, onto her wrist. She stared straight ahead, concentrating. She saw the loom of threads and staves curl in and become that tunnel. She cast her line out, to the coward, and it hooked. Then she shoved the power from her arms, into the three of them, and they disappeared from the bed, they dissolved into the loom, and they were

spinning through a thousand and more days to come. They shot past a blurred crowding of moments. Rin wondered, as they burst through time, where she would be, say, in the summer of 1928. Or the winter of 1932. Maybe she wouldn't even still be here to be anywhere by the fall of 1936. She couldn't see herself; she could barely see anything. It was a dark, spinning place as if they were having a waking dream or somehow stepping through the white space between lines in a book. Small flashes of things, then off again, and it all took less than a second. It didn't look like protractors or round squares anymore, but a backstage to time itself. A void of stars and imprints of moments. Rin didn't know what this all looked like to the other two, though she suspected Mauve saw a lot of it, and she had a fleeting moment to worry over what Mauve'd told them tonight, that her Spark and sight was getting stronger, because how much can one human take, even if that human is a Spark?

This jump, for Rin, was not as freeing as jumping the train. It didn't feel like flying between cliffsides, but instead like she took a massive breath, held it, and jumped off a diving board. It was that space in the air, not on land, but not hitting the water yet. She knew the splash was coming, she could see the world moving around her, and before she could stay too long, they

14

THE RINGMASTER, 1938

arrived outside a dashing restaurant. Its innards chimed with clinking glasses and a string quartet. It was a nice spring day, sometime in the future. It was April 30, 1938. The air was dry and cold, but still the winter was over and a reprieve hung around the necks of those who walked London without scarves or mittens.

It was 5:38 P.M. according to the big clock outside the department store. It was important to keep time straight.

By 6:00 P.M., the three women had found suitable clothes and hairpieces and jewelry and slipped through to the cocktail party holding themselves as if they were heiresses or some distant royalty. They'd learned women were not treated well in most places on the timeline, considered only a step above furniture. Tonight, it seemed to be working in their favor. What women would break into a cocktail party to chat to the PM's wife about theater? And Rin felt that familiar air of their group being stared at, but no one threw them out. Not this time. By 6:20 P.M., Rin had peeled off from Odette and Mauve with a stern look and unspoken warning from Odette to avoid the bar.

By 6:32 P.M., Rin had ingratiated herself to Mrs. Neville Chamberlain, who had been kvetching to a good-sized gaggle about how her husband, the prime minister, wanted to take a holiday, but if she had to hike with him through nature for another eight hours straight, she may assassinate him herself. Mrs. Chamberlain explained once her husband got walking, there was no stopping him. Like a windup toy, Rin imagined. A thin little windup toy of the man with the black crest of hair while the rest of him was gray. A man who was invigorated by nature and applause. There was a juxtaposition there, Rin thought. Nature was a worthy motivation, to see all of the world that one can. But applause was deceptive and easily dissolved.

She said none of that out loud to Mrs. Chamberlain.

By 6:35 P.M., Rin had mentioned to Mrs. Chamberlain that Stratford-Upon-Avon had beautiful parts to walk, but nothing too lofty that would damn her to an entire afternoon's worth of exercise. She then mentioned that the Scottish Play was being performed by the RSC, and her cousin was playing one of the witches, and it was quite good. Rin didn't have a cousin. But Rin herself was an actor, first and foremost. She said it so quietly, meekly, kindly, that Mrs. Chamberlain seemed intrigued by this mousey new addition to her evening's entourage and coaxed more information from Rin.

By 6:43 P.M., Mrs. Chamberlain had a new grand plan to take her husband to the theater in Stratford-Upon-Avon, to see a play about a man who must move the woods itself to stand up to the tyrant. By 7:01 P.M., Rin met back with Odette and Mauve who had pretended to enjoy themselves with the evening's music and drinks, and the three set out to the powder room. It was there they locked the door. Rin looked to Mauve. "Wanna check if it worked?"

Mauve bit her lip, scanning the flowery wallpaper of this ornate future washroom, and she then said, "She goes to the theater with him."

"Does it work though?" Rin said. She picked at the doorframe's carved roses. She shouldn't. But her nerves were killing her, especially with the smell of cocktail hour all around them. Odette was staring her down, Rin could feel it. Odette was cataloging her nervous tics.

No, they were all just nervous.

But it would be over soon.

Mauve's face fell. "I'm seeing him in a plane, on his way to Munich to talk to the evil man. He looks down, he thinks about Birnam Wood in the play. He asks a man how many bombs would it take to kill London . . . how long it would be to kill a million people. . . ."

Rin knew the play well enough to know what had gone wrong. Chamberlain didn't see himself in Macduff. He saw himself in the hapless king who lived in fear, the tyrant who thought he was safe only to be duped by the witches' prophecies of moving forests. A man who did not look ahead and did not listen to his mortality.

"I don't understand," Rin muttered. "It should have worked."

"We can't force people to see what we want them to see," Mauve said.

"I think he's a person under a lot of stress," Odette said.

"He's a coward." Rin burned inside. The washroom felt catastrophically small against the dark future they were discussing. "So I go back out there now and tell Mrs. Chamberlain to pay attention to Macduff, or that her husband reminds me of Macduff. They just need a shove in the right direction."

"You cannot gracefully reenter that conversation, Rin," Mauve said. "She's the PM's wife, not your bridesmaid. Oh hellooo, Mrs. Chamberlain. I did so forget to give you this study guide for this play so your country doesn't end up on a beach from hell, no reason. Just felt like it?" Mauve shook her head, and then turned to the mirror. She patted her braided bun to make sure the hair was still in place. "We have to try somewhere else."

"We have to get home and recoup," Odette said.

"No," Rin said. "No, what if I try again from the start of the scene? I can go back to an hour ago and do it again."

Mauve was saying something but Rin was already looking past the air, trying to find the thread hidden in between the rays of light and the sturdy walls. She saw it, the thread that held her here, that pulled her back, if she just took a few steps backward—

"Stop," Mauve said, suddenly grabbing Rin's arm and yanking her to attention. "Don't do that. You're gonna end up breaking something."

"I'm just gonna go back and try again." But Rin could already see as the thread faded, Mauve's intuition was right. The thread was humming, thin, pulled and fraying, like if she messed with it anymore . . . years and years of having a Spark and she still didn't understand it. The Sparks were not in charge of how things worked; time and space and reality still had their own rules.

"Even if you could," Mauve said, "what then? You go back and do the scene again, and if something else goes wrong, you go back and do it again, and again, until you're nothing and nowhere but stuck in a loop lost to time?"

Rin snapped out of something, her eyes focusing once again on this room and Mauve. A loop. That's the word Mr. Weathers had used to describe bad shell-shock episodes. One day, Maynard had been on the ground screaming at the top of his lungs like a dying wounded animal. Mr. Weathers shook his head and said, "There's nothing to do but let him tire out his loop." So Rin had readied some cocoa for Maynard and kept it warm and waited.

Maynard and Mr. Weathers had been in the war. Loops never left you, he'd said.

Odette rubbed Rin's back. "Focus," she said. "Be here with us."

But here wasn't home. Rin still had the bracelet around her wrist: *not today*. She was still on the job.

"If we can't redo this exact moment," Rin said, "there has to be another place we can try. One more. Where can we go? What other angle? What about the devil man himself? Who is he?"

Mauve reluctantly closed her eyes. She shook her head again. If just one time she wouldn't shake her head. Rin paced, between the trash bin and the vanity. Mauve finally said, "There's a banker we could save from a heart attack, and that might stop the rise of the devil but . . . you get rid of one devil, another one comes. You get rid of that one, another one comes. There's a long line of humans willing to do bad things."

"God dammit." Rin kicked the trash bin.

"Well, Rin, war is complicated," Mauve said. "It's not saving Zachary Cooper's mom or getting a fella proper medication decades from now. It's thousands and millions of people and they all have free will."

"What about . . ." Rin trailed off. "What about—"

"Let's go home." Odette's voice was soft, full of worry. She touched Rin's arm. Rin's feet ached in these boots sitting on small white tiles. "At home, we can think about the 'what abouts.' But right now, we're in a locked washroom halfway across the world twelve years too far." She put a gloved hand on Rin's tense shoulder. She put her other gloved hand on Rin's wrist. The bracelet was there. "Love, we have time. But you need to sleep."

Rin stared at the bracelet: *not today*. "We'll get a hotel here in London and we'll—"

"No," Odette said sternly. "Take us home, Rin."

Rin gritted her teeth. "One more chance. One more thing," she said. "Mauve please find just one more thread."

Mauve sighed. But she closed her eyes. "I . . . Berlin?"

"Berlin." Rin clapped her hands. "Berlin. See, girls? We've always wanted to go to Berlin. Art, cabarets, music, misfits abound, it's everything we love. What year, Mauve?"

"1933," Mauve said. "The university students are gathering in the square."

Rin closed her eyes. "Berlin," she said.

＊

15

THE RINGMASTER, 1933

White columned buildings. A fancier version of the warehouse district in Omaha, halfway around the world.

Smoke in the air. They followed the smoke like they were following a gunshot.

A crowd was gathering in the open square. A long line of young boys and college-aged kids, some in uniforms, some in street clothes, not looking much older than the three of them had been when they started the circus.

There was a searing fire, blowing heat into their faces. It coughed smoke into the air. It set the night aflame.

Rin peered over their heads. "What holiday is it?" she said.

Mauve flinched, giving it a side-eye as she took a step back. "I don't like this."

Rin pushed a little through the crowd, as if the three of them were Ebenezer Scrooge shoving through gravestones to find his own name. And then she saw it. White paper, bound together, a book flinging through the cold winter air and landing in the fire.

The fire was made of burning books. For how cold it was outside, for how warm the fire was, Rin could not feel any part of her body. The people all around the three women cheered.

"The books," Mauve said. "They're not just stories. They're philosophy. They're science and medical records. And some of them . . . the ones on the bottom . . . they're records of people like us."

"Sparks?" Rin said.

"Queer," Mauve said. "Outsiders."

"Outsiders? In Berlin?"

Mauve nodded down the street, out of sight past the bonfire. "They're from a hospital they burned down. A gay Jew ran the hospital. It made them mad. It wasn't just that he was gay, it was that he was Jewish."

This smacked Rin across the face. The future *was* the past. Over and over again. And in Berlin. *Berlin?*

"In the future," Mauve said, "Berlin will be rubble. Berlin will be known for being the epicenter. It can happen anywhere. And this is just the beginning," Mauve said. "This is one bonfire. This is one night. This is one place. But the people here, around us, they'll see more. They'll make more. And some of them . . ." She looked away. She said, "I'm seeing a star . . . what's the star that people sometimes wear on a necklace? Is that Jewish?"

"The Star of David?" Rin said. "Yeah, it's Jewish. It's got six points for G-d, Torah, Israel, Creation, Redemption, Revelation . . ." A sign of protection and study. That symbol was her mother on Friday night over candles, beckoning the light to her face, singing a blessing she would teach Rin. One that Rin still remembered, even years after the last time she had sung it out loud. She didn't know much, but she knew the prayer, the star. Her mother had made the jump from the Yiddish stage to mainstream, and after that, it seemed like they spent a lot of time praying in private. When Rin was little, there was synagogue. When Rin was a little older, there was the apartment. And then . . . there was nothing.

But there was always that Star of David. Even now, after it was lost and after the graveyard and all the years that followed, she remembered that necklace. "It's a good symbol."

But from Mauve's face, Rin saw that the symbol was like Berlin. It was going to change.

"I think something happens," Mauve said quietly. "People disappear. People are killed."

This was different than what Rin had seen of the Great War. But she'd seen it before, in the way her mother had stopped attending synagogue. She'd glimpsed it in the way her great-grandmother gripped her cane tighter when Rin was a little girl and asked her where *she* grew up and why she left. It was the humming, thrumming darkness that vibrated under the daylight. She wasn't naïve. She knew the world was cruel. She knew that wars did not mean only battles on battlefields and military men dying. There were wars every day.

But it was her job to keeping believing, keep hoping, that tomorrow would be better. But here was tomorrow, right in front of her.

"They're trying to clear out anything that isn't like them," Rin said. "That's what's happening."

"They're erasing it all," Mauve said, looking at the futures in front of her.

"I can see it, threads dissolving, millions of them . . . just this one bonfire." Mauve's eyes grew tired, her plump cheeks sagging in a brokenhearted scowl. "This isn't the first time something like this has happened, it seems. And it's definitely not the last."

When Maynard had screamed, Mr. Weathers looked to him with his big glassy eyes and something on his face that wasn't pity; it was empathy. He knew what that was like. In 1926, there was so much electric light to drown out the shadows. Before 1916, so many of them had never seen a war machine. But there had been a time where the world almost frayed, almost tore apart like a broken thread.

And it was coming back. No, no, this would not be the future she would find for her family. No, she would change it. That rush of adrenaline pumped through her as she balled her hands into fists, refusing to feel fear. "We have to do something," Rin said. But what? What could they do?

"If we stop this one," Mauve said, her eyes lost in the flames and smoke before them, "there's another one in Hamburg in a few days, and while we are jumping through time trying to put out the fires, we miss the war. If we stop the war, we stop all of this." Rin had trouble following the logic. They needed to stop the war to stop the burning, but how could they stop the war if they didn't put out the fires?

"No, we have to try. Someone will probably try to shoot us, but we can—"

"Rin," Odette snapped. "The books are on fire. We are surrounded."

"What else can we do?" Rin demanded.

"Don't get that tone with us," Mauve retorted.

"I'm sorry," Rin said.

"I'm not going out any further than this crowd," Mauve said, her eyes darting around them here and through time, trying to see everything at once. "There are terrible things on the outskirts, past this place . . . I'm going to stop looking now. We need to leave. It is not safe here for us, at all."

None of them moved.

Mauve and Rin held each other's hands. Rin looked to Odette. Odette looked to all the people cheering around them. Her eyes were wide, haunted. She shook her head, over and over again, unable to stop.

Rin wrapped her arm around Odette and pulled her in, holding her close in the sea of applause. She put her cheek on Odette's soft head.

The only way they could leave this scene, this madness unfolding, was to jump time. They were surrounded on every side. They were shoulder to shoulder with the strangers, the crowd's heat burning with the bonfire's blaze.

"They're happy," Odette whispered. "They want this. I am looking into their eyes and I can see them and they aren't evil, they're people. How. *How.*"

Evil has eyes, too. Evil has cheeks, lips, ears, toes their parents counted, holiday traditions, and a favorite song. Evil is human. Evil looks straight at you while they hurt you. Lots of people love a reason to do bad things and get away with it.

Rin saw in the faces of these humans a memory, far away from Shabbat nights and book burnings and anything as large as a humming darkness. No, this was a smaller shadow, but a dense, ugly thing. The Circus King wasn't here, but once he'd looked her in the eyes. *You're just as much to blame!* And the fire rose from the Ferris wheel.

And her mother dying—

"Rin?" Odette said.

They watched as ashes rose from the bonfire, drifting into the smoke that blocked the stars.

"You can make anything happen?" Jo had said. *"So you could make it so the war never happened?"*

"We'll go home for now," Rin said.

"For now," Mauve said.

The crowd had noticed Rin, Mauve, and Odette. They were different and they were not cheering. The crowd smelled them, like wolves smelling a dog. Then the women were gone, just as quickly as they had come.

In the scheme of history and time, even Sparks were small creatures.

16

RINGMASTER, 1926

The morning after Rin's mother died, the world kept moving. Her mother was still dead and that couldn't be changed. There were things that needed to be taken care of. But Rin had just sat, stuck, in the night before.

Rin had sunk in the grief she saw reflected in her mother's eyes as she died. Her mother had tried to pry herself from the bed, her eyes bloodshot and wide, not wanting to die, begging to hold someone she thought she could never hold again.

But Rin *had* held her. Rin held her so tight, and it hadn't mattered. Being a mother was a brave thing; pulling your light from your own rib cage, letting it breathe freely, in its own body, in its own life. And long before the death-bed, Rin had taken her mother's light and snuffed it out.

Rin would have spun the world backward for her mother. Rin would have held time in between her fingers and choked it, frozen it forever, if it would have stopped her mother from dying. But there was nothing she could do.

A dead body is uncanny. A dead body slacks and stiffens without a soul.

Her mother had been buried with her songs and her prayers and all the answers to questions Rin could never ask. Her mother's Star of David had gone missing. Her mother was gone. Many more people were going to die in the future. Rin had seen the books burning, the smell of ash and smoking paper, the sound of the cheers—how could someone cheer when people died? How could the circus keep on with the certainty of an apocalypse?

She saw the thread ahead of her, behind her, all covered in a bloodred sheen, death in the past and all the deaths to come. Rin wanted to reach out, grab the thread, grab her mother's wrist, tug her, yank her, force her up to the surface and . . .

"Rin," Odette said from across the caboose, far away in the present.

The room started to wobble in front of Rin's eyes.

No.

"Rin, stay here," Odette said. Like how Rin would push Odette to her side in her sleep when Odette started to snore; a small habitual reflex to protect.

Rin wasn't back then, she wasn't in that cold death room. She could see the thread but she wasn't there. Don't jump, Rin. She felt the light feeling of floating away, the rush of . . . no. Don't jump. Stay put.

Rin touched her bare wrist. No bracelet was there. Not right now.

Rin focused her eyes. Odette was eyeing her from the mirror where she fixed her finger curls and makeup. Rin was sitting on the bed, wearing the same shirt she wore last night.

"I'm fine," Rin said.

"Ground yourself, sweet darling," Odette said. "Don't you go wandering off."

The shirt smelled like a bonfire. It had been touched by a very real future.

No. No, the present. Come on, Rin.

The dawn sifted through the window beside their bed and Rin stared at their room. The caboose bathed in the dusty sunbeams of a six o'clock sunrise. It was the summer of 1926, and she ran a circus now.

With pyromancers on the train, they hadn't needed a fire car. So now the caboose was lined with wooden floorboards (good, good, keep focusing), pretty lace things, big sturdy oak furniture, the practical sort, and a hodgepodge of trinkets given between two wives over a lifetime of adventure. It was their space, Odette and Rin's.

This was her home. Odette. The caboose. This is where she was in her story. Her mother had been dead for years. The war was yet to come. Today, there was Odette.

They had lived the same amount of days, but Odette flitted like a butterfly and Rin was an old dog. Her aging body showed all the extra days she'd shoved in the corners of her life. Even now, she felt stretched thin; like her mind was dispersed between here, her mother's bedside, and Berlin.

For many of the circus Sparks, their lives had begun when they entered the circus. For Rin and Odette, their lives had begun when they met each other.

Rin stood and pulled Odette's locks out of her face. A soft gesture, like the wings of a hummingbird. Odette's eyes glowed like galaxies for her.

"My sweet love," Odette said with a gentle smile. She took Rin's hand in her gloved fingers. She squeezed her hand, trying to ground her with the pressure. "You can't function in a circus with no sleep. I can take the kids' training today, you need to rest."

"Nah," Rin said. "It's my job, you already have a job. I gotta earn my keep, you know."

Odette took her wrist. It was gentle. Rin stopped short of the door to the vestibule. Odette looked up at her. "You know one of the things I love about you is your stubbornness, your strength," Odette said. "But you don't have to earn your keep. This last night . . . this last *week* has been a lot. Between the war and the Circus King—"

Well, that was enough for right now. His name was a fire inside Rin, like she was a dragon. She didn't want to feel him. She didn't want to smell fire. Rin forced her creaking bones to the door and grabbed her velvet coat off its hook. It also smelled like smoke and burning. She put it back on the hook. Just for now. "I'll sleep over lunch, all right?" Rin said. "I'm just gonna get the kids settled into a routine and then I'll be back. Sound like a deal?"

Odette sighed. "Well, I can't seem to stop you." Then she said, "I'm sorry, I didn't mean to upset you."

"You didn't upset me," Rin said. "It's okay. It's not you. I love you. You're the big bright spot in all this shit."

Odette squeezed Rin's hand one more time. "So are you."

She's lying, the voice seethed inside Rin. *What is there to love about you? She apologizes to you for what? You manipulate her, you make her feel awful, look at her and look at you—*

No, not today. She looked out the window, and saw the summer sun and the circus grounds waking up.

Today, the Reed children's new lives began.

✳

17

THE RINGMASTER, 1926

Lawrence, Kansas, had one of the largest fairgrounds in the area, Bismark Grove.

Rin liked this fairground. They stopped here a lot. The other options were Woodland Park or the high school's field. Woodland Park didn't allow Black patrons, and the high school was surrounded by homes, which meant no emergency exit if someone decided they didn't like Sparks. Not to mention Lawrence as a whole was dangerous for "outcasts" because they were the hot spot for the Temperance movement.

But Bismark Grove was lovely. A few years ago, a Spark bought up the land and restored the fairground to its historical brilliance. Bismark Grove had grown up parallel to the circus, contemporaries, and that made it special. It was about two miles north of downtown, a straight shot down the main road and over the river; just a small bike ride or walk away. But far away enough to disappear if something went south, and right next to the tracks. It had treated them well.

The train, sitting on the tracks, ran parallel to the midway. The train cars now sat behind some of the glue-and-sawdust painted stalls that made up the main drag. Across the dirt and gravel was the box office, then the tents behind it. She could smell the syrup and melted butter from the cookhouse all the way over here on the other side of the midway.

She looked down the way and saw the big tent already raised high to the sky. Maynard wanted to get it up before dawn, every time, so to any towns-folk it would seem more magic than manual labor.

The white canvas flags atop the point of the king pole beat against the blue Kansas sky. Colors meant something new out here in Lawrence. Blue skies were a bold, sharp jolt of joy. The cut green grass contrasted the brown and gray pathways.

The circus was a place where many people would live their happiest day. And Rin got to wake up here every morning.

Mr. Calliope played his warm-ups from beside the Big Top as Maynard exited the sideshow tents, putting his hammer back in his tool belt. It looked like he was done.

There was something about circuses in the heartland. Most of the Midwest was full of unassuming fields and dusty streets, some muddy rivers, and thick oily train tracks. The wooden houses had living rooms that were more often than not full of old discount furniture with lace pillows. Comfortable, for those who could fit into the contours of the couch and match themselves to the wallpaper's purple flowers and the screen doors leading to long porches. But sometimes, there were oddities like Jo and Charles, who were born to the prairie but did not fit. They were too loud, they took up too much space, they looked different. They found a more fitting home here in between the ballyhoo posters and the Big Top.

They all needed this circus. Now the Ringmaster just needed to keep it for them.

Good luck, you haven't stopped the war.

Right now, today, the war was nothing more than a harbinger, a warning. It wasn't yet real. So she shoved it down. She could not think about impending doom all day while she was trying to function as the Ringmaster. She'd go mad and nothing would get done and everyone was counting on her to do her part.

You'll die along with them, a voice slithered. *Or worse, you won't.*

Jo Reed waited, one ankle crossed over the other, her arms folded over her stomach as she sidled a look to the midway that Rin guessed was supposed to look unimpressed and possibly bored. But she knew that Jo felt the magic here, just as much as she did.

"Good morning," Rin said, coming to a stop and shoving her hands in her trouser pockets. Now she had her sleeves rolled up, her suspenders out for all to see, her shirt buttoned high enough to be modest but low enough to get air on her collarbone. Her boots stayed on at all times walking the grounds, because she'd learned boots relieved the stress of stepping in just about anything and saved her trousers' cuffs. She'd also learn that putting a bounce in her voice and a grin on her face said to others that she couldn't be sad and would hide any cracks she didn't want them to see.

Rin took in a big whiff of air; the syrup and butter smells wafted into her nose. See? Not all in the near end of times was lost; flapjacks still existed.

"Morning," Jo said. "You're grinning. Why are you grinning?"

"It's your first day here," Rin said.

"And why does that make you happy?" Jo said. "What's that got to do with you?"

"I just know how much you have ahead of you," Rin said. And suddenly, she felt something clench in her stomach. Yes, she knew exactly what Jo had ahead of her.

Stop it, stop it.

"Why do you smell like smoke?" Jo said.

"Where's your brother?" Rin asked, keeping a chill off her face. And just as she asked, Charles Reed bounded like a golden retriever onto the midway, buttoning his shirt.

"Here! Present!" Charles shouted out.

So they marched forward, down the craggy gravel of the midway, the twin ragamuffins walking together one step behind her.

The morning shone with a quiet sunburst through the trees lining their lot. Rin kept an eye on Jo and Charles, who stayed close to each other and were trying not to seem overwhelmed by the hustle and bustle they weren't a part of yet. Jo looked mesmerized by the Maynard roustabouts working in perfect synchronization to put up the dressing tent, which they now passed. The smashing of the mallets hurt Rin's ears.

"I slept great!" Charles said. "It was like we were speeding through the air."

"Watch them," Jo whispered to Charles. Charles did so.

"So?"

Jo nodded to the gandy dancers all hammering the same stake in a perfect rhythm as a team. "They're all the same person." Identical men with thick green eyes and strong arms and flaming red hair, dressed in brown-green suspenders and dirty brown boots.

"They are," Rin said. "They're all Maynard."

Rin had met Maynard at her very first auction. Maynard's old employer was folding and selling off their assets for a cheap price. It was normal; one circus folds, another circus engulfs their bones and canvases. Maynard helped pack up the tent that day, and Rin had offered him . . . *all* of him . . . a job.

He'd taken it, and now he made more money collectively than any of them, what with the quantity of Maynards there could be and the amount of work they did to make the circus what it was each day.

"Hey," one Maynard growled at another, "what'd you maroons do to this pole? It's not going up right!"

"It wasn't me," said the other Maynard, in a quiet, kinder voice. "Here, let's try again. Keep an eye on the guy rope."

"It's fine," another said, exasperated. "It's absolutely fine."

Slowly, one stood straight back up and he whistled to the others. They each ran for him, and all collided into him until he was the only one standing. Maynard then walked across the yard like nothing happened, at first not saying anything to Rin and the kids. Not because he was angry, Rin had to remind herself, but because he probably didn't even notice them.

Maynard was an old-school circus hand, and Rin knew he still saw her as a newcomer to this world, an interloper come from theatre, even though it had been over half a decade that she, Mauve, and Odette had worked with him. But half a decade seemed like a drop in the bucket for the rich history of circus as an art form. Maynard scoffed at Rin's jargon, spit tobacco at her anxious choices, and knew better than anyone that without him, this whole operation would probably fall in on itself.

"Morning, Ringmaster." Maynard did eventually tip his hat to her as he walked past. She saw a flash of blue light across his face, a dream but she was awake. She needed sleep.

"Wow," Jo whispered, watching him disappear.

"His Spark is multiplication," Rin said, hitting her brain back into position.

"How does he multiply?" Jo said.

Rin shrugged. "How do you make wind pictures come out of your hand? How do you stop bullets, Charles? Now come on, let's look inside the Big Top." She gave a big Ringmaster grin and journeyed on through the tour.

The inside of the canvas tent was already thick with dust, although Maynard had erected it only about an hour ago. One work light was on, along with the ghost light, and Tina as an elephant was working on her choreo early.

"So there *are* animals in the circus," Charles said, his voice pealing with excitement.

"No," Rin said. "Shapeshifters. People can choose to be here, animals can't."

Tina jumped on one of her bull tubs and slowly melted from her elephant form and returned to her sequined, bubbly, sensual self. Her trunk became a dainty button nose, her gray skin melting back to pink, her armored chest and thick legs turning to a curvy, voluptuous Renaissance painting. She was wearing a leotard and draped in feathers like a cape. She waved at the twins and Rin. "Ringmaster!" she exclaimed in her Southern drawl. "Why hello! Who are these little dewdrops?"

As Tina rushed along the ring to meet them at the entrance, Jo turned to Rin. "So she's all the animals?"

"She's the Menagerie Woman, yes," Rin said. "Good morning, Tina!"

Tina beamed a rosy freckled smile. The same white-and-pink cheeks she would wear on the night she would die.

"Hello there," Tina said, coming to a stop still in the ring and extending her hand out for Charles to take.

"I'm Charles, ma'am," Charles said, removing his weathered hat and forgetting to take her hand. "This is my sister, Jo."

How did Mauve do this, stay calm when she knew how things ended?

"You twins, then?" she said. "Which one of you can be set on fire? I don't want to mix it up."

"That's me, ma'am."

"You?" Tina stepped over the ring curb and scooted closer. She was barefoot, but still looked like a main attraction. Because she was one. "Why, little Charles, you're not old enough to have played with fire."

"We're old enough, ma'am," Charles lied. "Twenty next March."

"It's June, darling."

"Can you turn into *all* animals?" Jo said.

"I can turn into any animal, but only one at a time," Tina said. "Sure did surprise my ex-husband when the Spark came and all of a sudden he had two dogs instead of one. Then I had no husbands instead of one!" Tina laughed at her own memory. Jo looked to Rin as if to ask for help.

"I'm just showing our newcomers the tent," Rin said. "Are we interrupting?"

"Naw naw," Tina said. "Just checking my new mark for the handstand. I think I've got it. But needed to check in the actual space, not just the rehearsal tent. Let *me* get outta *your* way."

"Good day, bully girl," Rin said, and Tina scooted past them. Rin looked out to the now empty Big Top. Even when it got real quiet, she could still hear its music. Like the echo of magic still sang.

There was nothing to fear in this place. Rin needed to breathe. There was still time to save Tina; no one was going to die.

That's when a faint *beep beep* came from behind her, and through the tent's main entrance a small clown car puttered onto the scene.

Charles shuddered. "I don't like clowns."

"Hush up," Jo said.

"Bad clowns can be scary," Rin agreed. "But real talented clowns? They are the connection between the audience and the heart of the circus. They make you laugh, and that's one of the hardest things a performer can do."

The car, which was about as big as a Cracker Jack toy, stopped in front of the three of them, and the door opened. Rin bent down and saw Mr. and Mrs. Davidson the size of needles enjoying their breakfast in the car's interior, which looked like the inside of a fancy flea's dollhouse. Mr. and Mrs. Davidson were a pair, graying white skin and bright red cheeks. They exited the little car, and grew. That is, the couple stretched high to the top of the king pole, filling the space like they were Alice in the White Rabbit's house. They leaned over and offered their hands.

"Those are some big clowns." Charles looked up at the couple, who slowly realized from Charles's terrified expression their spec wasn't for everyone. They shrank.

"Oh no!" Mrs. Davidson said as both clowns returned to an everyday sort of size. "Y'all are using the ring?"

"We are," Rin said. "Just for a minute, and Tina just finished up. Come back in five and it's all yours."

"The newbies!" Mr. Davidson laughed deep in his gut. "Good to meet ya! I'm Oscar, and this is the love of my life, as beautiful as she was fifty years ago. Susan." He nuzzled her.

"Oscar!" Mrs. Susan Davidson laughed, turning bright red. "Also, it's been forty-eight years we've been married, not fifty, Oscar!"

"Fifty," Mr. Davidson said. "I start the count at the moment I met her." He plastered a big embarrassing kiss on her cheek. "Used to chase her around to our favorite song, dancing. I never stopped."

Mrs. Davidson giggled as they got back in their car and the pair waved goodbye as they exited.

"Well," Charles said. "I did not enjoy that."

"Fifty years," Jo said, watching the car disappear. "Huh. That's a long time." But she said it genuinely, no mocking in her tone. Like she thought it was special.

"All right," Rin said, shoving her hands in her pockets and stepping on top of the ring curb. "Ready for some vocabulary?"

"We both dropped out of school," Jo said. "When do we get to the part where we get to do our Sparks?"

"Being a performer means learning your space." Rin kicked one heel onto her other boot's toe. And she waved to the tent. "This is the Big Top. Out there was the midway. Candy pushers work there. There's also the sideshow, but it's family friendly, very different than what you'd get at other circuses. Ours is more like a fun house. But you aren't gonna be in the midway. You'll both be here, in the Big Top. We got one ring. Some have three rings, but we've got one." She pointed to the big ring in the middle of it all. "Around the ring are these ring curbs." She kicked the curb under her feet. "They separate the ring from what we call the hippodrome track. On the hippodrome track, where you two are standing? It goes all the way around the ring, see?" She pointed to the big dirt track that separated the ring from the audience's bleachers. "On the track, we show our spec parade and interludes and a finale. Spec parade is sort of like a taster for the whole circus, a grand opening."

She waved her arms to the bleachers, shoddy yet sturdy wooden planks as if they were ready for a baseball game. "And there is where the audience sits. Some people refer to visitors as 'rubes.' Don't do that. Now the arena is in the round, so you need to make sure to turn your body and perform for all the folks, regardless of where they're sitting."

Jo nodded. "Why do you have one ring and you said others have three rings?"

"Three rings mean you got a lot going on," Rin said. "It's chaos. We're already chaotic enough with one."

"Sounds fun," Jo said blithely. Or was she serious? You could never tell with teenagers.

Rin jumped off the curb. Charles eyed Rin, as if he was Jo's bodyguard. Rin offered a step back. Then she said, "In order for any collaborative art to work, you have to have shared terms, traditions, old stupid reasons from old stupid stories passed down. It makes the art bigger than one person. So we do our energy circle before we go on, we leave the ghost light on through the night if we need to be in the tent after hours without the stage lights, and also superstitiously to protect us from wandering spirits. Yeah?"

Jo shrugged, eyeing the light bulb on a plank of wood stuck to wheels. "Sure. Ghost light." But her tone again didn't sound mocking. She said it like she was memorizing.

Rin was curious why Jo didn't snap back with something clever. She could have, Jo was as wily and sardonic as a hyena, but a part of her seemed to want to learn. Maybe Rin wasn't talking to herself after all.

"Ready to see the Back Yard?"

She led them to the left and pointed at the big gaping mouth made of pulled-back curtains as they exited into the dark. "The portal," she named it. "Our in and out from backstage."

Then they were outside. The bright morning sun hit Rin's face like a shade drawing up. Summer and her skin never mixed well, spattering freckles everywhere by July. And the heat of her hair was a furnace on her neck. But a small breeze cooled the Back Yard, even with the skillets from the cookhouse blasting full-speed.

In the clear blue Kansas sky, the backstage area was unpolished but alive. Everyone rushed to the cookhouse to eat, cutting through the smell of syrup mixing with the scent of body odor, old wigs, chalk, oil, and wood. It was the smell of theatre magic in the morning.

Rin pointed out all the bones of the Back Yard: the dressing tent, the rehearsal tent, the cookhouse. They were all white tents in a little circle surrounding them. And among the smells and sights were Sparks rushing around, a hodgepodge of fantasy.

"Lau Ming-Huá," Rin said, as Ming-Huá approached. Ming-Huá seemed torn between getting a good spot in the breakfast line or being polite and stopping to say hello. Food won out, and she awkwardly waved the unattached arm she carried under her other arm, as she piled into the queue behind Wally and Ford. She patted down her fringe with the rogue arm, her fingers working perfectly. Rin watched Jo try to piece together her Spark of removing limbs.

"She's also into poetry," Rin said. "Real knack for not forcing rhyme. I'm not a writer, but she's got this one about a tornado and it—"

"Blew you away?" Jo said.

"Wow," Charles said.

Then there was a gaggle of college-aged men that flew past them, their feet off the ground ("That's Herb, Dom, Dyl, Dave, Wesley, and Guy"). They weren't collegiates, though, they'd been run out of town. They seemed to laugh more, now that time had passed.

"And there's Jess." Rin nodded to the "Spectacular Shapeshifter" checking themself in a mirror as they transformed from masculine to soft feminine. "Jess is talented as all hell," she said. "They ride on Tina. The two of them have been working on a very impressive horse act. They also are a good friend to have on your side. They're shy, but ask them about card games and they'll spend the rest of the night teaching you everything there is to know about gin rummy."

Jess waved. Rin waved back.

Kell also arrived, cutting through the tents. When he caught sight of Charles Reed, he awkwardly lost his footing and one of his wings slammed into a support pole. He held back a yowl and nodded toward them like nothing had happened. Charles nodded back, a small smile cracking his young face.

Rin also smiled. "Good morning, Kell!" she sounded out. Kell nodded again and continued on toward the line. His eyes were still on Charles's face as he ran straight into Mauve, who'd been crossing through the cookhouse area, singing to herself and fixing the towel around her head. She was dressed in a robe.

"Kell, slow down!" Mauve said.

"Morning, Mauve," Kell muttered.

"Where's your crabby daddy right now?"

"He's getting some sleep," Kell said. "He said not to bother him and do whatever you want by yourself."

Mauve raspberried and continued along, singing a melody with an "aah" and an "ooh." Her voice was gorgeous as she twirled by.

"We're a small circus, but definitely not a mud show," Rin said. "Mud shows are wagon-based fly-by-nights. But we do try to stick near the rail, just in case we need to hightail it out of town. We don't like haul roads, uh, I mean having to schlep things across town."

"Do people usually come after us?" Charles said.

"There are lots of things out there in the world that aren't too keen on us," Rin said.

"Okay, so I've got a question," Jo said. "How come it's been rainy all summer, but every time you set up, the rain stops?"

Rin winked. "There's a girl who ran from the asylums and she works the arcade."

"Wait," Jo said. "So you've got a person who can *control the weather* and she's hiding behind the milk bottle game?!"

"Well, it's the duck pond, but yes," Rin said. "And she doesn't control the weather. She can move water to different states. You know, liquid, solid, gas. She likes to smooth out the midway so those who need accessibility can make it just fine. Otherwise, it'd be a big ol' mud pit. But she doesn't like her Spark, and she doesn't want to talk about it, so I wouldn't ask around."

"What's her name?"

"She calls herself Esther," Rin said. "That's all she told us and I'm not gonna pry. Sometimes secrets aren't some mystery for us to unravel. They're the journey the person is going on for themselves. All we can do is respect that. Now"—she clasped her hands—"you should eat. You've got to feed your body before you use it. Go get some flapjacks." Out of her pocket she pulled two vouchers, and she handed one to each of them.

"Here," Charles said and held out his hand. Jo handed both slips to her brother and he skipped off, joining Kell in line. Jo shrugged as she watched him go.

"Oh," Rin said. "Are you not eating?"

"Charles is getting it. Don't like lots of people shoving me around," she said.

Rin raised a brow. But she didn't ask, just considered the subtle ways Charles looked out for his sister as he bounded into line. It clearly was what he'd been doing his whole life.

"He's a good kid," Rin observed.

"Eh, I'm partial," Jo said. "Is the cook a Spark?"

"Yes," Rin said.

"Is the cook's Spark cooking then?" Jo said, bemused.

"No," Rin said. "They're lightning fast. And Cherry will be the first to tell you their skills in the kitchen came honestly."

It was true. Once, when Kell and Mr. Weathers first came on board, Kell said something about how Spark cooking was delicious. Cherry shot their thick-boned bronze body from behind the griddle to right in front of Kell in a split second and barked, "I went to culinary school! I was this good *before* any old Spark! How dare you!"

Rin always liked Cherry, because they were the kind of person who got a Spark to dart around the world in a flash, but then said to themself, "You know what I could use this for? Doing something I love even *faster.*"

"So you sure you want us?" Jo said. "What if our rehearsals go bad today? You gonna just throw us out or something?" Her words sang like a joke, but Rin heard the real fear underneath.

Rin shook her head. "We don't throw people out," she said. "We're a family."

"I've known families to throw people out," Jo said.

Rin looked to her. "Not this one."

And almost as if on cue, a big hand clamped down on Rin's shoulder. Bernard's thick fingers made the goliath Rin look more like a dainty mouse, and he pulled himself into the conversation. "Who do we got here then? New act?"

"Jo Reed," Rin said, "this is Bernard. He's Mauve's father and works as security."

Bernard held out his big hand for Jo's small, scrawny grip. "Put her there, Jo Reed. Nice to meet you."

"You're gigantic," Jo said. "Is that your Spark?"

"I'm not a Spark," Bernard said. "Just a supporter! And I get free tickets to the shows." He laughed his big belly laugh, then headed on toward the food line himself. "See you later, Spark gals."

Rin watched Jo watch him leave, and then Jo looked to Rin. "I don't trust nice people."

"I don't, either," Rin said honestly. "But I trust Bernard."

"And do you trust everyone else here?" Jo said. "Everyone's way too happy-dappy to be real, you know? What sort of cult are you running?"

Rin allowed a half smile, like her lips were caught on a jagged edge of anxiety. She had to believe everyone here was trustworthy. She had to believe they trusted her. And she definitely had to believe she was going to get them all out alive. She elbowed Jo. "A cult that has good breakfasts."

Charles soon came back with a plate full of bacon, a couple sticking out of his mouth to boot. Rin had never had bacon and just never felt the need to sneak one. But she understood a lot of people went batty for it.

Charles handed Jo a stack of flapjacks he'd rolled into his hand like a news-paper. Jo ate it like a hotdog. Sure.

Then they were off to the closest rehearsal tent. Jo and Charles both went to enter the space, but Rin's hand came down between them. "Charles will work in the tent with our archer, Yvanna. You, Miss Fancy Fingers, are work-ing with me out in the field."

"Yikes, sounds like a romp a minute." Charles patted Jo on the back. "Well, good luck with that vocab." Charles stepped into the tent, leaving Jo and Rin alone together. "Hello, ma'am," he said, muffled by the cloth. "I'm ready to be set on fire!"

Jo shuffled from one foot to the other, nervously inching closer to the tent where Charles had just entered, as if there was an invisible string that con-nected them around their wrists. When was the last time they'd been apart?

"It'll be alright," Rin said. "You two can tell each other how the rehearsals went, when you're all done."

"What?" Jo snapped from a thought. "Oh, it's fine . . . I just worry about him, you know? He can be shy sometimes."

"I think Yvanna is a good partner for him," Rin said. "So you like the cir-cus then?"

"I guess it's fine," Jo said. But her eyes gave her away. They were as big as saucers, drinking in the hustle and bustle of the Back Yard. "I mean . . . if you like that sort of thing."

Rin pulled one hand out of her pocket and offered it. "To rehearsal then?" she said.

18

THE RINGMASTER, 1926

The field was far away from the circus tents and the hullabaloo. Just thick Kansas grass against the thick Kansas trees that lined the grounds. This was a good day. Rin had seen Kansas in all sorts of weather, and summer was definitely the transformative season. In the winter it was nothing but brown grass, bare crops. But in the summer, it was a sea of green.

Rin took a deep breath of air. This, the wide spaces under a clear sky, far from the coasts and far from the cities and beyond anything in any book or film . . . the Midwest was home.

And she, the lady with her wild hair and her work shirt tucked into her high-waisted black pants, stood ready to welcome this little girl in a starchy faded blue dress that matched her violent blue eyes. They were a pair.

"All right," Rin said. "You have your first performance tonight. Today, I want to practice the illusions you'll need to show in the ring tonight. But more importantly, we need to work on your technique."

"Tonight?" Jo said.

"You wanted to be in the circus, yeah?"

"Yes," Jo said slowly. "But I just got here?" The brash sardonic act seemed to melt away to a quieter, softer Jo. Without her brother, she seemed like a deer in a meadow, unsure of being so out in the open.

Rin pulled her bushy hair back behind her ears and tied it tight. "Best to jump both feet in, right?" she said. "Now I've seen what you can do, but I brought us out here because I need to know the limitations." Jo looked confused. "I wanna see how big it can get. What are we working with here?"

Jo nervously looked out to the field around her. "It's not just pretty pictures. It can get . . . intense."

Rin waved her hand out to the field. "Well . . . let's meet it head-on, shall we? I'm gonna give you a word and you're gonna conjure something up. Alright?"

Jo, her black straw hair bristling in the wind, looked doubtful but still moved forward. Her hands were placed in front of her as if she was ready to fight open-palmed.

She always seemed ready to hit something, kick something, tear her way through an enemy only she could see.

"Where does your Spark come from?" Rin said. "Right now, as you prepare to do it."

"No one knows where the Sparks come from," Jo said.

"No," Rin said. "It's important to understand our Spark. I meant, where does it come from . . . from *inside*. Mine comes from my gut and my spine. Mauve says hers is in her head. Odette's is in her hands. So where do you feel the energy originating?"

"Didn't know this was a science."

"No one knows what it is," Rin said. "Now stop bluffing and tell me where you feel it."

Jo took a deep breath in and out of her nose, gritting her teeth, looking out to the field as if deliberating something. Not where it came from, Rin knew. But whether or not to tell.

"My heart," Jo said quietly.

It seemed to surprise Jo that this sentiment came out of her. But it didn't surprise Rin. Because she recognized that gritted teeth, that deliberation.

She once had been a girl with gritted, grinding teeth, who stood on the edge of a graveyard where she'd left her name on a tombstone.

She never wanted anyone else to ever feel that alone.

Rin watched Jo position her feet on the rich brown soil. She saw Jo concentrate on the grass.

"Ready?" Rin said.

Jo nodded.

"All right," Rin said. "The word is 'home.'"

Jo's eyes closed.

Light erupted from the young girl.

An illuminated tidal wave of stardust and sun pushed from her soul through her fingers and into the world. She was a dawn all her own.

Rin felt a rush of warmth blow past her. Her hair ruffled. She stood still.

The field transformed into a cold, dark room. The two stood in a wooden farmhouse.

In front of them sat two children, a boy and a girl, watching the front door from the stairs. There was another child, much older. It was a boy, and he scrambled around in the kitchen.

So many years between them and their brother; and those years dictated who would go die and who would stay and live.

Rin watched a smaller Jo on the staircase, turning her bare feet inward, the cold splintery wood making no sound as the older boy grabbed his pack, put his hat on, and opened the door.

Nothing had changed. On that night, and now on this day, it was all the same. She could do nothing but see her brother go.

Rin felt something inside herself, as if she was the one settled in this memory; something dark, bubbling. The room shook. The shadows became dark dangerous strangers. The floorboards disintegrated, and Rin fell and fell and screamed. Everything she never wanted to feel again, radiating from every pore of her body, curling in through the holes of her heart like poison, then shooting out like bullets. Fear. Grief. So much grief. Anger. It wasn't fair. What sort of a god would have killed her brother?

Brother? Rin had never had a brother.

She felt a panic in her throat. This wasn't hers. This grief wasn't hers. This wasn't her mind.

"Jo!" the Ringmaster shouted. "Focus! Bring it in!"

Her voice shocked Jo and she jumped back. As the spell broke, Rin felt ground under her feet and rump and hands. Grass. Dirt, wet from the morning dew. Everything else was an illusion, it wasn't real.

Jo dropped her hands and it all disappeared. Rin lay where she'd fallen. It was gone. It was a bad dream. But it felt so real.

It felt like before. It felt like . . . *him*. The Circus King.

Jo was powerful. *Jo is dangerous,* a voice said. And Rin felt herself detaching, leaving her body, disassociating, numb—

"I'm so sorry," Jo said, rushing forward.

No, no this wasn't Jo's fault. Rin couldn't shut down and leave this girl alone. From what Rin had just seen, Jo had been feeling alone for quite some time.

Jo looked down at the Ringmaster in horror, her eyes glassy. She was just a kid, and she was floundering. And then Jo broke down crying.

Both of them could not cry. One of them had to stand up. Keep going.

Jo was just a kid.

He was also once just a kid.

But Rin was grown. And so Rin could stand.

"I'm a monster, I'm so sorry." Jo's hands shook. "I . . ." Tears burst out of her like she'd not cried in years. She looked old enough to hold back hyper-ventilated gasps of air, and her Spark was enough to vanish a field. But she was trembling.

"You're not a monster," Rin said. She fixed her suspenders. She pulled up her sleeves. "You don't have control. That's all. If your Spark comes from your heart, then your heart is hurting. Those images . . ." She stopped herself. A part of her wanted to walk away. Something about this was too familiar. Her circus was a good place, a kind place. Nothing like this. This was like the horrors on display in the midnight black tents that followed them.

And if Rin didn't teach Jo to do better, that's exactly where Jo would end up. If not worse. Rin knew the blue light in the midst of war was not the only thing that could hurt this girl.

"Those images were fear," Rin said. "You're not a monster. You've *known* monsters."

Jo wiped her nose on her arm. She was so small, scrawny, chewed up and left to be forgotten. She was too young to be alone.

But she wasn't alone, was she?

Rin reached out to touch Jo's shoulder. "I want you to do it again," she said, "but this time, don't be afraid."

"So you want me to dampen my Spark?" Jo said, defensively.

"No, no no," Rin said. "I want you to find the joy in your Spark. What is the joy in the word *home*? Find those happy thoughts."

"All right, Tinker Bell," Jo snorted, her cheeks dried and her eyes still red, the smirk returning.

"So you know *Peter Pan,*" Rin said. "Good. Then yes, exactly like Tinker Bell. What's your happy thought? What makes you fly?"

Jo closed her eyes. Rin expected her to smarm back, but she didn't. Jo grounded herself by pushing her feet out under her shoulders. She raised her head. She squinted. Then she raised her hands.

Out of her fingertips manifested purples and blues and clouds and snow-capped peaks and a line of little boys climbing trees to the music of flutes. High above was a little girl and a little boy, flying beside each other in big loops, slowly melting into a dance.

Rin and Jo watched in awe as the image swelled from Jo's hands and high into the sky, as if the winds themselves had painted them and now they stood as real as any book had been in Jo's head. They were like music, a soft piano heard when the world was younger and safer.

Watching the boy and girl dancing in the air, Rin remembered what it was like to trust people.

Then it disappeared. A fizzle, like a candle's smoke dissipating in a room full of open windows. Ringmaster stared at the blank air with absolute wonderment.

Jo slowly closed her fingers into fists and shook them before rubbing her clammy palms on her starchy dress. "So, there's that," she said.

Ringmaster blinked slowly, as if waking from a dream. "Wow," she said. "I smelled the ocean. That's the second ocean you've made. You've never *been* to the ocean, have you?"

"Oh, 'cause I'm from Nebraska I haven't seen the ocean, huh?" Jo said. And then, "Yeah, no, I've never seen the ocean."

"So how did you know what it smelled like?"

"I just did a spring shower mixed with salt water and that stench that comes from a mossy lake." Jo shrugged.

"Don't shrug this off," Rin said. "Jo, that was gorgeous. That was . . ."

"M-m-m-magic!" Jo sang, doing a little wiggly dance. Rin chortled and batted her hands down.

"That," Rin said, "was you."

Jo froze. Something seized in her face, like Rin had jabbed something under her ribs. But she laughed it off. "Sure," she said, toeing the dirt with her beat-up black shoe. Then she said, "That second one was actually the farm, too. Just the good parts. Charles and me would play Peter Pan in the fields. It was a nice place . . . Marceline. I miss it . . . I mean, it's all Marceline. The good and the bad. Just like it's all me. I can be the ocean but I also can be all the other really scary things, can't I?"

"You get to choose who you are," Rin said.

"Yeah, I don't think it's that simple," Jo said. "I can't just say, 'Hey I wanna be Babe Ruth,' and then boom."

"You say you miss Marceline, even if there was sad stuff that happened there," Rin said.

Jo softened. "It was home. It . . . it still is." Jo rubbed her eye. "I think it might always be."

Rin made sure Jo was looking at her. Then she said. "Do you want to be someone who helps people? Do you want to perform in my circus?"

Jo slowly nodded. Jo's stringy bangs bobbed, her jaw strong and her eyes determined. Good.

Rin rubbed her back, looking out to the circus splayed out in front of their field as the sun rose higher. "All right," she said, wiping her brow of sweat. "Tonight, we introduce you. The Dreamweaver."

19

EDWARD, 1917

Edward could get anything for Ruth. Whatever sort of a life Ruth wanted, all he had to do was pull the strings behind the curtain and it would appear. He was a dream granter. He had a VIP card to life, and this meant the nicest hotels, the best dinners, and the most expensive presents. He showered her, and they lived a life of glamorous anonymity. They were alone, but their life together was magnificent.

"I don't want to stay anywhere for too long," Ruth said. "I want to travel the country, see everything!"

"As you wish," Edward said.

She shone like a lighthouse, and he was her rock.

But being the rock was difficult. Ruth was the one who was put out front, who was kind to those around them, who the waiters effortlessly laughed with and who the drivers gave handshakes to. Edward was left out of a club, unsure how to make others smile. And no matter how Ruth loved him, she couldn't teach him.

Sometimes, Edward would walk aimlessly around whatever Ohio town or Kentucky backwoods they'd landed in. Sometimes, he'd sit in a park and watch people walk past.

Something was disconnected. Something burned inside him to connect. But it reminded him of a time when he was a little boy, and he let go of a balloon and it would not come back down. When you let go of some things, you never get them back. And he'd let go of anyone outside of him and Ruth a long time ago.

Sometimes, he'd read the papers. He'd go to the corners. He'd find others who had a Spark. He would watch them, like a hungry apprentice plotting to outshine his master.

Some people had Sparks that would help others. They could heal, they could grow flowers. Others had Sparks that would hurt others. They could turn flesh into ash, they could scream until the trees fell down.

They could make people do things.

He would whisper small words to strangers strolling past. "Clench your fist." "Laugh loudly." "Hit that tree." He tested his teeth against his tongue, the vibrations of words against his lips, like an experiment kept in the dark.

What if he could bring them together in some sort of brotherhood? What if he could command them to use their Sparks for his and Ruth's gain? They would be unstoppable, and it would be lovely to have a group of people he could depend on. A family, one that would never leave.

One bright day, Edward and Ruth walked through one of these parks together. They saw a Spark freeze a lake to make it into a skating rink.

"I don't think this is fair," Edward said. "Some Sparks are good and some Sparks are evil. Some people can turn bones inside out, and others can make skating rinks."

"I disagree," Ruth said.

"Oh?" Edward said. Ruth shrugged and pointed at the lake.

"He can freeze things," she said. "That's not evil or good. He gets to choose what he uses it for. Think about it. He could freeze the whole city. He could freeze vaults open and he could murder people. But he makes ice-skating rinks. I mean, it's like me. I could transport into a bank vault myself, but I don't."

"You think you're a good person?" Edward said.

Ruth looked at him. "Yeah, I think I'm a good person."

And that's when something boiled inside him. Something turned his own bones inside out. Her smug face, her inner peace, she was nothing. She was a stupid girl who got lucky.

"You're not a good person," he growled. "You're just a person."

Ruth's eyes faded. Edward watched her wither.

And he didn't stop it from happening.

They kept walking. And when they saw a family, walking together and taking in the snowy day, Edward narrowed his eyes.

Pride would not get Ruth anywhere in life.

It was better she was taken down a few pegs by him, someone who cared about her.

"Go touch one of those parents and one of those children," Edward said. "Send them to the other side of the world."

Ruth didn't even look at him. It was as if it was her own idea. She sauntered over, with a plan. She touched the woman and the little boy, and they disappeared with her.

When she returned, she was alone.

The man screamed. The little girl howled. "Get us out of here," Edward instructed her. And she and Edward disappeared.

They landed in their hotel room. And Edward smugly raised a brow, as if he'd won a bet. "I guess you're right," he said. "You proved your point."

"What?" Ruth said, staring at her hands. Terrified at herself, her entire body shook.

"Any Spark can be used for evil," Edward said.

"I didn't . . . I don't know why I . . ." Ruth burst into tears. "I have to go back and get them. It wasn't worth proving anything. I'm so sorry. Oh my God—"

"Don't go after them," Edward said. "Come here. It'll be all right." He pulled her in close. She still shook. "What are we going to do with you, Ruth?"

Ruth sobbed.

"You're no better than me," Edward said, stroking her hair. "I keep telling you I'm trying to help you. But you think you're so much smarter than me." He tugged her hair gently, to pull her eyes up to look at him. "You aren't."

Ruth's blubbering got tiresome after a while. He didn't want her to forget what she'd done, but the tears needed to stop. They needed to move on with the night. So he eventually cut her sadness short. Like an artist polishing his masterpiece, he wiped away the tears and kept the minor chords he'd played into her heart.

He held her close, the reins back in his hand as they drifted off to sleep. "About the park, darling. I've been thinking. You shouldn't open up philosophical discussions if your temperament can't handle them."

Ruth nodded, lying on his chest.

"I do everything you ask of me," Edward said. "I have made your life *our* life. Where could I be if I didn't have you, Ruth? Have you ever wondered what I wanted?"

Ruth didn't say anything. And then she said quietly, "What do you want?"

He wanted her to light him up with that flame he saw in her eyes, give him everything he needed so he could sleep at night. He wanted her to make him bright. Him, and only him.

"I want you to love me," he said. "Please. Kiss me."

She did so.

And the two fugitives fell asleep.

20

THE RINGMASTER, 1926

Rin found Mauve sitting outside her own car, patching up her purple costume and singing to herself. Mauve's skirt hung above her boots and stockings as she leaned over the vestibule's stairs and onto her knees to catch the best light.

"I'm glad the rehearsal went well," Mauve said before Rin opened her mouth.

"Is there any point in even speaking when you know what I—"

"Not really," Mauve said, tilting her head up to grin at Rin. "But I like hearing your voice, so I'll allow it." Then she snorted. "No, I have no idea what you're going to say. My powers haven't grown *that* much. I'm razzing you." She was alive, here in the present, not drifting forward and backward and up and down through time. Rin was envious of how Mauve could ground herself without trying. Or maybe it only looked like she wasn't trying.

Rin was so tired. She remembered when she was younger, she could rehearse for hours, she could sleep on a board for twenty minutes and then be all right. Now every bone in her back ached. Now her knees hurt when she sat too long. Now she needed to rest before tonight.

"Are you okay?" Mauve said.

"Is the circus safe tonight?" Rin asked quietly. She didn't have to say from whom; Mauve knew. The threat of today. Black tents riding closer and closer, creeping up her spine with a cold shiver. The question had been on the back of Rin's mind the whole morning. Juggling was exhausting. Now that Jo and Charles were taken care of, she could and *should* worry about the Circus King. And after the circus was taken care of, she could worry about the world. Some days, she felt like an orchestra conductor whose arms were getting tired but was far from the coda. She could hear the instruments of her life straining from all the different sections of the pit, trying to make music out of cacophony.

Mauve looked into the air, as if pondering, and then gave a definitive nod. "As far as I can tell, the circus is safe tonight from the Circus King," Mauve said. "I do see something beyond that, some dark shape, a cracking . . . seems to be some sort of internal situation. Someone gets drunk, maybe? I see a bunch of imagery for body parts, a heart, a spine . . . but I think it's metaphorical. I keep asking is the show safe? And it keeps coming back yes."

"Well, that's ominous but positive? No one dies though, right?"

"No," Mauve said. "No death here."

Rin leaned in closer, so wandering ears wouldn't catch her words. Not that anyone was particularly close to their stoop, but she could see enough people wandering around, clanking things into place, carrying props here and there, jogging to the rehearsal tent as they taped up their wrists. And there were so many in the company it was just best to be safe. "Does the cracking have to do with . . . the war? We're going out again tonight, aren't we?"

"Odette asked me to remind you to nap before the show. And enjoy your opening night in Lawrence," Mauve said, pulling the needle and thread through her purple gown. "Then we'll worry about the future. So stop fussing, I'm already nervous enough without you coming in here throwing *your* nerves everywhere."

"You all right?" Rin asked.

"Yeah, it's not a bad day, just an anxious one," Mauve said.

"You need anything?" Rin asked.

"I need more sleep," Mauve said. "And remind me to drink water."

"You got it." Rin could feel Mauve charged with energy, but Rin could see how Mauve kept it buzzing right under her skin. Still in control. "How do you stay so grounded?"

Mauve grimaced at her needle and thread. "I'm not grounded," she said. "I'm every which way. Sometimes when I look at someone, I'm seeing them ten years ago and sometimes I'm seeing them ten years from now *and* remembering a good sandwich I eat in three years. And even worse, sometimes I look at them and know how they're gonna die. I'm not grounded, Rin."

Rin saw Mauve's steady hands pull at the thread. "You seem so calm," Rin said.

Mauve gave a small snort of a laugh. Then there was a hesitation, a pause, before Mauve said: "This isn't the first time the world's bled. If every time there was a war, I didn't stay calm, then I'd never be able to breathe. Do you know what happened in the summer of 1919?"

"That was when we started our circus," Rin said.

Mauve said, "Will Brown was murdered in Omaha. You know what happened in the summer of 1921? Tulsa. You know what's happened every single day since white people stepped foot on this continent? You know what happens across the world? Pain. The Great War? It was one blip. All that pain, all that loss, it was just a blip. So why did the Spark come then? Why not when the slaves rebelled in New Orleans? Why not at Wounded Knee? Why not in the summer of 1919?"

Rin shook her head. "I don't know," she said. Mauve had to carry this, and see this, every single day. That pain was something that was a part of Mauve's life, and no one, not even Odette, could remove it.

Rin didn't know the right words to say. There was pain she knew, that humming thrumming, and then there was pain she'd never know. Maybe there weren't any right words. So she stood beside the stairs, Mauve sewing and Rin breathing as they watched the lowering sun. Across the way, the midway lights clicked on with a whir. The generator was working, thank you Boom Boom. It glowed up like a carnival, the stuff of summer dreams. The yellows and reds and blues splattered atop the dim cobalt of dusk.

"The longer we have the Sparks, the more the Sparks grow. And my power's definitely grown since we met," Mauve said. She stopped sewing and looked to the back side of the midway ahead. "Hell, since we discovered this brewing war in the future. It's *really* grown since then. When I don't hone it in to just our little camp, I hear the whole world screaming."

"How do you stay sane with that Spark?" Rin said.

"What choice do I have, Rin?" Mauve said. She wrapped the string around her finger, fidgeting. "If this war comes, it won't be the last. If it doesn't come, there will be another. There will always be someone trying to snuff someone else out, because they're either scared or they're stupid or they're evil or they're all three." She cut the string. She tied the end. She set her needle back in her small tailor case. "And we just keep living."

"We can't stop the war, can we?" Rin said.

"If we do," Mauve said, "it'll be a blip. But it'll be our blip, nonetheless." She scooted over so Rin could sit by her. Rin took the invitation. The two women sat on the train car's stairs, Mauve fidgeting and Rin with her elbows on her knees. Rin's boots were so heavy. She wrapped her arms around Mauve, and Mauve reciprocated. Beyond them, the circus readied itself for the evening ahead. There was enough space between wagons and boxes that they could see some of the midway activity from their perch. Some customers had already come in from town to take a look at all the work and now formed a line beyond the fairground's gate. A gaggle of performers ran around behind and within the midway as Mr. Calliope struck his first chord. They laughed and pulled at each other's sleeves and showed off their final warm-ups. The nice thing about their circus: they didn't have to hide the magic. Because it was real.

Kell danced with Charles Reed, right out in the open, because here was home and here was hope and here someone could be who they wanted to be under the humming lights of an arcade booth.

It was a blip, but it still mattered. So maybe there was a reason why they all did this circus every day.

"They're all going to die if we don't stop it," Rin said.

"Yes," Mauve agreed. "But if it does go south, we still have tonight. And tonight is a lovely thing." Mauve's eyes sparked as she unraveled herself from Rin, picked up her sewing kit, and stood up on the steel stairs. "Jo," she said, "is going to be magnificent."

21

THE RINGMASTER, 1926

And Jo was magnificent.

"All right, curtain's up in five!" Maynard shouted backstage as everyone scrambled in the Back Yard. The floodlights buzzed above like an electric twilight, and then went dark and silent, bathing the waiting cast in anticipation.

Best get in quick, though. The mosquitos were fierce tonight and Rin's back itched under her velvet coat. For some reason, they rarely ever bit her, but when they did it was hell.

"Thank you five," the collective company said back to Maynard.

"Curtain meeting!" Rin boomed. "Come on now, the hair looks fine, Tina. Let's go, let's go."

The whole company gathered around as their eyes adjusted. They held hands. Rin grabbed Odette's and Odette thumbed her palm softly. Rin squeezed it, but there wasn't time to say anything. They needed to get the show on the road. Rin said, "In every theater there is a ghost."

"Of the past, present and future," everyone joined in.

"So we'll make them proud tonight," they finished.

And then with a deep, low hum, they all caught the same note. Even the ones that couldn't sing. They held that note together. They closed their eyes. From the different places they'd come from to be here now, they found themselves in the same story. Rin squeezed Odette's hand, then Mauve's hand, and as usual cheated a little, opening her eyes to see her crew all together in this moment.

But tonight, she saw something . . . really *saw* it . . . in the middle of the circle.

Something that had never been there before.

A yellow ball of light, illuminating the dark Back Yard and dancing across the circle's many faces.

It hovered there, as if all the cast and crew built it together.

But Rin knew where it came from. Her eyes flicked to Jo, who was dressed in a leotard and a pristine toga. The light got so bright, everyone opened their eyes and they stared at it. They weren't afraid, they were in awe.

Jo let go of the hands she held, disconnecting from the circle, and it disappeared. Her shoulders caved in, and she looked at the others in something between an apology and embarrassment. But Mr. Davidson on one side and Agnes Gregor on the other side, they grabbed her hands again. And Mr. Davidson nodded at her.

"Go on then, kid," Rin said. "Show us what we've got."

Jo, a quiet piano solo in the midst of an orchestra of Sparks, looked to where the light had been.

They began to hum, and the light returned. A crash of strings. A thumping of their hearts' percussions.

And there in the middle of the circle, Jo's Spark made their light real. A warm glow, gold and bright and as magic as the people in this place.

Rin smiled. "Break a leg everyone," she said.

Four minutes later, the Big Top burst to life.

Spec parade. The music. Mauve's purple gown perfectly patched up and her voice perfectly in tune, singing the opening song from above on her perch. Odette's acrobatics. Agnes lifting pieces of old farm equipment. Mr. and Mrs. Davidson. The jugglers and tumblers. Kell and Mr. Weathers. All the names spiraling together from one act to another in a dizzying display of imagination. The crowd squealed in all the right places, they gasped for the pony show when Jess nearly fell off Tina only to applaud when it turned out Jess had choreographed the whole thing to end in a flip.

Then it was time for the debuts.

Rin announced, "This is a first in front of your very eyes. Yes, you, Lawrence, Kansas, will be the first people in the universe to witness the Unkillable Devil."

Charles's performance was fine. The devil outfit they'd cobbled out of an old fire curtain made him look slightly ridiculous, and he wasn't a natural showman, but his skin made up for it, withstanding Yvanna's trick arrows and swords. Yvanna's Spark, to always do something perfect the first time (and only the first time), meant she could either change up her routine every single night or work very hard at one routine until practice made perfect. And

Yvanna had chosen the harder path when it came to her flaming arrow act, because she was a fire herself. Yvanna's igniting personality awed the audience enough to make up for Charles's shyness, and as Rin had suspected, they made a pretty good pair. Yvanna had created a wheelchair (on her first try) that could withstand the dirt floor Esther prepared, and tonight, Yvanna sped along the outer rim of the ring decked out in her painted flames. She held the audience captive as she lit her arrow—"a final strike to the Unkillable Devil!" she roared—then hit Charles with a burst of fire. As his costume caught flame and his hair burned, he looked like a phoenix, a demon. An Unkillable Devil indeed.

"He needs a better costume," Ringmaster muttered to Odette.

"Breathe," Odette whispered. "We'll fix it later." Ringmaster took a deep breath in and let it out slow. If she started analyzing the intricacies of the performance, she would lose her nerve. A pianist realizing she's playing a song note by note, finger by finger, in the middle of a hard concerto, she'd slip up.

Charles was followed by Tina sans Jess, so Tina could show off her entire internal menagerie. An interlude of chorus dancers filled the hippodrome track.

The audience was on the edge of their seats. The circus had found its rhythm through trial and error over the years. Ringmaster had learned to balance the stories and the brilliance of each performer, all connected by the ebbs and flows of feeling in the spotlight.

Ringmaster flushed in the heat of the tent as she and the audience clapped for Tina and the overlapping ballet.

It was perfect.

"Another premiere tonight!" Rin announced. "Our very own Oracle of Delphi, an Illusionist Persephone, the Dreamweaver!"

It wasn't canonically accurate. But people ate up Persephone lore. The spotlight turned from Ringmaster, spun to the center of the ring, where a shaking Jo had already hit her mark. Ringmaster had blocked—choreographed—Jo to hit her mark in the smack-dab center, hoping her illustrations would be big enough for the whole audience. They'd see how it went tonight, maybe she'd have to put her to the left or have her travel, maybe some mirrors . . .

Jo wore her thick toga, and she looked as if Hera was going to Gatsby's party. She had piercing blue eyes, and her black hair curled around her face. She looked uncomfortable, all parts of her tomboy demeanor scrubbed away. They needed to find something she liked to wear; they'd work on that.

Come on, kid. You can do it.

Jo raised one hand, staring out to the crowd. There was a flicker of fear in her face, and Rin knew that look. Rin wanted to run to her, pat her on the back, tell her it was okay, she was enough.

But Rin couldn't do any of those things. The only thing she could do was hold her breath and get ready to help guide Jo with a scaffolded narrative (*And now the Dreamweaver will . . . , then she will . . .*); she was used to doing this for new specs who weren't used to the limelight yet.

But the flicker of uncertainty disappeared, and a small impish smile curled on the kid's face. She had everyone looking at her, and she could do anything she wanted with that energy.

Jo, it turned out, was a natural. She wore gloves of golden rope, and she reached both hands into the air and began to pull out colors. Index finger and thumb together, she pinched the air, yanked down a long thread of blue, like she wove wind. She spun it around. A sky. A *cobalt* sky, just like the sunset tonight. She captured that feeling of a summer's night after a long baseball game, with the staccato sound of cicadas.

Then gray. The sort of gray that comes the evening before a thick, clean snowfall. She painted the sky with mountains. It happened so quick. She was a master.

This kid was full of multitudes. It spilled out of her like deep shades of ink, and so much, too, like she had been keeping it all inside for years, adding on rooms inside her heart for storage, waiting to surprise the world with her depths. And tonight, it all flew out, ribboning and gushing into the air, filling up the tent and the breath in all their lungs and the space inside all their heads.

And Rin got to see it.

She'd spent so much time with Odette and Mauve trying to look toward a brighter future, and here was a little sliver of that future. The future was laced with colors she'd never noticed. A quiet warm red found beside a campfire. It smelled like fresh laundry a plump, comforting grandmother folded against her stomach and set in a clean wicker basket. This world was made of the soft sheets of a bed curated by no one but her. It was the completion of a home unknown but hoped for.

A home for Jo.

Joy burst from every inch of the girl's smile, and she radiated like a brilliant lighthouse through the fog. It was a light Rin recognized from her own soul, like a song she'd not heard for years but still remembered all the words. There was her old heart, in the smile of a little girl.

Rin had to force herself to stop watching the performance to watch the audience. Especially one young man sitting in the front row, who had lost his composure and was now sobbing silently as he gaped at the spectacle above him.

It was exactly what he needed to see at the exact moment he needed to see it.

❋

"Did it work?" Odette approached Rin as she watched the audience file out and Maynard cleaned up the seats. The show was over, and the fantastical colored gels were now put away and replaced with work lights. Ringmaster sat on the curb ring, and Mauve drank some tea quietly beside her. Odette collapsed next to the two of them, waiting for an answer.

Ringmaster looked to Mauve, and Mauve nodded as she took another sip of her tea.

"The boy will go back home," she said. "He's left the gun behind in his hotel room."

"Will him and his girl make up and get their act together?" Ringmaster asked.

"Who can say?" Mauve replied. "But at least there's a chance now, isn't there?" She put a finger to her eye, rubbing off a smudge of makeup that seemed to be clumping her lashes. "Did I get it or do I look like I've got a black eye now?"

Odette checked. "You got it."

The three women leaned into each other as they took a deep breath and looked around the empty tent. It still echoed with the cheers, the ghosts of those who had performed a hundred times and those who would perform in days to come. It also was littered with discarded popcorn buckets.

"Sooooo?" A voice broke the moment of peace. Jo rushed toward them, her toga gone and her trousers and shirt back in place. Charles followed a couple steps behind looking very put out and hurried. Jo's black straw hair swept into her face as she looked around frantically. "The special person, did they already leave?"

Ringmaster nodded. "He went home."

"I don't even get to meet him?" Jo said. "I ran out here as fast as I could. What was he, a senator?"

"Oh my God." Charles caught up, his hair flopping in his face. "Was it Charlie Chaplin?"

"No," Mauve said. "His name is Thomas. He served in the war and had forgotten about mountains and sunsets. You reminded him."

Jo looked confused. "Was he the special guest?"

"You have beautiful detail in your work," Ringmaster said patiently. "The cicadas. The shadows on the snow. It's what makes your illusions real. The small things." She saw Charles perk up expectantly. "Charles, you were very much on fire and have lived to tell the tale. Quite impressive."

"Thank you, ma'am!" Charles beamed.

"Yes, thank you," Jo said, pushing on. "So . . . the special guests are just random people? The circus goes and helps random people?"

"That's what we do here," Ringmaster said. "Thomas now can grow old. Thomas can become active in his neighborhood, raise children, and plant trees. A ripple of good happens in the space where a black hole would have been." She stood and looked down to the girl who looked up at her. "You did good, kid."

"Yeah, she's a star." Charles patted his sister on the back, proud.

"Aw, shucks," Jo rebuffed. "So we do ripples of good, but how did you know this Thomas fella needed it?"

"Mauve tells us where to take our circus," Ringmaster tried to explain. "She guides us to people who need this light in their life. And now you, Jo, are an integral part of that mission. You will finesse the exact image someone needs to see in that exact moment. Of course, none of us can control the world. The people we visit still make their own decisions. But if they make a different or better decision, then they can change a lot. A beautiful moment of art can do much more for change than brute force." Ringmaster watched Jo carefully. "Does that make sense?"

Jo looked bewildered, but she took it all in. She shook her head, as if to gather her bearings. Then she looked up to Rin. "Aye, Captain."

Rin became painfully aware she was an adult that a kid looked up to. It was a heavy weight she hoped she was able to uphold.

Kell poked his head in. "Charles?" he said timidly. Charles lit up.

"I'll see you out there, Jo," Charles said. "I'll wait before doing any of the games, okay?"

Jo watched him leave, but then turned right back to the three women. "So who had you come for in Omaha?" she asked.

"You," Mauve said, without missing a beat.

Jo scrunched up her face again. "Me?" she said. "Not Charles?"

"Both of you," Odette said. "Charles would be happy wherever you are. You are the guiding star of your little team, you know."

"I'm not important."

"Everyone is important," Ringmaster cut her off. "And this circus needs you."

Jo stepped back and brushed her off with a laugh.

"Well obviously," Jo said. "That third act of yours was really lagging in Omaha. Gotta give it that pop pop va-va-voom of all this." She waved to herself, then slowly stopped, then turned on her heels. "I don't know why I did that. Good night!" She ran to the exit, into the lights of the midway outside. "Charles and Kell, you better be waiting or I'll smack you!"

After a second, Rin snort-laughed.

"They're both so sweet," Odette said calmly, holding Rin's arm as Rin slowly sat back down. "But that girl has been through the wringer and she's not as resilient as her brother. We must tread gently."

"The thing is, she's been through the wringer and she still shines." Rin fixed her cuffs. "Mauve," she said, "you told me she was the special guest. You didn't tell me how powerful her Spark was."

"Sorry," Mauve said, obviously not sorry. "I can't tell you everything. You gotta make decisions based on living in the moment, or else I have too much power over you. I don't want that much power. You're my friend."

"You didn't know, did you," Rin said dryly.

"I did not," Mauve said.

"Should we be concerned that she can fill up the entire tent with her Spark?" Odette said. Just that evening, Rin had worried Jo's Spark wouldn't be strong enough to the act they'd set for her. That seemed silly now. "Rin, you said she lost control for a second and it wasn't pretty."

Mauve shrugged. "I just know she needs to be here."

"When others go along with things, she questions them," Rin said. "She's a brave one. And if I'm right, and if Mauve's right, we're gonna need her as much as she needs us."

Mauve was quiet. "Around her is darkness and light. Both possibilities of both futures. But that's everyone, isn't it?"

"She's strong-willed," Rin said. She had also lived with one foot in the dark and one foot in the light. She remembered a train car, far away from here, sobbing in the doorway, a suitcase in her hand.

Honestly, look at yourself. Do you think I made you do every single thing you've done? And once you get out of here and you're no longer near me, and you go off and do things you're not too proud of, who are you going to blame then? Huh?

Who had she blamed when she kept stealing after she left? Who had she blamed when she kept shoving Odette away? When she couldn't sleep at night and turned to a bottle or took it out on a neighbor? She'd hit him. There was violence in her, unrest. All the small moments before Odette, and then even after . . .

Jo had never been shown kindness, and yet she was kind. So there was more hope for Jo than there had been for Rin at that age.

"That's the fun thing about strong people, they have control over what happens to them," Odette said.

"Sometimes," Mauve said. "Not always. She's full of fury, rage, red-hot flames." Then she blinked, narrowing her eyes far off at something Rin couldn't yet see. "We should go now."

Odette pulled her hair back and rocked to her feet. "It would be nice to just live one night all the way through."

Rin set the ghost light. Then they were gone.

*

22

THE RINGMASTER, 1941

Rin, Mauve, and Odette stood on a street corner, looking down a long line of houses. From the technology and the architecture, it was clear they were in the future. She didn't even have to feel the bracelet around her wrist.

And yet, although they were in the thick of war, it looked like this neighborhood had been spared from smoke and death. The houses were pristine, all pretty white and primary colors. The grass was cut and a rich deep green as kids ran on uncracked cement. The air was so clean and crisp it could have been a dream. This future smelled like soap and lilacs. Rin didn't trust it.

"Sparks are taken," Mauve whispered, as if that explained why they had jumped to this quiet, peaceful-seeming street. "Those without Sparks are taken. Anyone they don't like is taken."

"What do you mean taken?"

"They're cleaning, they say," Mauve said. "They're making everything 'perfect,' 'pure.'"

They saw a big black truck with a motor that purred softer than any automobile Rin had seen back home. It appeared on the horizon then pulled to the curb outside a nice white house with blue trim. A man next door watered his plants, a woman across the street played with her baby.

She had thought darkness hadn't spread here yet, but now Rin realized everyone on the street avoided looking at the house with blue trim.

Something bad was in there.

"Are they picking up a Spark kid?" Rin whispered. Mauve shook her head.

"No." Mauve stood in silence, unmoving. The three of them were like shadows in the background; far enough away that no one would notice them, close enough to see everything that happened.

The black truck cut its engine. Now that it was closer, Rin registered that the truck's bed was covered with a canvas tarp, like a little circus tent. Two soldiers with guns sat in the front seats. They got out. They marched to the door. They disappeared inside. Five minutes later, a family came out with suitcases in their hands. The little girl carried a Snow White doll and the woman was still dressed in her house clothes under her coat, as if the soldiers had interrupted their lives in the middle of a sentence, in the middle of a breath, and they'd not been given time to start breathing again.

The soldiers weren't wagon men. They were kids, boys stuffed into stiff uniforms. The girl and the woman who followed them, Rin saw the Star of David on their coats.

Rin's stomach dropped, further down than the ground. There was something sinister with gnashing teeth that stood behind its yellow cloth. Something horrific stood before it, down the road, past this place with the blue and white houses.

The Star of David was known in Hebrew as the Magen David. *Magen* was the word for shield. But now it had been made into a target. She felt it, the humming, thrumming march of years.

She had to do something. What could she do? She could take them into next week. She could . . . get shot. She could take them where she took some others who came to the circus for help, to the future, but what about the immunizations? She hadn't made any prior arrangements . . . she could take them back . . . she could . . . get herself and Odette and Mauve *and* this family killed.

The neighbors weren't doing anything. They were trying to avoid eye contact, like they'd not necessarily expected this particular visit but also weren't surprised. If the neighbors knew what was happening, and this was done like a dance . . . then this had happened millions of times before and would happen millions of times after. It wasn't just this family.

This was something that was larger than what she could see, something that to the people of this time already felt baked into the everyday humdrum.

She swore the mother saw her, eyes flashing in the three women's direction. The woman didn't plead with Rin, she just stared, as if she were already looking through dead eyes.

"Where are they taking them?" Rin whispered to Mauve.

Mauve shook her head. "Don't ask me to answer that."

That was enough to know.

And it wouldn't just be these two. If the soldiers knew what Rin was, Rin would be in that truck, too. Odette and Mauve as well. None of them were safe, none of them fit in.

She remembered her great-grandmother, clutching that cane.

She remembered the blue light in the war-torn village. Jo's face—

Rin felt her heart and her throat tangle in what had happened and what would happen, and she couldn't breathe. It hadn't felt completely real, she had hoped it wasn't real—but now she was here in the future and she saw it, touched it, heard it . . . and why did the air smell so good here?! An apocalypse shouldn't be this clean. An apocalypse shouldn't be silent, shouldn't *be* at all. But it was as real as the circus, which smelled like sugar and sweat and sounded with music and children. How could both of these places exist in the same world?

No, no, take a moment. Understand all of these were not things that would *have* to happen. They could still change it. They could still make it so black trucks didn't ever exist and never would again. She had a Spark, didn't she?

"We'll stop this whole thing from happening," the Ringmaster said to Mauve and Odette, for the hundredth time.

Now the words sounded tired. An old battle cry for a platoon that had already been gunned down.

"Rin—"

"No," Rin said. "We're not just sitting here. Tell me, how do we stop that truck?" But Rin was already on her feet. If all she could do was teleport that truck to Timbuktu she'd do it.

"We can travel back," Mauve said. "A few years. Warn the family, and hopefully they'll listen? I see the mother has a cousin in London. Maybe they can go there." She fell back, as if a giant animal had reared its head in front of her. "There are so many threads going where that family is going. There are so many people. Not all of them have cousins in London . . ." Mauve's eyes dilated.

Odette grabbed Mauve's arm. "Mauve," Odette said, sharply, worried.

Mauve snapped back. She shook her head. "We . . . we can try."

It would be more than what the neighbors had done.

Rin glared at the truck, now closed and locked around the little family. Just because it drove away right now did not mean that it would drive away for good. This was not the final draft.

But what good was she, jumping around and staring at scenes like a tourist? The future was a jewelry box full of tangled necklaces and every time she touched a chain, the knots got worse.

The truck drove away.

And the three women reluctantly disappeared from the street, just as haunted as the white house with blue trim that was left empty.

Now years before, the street still looked the same. Rin and Odette and Mauve watched with wide eyes as the neighbor kids and the little girl played together; it looked like one of those afternoon games that are organized by children on summer break. Rin imagined there was some sturdy tree house somewhere or maybe a good mulberry bush they'd make home before their parents called them in for supper.

In front of the white house with the blue trim, the mother was pruning the row of healthy-looking bushes that lined the walkway to the door.

Odette volunteered because, of the three of them, she had a way with people.

"I hope with a cousin in London," Odette said, "someone in the family knows English. I don't know any other languages."

Rin and Mauve watched in silence as she approached the edge of the lawn and spoke softly to the woman, wringing her hands as she uttered words Rin could hardly even imagine. The mother just stared, pruning shears in one hand, bushes forgotten.

Then Odette walked away, leaving the mother with a pale haunted gaze.

To know the end is coming—it was one of the worst feelings in the world. Rin, Mauve, and Odette all knew that stone in their stomachs.

"Did she listen?" Rin asked desperately.

Odette shrugged, near tears.

Mauve looked to the future. "I . . ." she said. "I see this truck doesn't come here anymore. But it goes somewhere else. And there are many, *many* trucks."

"Well," Rin said. "We have lots of time."

The three of them stood, lost, on the street. Rin's body hummed with nerves.

"It would make more sense," Mauve said, "to pull the plant up at the root. We trace the root, we stamp it out before it even begins. We gotta find a way to do that. We might get to resurface from this nightmare with all our wits about us. If we could muster up one gigantic ripple that touches everyone . . ."

The women were silent, and Rin was sure they were all picturing what she was—a million more trips like this one. She felt dizzy and helpless, like trying to grasp water in her hands and never being able to hold all of it, or any of it, for very long.

Rin looked to the woman staring at them from her lawn. Then the woman ran for her daughter. They knew, they understood. Sometimes, it felt like as soon as you outran yesterday, it was right back in front of you.

There you are.

"Mauve's right. We go to where it started," Rin said. "Tomorrow night, we finish this."

✳

23

EDWARD, 1917

Edward thought on his wedding day he would feel excited. But he was just a bundle of nerves, and nerves were not the same as happiness.

He stood outside the judge's quarters. He fixed his shirt. He checked his hair once more in the glass of a framed picture in the secretary's work space. He fiddled with his pocketknife. He waited.

He'd waited for months before bringing up marriage again. He'd waited for her and him to grow accustomed to their new beautiful life. He wanted her to want this.

It seemed like she wanted this.

"Ruthie?" Edward had said quietly one night, and Ruth stretched beside him, the moonlight on her and the bed, and she smiled up at him.

"What is it?" she'd said. "You've got that look on your face, like when something's eating you from the inside."

She knew him. He knew her. There was a pinnacle of existence with another human, when two pieces of twine twist together to make something bigger and sturdier. He pulled a lock of hair out of her face.

"There's nothing eating me up tonight," Edward said. "I'm just happy. I think we've had some great adventures together."

"We have," Ruth said. She stroked his arm.

"When you sleep at night," Edward said, "what do you dream about?"

Ruth shrugged. "I dream about us, sometimes," she said. "I dream about flying. Colored lights. It sort of looks like a kaleidoscope that we're falling through."

It sounded nice. Nicer than what he dreamed about. It was like the gas was still coming for him, even after all this time. But sometimes, Ruth would be there, saving him. *Choosing* to save him. Maybe she had wanted to, all along, regardless of what he said or what his Spark may be.

He touched her cheek. "You're beautiful," he said. She was his person. She was his life. She was all the parts of him that were worth anything.

He made them cocoa in the presidential suite's kitchen. Ruth pulled a book off the shelf, and Ed carried two mugs to the bed, where they sat and drank and she read him a playscript about King Lear and his three daughters, and it was touching and lovely. Looking at her in the firelight, he'd asked, "Tomorrow. Do you want to get married?" Then he said, "If you want to, then I'll do it. I'm not going to make you do this."

Ruth's nose had crinkled. "Well, of course not. You can't make me do anything."

"Right," Edward said. Maybe marriage could be a new start. If he could try harder for anyone, it would be Ruth.

They talked over the logistics of how they could get married. Edward argued a courthouse would be best, although Ruth mentioned she wanted a myriad of odd impossible things because they were traditional.

"We aren't doing any of that," Edward said. "It makes no sense. It's not us. You don't need all that old-fashioned stuff. Now we should sleep."

"Good night, my prince of the Franks," Ruth said. She smiled.

"Goodnight, my beautiful Cordelia." Edward smiled back.

They had lain side by side in the large king bed. Ruth had fallen asleep first. Edward didn't. He'd watched the wall, thinking through every single thing he'd done since the war, and sometimes his mind slipped further back. His stepfather's fist slammed into his conscience, and he remembered the one time he struck back. He remembered his mother screaming. Once, he even remembered before his stepfather, when his mother's eyes looked at him like he was a monster. She'd found Edward in the kitchen the night after an argument. He was leaned over the sink with a match, burning her parents' only daguerreotype.

But most of all, he would remember the trench.

Night was the worst for his mind, racing through the frayed ends of his conscience. At night he was alone. Ruth wasn't awake to keep him at peace. He could wake her, but if he wanted her to function well the next day, he did have to let her sleep.

Now, in the courthouse, Ed stood waiting, his eyes roaming the hallway with its cheap framed art. She would come. Of course she would come. They were two fires engulfing each other, the only two people in the world who understood the other's heart. Once he had heard a story about how the moon was two rabbits who had been stuck together, one dark and one light. That was Edward and Ruth. Not whole without the other.

What if she didn't come?

He'd given Ruth too much rope to hang him with. She could run now. She could be in another shit town in Ohio by now.

What if she didn't come?

The terror rose in his chest like vomit. His knife felt clammy in the hand he'd shoved into his pocket.

And if she did come? Would he ever be sure she'd truly wanted to come? Had he worded his request correctly to give her the choice?

Had he ever done anything worth loving?

The judge's door opened. A portly fellow, exactly how Edward had imagined a judge would look, sauntered out of his quarters. "Ah, she's late." He nudged Edward's stiff body. "Looks like we got a runner!" He laughed. Edward did not.

"Stop trying to be funny," Edward said, bored.

The judge grew solemn.

And the hallway suddenly sounded with the clicking of expensive heels. Ruth had managed to find the sort of shoes a wealthy beau could afford, even with only a day's notice.

She wore a modest, silky dress that hung off her shoulders and cascaded down her arms and her breasts. Her hair was forced into tight curls, as if she'd tried to make a bob and had instead succeeded in creating a whole new style altogether. Her eyes looked down the hall, and landed on Edward.

She smiled. But he did not smile back.

The way her hands clutched her fresh flowers, the way her eyes creased in a worried frown . . . she was not completely sold on being here.

This was not how he'd imagined it.

But she was here. She was here, and she was ready. He could take it from here, she just needed to say yes.

"Hi," she breathed, reaching for his hands and pulling herself closer. She kissed him. And he allowed himself to receive it.

She loved him. Of course she loved him. They were connected by more than his sham. This was deeper than Sparks.

The judge began. Two women in the hallway were their witnesses.

Edward said, "I do," and he meant it.

Then it was Ruth's turn, and the words came out rushed and then slow. "I . . . do." Edward tried to read it closer, but it was a quick second in time and then they were off to the next moment.

As they stepped forward, together, they were married. Mr. and Mrs. Edward King. It was legal, on paper. And there was no taking that back. Not now. Not ever.

✳

That night, Edward whispered to a man at the hotel bar: "You think she's beautiful."

The man looked up and saw Edward's bride in her white dress. The man set his drink down and went to Ruth. They spoke for a while. Edward watched, like a hawk, from his perch at the bar.

Ruth pressed away from the man, until Edward had to step in and punch him to the ground. Edward pulled out that piddly knife and waved it around like it was something. He told the man to get lost and never look at Ruth again or else the man's body would feel like it caught fire. The man ran out of the bar, screaming and crying. Then Edward told the bar . . . and Ruth . . . to forget about it. But something still gnawed away behind Ruth's eyes. She still felt she'd been scared, even if she didn't know why. An anxiety with no name. Good. She would learn to stay away from men like that.

It was stupid. Edward knew it was stupid. But he'd felt better, watching Ruth push the man away.

But it wasn't enough. The fear was back as soon as they lay in bed again.

Their backs touched one another, two beautiful statues settled together like lovers in a grave.

Edward broke: "Tell me why you looked nervous at the courthouse today."

Ruth took a minute, and then she said, "I sometimes feel as if the whole world is out there, and we are here, siphoned off. I don't want to be siphoned off."

"But you love me?"

"Of course I love you."

"Did I make you marry me?"

Ruth situated herself in bed to a more comfortable position. "No."

"Do you want to be married to me?"

Ruth situated herself again. She coughed. "I don't know."

Edward threw his hand out to the nightstand and shoved it to the ground with a crash. Ruth squeaked. Edward shot out of bed, grabbed his trousers, threw a shirt on, and marched to the door.

"Ed, please!" Ruth struggled to untangle herself from the peaceful sheets. "I'm sorry, please don't go. It's our wedding night."

"You went of your own accord!" Edward shouted.

"Yes, yes, darling, I did, of course I did," Ruth begged him. "Please keep your voice down, sweetheart."

"Tell me if you love me, do you really love me?" Edward asked.

The rest of the night was a blur. Edward finally settled back into bed. Ruth settled back near him, now holding his chest in her arms and her naked body pressed against his.

"I don't know who I would be or what I would do without you," Ruth said. "Please don't leave."

Edward allowed her to feel his hand up and down her arm, a rub of affection.

"I love you," he said quietly.

"I love you, too," she said.

They left the night at that.

❋

In the morning, Ruth was not happy. Edward could see this. And it was causing him problems. She was wilting like a poorly kept plant. No flowers burst from her, and so no flowers burst from his life at all.

So he bought her flowers.

She woke to a beautiful bouquet on the suite's small tea table. The curtain was already opened to let the city sunlight in through its sooty windows. Edward was already dressed, waiting for her with breakfast: a croissant fresh from the bakery down the street.

She rubbed her eyes. "Good morning?" she said.

"Good morning, wife," Edward said.

She slowly crawled out of bed, her long, young legs slipping out from the white sheets. She tussled her hair, grabbed a robe, and came to gingerly sit across from Edward and in front of her croissant.

She was beautiful.

Edward waited for her to eat, wake up a little bit, before he began speaking.

"I have been thinking," he said, "perhaps we should do something a little bit like a honeymoon, seeing as that's customary after a wedding."

Ruth took a bite of her croissant. "Where are we going?"

"Well," Edward said, "I thought we could decide that together."

Ruth swallowed and reached for the milk he'd brought alongside her breakfast. Her robe dangled dangerously, almost rolling into the flowers. But he said nothing. Not this morning.

"I was hoping you'd say something," Edward said.

Ruth shrugged. "I would like to see my mother, perhaps," she said.

Rage filled him up. And he said, as if putting a toy train back on its rails, "No, you don't. Go on, where else? Niagara? The mountains? Grand Canyon? Paris? Polynesia? Iceland? You had all those pictures on your wall back in New York. *Those* are the places you really wanted to go. So where do you want to go?"

"You'd really take me to all the places in the photographs?" He'd found her true desire, hadn't he? "Anywhere on that wall would be wonderful. I've always wanted to go there." She said, as if in a trance. This was pleasant. She was happy. "You're good at picking those things out, how about you pick?"

Edward smiled. "All right," he said. "I'll pick an adventure for us."

"Thank you," Ruth said, eating the croissant. "It should be fun."

"And don't you worry about anything," Edward said. "I'll get the whole thing sorted. All you need to do is enjoy yourself. Croissants and hot chocolate every morning, any sort of gifts you see are yours. And then at night, I'll make sure you're tucked into the most comfortable beds. Ruthie, it'll be grand."

"It will," Ruth said. And it was as if she believed him. There was something left, under all that grime, like the sooty window. Outside, the sun still shone. Inside, Ruth still loved him.

She had to.

And if she didn't, then he would make sure she did.

24

THE RINGMASTER, 1926

Rin sat alone on the top of an arcade box. She looked to her bare wrist.

Her body shook. She tried to take deep breaths. She tried to center herself in the now.

Her mother had lit candles on Friday nights. Her mother wore a Magen David around her neck. A long line of women before Rin knew the prayers for Shabbat. She had learned the notes without seeing the notations, just listening. The lilts up and down, the fun ha'olam phrasing that felt like a roller coaster to sing. She didn't know any prayers other than that, but she knew there were many. She knew they'd been sung for centuries back.

Did all of that die in a few years?

Maybe the Sparks would die, too. Maybe by the middle of this century, all the magic in the world and all the people who lit up the nights with their lives would be destroyed, and even worse, maybe forgotten.

Rin was certain she was the only person in the world who remembered the sound of her mother's singing. The memory perched in her brain, so delicate, so easily plucked out by time or illness or a possibly difficult concussion. The lullabies, the prayers, the soft hands on her head, pulling her hair out of her face and whispering that everything would be okay.

After the Spark came, when Rin would get scared, her mother would say she wished she could hold it all for her.

Rin remembered the outside of her mother's old synagogue. It was surrounded by names of the dead. They sang of the dead every Shabbat. When someone died, close family members tore kriah, or ripped a piece of clothing to remind the living that the physical body may be gone, but the soul continued on. There were memorials for the dead during high holidays. The dead were ever-present in a congregation, in a household; that was part of what it meant to be Jewish: to hold the others' light who had come before and then had to leave. Even after Rin and her mother stopped going, and even after Rin lost herself in the black tents, that synagogue kept saying the names of the dead.

But what if everyone was gone? Then who remembered?

Where had her mother's Magen David necklace gone? It must have gotten lost along the way, back before the graveyard. Before Odette and Mauve and the circus. Had they pawned it? Had he forced her to drop it in a gutter somewhere? Even if she could buy another, it wouldn't be her mother's. Precious things were so easily destroyed and never replaceable.

She breathed in. Ground. Ground in the now. Grounding her like tearing kriah.

Sometimes, she forgot she had a body. She'd realized this one day when she watched Odette rehearse. Rin had started to think through every single thing she'd have to do with her hands and feet and abdomen and thighs in order to succeed at aerials. And she realized Odette had to be so very grounded to succeed in the air. Mauve could somehow do it, too. Keep one foot in this world while exploring others. Ringmaster could never. She used her body for walking, for sleeping and eating, for speaking, and for jumping through time. But she didn't use it to celebrate, to feel, to pray, to dance.

So now Rin sat atop the arcade stalls of their circus, looking up at the stars over the field. She tried, *tried*, to ground herself.

The midway lights were turned off, and she hugged her knees, the warm summer breeze whistling on her cheeks.

She'd gotten up there by jumping from one minute ago on the ground, to two minutes forward on the top of the stall. It was faster and less painful than a ladder. What had been a miracle a decade ago became a stepping stool today.

There was peace being just a little closer to the stars. There was no trace of the war to come. Today was today.

Tomorrow would be their last show in Lawrence. She'd give her marching orders to Jo, who was still young and very much alive and had only just gotten here. Rin had helped her perfect an image for one last soul in the town. A woman who had just lost her dog, one of her last companions in this world, and who needed to see bright clouds and rolling fields and her father bringing home her first puppy seventy years ago.

It seemed, Rin realized, that most things Jo showed the people they were saving had to do with other people. In their hour of need, people didn't need to see castles or magnificent golden thrones. Even those who needed cash, the cash was a way to help one another, to heal one another. People needed people.

"Can I join you?" Odette asked quietly, shimmying up the pole of the awning. Rin scooted over and let her sit. Odette didn't take up as much space as Rin did, but she was sturdy, not worrying about her kneecaps popping wrong or cracking her back if she was stiff for too long. She looked at home next to Rin, clumsy old Rin with the painful leg.

"Penny for your thoughts?" Odette asked, pulling her sweater down around her fingers. She was dressed in a knitted gray getup, with a flowing skirt she'd hiked up around her knees to climb up here. She was talented. Her hair wasn't curled or bobbed, it sort of frizzed out like she'd brushed it in the dry heat and it bunched up a little, from the static.

She was beautiful.

"I was thinking about what Mauve said to me," Rin said. "Back in Chicago."

They'd weathered the storm of the flu pandemic together in Chicago, back in 1918. They'd battened down the hatches at a boardinghouse, waiting for it to be over. Not knowing *if* it would be over. It was a total possibility back then that the rest of their lives would be hiding from an invisible death, a weapon on the wind.

"She knew I was hurting myself," Rin muttered, embarrassed. Odette softly touched Rin's arm; the same place where Rin used to pinch herself when she got stressed or drunk or both. "She knew what I was planning, and one night she came up to me, and she said people were going to need my help, and I should stop hurting myself. I told her I was the last person on earth who should be helping anyone. And she said . . . she said those who hurt the most are the best at protecting others from the dark, because they know what the dark looks like."

"What were you planning?" Odette said.

"You know what I was planning," Rin said.

"I'm glad she stopped you," Odette said.

"That's not what did it," Rin said. "She planted herself in the courtyard right outside the bathroom window, the bathroom I'd locked myself in. She sang a song my mom used to sing to me."

That was the first night Rin had jumped through time. She'd given up on Sparks, she'd given up on herself, her brain pounding with a voice screaming she was useless, she would be nothing without *him*. She was nothing to begin with.

But that song. That one little song had started to move her out of time, send her back to the day in the graveyard when she buried her mother, and Rin had to hold on to the bathroom walls to stop it. No, no she could not go back there. If she went beyond the places of the now, then *he* would find her again. That would become one of her very first rules, even before she realized her Spark had grown that night. She could now time travel.

With all of this weighing down on her, she'd found herself screaming. Then someone had moved her to the living room, and she sat there soaked in her own tears, her hair matted and unwashed. She'd said to her little found family; Mauve, Bernard . . . Odette. Rin had said, "I've been this powerful all this time?" Because *all* this time, she had seen herself as a shriveled-up shrew, a useless, ugly thing, and the deep voice in her head made it a fact. She was weak, she couldn't even boil water right, and here she had jumped through tomorrow.

"Yes," Bernard had said.

"And what am I supposed to do with that?" she'd said, desperate.

"You can believe it," Bernard had answered. Rin had never forgotten those words, but she also hadn't ever been able to swallow them.

Now, under the stars, Odette rested her head on Rin's shoulder. "We got through it," she said. "The pandemic ended. You got better. We got married. We started a circus. Everything was alright. And everything will be alright again."

"If we're so powerful," Rin said, "then why can't we fix it?"

"Before we do anything else," Odette said, stroking her hair very carefully, "you have to rest. You have to focus. Right now, you feel like a whirring engine, or one of those plasma balls."

"Plasma balls don't feel like anything," Rin grunted.

"Well, if they did, they'd feel like you."

So Rin tried to focus, digging her heels and her roots into the soil of the present . . . or the top of an arcade box. Rin looked down and saw Mauve humming to herself, holding a flower and smiling at it like it was the most beautiful thing she'd ever seen. Tina, like she'd smelled some sort of gossip, was hot on the trail and had arrived at Mauve's side to walk back to the train together as Mauve giggled about something.

"It feels so far away," Mauve said, excited. She was talking loud enough for Rin to hear on her perch, but only as they passed. "But he'll come. He'll come soon enough."

Rin smiled softly. She did appreciate the midway, this moment, just feeling Odette on her shoulder.

There was one night, back when Rin was still coming to terms with the fact that she was a useless sapphic and not the "normal" girl she always assumed she was, when she stood in the kitchen of the boardinghouse and watched Odette flip pancakes for a late-night/early-morning breakfast extravaganza.

This is wrong, something whispered inside her ears.

This is too gentle to be wrong, Rin thought, content. *But if it is, let us be wrong, let us live in love.*

It was going to be a hard life for them. Their wedding was secret, without a certificate. In the ledger of the outside narrative, they had no say in each other's stories. But Odette and Mauve and Rin had all done hard things before, they could take anything that was to come. They were powerful.

Mauve looked up and saw them. She waved. And she joined them with a hop and a skip. Her body was still much younger than Rin's. She swung one leg up over the top and then crouched to scoot closer. "Let's hope it doesn't crumble under us. What're we doing?"

"Talking about the pandemic," Rin said.

"Not a fun time," Mauve said. "Although I do miss our little boarding-house bubble. That one girl, she was an amazing cook, what was her name? The one who could regurgitate? Was she a Spark or just a really good sword swallower?"

As Odette and Mauve reminisced about a girl from their boardinghouse that Rin couldn't remember, her eyes drifted to where Charles stood below, flirting with Esther as she cleaned her duck pond booth. Esther was a quiet one; someone who had joined the circus to disappear. But Charles made her laugh.

Rin felt another small smile creep over her cheek. And then she lost that smile as she looked over and saw Kell, smoking near the entrance of one of the barker boxes, leaning up against the red-and-white stripes. His eyes looked wide to Charles and the girl. His shoulders sagged, defeated.

Ebb and flow, love and pain, war and peace. This is what the experience of living was. And sometimes, that uncomfortable dissonance pulled some-thing deep inside Rin up to the bubbling surface and she'd go looking for a hidden flask. But tonight, she just watched. She just smiled.

Even the sorrows of the scene below were illuminated by the stars in a country sky above, scored by the music of laughter.

When the world is so dark, there is a bravery in laughter.

And if the three of them were nothing else, they were brave.

Something clanged, loud. Rin jumped in her spot. Odette straightened up, looking around.

"What in the blazes . . ." Odette gasped.

Rin peered down, past Charles and to the left where the entrance gates still stood, stuck in the ground. There Mr. Davidson entered in his street clothes of overalls and a nice hat. He stumbled, his eyes straight ahead, like an invisible string pulled him forward. He must have tripped, run into something in the dark.

He looked up, past the arcade signs and right at Rin.

Rin gave a small friendly wave.

Mr. Davidson did not wave.

Mr. Davidson took out a gun.

✷

25

THE RINGMASTER, 1926

Mr. Davidson, his eyes trained on Rin, aimed a black pistol at Esther and Charles.

"Charles!" Rin barked.

Charles saw Davidson and, faster than Rin could think, he slammed Esther to the ground and ran for the man. Davidson shot again and again and again. *CRACK. CRACK. POP. POP.* Charles kept running for him.

So Davidson pocketed the gun, and started to grow.

No no no no. Rin jumped from the arcade box, soaring through a small tear in time to kick out the other side and run at Davidson. She needed to shove Davidson down on the ground before it was too late, but it was too late. He roared above her, transforming into a titan.

His entire body swelled, shot up to the sky, a small man to a giant. His Spark that had made so many laugh now looked like a nightmare, casting a growing shadow as he towered over the midway.

"STARS AND STRIPES!" The Ringmaster roared out the emergency call. "STARS AND STRIPES!" She couldn't see it, but she knew help was on the way, she knew Odette and Mauve were only steps behind her. "Get back, Charles! Run. Go!"

She rushed for Davidson again, now taller than the booths, taller than the tents. He jerked his foot out to ruin the box where Rin and Odette and Mauve had just been perched.

Everyone spilled out into the night, some holding lanterns and peering into the dark. Rin heard a shout.

"Davidson! What the hell are you doing?!"

Davidson reached the end of the midway and the Big Top. He pulled the tent canvas, tossing it aside like a napkin. The harnesses snapped, bringing razor-sharp anchors with them. Screams of pain echoed from the grounds, and the skeleton of the Big Top stood unsteady, bone white in the moonlight. An angry cry rang out from down beside Davidson's feet.

That's when Rin saw Jo rushing toward him. "Jo!" Rin shouted, pumping her arms forward. "Jo, no, get away from there!"

But Jo either didn't hear her or didn't listen. Jo sprinted forward into the rising dust where the Big Top's remains were collapsing, people scrambling as fast as they could from the demolition. "Mr. Davidson!" she shouted.

Jo raised her hands high; she breathed out and unleashed a cloud of her own. A cloud of dragons, larger men, big tanks, anything she could think of to make him stop. But he did not. So Jo tried to make what looked like a box around him, but he batted it away, turned around, and looked down at her, like Jack's giant.

"You gnat . . ." He started to say something, but Rin shoved herself forward, through the air like space was nothing but water and she swam forward, jumping between him and Jo.

Rin shot a sharp: "Davidson!"

Davidson's large eyes turned to look at her. Rin shoved Jo back, behind her, back into Odette's arms, back to the crowd that huddled together in the dark, covered in dirt and grime.

The Ringmaster glared up at him, unafraid, a giant slayer.

"What the hell do you think you are doing?" she roared. "Lay off your Spark and explain yourself!"

"I have nothing to explain, my little Ringmaster!" Davidson roared, but he stumbled back as well. "You think you can make me look like an ass? You think you've won? *You've won shit!* You will never get rid of me!" Davidson laughed cruelly.

A kite on a string. Rin's body numb. Her life passing out of it, like a ghost who had been clinging to life, begging to stay just a little longer.

You think you've won.

No. No no no.

The Ringmaster faded from Rin, and the circus—her circus—melted from her grasp. Everyone she loved was behind her, but the threads were severed between them. Rin floated loose in her own black hole.

This was Mr. Davidson. But it wasn't Mr. Davidson. *He'd* found him. *He'd* found *her.* The Circus King peered out from behind Davidson's eyes. It was his face, his contorted grin that wanted to eat her, gulp up everything and bite down to make it spray blood just to scare her. She knew the Circus King well enough to know he wasn't here, but he must have been close. In town, even, maybe . . . He could have found Davidson at a gin joint or had come to the show right under her nose and had recorded in Davidson's head how to smile, what to think, who to become.

"Everything here belongs to *me!*" The Circus King's words snarled from Davidson's lips. "Stop this fucking charade. You lied to me! You made me a fool! You took my circus of Sparks! You *took everything from me!*"

"I've taken nothing from you," Rin said, speaking both to Davidson and the dark voice currently in his head. "This circus has nothing to do with—"

"*It has everything to do with us!*" Davidson roared. "*I am going to take your heart and rip it out from your chest. I am going to break your spine. And you will feel it all.*"

He turned back to the Big Top's skeleton. He snatched the king pole. The other poles either fell or looked ready to fall. Everyone stepped back in fear. Rin watched as Davidson took the king pole over his knee and cracked it in half like a twig. Six years of toil, all the marks and signatures they'd etched on it. It was no longer her king pole, but his debris.

Davidson threw it aside like it was a toothpick. He finally shrank then, sinking down into the dust until he disappeared, ten feet in front of her and now nowhere. Everyone was frozen. Bernard shouted something but Rin couldn't hear him. She was underwater and in space all at once, was she still breathing? She had to do something. Move, Rin, do something!

Where was he? She couldn't stop him if she didn't know where he was.

And then it was too late. Davidson shot out of the soil like a daisy, right in front of her, with the pistol to her head, like a ghost jumping out of a shadow.

"I'm going to ruin you." Davidson's words seemed to slither, inches from her face. Rin could smell the whiskey. "I'm going to do what you did to me. I am going to burn you from the inside out without ever touching you." He touched her chest. His clammy, warm hands. The ones that belonged to Davidson. They were heavy on her collarbone, too close, too familiar.

"I'm not going to speak to him, Davidson. I'll speak to you, but not him."

"*I am him!*" Davidson snarled. Impetuous. "Dumb-shit clown told me everything. I know about your life. I know about your *wife.*"

Her stomach clenched. Odette. She saw Odette in her mind, stained in red, unspooling into threads until she was nothing. She shoved the image back. Instead of fear, a rage built up deep inside. Her body felt hot, like a fire flared through her. She'd rip the Circus King apart.

"Darling?" a woman's voice sounded from the crowd. "Oscar!" Mrs. Davidson rushed forward from the broken arcade boxes to the right. "Stop this now! What are you doing to him? Get off him!"

Davidson coolly, calmly relayed a message as if it was a telegraph being read off. "It's been a fun game, but I am losing my patience and we are getting older. So it's time to end this silliness. I know where you are going. I know how your circus works. And I am coming to ruin you. I have my hands around your heart and I will squeeze until you won't *want* to live. Unless you come to me *now*."

Then he broke into laughs, so many laughs, and they wouldn't stop. Odette sprang forward, gloves off. She touched him, and Davidson crumpled. Odette jumped back from him like she'd touched a hot stove.

Or worse, like she'd seen something horrific.

No one said anything in the breathless moonlight. Rin tried to steady herself as her leg muscles strained, shivering with exhaustion. She turned to face the others. Jo shook, looking at the crumpled man beside them as if she'd just seen a public execution. Rin saw the broken tent behind her. An eerie silence filled their circus.

The Ringmaster couldn't be afraid. The Ringmaster was strong enough to get them all away from him.

The Ringmaster, standing still in the dark, said to the company behind her in low and steady words: "Pack everything onto the trains. Odette, help the injured. We're leaving now."

26

EDWARD, 1917

Edward knew he was lucky to have Ruth in his life. Not everyone got to meet their soul mate, someone they'd so clearly known even before they met, someone who matched them in a way that couldn't be explained by man.

Sometimes at night, when he was in and out of sleep, he would clench with fear, afraid he'd forged that love between them. But no matter how it had started, back in France, back in New York, they were inextricably a part of each other's lives now.

He'd tried harder, to see if Ruth still loved him when he watched his words. And she did. They had good moments together. As they hopped a first-class train to the Rocky Mountains for their honeymoon, Ruth taught Edward a song from a musical and it made him laugh.

The two of them, children out in the world on their own, watched the trees turn from barren to pine outside their moving train car, and he held her in his arms and she stroked his hand.

"Two against the world," Ruth said quietly, a small teasing in her tone. "Me and my big brute."

"I'm not big," Edward said.

"Well, you're a big man in character," Ruth said.

Their accents had even joined together, Edward's becoming more New Yorker and Ruth's becoming a tad English. And after intertwining their past worlds, they both had picked up an ever-growing Midwestern dialect that came and went like clouds on a clear day.

Their story was one. That was the beautiful thing about marriage.

"There," Ruth said, pointing out the window at the Mississippi River as they crossed into the West. "The biggest river in the entire country. Have you ever read Mark Twain?"

"I haven't," Edward said.

"He uses that river as a symbol of our country," she said. "The good and the bad. I've never seen it before." Her eyes were wide like a child's on Christmas.

Edward warmly smiled. He pushed the hair out of her face. "Every time I think I have your face memorized," he said, as she kept gazing out the window, "I find a new angle. I see a new light. You're mesmerizing, Ruth King."

Ruth beamed. Her eyes met his. And she kissed him.

"And I love you, Edward King," she said. "Thank you for this adventure."

She meant it.

"I have an idea," she said, nearly bouncing in her seat. "You're going to think it's crazy, but hear me out. I have another dream . . . of something I want to see."

"Anything," he said.

❋

He sat beside Ruth at a circus, part of a dusty audience on dusty bleachers. The performers flew through the air and sang and danced.

Ruth showed him all the sorts of lights they used, pointed out how the ballasts worked, and hypothesized how the tent was brought up and down so fast.

"My mother would have loved this," she whispered to him. Edward tensed. But he didn't tell her to stop talking.

My mother. My mother. It chimed in his ears, pricking the inside of his skull like a crescendo on a timpani. My mother.

That night, Ruth jumped them to Florida for another circus. Then back to Georgia for another. Then up to Vancouver. They saw four circuses in one evening, and she was in love.

"Let's join the circus," she said.

"Why?" he said.

"Because it's beautiful," she said. "Don't you want to be part of something beautiful?"

Wasn't she already a part of something beautiful?

Edward drank his beer stoically. He wasn't much of a drinker. But something hit him hard with that word, beautiful. It was like the sharp edges of the *b* and *t* were sticking in him like daggers in the back.

Beautiful. The world was supposed to have been beautiful.

"Ed?" Ruth said quietly.

"You remember the day we met?" he said.

"Yes, in France," she said. She said it as if it was only one meeting in a million lifetimes of two soul mates. He wanted that to be true. He ached for that to be true. He wanted her to be his and he wanted to be hers.

That would have been beautiful.

But the world wasn't fucking beautiful.

After all this time, that word *mother* still dangled from her lips. A monster in the background of his false happiness, clanging against jail bars. Wanting to be let out, wanting to kill him. This was all a sham.

Mother.

Would Ruth still be here if he let her go?

He knew the answer to that.

He had seen the underbelly of everything. There was always a catch. And anything like this circus that sported any other truth was a liar. Smoke and mirrors.

"France was terrible," Ruth said.

"Do you ever think about what you saw there?" he asked.

"Sometimes." Ruth swallowed. "But not too often. I was only there for a moment really."

"Then you were spared," Edward muttered. He took another drink.

"Do you need to talk about something?" she said. "You've been rather off tonight."

"Don't ever ask me about the war again," Edward said.

"Okay," she said. And of course, she never asked again.

If he said, "Leave me now and never come back," she would. It was all as fake as the gelatin-covered lights and sawdust cutouts of a three-ring circus.

"But what do you think about the circus?" she said, like she'd already forgotten the war talk. "With your luck Spark and my theatre background, we'd be shoo-ins, yeah? You and me, traveling the train tracks and playing in all the nice cities? I know it's not a glamorous life, but I wouldn't mind some dirt under my nails. It's an adventure! I've never seen—"

"Why do you mention your mother?" Edward asked her.

Ruth bit her lip. "I miss her," she said.

"Am I not enough?"

"I didn't say that," Ruth said. "I'm sorry, I didn't mean to upset you."

That night, after she'd fallen asleep in a hotel in Boulder, he went down to the bar and got drunk. He went out on the street, and he found a mountain man waiting to start his trek in the morning. Edward listened to him talk about his wife and kids back in Denver. He listened to the story of a fella who loved the outdoors and how beautiful the world was.

"Beautiful," Edward sniffed. "You think it's beautiful?"

The war had stripped that beauty from the world, and now there was only the ugly skull and sinew and muscles and the truth. The truth was, this world was made of mud and corpses and men willing to take other men's gas masks to escape it. The truth was, Ruth didn't love him.

"Rip your face off," Edward said.

Without another word, the mountain man calmly clawed at his face until the skin peeled back in long hangnails, like a dirty wooden floor being refinished. He didn't even shout. Not until Edward walked away and his cheekbones were already showing.

Then he shouted quite a lot.

Somewhere between the man's screams and his bed, Edward took out that old knife from his pocket. He held it in his hand. A small thing. A useless thing. He could throw it in a trash bin. He could chuck it into the river.

When Ruth woke, Edward stood above her. He was drunk. The knife was gone.

"Sure," he said. "We'll join the circus. We'll show them what the world looks like."

27

THE RINGMASTER, 1926

None of them had seen the Circus King, not even Mauve. But somehow, he had gotten too close. So they had to run.

The Ringmaster implemented their alternate route immediately as they wildcatted out of Lawrence. They had two safe havens, one in Estes Park, Colorado, and another in the prepaid fairgrounds of Missouri Valley, Iowa. Davidson had thought they were going west, so that's what he would have told the Circus King. They went north instead, to Missouri Valley.

The second thing that needed to be done was getting a new king pole. Mauve found one, in the year 1928. It was in good condition. They took some money, purchased it in the liquidation auction of another circus, jumped back, and left it on the edge of the field for Maynard to lug in as he patched up the rest of the tent.

The third thing that needed to be done was to speak to the circus. As a whole.

They collected outside the train, which now sat off the tracks in a muddy field in Iowa. The Ringmaster stood on the stairs leading to the pie car. She reminded everyone of their contracts, that they could leave whenever they'd like. She'd warned them when they came on this may happen someday, and now that someday was here. Anyone who needed to leave should please do so by alerting one of the three owners of their termination and collecting their personal things by Wednesday morning. They would receive their payment for Missouri Valley and one train ticket to make their way to Des Moines to find a connecting route. If they were staying, they had until Friday to take an R&R, and they would resume performances at that time.

The fourth thing the Ringmaster needed to do was talk to Odette.

"I'm not going anywhere," Odette said calmly. A lot calmer than Rin felt.

Rin stood shaking in the corner of their room, looking out the window like the Circus King was about to jump into view with another gun.

But right now, Rin wasn't afraid. She was shaking with rage. She was full of fire.

"He's coming for you," Rin said. "I know him. He said he was gonna take my heart. He wasn't talking about a king pole, Odette. He is going to take you to hurt me."

"Let him," Odette said. "I'd like to see him try."

"No." Rin said loud and sharp. She turned on her heels. "No, Odette, you don't know him. If he gets near you, you're done. I'm not letting that happen. You have to leave."

"Absolutely the hell not," Odette said.

"I buried my mother." Rin stepped closer, slamming her finger into her own chest. "I watched her die. Her light went out, Odette. Do not ask me to watch you die."

"That fool can't take my light," Odette said, dead serious. The way Odette scoffed at the devil, it almost made Rin believe her.

Rin's mouth formed a firm line. "He can, my love. He almost took mine. And I've seen him snuff out powerful men like birthday candles. He finds the thing that keeps you getting up in the morning, and he tears it apart. You need to leave."

"I'm a grown woman, it's not your choice to make."

"I'm not going to lose you!" Rin roared.

"I knew what I got into when I married you!" Odette made herself taller, her voice just as loud as Rin's. "You think I'm just walking away when it gets scary and leaving you alone with this? Stop, Rin. No, don't say another word. We do this together. And if he comes for me, then I made my choice, didn't I?"

Rin saw Odette stand there like she was made of steel. The trapeze swinger was unmoved, and her gloved fists were clenched like she would rip the world in two. That fire inside Rin was inside Odette, too. Odette was soft, but never weak. Rin would never let the Circus King touch Odette. And Odette would never let him reach Rin.

Rin closed her eyes. She took a deep breath. She felt her wrist under her fingers, bare and thinning, the bone on the joint, her skin wrinkled and dry. She said, "If he comes for me, let me go. Do not follow. Do you understand?"

"Rin I'm not going to let—"

"If he comes for me, let me go," Rin said again, louder.

Odette stopped, as if Rin's command was a wall she couldn't walk through.

She didn't say anything. But Rin knew that was the best promise she could hope to get from her.

"And if he comes for me," Odette said softly, like a songbird's wings fluttering as it perched. "Then you let me go."

Rin slammed her hand down on the wooden desk. She scooped up her brass knuckles, for protection. She shoved it onto her hand, and swung open the vestibule door.

"I'm going to see Davidson," Rin growled.

"Rin," Odette said. "Stop. Will you *stop for a second*?"

Rin stopped in the doorway, looking out to the field. Her shoulders tensed.

"I'm going with you," Odette said. She took off her gloves. Her hands were more dangerous than any weapon Rin could hold.

✳

The two of them charged down the side of the train through the freshly cut grass, Odette in her slippers and Rin in her boots, tense and with purpose. Rin liked to think they looked intimidating, but they probably just looked tired.

Odette jumped onto the LQ car's stairs, wrapped her skirt around her hand, then grabbed Rin to hoist her up. They opened the door. The sun immediately left their faces. They were met with dust. A long metal and wooden corridor that branched off into closet-like bunkbeds. Everyone had moved out and into the second LQ car to give room for Davidson.

Davidson lay on one of the bunks in one of the cubbies, tied down, his wife keeping vigil beside him. The Ringmaster squeezed next to Mrs. Davidson in the narrow corridor. Recognition flashed across Davidson's face when he saw Rin, a wicked smile seeping through like a soiled cloth. He laughed. "Still here, starling."

Rin wanted to hit him. But she knew it wasn't him.

"Odette," Rin said. Rin gently nudged Mrs. Davidson to the right as Odette took her bare hand and placed it on Davidson's sweaty brow. Davidson went calm. But Odette jumped again, like last night, and stumbled back into the wall behind her.

"Odette?" Rin said.

"I'm fine," Odette said. "I . . . there's nothing for me to remove. I can't take it. It's just Davidson in there. How is that possible?" She looked to Rin, her eyes big and glassy. She was afraid. For Davidson, yes, but for the Ringmaster as well.

Rin had once been like this. And Odette's eyes said it all, like she was finally cracking the surface to understand the horrors of the Circus King.

"Was it like that for you?" is what Odette's eyes silently asked. Rin nodded.

"When I hear his voice, in my head," Rin said, "it's not his voice. It's my voice. It's me."

"You . . . you know it's him though, don't you?" Odette said.

Rin shook her head. "It's not him," she said. "It's never him. He brings something out in you."

"No no no," Odette said. "You know better than that. You know he is making you think it's you—"

"Well, can you do anything to help him?" Mrs. Davidson pleaded. "Oscar, please snap out of it."

"Quiet, you old bitch!" Mr. Davidson snapped.

"Hello?" a new voice came.

Rin swung around to look at the door, her brass knuckles out and her sleeves already rolled up. But there stood Jo, with the light behind her and the dark of the corridor clouding her face.

"Ringmaster, what the hell happened to Mr. Davidson?" Jo said, stepping into the dusty air of the inside. She had the swagger of a production manager asking why Davidson had missed his cue.

"Go meet me in the field," Ringmaster said. "No one is supposed to be in here."

"Hey hey hey, I helped last night." Jo kept coming forward. "If you're gonna have a party in here, I think I can help out."

"Sweetheart, you need to get out of here," Odette said stiffly.

"Where is your brother?" Rin asked.

"He told me not to stick my nose into things that weren't ours," Jo said. "So he went ahead to the cookhouse with Kell."

"Your brother is smarter than you," Rin snarked.

"I'm not gonna leave y'all alone until you tell me something."

"Oh, is that right?" Rin said.

"*Have you triiied Wheaties,*" Jo sang off-key. Rin marched to her. "*They're the whooole wheat with all of the braaaan. Have you triiiiied Wheat—*" Ringmaster's hand clamped down on Jo's mouth. "*mmm mmm mm mm—mmm.*"

Ringmaster's eyes narrowed. Jo stared right back at her and stuck her tongue out, licking Ringmaster's palm. Rin jumped back, wiping her hand on her coat with an "urgh!"

Odette and Mrs. Davidson were silent, waiting to see if the girl would be let into the world of grown women. Mr. Davidson just laughed to himself, unhinged.

"We'll be right back," Rin said. Rin pushed Jo out the door and onto the iron vestibule. The door closed behind them. Rin sighed, brushed her hands off on her trousers, and then looked at anything that wasn't Jo.

Everyone in the circus had been warned about the Circus King. It still hadn't been enough to protect Davidson. With Jo as powerful as she was, Rin was scared.

Rin finally said, "The Circus King got him."

"And the fella cut him a deal so good he tried to shoot us and break our tent?" Jo said.

"No," Ringmaster said, taking out a toothpick and sticking it in her mouth. She nervously clamped down on it. Better than a cigarette. Or a bottle. "No, that was the Circus King's Spark. He must have made Davidson think like him, planted ideas in his head like a bomb."

"So that's his Spark?" Jo followed her.

Ringmaster rubbed her eyes. She'd not slept. But it was true, Jo had helped last night. She'd been very brave. If she was old enough to be in the circus, she was old enough to know. Rin said, "You see how quick we picked up last night and got out?"

Jo nodded. "Uh-huh."

"If the Circus King gets near you," Ringmaster said, "he can make you do anything without you even knowing. If you can hear his voice, if he can see you, then he can warp everything you see, everything you hear, even everything you think."

"Wow, talk about a circus rivalry," Jo said.

"Ringling Brothers set Barnum and Bailey trains on fire," Rin said. "And that's without Sparks. They don't control minds."

"So we just run?" Jo said. "We don't fight back? He's a bully!"

Ringmaster breathed through her nose, biting hard on the toothpick. Calling the Circus King a bully was like calling a tornado a breeze. She'd seen twisters from the train and outside the tent. Once they'd had to stop a show because the sky got black and the clouds came down like walls and started to churn like a whirlpool right above them. It never touched down, but Rin couldn't believe how many people would not run for cover. So much of the crowd just stood outside the tent on the midway, staring up at something that could kill them like it was a lion in a zoo.

None of their Sparks could stop a tornado. None of them. When a bad twister hit, they could stop the hail, they could stop the rain. The rest, they just tried to hide in ditches and wait.

Rin said, "It's one thing to fight back against the everyday injustices of the world. But some things . . . some people . . . are just insurmountable."

"I guess it's lucky he just wants to ride the rails and not take over the world or something." Jo gave a scrawny shrug, her hands digging into her beat-up overall pockets.

"A man can do a lot of damage with art, Jo," Ringmaster said. "We try to help people, show them good things. He says his circus is the 'truth' when really it's just one shitty way of looking at the truth while omitting all other possibilities. He makes his mark on his audience, all right. While trying to make our lives a living hell."

"He's evil?"

"Sparks are like anyone else. There are good and there are bad and there are those still making their minds up," Ringmaster said. "He's made his mind up."

"So why don't we stop him?"

"We've done what we can, taking back whoever we can save from him. Some of the girls who work in the midway are from the asylums, and some are from his circus. Paulie McKinley, one of our best acts, is from his circus. But—but if the Circus King had his way . . ." She trailed off. She just saw a big black void in her head . . . "Imagine what he could do with all of us Sparks under his control. So the only way we stay safe is by staying the hell away from him. Understand?"

"All right." Jo sloughed the words off her shoulders.

"No, Jo," Ringmaster said, dead serious. "If he knew about your Spark, he'd kill to have it in his program. And last night . . . I couldn't protect you." Those words stuck on her teeth, like a nightmare. She just realized that was true, just as it came out of her mouth. If Davidson had wanted to pull that trigger, he could have. If Davidson had wanted any one of them dead, they would be dead.

Which meant the Circus King was toying with them.

No.

"Me?" Jo said. "I'm just an illusionist. I can't control minds, I can't heal people—"

Ringmaster shook her head. "You can show people the way the world *could* be. The world they *deserve*. And that is more powerful than any of our schtick."

"You're giving me a complex with this, like my Spark is nifty."

"No," Ringmaster said. "The magic in you is not your Spark; it is how you choose to use it."

Jo opened her mouth, but nothing came. Ringmaster set her hand on Jo's shoulder, and she said quietly, "You are still a kid. You worry about shining and let me worry about the rest."

"Davidson's not all right, is he?" Jo said.

"No," Ringmaster said. "He's not. And there's not much we can do to heal him. But we'll figure it out."

Jo pushed past Ringmaster, her beat-up boots scuffling on the grating, and she slipped into the train car.

"Jo!" Ringmaster shot, but Jo shot back:

"I can help. You said I can help people, so let me."

"It's not on your shoulders to fix things, kid," Ringmaster said, grabbing the door before it closed. "Let me do that."

"Let me help!" Jo squeaked.

Rin followed Jo back into the car, the dark hitting her harder this time so her eyes ran with spots. Mrs. Davidson was sobbing, Odette was watching and thinking, and Mr. Davidson was still laughing at them like a deranged demon.

"You'll never have your husband back," Mr. Davidson said. "I never loved you. I'm glad our boy died. You fat, ugly bitch."

"Stop," Jo said sternly.

Mr. Davidson looked to her, and then laughed that laugh that was not his. He opened his mouth, but Jo raised her hands.

Without another word, she shot out a swirling image that curled like fire in a chimney, filling the room. The music from the Davidson's clown car sang from the dust. Mrs. Davidson's visage unraveled from her colors. She was young, dressed in a bridal gown. Then she laughed as she was chased around an old house that had been made a home, and that laugh was something so different from the one that had filled the LQ car a moment before. The image of Mrs. Davidson aged, the beauty of a story unfolding.

Mr. Davidson stopped smiling. His teeth gritted. He shook, like he was fighting something inside of him. He grew red; he looked in pain. Then a burst of tears.

Rin watched the images float into the air like bubbles, like the wisp of dreams. It had been pieced together by a mention in passing. Fifty years together, how they used to dance . . . Jo had paid attention. Jo had woven it into a reality.

"You remembered their dancing," Rin said quietly to Jo. The illusions were gone, but the two old bodies were wrapped around each other in reality now, Mr. Davidson shaking but crying, trying to claw his way out of that hell Rin knew too well.

Rin put her hand on Jo's shoulder, dazed. Jo looked up at Rin. "I'm sorry," Jo said. "I couldn't just do nothing."

"I know," Rin said. G-d she knew.

Rin, Odette, and Jo stood there beside the Davidsons for another moment, then left them to sleep, Mrs. Davidson curled up next to her still-restrained husband. They stepped out into the day once more.

Jo said, "I hoped . . . if I could get him to remember something that wasn't the Circus King's . . ."

"Very smart," Rin said. Rin remembered the night she finally escaped the Circus King's spell. She'd . . . she'd . . . barely made it out. It was something deeper than remembering something, wasn't it? It was something much more complicated than visions of dancing. And even after Rin had gotten out, she wasn't all right. She still felt him pulling at her veins, gripping her lungs . . . the only way to fight the Circus King was to claw your way out of a deep dark hole and pray you make it.

Some days, she still wasn't convinced that she'd escaped.

"You're getting all mushy on me," Jo teased. "Look at you, ya big lug. Tell me again how smart I am, come on now, keep it comin'. I like the compliments."

Ringmaster forced her own laugh. Her laughs were so rare, they sounded covered in cobwebs. "You paid attention to the little details about the Davidsons. That's something special."

"Well," Jo said, shrugging. "When you were introducing me to everyone, you were telling me all the little things about them. So . . . maybe your goodwill toward men routine is rubbin' off on me." Jo winked.

Rin hadn't even noticed she'd done that. Her brain snagged on the compliment. She imagined she looked like a fried light bulb, shorted out in a pregnant pause as her wife and her mentee waited for her to say something.

"It seems like you're always trying to fix things by yourself," Jo finally said.

"That would be correct," Odette said, rubbing Rin's back, gloves in place.

"We all play a part," Ringmaster said. "My part isn't any more important than anyone else in this circus. But it is my part. And it's one that not everyone can do. Just like Odette. She is a healer, she is a comfort. And Mauve, she can see things, she is a planner and good with finances."

"And you are a leader," Jo said.

"And so are you," Ringmaster said.

She hoped the kid could tell Rin was taking her seriously.

"All right then," Jo said, stepping back and puffing her shirt as if she had a coat collar to pop. "My work here is done."

"Not even close," Ringmaster said to herself as Jo scampered off, and Odette rubbed Rin's back again.

"I need to tell you what Mrs. Davidson said to me about Jo while you were out on the vestibule," Odette said. Her tone broke the sunlight, as it sounded like another warning.

Rin looked to her.

Odette had already locked her stare to her love. "The other performers in her LQ car," she said, "are afraid of her. She conjures nightmares in the air while she sleeps. Charles has to wake her up to make them stop. I had to assure Mrs. Davidson she wasn't going to hurt Mr. Davidson. She nearly didn't let her anywhere near that bed."

"So you're saying the kid's dangerous. Aren't we all?" Rin said. "She just did a good thing in there."

Odette nodded, in agreement. "I'm saying the kid is complicated."

Rin looked out to the field where everyone was sitting down for lunch. It was bustling. Maynard had multiplied to devour more than one sandwich at a time. Tina and Ford talked in soft tones while Agnes boasted she could run over to the pool across the way and swim the length of an English Channel. Kell, Jo, and Charles now all huddled together, Jo bargaining for Kell's potato chips. Jess and Yvanna chatted about something that looked costume related. Ming-Huá scribbled in her journal. The tables were crowded; the mustard got thrown around instead of passed politely. Once in a while someone would venture a glance to the LQ car, as if wondering when the Davidsons would be okay.

"Why is it so crowded?" Rin asked. "Why aren't they packing? I gave them a deadline to terminate and they're all dragging their feet. They need to get going. Are they waiting to leave after they eat?"

Odette raised a brow, as if Rin had told her she believed in Santa Claus. "Rin. They're all staying."

"What?" Rin said.

"Are you really that surprised?" Odette didn't smile when she said this; she looked shocked that Rin was shocked.

"Well yeah!" Rin said. "Do they not understand we are in real danger, we—"

"—are a family," Odette said. And her eyes grew sad. "We are your family."

✳

28

THE RINGMASTER, 1926

Missouri Valley smelled like dirty water, wide open prairies, cows, and the hottest day of summer. The sun beat down on their necks as Rin and Jo quietly took position in the field to the west of the fairgrounds and the train. Some townsfolk had come to swim at the fairgrounds, watch the trains go by, and try to catch a glimpse of a Spark doing magic. But this far away, behind the trains and the tree line, no one would see Jo.

"Uh, are we trespassing?" Jo said, looking down at the lines in the dirt and the little cornfield stalks that came to below their knees.

"Just don't step on the crops and we'll be fine," Rin said. She steadied herself in the dirt, boots slipping a little in the mud. Luckily they'd missed the rain but snagged the mud for landing off the tracks. "So I heard about what happens when you sleep. Nightmares?"

Jo glanced off into the sky as if to gingerly check where the sun was. She shielded her eyes, and looked caught. She shook her head. "I thought they'd stop when we got away from Omaha."

"Do you want to tell me what's going on?"

"They're doors," Jo said. "Charles says they're a bunch of doors and they're all screaming terrible things."

Rin's first inclination was to snort-laugh, imagining a grown woman like Mrs. Davidson scared of anthropomorphic doors gnashing their doorknob teeth and howling. But she knew better. Doors could be some of the most frightening things; there was always something on the other side.

Jo shrugged. "I don't know what to tell you. Maybe hook me up with a nice private caboose like yours, eh?"

Rin allowed a slight smile. "When you start your own circus and balance the checkbooks, you can have your own car. Until then, you need to learn how to control this."

Jo rolled her eyes. "Oh, that easy, huh?"

Ringmaster raised her hands in front of her, like she was touching the morning light. She closed her eyes, took a deep breath in, and a deep breath out. "If you are very quiet, you will feel that electricity in you. The Spark you've been given. And you must make peace with it."

Jo raspberried. Ringmaster elbowed her. "Ow!"

"Put your hands out."

"If we're gonna go up against these doors, can Charles be here?" Jo said. "I . . . never mind. I'm fine. I'll . . ." She closed her eyes, a wavy breath escaping through her teeth. "All right."

"Are you sure you don't want your brother?"

"I do, but I don't want him to see what might come out . . . if he doesn't have to . . ." She trailed off. "He's already been through enough with me." Then she popped up, shaking her hands. "Now tell me what to do. I don't feel anything. I'm too nervous."

"For some reason," Ringmaster said, "out of all the people in the world, you were one that was chosen to hold on to something special."

"Yeah, real special," Jo said. "Everyone's bully jealous of our lot, they are."

"It's frustrating," Ringmaster agreed. "It is. All our lives would be much simpler if we didn't have this Spark. But we can look at it as a curse," and Ringmaster took Jo's hands and guided them up slowly, gently. "Or we can use it as a gift. Just like you did with Davidson."

Jo opened her eyes to see, sun softly illuminating her pale cheeks and skinny nose, her guarded frown. Rin kept holding on.

"You," Ringmaster said, "get to write your own story now."

"Write my own story?" Jo said. She didn't try to tug away. "The world wants me dead. My dad sold me. One time I tried to wear pants and the names he called me . . . he'd have seen you as a bad influence, you know. He would've hated this circus."

"Well, this circus wouldn't have been fond of him," Rin said flatly. She patiently turned Jo's palms upward. "Your dad seems to have been wrong about a lot of things. So don't you think he may have been wrong about you?"

Jo looked away. But she didn't pull away.

"So," Ringmaster said. "What do you need to see, to make the doors go away?"

Jo swallowed. "I don't need to see nothing, I'm fine."

Ringmaster did not let go. "You don't need to act tough in front of me, I'm your teacher. Now release it, whatever you need to see."

Jo narrowed her blue eyes, probably sizing her up to see if she was enough of a teacher. Rin tried to remember how it was to be that young, to look up to her mother. It was like standing under an oak tree, weighted and grounded and rooting down something in her.

Well, Rin may not be an oak tree, but she was here.

Jo nodded. "All right," she said. "Don't run away."

"Of course not."

Jo looked to her fingertips, raised high and supported. She breathed in, and she breathed out. The colors in the sky melted from bright dawn to a dark musty Omaha apartment. It leaked out and showered around them until they stood in the old living room she'd run from.

Jo glanced at it, and then to Ringmaster. "Well, I did it." She gave an apologetic grin. "*Good job, kiddo,*" she continued, in a voice that was supposed to be Ringmaster's. "*You're a real special genius.* Welp, look at the time!"

Ringmaster did not smile. She did not let go.

Jo looked down, not able to meet her eyes. That's when the door to the illusionary living room Jo had painted started to open.

Slowly, the door swung inward, and there were Jo's parents, staring through her. She was nothing, she had no thread between her and them, no matter how much she'd wanted to have some sort of unbreakable chain keeping them all together. Rin could feel that tug, that need that tripped her inside like she missed a step. She just wanted to be wanted.

But Jo had dragged something in with her from the outside, like she was seeping toxic goo. Her parents were sad and lost, and they glared at her with a fury she had created in them. She'd tried real hard not to; she'd tiptoed around when she could, she tried to be better. She wanted them to hold her. But they couldn't. She couldn't be held.

Then the room melted, the scene fading to a quiet conversation outside the apartment Jo's family lived in, with Jo and Ringmaster looking down at the street from beyond the door. Like they were ghosts, or eavesdroppers, or both.

Rin remembered this. Somehow. Even though this wasn't Rin's life.

"A girl with that much power," her father had said to her mother as they shared a smoke. Her mother took a long drag, her lips pursed.

"They say there's peace," her mother said. "That they might be good?"

"They're not good," her father said. "I see what she does at night." Then a gruff, "She was already acting like a bulldyker before all this and now she—"

"They hated me, to begin with," Jo said. "I was another mouth to feed, I was a waste of a daughter, and I was a pain in the ass."

"You were a child," Ringmaster said.

"Well, they hated this child even more after she could spray a room with nightmares," Jo said.

"And do you think that's what you do?" Ringmaster asked. "You think this is who you are?"

Jo shrugged. She looked at her mother. Something crawled inside Rin, a festering parasite churning her stomach. Rin could almost empathize with the father's cruelty; Jo's father had kept himself removed, always too far away to touch. But Jo's mother, her mother had given birth to her. Her mother was a girl once, too. Her mother was supposed to have held her close, shielded her from people like her father. And yet.

Jo's mother's face took the focus, the rest of the image breaking away, a feeling sweeping over her and Jo and the field they stood in as if it was a plague. It was the feeling of being betrayed. It was the feeling Jo had felt (and now somehow Rin could recall) when Jo had told her mother in confidence she'd been the one who forgot to latch the gate and the pigs got out into the field, only to watch her mother throw her under the wheels of her father's fury. "Well," her mother had said with no remorse. "You know better than to not latch the gate. You're the most selfish, dullest thing I've ever seen."

There was a longing to touch her mother, but her mother felt nothing. Worse than nothing. What is the absence of love called? It's not hate. It's not even apathy. The word lives in the anticipation of waiting for someone who will never come home.

No, this was just an illusion. Rin's mother had loved her with all her heart. Rin had not known this loneliness from her mother. She had known many things that hurt, she had stood at many doors not wanting to see what was behind them, but never with her mother. She had to pull out of this dream.

"Jo," Ringmaster said suddenly. "Jo, concentrate."

Jo closed her eyes. She balled up her hands. Rin knew Jo tried to bring the pain back into her, tried to swallow it all in from the world. But it was out there now, and to cram it away again was impossible.

"Let it go," Ringmaster said. "Don't take it in, shove it out." Ringmaster took Jo's hands, and she gently pried her fists apart. "Relax your fingers."

"Why didn't she protect me?" Jo said, eyes still closed. "Why did she love him more than me? Why wasn't I enough? I did my best."

"You did," Ringmaster said. "*She* didn't."

Jo opened her eyes. The apartment and the mother dissipated.

Ringmaster lowered Jo's hands, tired. But no pity. She felt something softer. Or maybe something rougher. The fire she'd felt to protect Odette, or the fury she had tried to shove back when she had realized the Circus King should have never met her.

Jo should not have known these nightmares.

"That's not how homes are supposed to look," Rin said. "That's not how all parents are."

"I've never met anyone with a happy childhood," Jo said.

"I had a happy childhood," Rin said. "And you deserved better."

Something passed between them.

"The answers don't always come in one day," Rin said, letting go. "But I hope you know that we . . . we see you."

"All right, well, whatever that means," Jo snorted, pushing Ringmaster off with a brush of her hand.

Rin's eyes narrowed. Jo wanted to walk away. Rin wouldn't let her.

"Well," Rin said, turning out to face the field. "Then let's see, shall we? Show me you."

Jo stared at Rin. "Ta-da?" she said, pointing at herself.

"Take your hands," Rin said genuinely. "Raise them up and show me you."

"I'm right here."

"I know this dog and pony show of smart-assery," Rin said. "And we can waste our entire rehearsal standing here, or you can just do it. Raise your hands. Show me."

Jo raised her hands, but nothing came.

"Come on now," Rin said.

"I'm not being ornery!" Jo said. "I can't get my brain to think! I . . ." She trailed off.

She'd been her father's daughter. She'd been her mother's shadow. She'd been a show pony. She'd been a problem. She was Charles's twin, Ringmaster's student. Now she was a performer in the circus.

"I don't know," Jo said.

Rin looked at her own hands. "I wish I had your Spark," she said. "Then I could show you at least what I see. But unfortunately, you're the only one who can conjure that picture for yourself. So you're going to have to do it."

Jo was quiet. And then she said even meeker, "Can you tell me what it would look like?" Ringmaster turned to her, confused. "I mean, if you could conjure a picture of me, what would it look like?"

Ringmaster wasn't expecting this from Jo. She awkwardly stood there, like a broken-down jalopy. If she expected Jo to bare her own heart, Rin had to be open with her as well. But what if Rin opened herself too much, and then Jo wouldn't have the Ringmaster. Jo would have a human with cracks in her foundation. She needed to be more than human for Jo; she needed to be a teacher.

"Please," Jo said. "What would it be? You say you see me, so see me. I'm not being a smart-ass, and I know I gotta see it myself and blah blah love myself so others can blah blah but sometimes we can't love ourselves until someone . . ."

Until someone tells us we are deserving of love.

A quiet breeze picked up the field's grass, the ocean of the Midwest. And the two Sparks watched each other, carefully. What would Odette say?

What would Rin's mother say?

She'd spent so much time thinking about her mother's death, so much of her mother's life fell away like those helicopter leaves. But Rin could still see her, standing in that park, looking down to her daughter with a warm smile.

Rin cleared her throat, and said solidly, "I would paint fireworks. Put to music. I would paint you and your brother and all the things and places you love. Swirls of color all around, reaching out and healing the world. You are your own story, not a character in someone else's." And then she said, "I would show you the way you shine."

Jo said nothing, like she was swallowing something back. "If I shine, I wouldn't have scared people when I got mad, back in Omaha. I wouldn't have wanted to . . . to hurt my dad when he sold us. . . ."

Rin came to stand beside her, resting a hand on her shoulder. "You feel bad about those things, huh?"

"Yes?"

"There are people out there who would never feel bad," Rin said. "You've learned. You will grow. And someday, I hope you can learn how to forgive yourself. You deserve that."

It was like a waterwheel churned the contents of Jo's heart toward her head, flooding her eyes. The girl hid her face and gave a small sob.

Rin was jarred, but she only said, "Let it out."

It came out of Jo, tears woven from so many things Rin had felt only minutes before. Her mother. Her father. The doors. The fear. The anger. No, not anger. Fury. She and Charles had been alone.

They shouldn't have had to be alone.

Rin pulled her in, and she held her. In turn, it felt like Ringmaster held that pain for her, in her arms. She held as much as she could.

And Jo clung on like she'd been searching for that hug for fifteen years.

29

THE RINGMASTER, 1926

Rehearsal days came before show days. It meant the day was full of "cue-to-cues" and doing "cleanups" and fight calls. Then that night, they would have time to unwind.

"Cut the work lights, Maynard," Rin said.

Maynard did so. "Blackout!"

"Thank you blackout," the company of performers shouted back up to the Maynards above.

The work lights' weird, fluorescent luminosity cut short, and they stood in the dark.

"Cues are all yours, May-May," Rin said, digging her toe into the dirt floor like a horse at the starting line.

"Cue one standby," one Maynard said from above on her left. "Cue one go!"

One spotlight clicked on, there in the middle ring.

Rin jogged to the spotlight. "And we're walking majestically, walking walking walking—hit the spot," Rin said, coming into view. "I'm covered?"

"Yup," Maynard said.

"Blah blah welcome to the circus introduction," Rin said. "Giving you the cue line, Maynard."

"I'm on it, thank you," Maynard said. "Cue two standby. Music, you're on cue three standby."

"Circus of the Fantasticals!" Rin shouted out, waving her hand.

"Cue two go! Cue three go!"

All the lights clicked on. Calliope Man boomed into a rousing march.

And all the performers rushed out to start the spec parade. It, of course, looked different than it did for performance; they all were dressed in jeans and work pants, parts of their undergarments and corsets, as if they'd all rushed out of bed for a jog onstage.

This was Rin's favorite secret of live performance: people would come dressed to the nines at night, paying top dollar to see a show put on by Bohemian rascals who had, just hours earlier, done cue checks in their underwear.

"Cue four standby," Maynard said.

"Why do we have cue two and cue three on two different cues? Why can't it be the same cue?" one Maynard asked another.

"Hold please!" Maynard shouted out.

The whole cast and crew froze. "Thank you hold."

✳

Rin had learned the fine art of living in the Midwest while being different. She learned how to live between the cracks in the sidewalk, find beauty in the shadows of alleyways, and how to get to the underground without letting anyone above in the real world know that an underground existed. And yes, it did exist.

It surprised those who had come from the coast that even out here in the sticks there were pockets of Sparks' joy, tucked between the Loess Hills and fields of soybeans. But Sparks lived everywhere, so their joy was everywhere; you only had to look for it.

Tonight, a group of circus Sparks appeared in the alley beside a small blue theater on Broadway Avenue in Council Bluffs. It was always easier to jump directly to wherever they were going, but there were other reasons tonight for transporting everyone with a Spark. Walking from Missouri Valley to the Chandelier in Council Bluffs would be dangerous. The best-case scenario: a buzzing worry would follow them down the main drag as eyes followed them.

The alley was settled between two old brick and wooden buildings, where thick summer grass and dandelions were growing between concrete slabs, and accented with the pungent scent of old trash from the dumpster at the mouth of the alley.

But deeper into the alley, hanging from an iron awning, was an ornate lantern. Rin pointed and Jo looked up at it, dubious, her paperboy hat casting a shadow across her face. The lantern didn't quite fit here, but it didn't stand out enough for someone passing by to notice. But Jo watched in awe as everyone walked toward it and disappeared into thin air as they crossed under the iron bars.

"There," Rin said. "The mark of a safe place for us. If you're ever in a place that feels unsafe, look for an iron lantern. Iron because it supposedly keeps bad things out, a lantern because of the Sparks."

"But how is it safe if all Sparks aren't safe people?" Jo said. "Can't the Circus King just come waltzing in here?"

"He could," Rin said. "Every group of people has its lemons. Even when we're in a place that's safe, we need to keep an eye out for each other."

Jo nodded. "A secret society. Swanky!"

"Oh stop," Rin said.

"No, really, the cat's pajamas," Jo said dryly, winking at Rin with a finger gun. Rin pushed Jo's cap down over her face and Jo pushed her.

"Come on," Rin said. "It's a concealment under the iron bars. They haven't disappeared, they're just out of our line of sight."

"Hello!" Mauve shouted from the other side.

"Oh no, I definitely thought they were dead," Jo said. Then, "Cat's meow?"

"Get in there." Rin shoved her forward and kicked up dirt with her shoe behind the cheeky ragamuffin.

Mauve and Kell and Charles had already passed through. Behind her and Jo was Odette, speaking quietly to Agnes and Ming-Huá and Jess. Bernard was behind them, laughing loudly with Maynard, who he had forced to come . . . or at least partially come. There was a part of Maynard back at the circus, another part of Maynard working as an advance man somewhere down the tracks, and a small portion of Maynard trying to enjoy the night here.

Odette looked around as she trailed away from the other girls, making sure no townsfolk were watching, then she took Rin's hand with a mischievous bite of her lip. They stepped together over the threshold.

It didn't feel any different, other than the fact that it no longer felt like they were on stage but had slipped into the wings, out of sight lines, where they could do what they damn well pleased. They could be whatever they wanted to be, and for Sparks, that was usually just who they had been all along.

Rin felt her shoulders relax.

Before them was a large gaping arch of bricks and an ornate chandelier hung from the keystone. Its golden brass curled in spirals like a blooming flower, and its fashion felt somewhere between art deco and the old Edwardian guard. Instead of candles, the chandelier was lit with electric bulbs that flickered. Oversized jewels of every color, red and blue, green, purple and orange, dangled like a rich duchess's jewelry. This was, of course, the entrance to the Chandelier Dance Hall.

Rin pulled Odette closer, wrapping an arm around her. Odette kissed her hard, out in the open, and there was no fear. Here, Rin could drop the anxiety she usually held like a tightly spinning top. She allowed herself a small laugh, then she laughed honestly, kissing Odette back.

She saw Charles and Kell ahead of her, and Kell offered his hand. Charles took it.

Mauve and Jess were linked arm in arm, dancing, as Mauve led the group deeper into the arched brick corridor. Stairs greeted them, and they shuffled down into the dark to find light underground, more ornate chandeliers illuminating what looked like an old abandoned wine cellar.

It was hitting on all sixes, brimming with Sparks dancing and laughing and milling about getting something to eat. On one side of the tavern was a small stage where people could show off their Sparks. Currently in the spotlight was a thin femme person with a receding hairline and a beautiful flapper dress. Their stockings glittered above their black buckle shoes, and their soft, light brown hands were outstretched as static crackled between their fingers, conducting a small fireworks show for the onlookers crowded around.

On the other side of the brick cave was a speakeasy bar, at which Rin shot Jo's hopeful face a look that said "absolutely not."

Directly ahead on the long wall was a group of older Sparks who played loud, bouncy covers of songs from all through time. One of them must have at least an ear to the timeline. Rin always loved the Chandelier in Council Bluffs because it was the only place in the world she could hear these songs in 1926. It reminded her she wasn't crazy; she *had* heard these songs that no one today knew.

Kell pulled Charles onto the dance floor. Rin gave Jo one more warning, "Do not even think about going to the bar." And then Rin took herself off duty. For just one night, she wasn't the Ringmaster; she was simply Odette's wife.

They held each other close as the band played on. Rin's hands slipped to Odette's hips, and Odette's hands hooked behind Rin's neck. Odette smiled up at her. When the beat picked up, they jumped up and down, because neither of them had the time to learn the dances of the day. They laughed, they spun each other around, and even though Odette didn't have to worry about her kneecaps giving out and Rin was running out of energy, they kept a beat with each other.

Agnes climbed onto the stage and bench-pressed a large man. Jess let their hair flow long and talked excitedly to people about the newest pulp they'd read. "The wife for sure did it!" Jess shouted over the din of the underground. "She did it in real life, which is what it's based on!"

Ming-Huá sat in the corner, watching everyone around her, writing things down.

Bernard was at the bar, boisterously telling stories about Mauve's childhood and how he once saved the train single-handedly. "Free tickets for everyone!" he said, before Maynard shot him a glare and he said, "Partially discounted tickets for everyone!"

"It's good to see you smile," Odette said, beaming up at Rin. Rin felt her world gravitate toward home, the center of everything: a small trapeze swinger with eyes made of stars. Rin held her closer, their hips touching.

"Excited to start performances back up?" Odette asked.

"More than excited," Rin said.

Odette gave a small smile, like the kiss J. M. Barrie talked about in *Peter Pan*. That was one of the first things Rin had thought when she'd first met Odette; the kiss that girls hold on to and won't give to the world except the soul who matches theirs. Odette had been familiar even as a stranger.

"I'll never understand why you look at me like that," Rin said softly.

"Like what?"

"Like you love me."

"Because I love you?"

"Yeah," Rin said. "I'll never understand that."

Odette narrowed one eye, sizing Rin up. Then she said, "Well, for starters, when I was a little girl, I would look up at the moon and think, 'My person is out there waiting for me, and if they're my person, they do silly things like looking at the moon, too. So maybe we're looking at the same thing right now.'" Odette reached up with her gloved fingers and pushed Rin's hair out of her face. "And you were looking at the moon, too."

"I mean . . . it's pretty big, you can't miss—"

"Don't deflect," Odette said, and Rin stopped. She nodded.

"I was looking, too," Rin said, her mouth feeling like cotton. Down deep inside her was a part that felt stupid. There was a part with a deep guttural snarl that said she was *stupid, childish, no one is impressed.*

But there was also a part of her who thought, *Maybe this world isn't as cold as I see it. Maybe, just maybe, she finds joy in me.*

Odette pressed her hand on Rin's cheek. "My love," she said softly. "The woman who built me a circus so I could fly. And I have the honor"—she drew in nearer, their dancing forgotten—"of seeing you shine, Ringmaster."

She pulled Rin close and kissed her long. She pressed her soft lips to Rin's, and the two melted into one another. Nothing else mattered outside of this moment. All of the buzz of all the things Rin hadn't done or needed to do or would never be . . . it all drifted away and she returned.

A word came back to her, from a faraway place in her mind where all the days in the sunlight lived. *Teshuvah.* This dance, to her, felt like teshuvah; a kind of repentance, a return, a remembering of who she had once been and who she may have been this whole time . . . who they were. They were in the center ring, they were the crescendo of an orchestra, they were the soaring swelling in the audience's hearts, mouths agape, as everyone realized, "It's going to be okay. Magic is real."

For a brief second, Rin swore the cellar went silent, still, frozen.

She opened her eyes. No, everyone still moved, everything was the same. The beautiful people with their beautiful Sparks, lighting up the night with their laughter and their gesticulating, their big stories and big ideas. Jo squealed as she danced around Kell and Charles, who spun with each other. And there was love.

But it had felt like it had all frozen, just for a second. Like all of it could coalesce in a small photograph, if Rin could hold on to it just for a moment longer. . . .

"What's wrong?" Odette said.

"Did you feel anything weird?" Rin said.

"I wasn't paying attention."

Rin shrugged. "Kiss me again, lady." And she did.

✳

After a long night, they returned home to the familiar hodgepodge of dusty circus wagons, and warm tents and train cars that smelled like makeup and sweat. The sun had gone down, and lightning bugs blinked on and off as they swirled through the lazy ash trees. Locusts were the sound of Iowa in summer.

"How's Mr. Davidson?" Rin asked quietly as Mrs. Davidson watched them reenter the camp. Mrs. Davidson nodded.

"Doing better," Mrs. Davidson said. "Still in bed, but still stable."

"Hey Ringmaster!" Jo laughed, jumping up on a barker box and puffing her chest out. "Look! Who am I? Rah rah rah, everyone is fancy, rah rah!"

"Get down." Kell pulled her down, his laughter mixing with hers, and Charles threw his arm around the two of them, his sister and his new dance partner.

Jess and Agnes still talked books, Agnes throwing a big arm around Ming-Huá to rope her in, too. Maynard yawned, checking the tethers on everything he walked past like his brain wouldn't rest. Bernard and Mauve stopped at the edge of the train, and they gave each other a long hug, like they'd not seen each other in years. Bernard kissed the top of her head and whispered something to her.

Family finds us, even if we're born in different places to different homes. Rin wished that when she was scared and young, alone on the street and grabbing at anything that would make her mind stop screaming, she could have seen this night. All of them with little strings binding them together, bringing them closer to this home.

Odette headed for the caboose, but Rin grabbed her hand as the others filed back to their LQs. Tomorrow would be opening day for Missouri Valley. Some would sleep in, all would be ready by the evening. Odette looked back at her, quizzically, and Rin offered her a conspiratorial wink.

"Our night isn't finished," she said. She pulled Odette closer and Odette swooned, laughing.

"Oh, dear!" Odette said. "What are you up to, Ringmaster? You have that look in your eye, the one that says we have a Rin Plan."

"We have a Rin Plan."

Rin kissed her again, took one more look at the circus, and then looked away to see time open before her. A string waited for Rin to hold on to and swing them into that night's adventure. That one last look should have been longer, the goodbyes should have been sweeter, but even though Rin could jump through time, she couldn't *see* through time.

She held on to the gold thread, took Odette in her arm, and like Douglas Fairbanks as Robin Hood, a swashbuckling pirate with a fair maiden in her embrace, Rin jumped off the cliff of Missouri Valley and through the cosmos, charging forward through the light

and the ride was beautiful.

She had learned over time how to slow the teleportation down. So she said to Odette, "Open your eyes."

Odette's eyes fluttered open, and she gasped and grabbed onto Rin's collar.

It was as if they were in a cave full of stars, flashes of scenes playing out around them in bursts of firework-like lights. There were echoes of pieces of conversation, laughter, screams, sobbing, whispers, and shouts. Throbbing reds, flowing blues . . . it was as if Rin had snuck them backstage to the greatest show in the universe.

Rin and Odette, the Ringmaster and the Trapeze Swinger, soared outside of time and space, clasped onto one another.

Below and around them was their story. Rin could feel the warm late summer afternoon sun on her skin from their wedding day. She could taste their favorite dessert on her tongue; a spongy faulty tiramisu that didn't taste anything like coffee. Her chest bubbled with the laughter from the time Odette screamed out "Boooo!" at the wrong name during Purim, and how for months afterward whenever anything was absolutely inappropriately timed, they'd shout "Boooo!" at each other. Odette looking up at her the day she'd asked Rin to marry her. Odette's galaxy eyes, knowing how exactly to word such a proposal for someone with scars the shape of Rin's. The absolute adoration, and how just for a minute, Rin had forgotten to be afraid. A thousand moments between two people, swirling around, happening all at once.

Then they flew into a light ahead, and they descended

onto the cobblestone of the Latin Quarter.

Rin had never been to Paris, but she knew pictures of it and where it was on a map. So she'd pictured a globe in her head, drawing a line from where they were to where she wanted to go, then she'd grabbed onto that line and followed. And now they were here. Best travel agency in the universe; no steamer trunks necessary.

She'd pictured a Paris that was the same time as Council Bluffs, so scooting backward to make up for the time difference, she would say it was what, half past nine here?

Rin pulled out her bracelet. She bound it around her wrist. She checked her boot, because one sock seemed to have scrunched down to her toes. The cobblestones were uneven, which wasn't great for her knees, but she'd manage.

"I'd never opened my eyes before!" Odette said. "We usually go so much faster! You show-off." And then Odette said, "I felt the sunshine from our wedding."

"Me too," Rin said.

"It was such a nice day," Odette said. "I mean, Bernard got the carriage stuck on that log but . . . he got it off."

"It was a good day," Rin said. "One of the best." Then Rin nodded ahead of them. "Look where we are," she said. "Look at the river and beyond."

Odette's jaw dropped as the streetlights caught her eyes. Beyond the light, on the riverbank across from where they stood, was Notre Dame. It wasn't a painting, it wasn't a replica at some carnival in South Dakota. It was the real McCoy.

"Paris," Odette gasped.

"Paris," Rin said. "Now I hope you know French, because I hear no one speaks English here. But I heard a certain Odette Paris used to think that someone had built her an entire city, back in the day. I remember that a *certain* Odette Paris used to collect Eiffel Tower miniatures."

Odette laughed as she took it all in, looking like she might start to cry.

Rin shrugged. "My mother taught me enough French to understand *La Bohème*, so I guess that'll have to do."

It would not do.

They passed a very packed café near the street where vendors sold little Eiffel Towers and chalk drawings of passersby. Rin was able to procure an Eiffel Tower for Odette, but it was more a game of pantomime than a fluent conversation. They asked a woman sitting at a café if she knew where Le Monocle was; Rin had heard about it in a travel book once. The woman just stared at her, confused.

"Then Montmartre?" Rin asked, pointing in all directions. The woman rolled her eyes.

"America?" she asked.

"London," Rin lied.

"American," the woman called her out, and then said, "*Montmartre.*" Or at least that's what Rin thought she said. It didn't sound like any pronunciation of the word she could have imagined seeing it written out, and the woman's lips and tongue bent and wrapped around the vowels in a way Rin had never learned and probably would never be able to master, even if she lived here for a thousand years. Rin tried the word in her mouth properly.

"Mont-mar-truh?"

"*Montmartre.*"

"Mon . . . maw . . ."

Then the woman waved them off with her silk gloved hand and said something disparaging. Rin and Odette, disheveled, kept walking, over the river, until they saw an iron gate with a familiar-looking lone lantern.

Then another, and another. They treated them like bread crumbs, and the annoyances of the night turned into adventure.

Finally, they found the winding hills and tall corridors of Montmartre. It was a place of artists, crammed in every niche and cranny of the larger-than-life bohemian-ness of the streets. The whole city had a gothic feel to it; it reminded Rin of the chandelier in the arched brick threshold. Everything here seemed to be in a stylized painting. And there was no threshold; it was all out here on the street. It couldn't have been more different than the prairies.

"Look," Odette said, "they're . . . holding hands."

Two women, walking down the street, their hands linked like lovers. No one batted an eye. Rin smiled. And she threw her arm around Odette's shoulders. She could touch her here. This whole place was right out in the open without a cloak to protect it. It didn't need to be protected. It was an entire neighborhood. And yet it felt safe.

"There's a place in the world where we can be ourselves," Odette said quietly. "Oh, Rin, I had no idea."

"This is the epicenter of the outcasts," Rin said. "And where there be outcasts, there be Sparks."

They turned the corner, entering a square full of people clapping and cheering each other on as they took turns in a circle. Right there in the open, they showed off their Sparks. One turned into a bird. Another manipulated metal to melt into a replica of Michaelangelo's statue of David. Another disappeared altogether to return a moment later. Rin coaxed Odette to join the fray as Odette looked nervously around.

"There aren't any wagon men in Montmartre," Rin said.

Odette nodded. "Shall we recruit?"

"No," Rin said. "I mean, well, I would offer jobs if anyone wanted them, but these folks don't need us. They have a home. They do good here. We . . . could also do good here."

Rin waited for Odette to understand, but she didn't. She was busy watching the Sparks. Or maybe she'd not heard her over the din.

"I'm saying when it's safe to do so," Rin said, "I'd like to come here and live out a life with you."

Odette startled, and she looked to Rin. "Don't you toy with me, Ringmaster. You know our home is the circus."

"It is," Rin said. "And when the circus doesn't need us anymore, I want to move here. I want to have a life with you."

Odette's eyes welled up. She nodded. "Happy anniversary," Odette said softly.

Rin smiled. "Happy anniversary, my love."

They lost themselves in the streets of Montmartre as the streetlights glowed, lit by a woman who could create fire from her wrists. The drunken bars spilled out onto the street. The hot summer air stuck to the back of their necks. And here, they kissed in the middle of the street.

"When the circus doesn't need us anymore," Odette said. "Do you really think that's going to ever happen?"

"I don't know," Rin said.

"Moreover," Odette said, "do you think there will ever be a day when *we* don't need the *circus*?"

Rin held Odette close. "It is our home."

Odette nuzzled into Rin's collar. "So, let's go home."

They didn't have to lurk in an alley to not be seen. They could disappear right here, in the middle of the street. And Rin's heart ached for a place where she didn't have to hide in the shadows.

But her work wasn't done.

In one moment they stood in Montmartre, and

the next, they were back to Iowa.

If there was one thing she'd seen in her time jumping through the backstage space of the world, every person had their own story. Every person was attached to different strings, different places, different people. And she followed the strings that would lead her back to the lamplight of the rehearsal tents, where their own Spark family would be laughing and dancing and warming up and putting on a hell of a show. It wasn't Paris, it was hidden among the cornfields and constantly moving to dodge the shadows of wagons and Circus Kings, but it held the same holiness they'd felt in Montmartre. And that held some magic on its own.

They still held each other when they landed, the smell of perfume and hash on their clothes. Rin kissed Odette. They were forever wound around one another, the red string of fate not shackling them but adorning them. And nothing in the world could change this moment.

Not even the next moment.

Let this night be a love letter for Rin and the woman she loved. Let the world write this dance into a memory, forever remembered by someone.

She opened her eyes. She slipped off her bracelet. They were home again.

Behind Odette, peppered along the side of the caboose, were sticky black posters covering the purple skin of the train. On the posters were red top hats. Red blood dripping down them.

No. No no no no—

"No," Rin shoved Odette back and said, "Run, get out of here." Odette spun around, confused, then she gasped and Rin could hear Odette's footsteps behind her, following as Rin ran into the heart of the circus.

Rin's vision blurred. She felt like she'd ducked into a dark tunnel. Everything was one action, and then another. One observation, then the next. The stench of what used to be was here. The terror in her chest, the tensing of her shoulders, the darting eyes to find the wolf in the woods, stalking her.

Was he still here?

"You're a coward," she snarled to him, if he could hear her.

It was silent. Everyone was gone. No, hiding. They must have gotten to the panic room she'd made for them in one of train cars. She'd prepared. They were going to be okay.

The Big Top was untouched. The popcorn stands and all the wagons were only papered like a town expecting the circus. Red hat. Red blood.

"Rin." Odette had rushed into the caboose and returned with a shotgun in her arms. She had never fired a gun. She was going to get herself killed.

"Get out of here," Rin said. "Please."

Odette didn't move.

"Give me the gun," Rin said, and Odette held the gun closer. "Odette, please, I'm a better shot." Odette reluctantly relented.

"I haven't seen him anywhere," Rin said. "But that means nothing."

She stepped into the middle of the abandoned midway, and she cocked the gun. "Come on now, King," she said louder than she felt. Nothing.

Nothing.

The word sounded like a heartbeat in her head. Nothing.

"It's a trap," Rin whispered.

"We need to find the others," Odette said. "He's gone." Odette pointed to the dirt below them.

Rin looked down. There was a small dripping trail of blood. It led down the midway and to the entrance of the park. No one in her circus would leave during an attack. It had to be the Circus King's.

She stepped forward, and she looked down at the boot prints in the dirt. Big black boots. Just like hers.

"He's gone." Rin sniffed. "So, he's still human enough to bleed," she said, her lip curling. Rin grabbed Odette's gloved hand and jumped them into the one car on the train, an LQ, that was soundproofed and had thick locks on the inside, their safe room, praying everyone had made it there.

Inside, they found Mauve standing sentinel by the locked doors on the other end of the car, a pistol in her hand. She had ushered everyone else in, where they all waited now, some asleep in the bunks, like Jo, and some very awake and scared, like Charles. Everyone was safe, though.

Everyone but one.

"Mauve, where's Bernard?" Odette asked.

Mauve did not look at them. She just shook her head, tapping one finger on the door panel behind her. Odette looked to Rin, who silently moved to the door and reached for the first of the locks. One by one, the locks released. Mauve kept her back turned as Rin pushed the door open.

There, on the steel vestibule, crumpled between the railing and the outer wall of the car, was Bernard.

Dead.

※

30

THE RINGMASTER, 1926

Bernard was dead.

The circus wasn't safe. She had to take them away.

Had they ever been safe? Where could they go? Just somewhere away from this place.

Bernard was dead, and Rin couldn't breathe.

She jumped the train back to winter quarters. She took them to a rocky beach far away. But her mind was already racing to somewhere else. She was going to find him.

She was going to make the Circus King pay.

Rin ran outside the train. She screamed, snatching the flyers, tearing them down one by one, his red hat crumpling in her fists. *We'll make a hell of a team,* he'd once said.

She ripped up the flyers. She ground them into the mud. There was nothing else she could do.

The others fell out of the train into the cold ocean wind and salty night. Rin watched as Mauve saw Bernard lying slumped down on the side of the vestibule, with red down his white buttoned-up collared shirt. His gun smoked. Bernard had gotten a lick in. It had been too late. His life had been full of his joy and his starlight, but his death had been written by the Circus King.

Mauve refused to leave the car, refused to cross the threshold of Bernard's body. She held on to the doorframe, screaming for her fathers; she howled; she slowly untethered herself to find Bernard in other times. Rin could see her looking at the air, searching, muttering, shifting her brain from the day they met to the day they may die, to the days before and after and somewhere in between.

Rin tried to hold her, hug her, get her to look at Rin in the eye and tell her she was okay.

But Mauve shook and screamed. Odette caught her and fumbled to take off her own gloves. Mauve stopped her. She screamed, "No. No, don't you dare take this from me."

Because grief is intrinsically, painfully, tied to love.

Rin stormed from the train car, her body as tense as steel, her fingers curling around the barrel of that shotgun, her heart pounding with the sound of war drums. Odette shouted after her. She did not listen.

She took one step into the air, and

she landed back in Missouri Valley a few hours ago, the shotgun still in her hands. She kept walking, not missing a beat as she marched into her circus; *her* circus. The people and things *she* was supposed to protect. She and Odette had left for Paris already. But now she was here, and nothing was going to touch this place. Bastard.

Once a part of my circus, always a part of my circus, he'd said. *You don't run from me. You run to me. Even if you don't know it.*

The muddy grass gave way under her hard boots. Tina and Kell saw her march past. "Hey love," Tina said. "I thought you went with Odette? What's wrong?"

Rin ignored her. There was no time. Soon, the Circus King would come.

And she would be ready this time—

Hands grabbed her from nowhere and yanked her between two tents. She lost her breath and shoved the unknown assailant away. But then saw it was Bernard.

Bernard, *Bernard alive*! but somehow looking like he knew he would soon be dead. He looked so gray, so old, and it was only then Rin realized how much he'd aged taking care of all of them over the years. She hadn't noticed the new wrinkles, the gray deepening at his temples. Bernard was the strongest man she knew, and she'd only seen him as very much alive. She grabbed him now and stuffed her face into his warm coat, his old sturdy frame, the smell of an old attic. She was not going to let him end.

"Go," Bernard said. "I know what you're doing."

"You have no idea, I assure you," Ringmaster growled. "Now listen, you—"

"I know," Bernard said. His hands shook around her. "I know, sweetheart. We had this conversation tonight already." Somehow, he knew? Rin stammered in his embrace:

"What? How . . . no we didn't."

"Mauve."

"No. She never said anything. I'm here now, I'm gonna face him and we're going to get out of this. All of us."

"No," Bernard said. "We're not. Mauve and I have looked into it, all the different spiderwebs and nooks and crannies, and the way it happened was the best way. That was the least pain, for everyone."

"No," Rin started. "I'll—"

"Come back a thousand times, try a thousand different ways to save me. You will lose yourself looping, Rin," Bernard said. "You won't be able to keep track of your thread. Please, protect your future. Keep going forward. They can't lose both of us."

"No." Ringmaster boiled. "You're wrong. They're not going to lose *either* of us."

"I'm not wrong," Bernard said. "You can't stop every bad thing from happening."

"Watch me," Ringmaster said.

Bernard took her hands in his. "No. Listen, my little bear," he said. "You can't stop every bad thing from happening. But you *can* choose what you do for the people who have to go through the bad things. Do you understand?" He squeezed her hand, his eyes glassy and so alive and so *here*. "Be there for Mauve for me, all right? She needs her sisters. Trust me. Trust *her*."

That's when the lanterns were dashed. And everything went dark.

"He's here," Bernard said. "You can't take him out. You know you can't. Take the circus. You girls can protect them. Run."

"No," Rin said.

"Say goodbye to me, Rin," Bernard said.

"*No I am not going to*," Rin said.

Bernard pulled her in deep, to a hug. The sort of hug that only old arms can give a young body. One of support, of protection, of love.

It was an embrace she would never feel again.

"Go," Bernard said. "Mauve knew. I knew. I love you."

The cackling laugh of a madman sounded from the entrance of the circus. The sound of a gun.

Rin grabbed Bernard one more time. She held on to him, knowing this was the last time she would feel his tweed coat, his bristly beard. It was her fault. The Circus King wanted *her*, not the people he would hurt to get to her.

"This isn't your fault," Bernard said. "You are not responsible for him.

Please, please remember that. Now my girl, focus on the train. Go back home."

She almost took Bernard back with her. But he shoved her off, as if he knew what she was thinking. Before she could get time to stop bending to her will, she fell back into the in-between space and

knew from this moment on, Bernard was part of the past. He would never see a present again. How quickly sturdy men turn to ghosts. She saw the thread between them fizzle, disintegrate, become stardust. And he was dead again.

"No," she growled.

And she shoved herself forward again. The thread tore, her head spinning, her bare wrist without a tether . . . Odette and Mauve and the train on the rocky beach alone . . . she

landed back in Missouri Valley a few hours ago where she'd landed before, the shotgun still in her hands. She kept walking, not missing a beat as she marched into her circus; *her* circus.

Wait.

Dizziness settled in like vertigo. Wasn't she here already? It was like watching the same nickelodeon over and over again, reading the same page in a book so much that the words looked like black garble on white. The same drawing traced over and over again, line on top of line, not the same but the same.

"Hey love," Tina said. "I thought you went with Odette? What's wrong?"

Rin ignored her. There was no time. Soon, the Circus King would come.

And she would be ready this time—

Hands grabbed her from nowhere and yanked her between two tents. She lost her breath and shoved the unknown assailant away. But then saw it was Bernard.

"Rin," Bernard whispered, holding her by the collar. She couldn't look at him straight, her head was pounding and her vision doubled. "Rin, how many times have you jumped tonight?"

"I'll keep doing it until you come with me," Rin forced herself to say, finding his wrist and readying herself. She stumbled. He held her steady.

And he didn't yell at her. He didn't do anything but hold her tight.

"I'm already gone, Rin," he whispered. And he took the collar of her shirt. He ripped it, tore it on the left side, right over her heart.

Her mother had torn Rin's collar when her father died. She saw her mother, her father, the Circus King, Odette, Mauve, the twins, all of the circuses she'd seen, all of the spotlights she'd felt on her cheeks . . . like her entire life was happening all at once.

Then Bernard's hands clamped down on her hot face. "See Odette and Mauve," he said. "Do you see them?"

A thread attached to her heart.

"Go to them," he said. And he pushed her back and she went back and back and

she landed on her back, in the sand, looking up to where Bernard should be. But it was now late at night, across the country, near the ocean, too late and too far away to save anyone. Her head settled. The waves whispered beside her, licked her fingers. She felt her collar. It was still ripped. She was alive. He was dead.

The world had shifted in ways she could never change.

31

EDWARD, 1917

Edward was not a fan of circuses. But he stood in this Missouri pauper's Big Top all the same.

He was full of massive potential. Why was he here?

Well, why does any man do anything? He does it in the name of the best character in his tale; not him, but the girl he loves.

Mrs. Dover said Edward dimmed Ruth. But Ruth had followed Edward through this world, and he'd brought her to the brightest kindling of all. She beamed like the sun as they entered the ringmaster's tent.

"Oh my goodness," Ruth breathed, rushing into the center ring. "Edward, look at the canvas making the walls!"

"That there," the ringmaster said, raising his cane high to point to the largest point of the tent, "is called the king pole. You're a spec, but I want you to help out where you can. Best know the terminologists."

Terminology.

Ruth laughed, spinning around in her short blue dress, her curls bobbing and shining. An angel in a halo of light, bursting with a happiness that lit up the tent.

"This girl." The ringmaster patted Edward on the back, which must have looked a little odd, since he was a short, stout hairy man who was at least two feet shorter than Edward's long, lanky body. "She'll wow them by just standing there."

"She has a lot of offer," Edward said.

"I'd say so," the ringmaster agreed, and waved his hand to Ruth. "A real boob tickler, she'll—"

"You don't talk about her that way," Edward said.

The ringmaster stopped in mid-sentence. "Here we've got three rings, now up above you'll see the lyras for our acrobatics acts, and—"

But Edward wasn't listening.

Edward was watching Ruth smile.

Finally, he'd found them a home.

✳

Edward never wanted to perform at the same time as Ruth, because he wanted to watch her sublime joy.

Ruth was the Des Fantômes, which meant *The Ghosts* in a garbled Midwestern version of the French language. She would haunt the tent from the shadows, slipping between the audience members and scaring them. She'd be somewhere, and then somewhere else.

Edward was the Hypnotist. He could get anyone to do anything, on pure luck. He bought books on hypnosis and way too many pocket watches, leaning into the role, paranoid someone would realize it had nothing to do with luck or skill. He grew fond of the black obsidian pocket watch he bought in a small rummage sale out by Indianapolis and began wearing it on his belt. It didn't keep time, but it was a stunning piece.

The rest of the circus did not know what Ruth and Edward really were. This was not a Spark circus, because such a thing didn't exist. This was where magic was made with smoke bombs and sleight of hand. Except for Ruth and Edward; they were real.

It was probably for the best no one caught on, because then they would struggle when he tried to speak to them.

"You will make her the top bill," Edward told the ringmaster, and the ringmaster agreed.

"She has definitely earned it. Our strongest act."

"We are here for her," Edward said. "And I know how to do that the best. Don't you think you're heading toward a more hands-off role? Give younger, fresher faces the chance for ringmaster?"

"Are you interested, Eddie?"

At first, Edward had thought it would be fun to pretend the ringmaster had any say in all this. Of course, Edward could just come right out and say he wanted to be the boss, but he liked the game of manipulation, the power that came with word choice and making someone believe they had any say. It was tantalizing to think Edward could be quick-witted enough to navigate a true negotiation with this old geezer. But Edward quickly got bored of pulling the strings. It was beneath him. There was no reason to negotiate. He held all the cards.

"I will be the ringmaster," Edward said. "I will take the money. You will run the parts I don't like. You will run box office. You will get the crowds. But then the crowds are mine."

The ringmaster nodded. "Of course!"

"And you will spare no expense," Edward said. "If you have to sell your arm or rob a bank, you will get us better accommodations and bigger tents."

The ringmaster giggled. "My arm. Of course, Eddie, anything for you. You and Ruth are the heart of this circus. We're so glad to have you."

This would be their home. On his terms.

One evening, Ruth asked Edward for a night on the town. So Edward followed her down to Maryville's county fair.

The town hall stood on top of a large hill right in the middle of the main square. Little mom-and-pop shops surrounded the town hall with its clock tower like a fortress. The streets were brick, the lampposts were black, and it looked exactly like every other small town in the five-state area.

But tonight, with the fair in the square, Maryville stuck out like a bright planet in a sky full of stars. It peppered this small world with blinking bulbs and organ music and screaming teenagers and a Ferris wheel that hulked over it all.

Ruth begged for some cotton candy and Edward obliged.

"We need to see the top of the world!" Ruth rushed to the Ferris wheel with a mouth full of pink.

They curled into each other as the seat swung and the carnie shut the latch. The wheel shot them forward and up. Ruth bounced in their seat.

"We're going to . . . I mean I'm afraid we may die if you do that," Edward said. But he didn't say *Stop.* He didn't order her. Not tonight. Maybe never again.

He was trying. At least with Ruth, he was trying.

Mrs. Dover was wrong about him.

Pop guns went off below. He jumped.

Ruth jumped a little, too. She looked down, and Edward felt sick. He said, "Please si . . . It would be safer if you sat back."

"I don't understand why they have those pop guns at these things," Ruth said, not sitting back. The chair rocked. "There are people who are affected."

"I thought I said not to talk about the war," Edward said. "Didn't I say that?"

"No," Ruth said quietly. "You said not to ask you about it."

Edward stopped. "Well, I find Americans like to forget that misery exists," he grunted. This decade was now full of cars and fast lights and faster dice and big houses and carnival rides. Everyone was trying to move forward and gloss over the reality that had been dug up in those trenches.

"I disagree, I think," Ruth said. "It seems like Americans very much remember the war. That's why we need Ferris wheels."

"To forget," Edward said.

"No," Ruth said. "To survive."

Edward snorted. "To survive."

"Yes." Ruth turned to face him. The chair shook. Edward gripped the bar. "Because what's the point of living through life looking at all the bad things, Ed? What did we fight in the war for if we aren't going to ride Ferris wheels?"

"*We* fought in the war?"

Ruth shrank back. The Ferris wheel stopped. They swung in midair, and then lulled. Edward looked at his knuckles. "I'm sorry."

"No, you're right. I wasn't really there."

"I didn't mean—"

"I know."

Edward sighed. He can't. He shouldn't. He couldn't.

And then he did.

"Forget what I said about the war," he said. "Forget everything that happened in the last minute. And I suppose I wasn't clear enough. I need to be clearer. I said before I don't want you to ask me about the war. I don't want you to *talk* to me about the war. At all."

Ruth's eyes burst with the excitement of stepping onto a Ferris wheel. She smiled. She leaned forward. "Wow, look at how high up we are. Almost as high as the Eiffel Tower!"

"A little shorter," Edward said quietly. He'd done it again. He couldn't even get through one night.

Ruth turned to him once more and nearly bounced out of her seat. "The ringmaster told me about you taking over. And I wanted to approach you with an . . . well, an idea." She nearly sang this out. "What if we used your luck and my impeccable sense of placing, and we recruit fresh faces?"

"What?"

"We get more Sparks to join the circus!" Ruth beamed. Edward stared at her. "It can be so much more. *We* can be so much more! One of a kind! Think of how much real magic we'd have! Think of the daring feats and dashing destinies in one tent! Unless you think someone's thought of it already, a Spark circus. . . ."

"We would sell out night after night," Edward said quietly. Especially with his "luck." And with all those bodies, he could make them do anything. He could do anything. He could make a beautiful dollhouse for his beautiful ballerina.

"We'd be a beacon of amazement and astonishment," Ruth said. She wasn't a meek little thing right now, riding this Ferris wheel and professing her love for a dream. She was something bigger. Something much more like her mother. "The audience would love us. Especially with your luck, you could keep us safe!"

"Stop talking about my luck," he barked.

She went quiet.

God damn it!

Edward forced a smile. "You can be top bill and we can find these . . . other Sparks, I suppose. Get rid of the regular folk. Build up the circus the way we'd like. Is that what you want? Will that make you happy?"

"What do you mean get rid of the regular folk?" Ruth asked.

"I'll figure it out," Edward said. "Don't worry about it. You just need to worry about being my main attraction."

"I always have been," she said.

Edward took her hand. "We both have the same idea, to make the circus our own. We work so well together, Ruth. This moth-eaten circus will be ours. We will find our own way. Make it for both of us."

"Really?"

Edward nodded. "I can compensate for your childishness and you can ground me. I'll make it happen."

Ruth kissed him.

He didn't like circuses, but he loved her. He wanted to feel the happiness that radiated from Ruth.

So after Ruth had fallen asleep, Edward crept out into the night and found two circus workers out in the midway. He tore them apart with his words, leaving them for dead, their own bloody hands burying themselves under the soft Missouri soil. Because he could. Because it was better than tearing himself apart for what he'd done to her.

Two down. The rest of these dusty circus rats to go.

"Edward?"

He spun around. There was Ruth. Ruth stared at him, and the dying people underneath the ground. They didn't scream, but maybe that made it worse? Should he make them scream?

In her eyes, this was a gruesome, irredeemable scene.

"Ruth," he breathed, "what . . . what have we done?"

Ruth's eyes got bigger. "W-what?" she hyperventilated.

"They're dead, Ruth," Edward said. "It's okay. No one will know what we did, if we just keep it between us."

"I don't remember—"

"Ruth, I will protect you, whatever people say, however they come after us, I will protect you," he said. "I understand your temper gets the best of you, but there are other ways to get rid of those less than us."

"I *what*?!" Ruth couldn't breathe. She ran for the shallow graves, but Edward grabbed her around the waist and held her in his arms. She kicked.

"Ruth, stop it, *stop it*," and she did. She stood, wrapped in his arms, staring like a ghost, like those graves were her own. "Ruth, I understand that you wanted this. You and I are the same. I get it. We're okay. We're safe. I love you. We're going to be okay."

Ruth didn't say anything.

"Now take a big breath, keep breathing, and go back to our bed," Edward said. "Don't tell anyone and we'll be okay. But if you open your mouth about this, we're done for. The world will end."

Ruth was horrified, he could see it in her eyes. This would drive her mad. She couldn't handle it. So Edward said, "You don't need to know what we did, you just need to know it was something that makes us both powerful. It will be alright, as long as we stick together. Now go to bed."

Ruth, in either shock or in a dream, followed his instructions.

He could set Maryville on fire and get away with it, he could be whoever and whatever he could fathom and Ruth would still understand him. He could walk down to that Ferris Wheel and strike a match to it and when men came to put it out, he could tell them to let it burn.

But he didn't set the Ferris wheel on fire. He set the ringmaster on fire.

He was the author of this story. It was a power he'd never allowed himself to have. He did not have to play by the small rules of a constricted world. So he set himself free.

There was a moment, in this blaze, where he had a small sliver of a thought. It tugged at him; a final attempt to pull him from the edge. It was made of the man he may have been if the Spark hadn't poisoned him. If the Spark hadn't possessed him, given him no choice over his own fate, removed him from the tapestry of normalcy's illusion. Who would he have grown into, where would he be? Maybe that Edward King was somewhere far away from circuses, fires, and these streets. Maybe he was happy somewhere.

Maybe he could still be that person.

He went to the bar. He drank strong things. Then he said to someone, anyone, maybe the whole bar, "Tell me about the most frightening Spark you've ever heard of, and point me in their direction."

He had a circus to recruit.

*

32

THE RINGMASTER, 1926

Circus folk never say goodbye. They only say, "See you down the road." Even when they knew damn well they never would.

As they prepared for the funeral, the dust of Bernard's death settled around them, kicked up by an air of uncertainty. Rin felt shaken by that frayed thread, the spinning in her head as Bernard held on to her. She felt so useless against the tides of time. She did not dare tell Odette or Mauve about her getting lost.

The three of them didn't talk about any of it. Rin would never know what really happened outside that soundproof train. She would never understand why Mauve hadn't told her, why Bernard and Mauve went to the Chandelier on his last night and why Mauve didn't . . . Mauve knew. But Rin wasn't going to ask her to relive it. She felt so small, so useless. But she had to trust Mauve, she had to trust Bernard.

She sure as hell did not trust the Circus King.

The Circus King could have killed them all, if he'd wanted to. He could have left Bernard alive, like Mr. Davidson. But Bernard had stood up to him. Bernard had protected the others. So Bernard was dead.

The Circus King orchestrated all of this. He was toying with her, a cat circling and batting with its claws still pulled out of sight until it tired of the fun and got hungry. She had hidden from him for so long, had hoodwinked him with an empty grave and a headstone with the name he'd known her by etched into it. Now she was going to pay. And so was everyone around her. He had written Bernard's name on a grave, just like he had others before. Just like *they* had . . . no, no it wasn't her fault.

It was her fault.

But maybe Bernard had gotten a good crack at the Circus King and shown that dark shadow a moment of mortal fear. So there, that was the story Rin could hold on to, just long enough to get through this funeral without completely breaking down.

She shook off the nails-on-a-chalkboard memory of getting lost. She dampened her fury, her fear. Today was not about the Circus King. And it wasn't about how Bernard had been his victim. No, a man like Bernard would not be defined by something as mortal and dark as a murder. His life had been a spec parade, a beautiful circus, and so they raised the tent for him.

They buried Bernard at winter quarters in Florida. It was the closest thing the circus had to a plot of its own sturdy, stable land. Rin had learned through the years that homes were temporary. Homes were nothing more than a cluster of people desperately holding on to one another, pretending their love made a space sacred. But homes are only made of wood, steel, and short passages of time before things begin to rot. It can all come tumbling down.

They held the memorial service inside the tent. It was dark, the lights dimmed, except for the candles they all held as his coffin lay in the ring adorned by flowers. The people of Sarasota had helped them in exchange for a few "miracles." Mauve sang for Bernard, standing beside him, her hand on the polished wood, her other hand on her diaphragm. She sang a song from the future, one Bernard would never live to see but that Mauve had brought back for him and he'd loved before its time.

Mauve kept herself together, her darkest, longest dress draped over her legs, hugging her arms and torso like a sturdy embrace. Her hair was done in braids, pulled out of her eyes. She looked ghostly in the candlelight, with no rouge, no eyeshadow, no lipstick, like she might just fade into the next world alongside her father.

It was customary for the ringmaster to speak at circus funerals, but Mauve did the honors and that made more sense. Mauve stood in front of the crew and performers, all their friends, all the hands that had shaken Bernard's, and she said, "I've been thinking about the first wish we granted. Back when we started this circus, and we were first recruiting. There was a boy whose brother was trying to sell him off to us. You remember that, Odette? Rin?"

Rin nodded, Odette's gloved fingers intertwined with hers. They sat among the audience for this performance.

Mauve reached out to touch the coffin beside her. She looked so young. Her fingers couldn't move, she was stuck there, touching it, not ever wanting to let go.

"That's when Rin came up with the questions," Mauve said softly. "Do you really want to be here? Do you really want to do this? Is there anything else in the world we can give you? And he said yes, he wanted his mother back—" She stopped.

Rin saw Tina put her head down, breaking contact with the uncomfortable silence of grief.

But Mauve collected herself enough to say, "Odette." She said the name like she was reaching out for help. "Odette, you were worried that if we did that, if we brought his mother back, then there'd be consequences, and I said that's not how time works. It's not a tit for tat. It's not a Monkey's Paw. Well . . . we saved his mother. We went back to our present day, and he and his brother weren't even at the factory we'd been told to meet them . . . we'd seen them at that morning. They'd never been there. They were at home, with their mother. Like they should have been."

Another pause.

A longer pause.

Rin swallowed something back inside her.

Rin knew what it was to say goodbye. A goodbye was a patchwork quilt of the leaves rustling, the rain falling, the wind pushing the clouds along, all the small spectacles that created the performance of life. And the heaviness, the stopping of time at a grave, was the thread weaving in between, stitching it all together in a new way. Because no matter how many days Mauve DesChamps lived, Bernard would be in no more of them.

If only they could leave the past in the past. But that's where some of the best people lived.

"I wondered, that night," Mauve finally started again. "I wondered if I could go back and save my father, Bernard's one true love. We all have reasons why we're here at the circus, and my reason . . . my father died, and Bernard and I had to run. I thought, hey, I brought this boy's mother back. I could bring my father back. I could stop running." Mauve looked to the coffin.

Rin remembered this conversation, that evening, years ago. Mauve had been at the washbasin. She had stopped, said, "If my dad hadn't died, I'd never have joined the circus. So which one is the selfish choice? To let my dad die or . . . hurt everyone else?"

"We can go back and save him," Rin had said without hesitation. There wasn't anything in the world she wouldn't do for Mauve.

"We love you," Odette had echoed, "but if you need to return home, we of course understand."

"Y'all think I'm here just for you?" Mauve had teased them like a joke between sisters. "Ten years from now, I meet Clyde Parker. Looks just like Jackie Robinson."

"Who?"

"Ah, right." Mauve had laughed, because there had been laughter on that day. "Baseball player in about thirty years."

"You marry a baseball player?"

"No!" Mauve had said. "I marry a juggler. He joins us at some point and we fall madly in love. Soulmate love. The once-in-a-thousand-years kind of love. And if I go back to save my father, I don't go forward to find him. See, I'm on the track right now. And I can't get off the track. Not now. So . . . I guess the universe *can* be a tit for tat or a monkey's paw. I guess the universe can be anything it wants to be."

"I always thought you had eyes for Rin," Odette had said. "Or me. Or . . . I . . . thought we might all end up together."

"Oh please, you both wish!"

"Huh, outdone by a juggling baseball player."

"He's not a baseball player!" Mauve splashed water at them.

Water everywhere.

Odette gripped Rin's arm, bringing her mind back to this terrible place with the coffin in a ring that should have held live bodies, dances, music, glitter, and Sparks. Rin felt the black mesh veil over her face. Her eyes burned. No laughter was here on this day.

Mauve was staring at nothing, straight ahead, maybe the back of the tent, maybe at their faces all blending together like audiences do when you're so far away in the ring. She seemed to sway in a rhythm, as if the tears inside her sang a song she couldn't stop feeling. She softly hit her fist on the coffin, and she said, "I'm rethinking it all now, Daddy."

✳

They buried Bernard under the sky on their lot, under a marker on fresh green southern grass. It was close to his home in New Orleans, it was closer to Mauve's heart.

Rin stood silent as she saw Mauve step out from the crowd, their family, holding an old baby blanket of hers that Bernard had kept. She knelt beside the small stone they'd etched his name into. She touched it, gently, with her hand, settling the blanket underneath it. She whispered something to the grave.

Rin tried to remember that families can't be broken. Homes can be broken, houses can fall down, bodies can turn to ash. But a family can be in different places, times, realms, but they're still bound together.

Rin's mother had said something, whispered it between her teeth before she died. "We always have a way of coming back together."

It was a memory that swept Rin's mind backward to see that room again, her mother dead again, Rin standing at the door staring at the lifeless body one last time before they carried her from the bed. Waiting to watch someone die was like the last leg of a long trip; the story is over but you're not yet home. All of the good things can't be remembered yet because it's still happening, but there's nothing to hope for. It's an ending that is coming too fast and too slow all at the same time.

The moment of death itself, when the body is there and the person is not, the moments that make up funerals are uncomfortable. That's the thing about the big important moments; they're sad when they end, but they also were full of wind and hair in one's face and achy feet. There was a feeling of both wanting to leave and wanting to never leave.

She shouldn't have left Bernard.

The wind blew through Rin's hair, and she pulled it back into a messy ponytail. Mr. Calliope began to crank up his song for Bernard, and Rin knew the funeral was winding down. It would soon be time to go.

But where would Bernard be, once they left this grave? Would his smell, his touch, his memory, his spirit follow them or was this really the end? After a funeral comes the real mourning. Rin knew the steps to this dance and she did not like it.

"I buried my mother the day we met," Rin said.

"I know," Odette said softly.

"She was Jewish," Rin said. "And I've been trying to remember more about what she tried to teach me. How we lit candles . . . the blessings contained so many nice things to someone we couldn't see . . . I remember she always kissed me on one cheek and then the other, when Shabbat came. She gave a little blessing to me. And I wanted to give her a blessing or a prayer when she died . . . and I couldn't. I couldn't remember it, but even if I could, I wouldn't have been able to."

A moment passed.

"I was the reason she died," Rin finally said. "Just like Bernard."

Rin left it at that. She walked to Mauve as the crowd dispersed. Jo stepped toward them, but Rin held out a firm hand. "We'll talk later," she managed.

Rin stood behind Mauve, giving her space but there if she needed her. She saw the mound of dirt where the grass had been upturned to return Bernard to the earth.

He was under there, and he would never be anywhere else. Just out of sight, forever.

Come back, she wished to no one who was there. There was no closure when someone who was loved is lost, not even if there was a goodbye. The goodbye was never long enough.

"I have to carry this now," Mauve said, still kneeling. "He's not coming back."

And they let silence lie over Bernard's grave.

The crowd dispersed, and Mauve and Rin still stayed sentinel. Until Mauve stood up, turned around, her eyes full of fury, and said, "Are you willing to break a few rules?"

＊

33

THE RINGMASTER, 1926

The three women gathered in Mauve's room. Odette eyed the two of them tepidly. "Where are we going tonight?" she said.

Mauve took her hand. "We talked about cutting it at the roots," she said. "So we're going to go back further. To the beginning."

Rin and Mauve had come up with the plan, and then Rin sort of just stepped into it without thinking it through. Or maybe she had thought it through, thought it through too much, but hadn't really internalized it anywhere other than her brain.

"We're going to Bosnia in 1914," Rin said.

Odette shook her head. Like she'd just been hit by electricity. "Excuse me?"

"The Great War started with an assassination of Archduke Ferdinand," Mauve answered, using facts to pull herself forward, as if words were handholds and she was on her stomach scraping against the ground trying to keep going. "So we're going to save him."

"Wait, no," Odette said. "No, you're talking about going past the graveyard, *past the Spark*. What if we do something that ruins the Spark? Will we even be able to get back? Would we even be there in the first place? This makes no sense."

Mauve narrowed her eyes. "We all three agreed to this, when we watched that family loaded into the truck. We *all three* said to go to the root, so we do."

"And when we go back to '26," Odette said, "what if the Spark is gone? What if we can't get *back* to '26 because we don't have Sparks anymore?"

"I refuse to think we got the Spark because of a trench in France," Mauve said. "It would have happened anyway."

"You don't know that."

"Neither do you!" Mauve said.

"It's too big a risk! If we lose the Spark, we lose the circus, and we lose the chance to do good!" Odette said. "When we started, all *three* of us agreed the Spark was a gift. We don't have the right to take away that gift from the world!"

"But we have the right to just let the war happen?" Mauve said. "Maybe it's about making a world where we don't need the Spark to begin with."

"We have rules!"

"We don't know, Odette!" Rin spoke out, in a loud bark. Her jaw was so tense. "We are trying. And this is what we have."

Odette looked to Rin, and then Mauve, and then Rin again. She said nothing.

"Your job," Rin said matter-of-factly to Odette, "is to convince him not to come back to the road that's planned for the route, but to go another route. If he doesn't, he dies. You're going to need to be even more persuasive than you were back with the mother in Germany."

Odette stared at her. "You know what you're asking me to do?"

"I do," the Ringmaster said. "And I'm sorry."

Odette's body tensed, as if she was on a tightrope about to fall into the dark. But she took their hands. She always would. Rin felt a pang of guilt.

It had to be worth it, in the end.

34

THE RINGMASTER, 1914

Ten minutes later, or really more than a decade before, the three women arrived on a street filled to the brim with people pushing and jabbing their way
to the side of the road as if a parade would start at any time.

"You've absolutely lost yourselves," Odette said, looking down to her
gloved hands. "My Spark is not for this sort of thing."

"After you touch him, you'll need to tell him where to go, a different route,"
Rin said. "It's to help him."

"It's to control him," Odette pushed back, starting like a flicker on a flint.
"Just like someone did to you once."

That was a cheap shot that Rin knew she deserved. It stung. She took it.
She let it hit her deep.

Odette is learning who you really are, isn't she?

"Does this scheme even work?" Odette asked Mauve.

"I can see that you can do this, and you can change his route," Mauve said.

"If you can bend your rules, just this once," Ringmaster said.

"*My* rules," Odette said, looking to them both. "Just my rules. No one else's
rules? I made these rules on my own to be a pain? Listen here, I heal people,
I calm people. Not this."

"I know," Rin said.

"*Do* you know?" Odette said. "You *don't* know, because you're asking me to
do this. The one thing you asked me to wear gloves for, so *I wouldn't do it to you*."

Rin felt the hairs on her neck prick up. It wasn't a threat, she knew that,
but her body felt it as a threat. Like Odette was reaching out, ready to touch
her, take her thoughts—

And like Odette could read her expression, Odette quickly said, "I'm not
threatening you, Rin. I love you. I am saying I don't want—"

"Do you want him to die instead?" Rin snapped. "You either bend the rules, or he dies."

It came out more brash than she wanted it to. Or maybe there was no other way to say such a terrible, manipulative thing. She could hear the Circus King's voice in her tone, the way he knew how to find the thing someone fears the most and use it to his advantage. She'd learned these tricks from him, and now she still used them?

But before Rin could take it back . . . or maybe she really didn't want to take it back, maybe she needed to let it hang there in the air and she needed to not worry so much about how good of a person she was if they were going to stop this war. Maybe the Circus King had taught Rin a thing or two about cruelty because it was efficient.

Before Rin could take it back, Odette said, "This once. This once, and never again."

Odette took off her white gloves. Soft, thin hands that Rin couldn't bring herself to ever touch.

Odette's big eyes looked to Mauve, and then to Rin, and the pain on her face . . .

Ringmaster watched her march across the barricaded street, touch the shoulder of the closest guard with her bare skin. The guard sighed in deeply, smiled, and dopily escorted her in.

Ringmaster and Mauve stood on the sidewalk, waiting. Ringmaster looked to the faces around her, now persons who were dead.

Or maybe now, they would live. Maybe the boys would grow up.

"That man over there looks like Dad," Mauve said suddenly, like the thought had just smacked her between the eyes. "It's not him. It just looks like him." She didn't add anything to this. She just let it sit in the air in front of her, a thought she didn't want to digest.

Rin didn't say anything. She gritted her teeth harder.

"I always thought the Spark gave me what it did," Mauve said, "because I was tired of being afraid. Now I can see everything happening, and it's worse than not knowing."

Rin took her hand. She squeezed it. Mauve squeezed back.

It wasn't long until Odette slowly sauntered out from a side door and motioned for the two to meet her at the corner. They bustled through the sea of limbs and sweaty smells and reconvened under a tree a block away.

"I told him to go check on his wounded men in the hospital," Odette said. "That will hopefully get him on a better, less fatal route."

Ringmaster looked up to the tree. It was as if it was one of Jo's illusions; not really here belonging to Rin and her time. Or perhaps *she* was the illusion; the thing that was not supposed to be.

1914 had been so long ago. It didn't smell stale, but it was outdated. Maybe time moved forward because there was no room for the things of the past to live in the present. So what then, everything and everyone was just forgotten? No, she'd remember all of this. It still mattered, just as much as any other time.

Odette shoved off from her standing place and stalked away.

"Odette?" Ringmaster shouted.

Odette stopped at the street corner, and she turned away, hiding her face. Then she tore around, angry, marching back to her.

"I am not that sort of Spark," Odette said. But the words did not come out soft or hard; they came out in a delicate shatter of a sob. "I don't know what's worse, that we went back so far and could have done some major damage, or that you . . . you made me touch him and make him do things like . . ." She broke. "Like the Circus King does. I touch people to calm them, to *heal* them, not . . . not to *control* them. You *both* know that! Was this *both* your idea?"

Rin felt sick.

"You both are forgetting who we are," Odette barreled on. "This is about staying true to ourselves as we—"

"Bernard is *dead*, Odette," Mauve said. "If we don't do this, everyone dies. Just like him! You don't understand, it's everywhere! But if we go back far enough, we can fix it all."

"I agree," Rin said. "It hasn't worked to play footsie with the future. It was a good idea. And we came up with it together."

"So what, Mauve, the next stop on our whirlwind devil-may-care tour is to save Bernard?" Odette said. Mauve said nothing, but her fiery eyes gave an answer. Rin felt a chill roll through her bones.

"We can't save him," Rin whispered. "We can't. I tried."

Mauve's jaw set. She said, "I know we can't."

Odette stepped forward. "I know you're upset, but Mauve, you're always talking about Clyde and how we have futures. This isn't—"

"Stop telling me what is and isn't," Mauve said.

Two shots rang out.

Bang. Bang.

Ringmaster and Mauve fell on the ground, covering their heads. Odette covered them with her arms, like a blanket.

An uproar.

"You can make anything happen?" Jo had said. "So you could make it so the war never happened?"

Mauve reached out and grabbed them both by the wrists. "Go go go!" she screamed. Rin shoved her feet to the side, dragging the others with her.

The tree disappeared in the flash of light.

There was an answer in the silence, even if it was uncertain silence.

"Then you can't make anything happen," Jo said.

✳

35

THE RINGMASTER, 1941

They arrived in sunlight. On a beach, far in the future and halfway across the world from the archduke and those gunshots. The jungle crawled up the mountains behind them, the Pacific Ocean cooed at their feet. Rin breathed in deep, sea salt air untouched by the mainland. Untouched by war.

She'd come here, when she was very young. She'd read about such places in books, and when she saw it for the first time and saw it was real, she could barely believe it actually existed.

On the day she received her Spark, this was one of the first places she jumped to. A safe place, far from war. Somewhere she'd always wanted to go.

Mauve closed her eyes, crossed her legs in the sand as she sat. "The archduke's chauffeur did not hear he was supposed to go to the hospital. The archduke died."

"So we go back and try again," Ringmaster said, but immediately regretted it. She couldn't. She'd *seen* she couldn't. The dizziness, the lost timeline, she couldn't . . .

She was nothing but a broken record.

Something was quiet in Mauve. Something had shifted since her firm words in Bosnia. Something in the shots of the gun, something in the way they had all fallen to the ground, it had thrown her back into a place Rin couldn't follow her: a well-composed, critical mind.

Mauve took a deep breath, and then let it out, as if sending it out with the ocean breeze that moved the waves from here to the horizon. Mauve opened her eyes. "I . . . I had seen that there was a chance to change his route. So I said we could try, there was a chance. But now I understand. Even if we'd saved him, the archduke is murdered the next day. Or the next. Or if not then, a week later, as he is standing on his balcony. The Black Hand is the group that wants him dead, so dead he will be." Mauve rubbed her eyes. "Why won't he just live?" And she burst into tears.

Rin was sure Mauve wasn't just talking about the archduke. Mauve looked so heavy sitting in the sand, looking out to a sunset in the future that they weren't even supposed to witness. The Spark had brought them here. The Spark would send them into the front lines of this new war. But the Spark couldn't save them.

"This is too much," Odette said. "Rin, we can't go back before the Spark shows up. It would change too much. We can't . . . Rin? Rin are you listening?"

Rin was listening, but her brain was also on overtime. "Maybe then we go back to when the Black Hand was created."

"And then if that doesn't work, then what?" Odette said. "The Black Plague? Maybe we should just go back to Moses and see what butterfly he may have stepped on to start this whole thing off. And you get older, you stubborn ass, and the circus gets less of you."

"The circus is fine, and we are not having another conversation about my aging! Stay focused."

"The circus is not fine! *You* are not fine! What is going on with you! *Both of you!*"

"We are not ourselves," Mauve muttered. "We can't lose each other, especially not here . . ." But then Mauve stopped like she'd been shocked by a loose wire. "Oh no," she whispered.

"What now?" Odette said.

"It's here," Mauve said.

That's when the rumble came from the clear crystal blue sky.

Like black ravens, too stiff to be birds, too real to be a dream, the rumbling cut into their view. Rin looked up above the beach, the quiet beach, to the black planes. No, green. With big red circles like the black spot from *Treasure Island,* pirates coming to claim their blood debt. This was no machinery her world of 1926 had known, or any world before hers. These were death-dealing reapers, precisely fitted to the sky, methodically planned to kill.

The planes disappeared as soon as they'd come, over the ridge to the east. Then explosions. Then billows of black smoke. Big thick smoke. Like a bonfire.

Ringmaster took Mauve and Odette's hands. They stepped forward, off the beach and onto a hill in Honolulu, only a few miles away from the beach.

In silence, the three stood together on the tall hill as a sunrise tried to stab through the smoke of fallen buildings and screaming, sinking battleships. Rin felt stuck in a spiderweb, drowning in sticky threads that moved and shifted all over every time she touched just one strand. It was impossible. It was everywhere. Even here.

In their stillness, Ringmaster could hear the rumble of a second wave of aircraft, far off beyond the horizon.

Mauve swallowed, and she looked out to the sounds gathering closer. "We make sure we wash our socks. We get good sleep. We eat our breakfasts. We don't go that far back again. We do not loop. We follow our rules. And we give this future a run for its money." Her big brown eyes scanned Rin's face like she was trying to read her, trying to see if she agreed. "But we don't forget ourselves. Or it's already won, Rin. Odette." She snorted. "Mauve," she advised herself. She looked back at the air. "I refuse to believe this is the only way people can be. The only way it can go. People are stubborn, hateful dangerous forces. But I'm not going quietly."

Rin nodded.

Odette nodded as well, but her gloved fingers grabbed Rin's as if she didn't believe Rin would stay with them. Rin looked down to her, and Odette radiated something like worry. No, love.

This is what love looked like.

"I'm sorry," Rin said quietly.

"I won't apologize for this," Mauve said. "But I am sorry."

"We can't lose our souls to save the world," Odette said. "We can't forget who we are, and we can't hollow ourselves out. I won't let us."

Rin detached from the conversation. She'd apologized. It's all she could do. It would be fine. She needed to keep her wits about her. She was the Ringmaster. She had to find their way home.

"Rin," Odette said. "Take a breath. Look at me."

Rin, in a haze, did so.

Odette still held her arms across her chest, like she was trying to soothe herself. But she looked right at Rin, in that brave way that was void of fear or anger. It was brave to not be afraid, to not be angry. It was more than Rin deserved.

Rin could have said something. She could have allowed herself to have this moment with her wife. She could have connected.

But the planes came closer. Another whirring, another round of sirens, the black smoke still pumping upward into the blue from the last attack.

The planes crossed over their heads, torpedoes birthing from their stomachs, falling falling . . .

The island erupted in smoke and sirens, just like everywhere else they'd seen.

✳

36

EDWARD, 1917

Mrs. Dover had found them.

Edward recognized her immediately. She looked older, more haggard, but she still wore that red velvet jacket, and it made her stand out in the dingy crowd of Red Cloud, Nebraska.

She sat in the front row.

Edward knew Mrs. Dover couldn't see either of them. Her brain skimmed over their faces in the spec parade. Her mind filled in the gaps when he guided as ringmaster, when he did his hypnotist act, and her eyes wavered when Ruth glowed in the center ring.

Edward had done this.

He watched Mrs. Dover, unable to see them but there all the same, and Ed realized no one had ever crossed the world to find him. Once, he'd thought Ruth had done just that; he had been a very foolish boy.

But tonight, these shadows of past pains didn't charge him with fire. It made him feel heavy.

He watched Ruth glow like a thousand suns, the spotlight hitting her sequined gold leotard as she flitted around the circus tent.

She was special. He had kept her for himself. And somewhere under that admiration, he felt guilt.

So backstage, when Edward and Ruth stood next to each other, waiting for the finale, he quietly said, "How are you?"

"There's a terrifying thing in the front row," Ruth said. "I can't make it out, there are spots in my eyes . . . I think I might be going mad, Ed."

That's right. He'd told her once that her mother was a monster.

"Ruth," he said. "Your mother isn't a monster."

"What?" Ruth looked at him, startled.

"Your mother loves you, as much as I love you," he said, his teeth clenched, his eyes hot. "She came all this way to see you."

Ruth looked out through the dust and the peanut shells and the turning glistening lights. Edward saw her light up when her eyes finally connected with the face of Mrs. Dover.

"Oh my God," Ruth said. "Ed, she's here."

After the finale, Ruth rushed out of the dressing tent to find her in the crowd. Edward lifelessly followed.

He took one last look at the world he'd built for her. The expensive tents raised up, the masks on the faceless Sparks that played in the ensemble of their pageant. He'd collected them from all over to make the most moving circus. It revolved around Ruth. And what good was it without Ruth?

They were going to ride the tracks forever, Ruth happy and Edward happy . . . and now it was going to end.

No, he couldn't allow her to leave.

But how could he look at himself in the mirror ever again if he kept her here against her own will?

No, she would understand. She wouldn't leave him. He was her husband.

It happened like a silent movie, Edward watching from afar and through the crowd, as Ruth ran to Mrs. Dover and jumped on her, hugging her and kissing her and crying and . . . Mrs. Dover did nothing. Mrs. Dover couldn't see her.

Edward swallowed. It would take one word. He could undo this. He could let her go.

Ruth slowly removed her hands from her mother. He could see her face. Even past the crowd, he could see her horror.

A veil had passed between them.

Mrs. Dover couldn't feel Ruth, couldn't hear the words she was saying.

Edward could stop this. But he allowed Ruth to shout and scream. He allowed Mrs. Dover to walk away in a dream, empty-handed, still wearing her red velvet coat.

He slowly stepped away, back through the tent, and he found something to drink.

He drank a lot of it.

At some point, Ruth made her way back to him. He was deep into his bottle, the pumpkin-head clowns' hardest stuff now sitting in his gut and his eyes raging with tears and fire.

Ruth had looked beautiful in that trench. If only she'd really wanted to save him.

"Do you want to know what my Spark is?" he said slowly. Ruth, her face streaked with her stage makeup, raised her chin, her eyes questioning. "I told you it was luck. I lied."

Edward didn't remember much after those words. The truth spilled out of him like vomit. Like daggers that sliced Ruth open with a million little cuts.

Ruth stood over him, raged, turned away, blurred in his vision, and then at some point, he shoved her, and she fell.

The circus showdogs, big black mutts, rushed out of the tent; hellhound harbingers of an end.

That's when his mouth opened and he unleashed the truth. He shouted their story at her. His Spark was something dark, something that took her from her mother and walked her through their wedding day. It was probably the reason why she saved him to begin with.

He held out his arms and told her to kill him if she wanted.

It was a mistake, a miscalculation because it could have meant his death.

But she couldn't do it. Even with his permission and with complete freedom, she couldn't kill him.

"You think you're so much better than me," Edward spat. "*You told me to take you from her. This is all your fault, too! You stupid girl, you're just as responsible as I am.*"

Ruth broke into tears.

He told her to go to bed.

And that was that.

37

THE RINGMASTER, 1926

Charles, Jo, and Kell returned to the Sarasota grounds after a day on the Florida beaches, tired and sun-kissed, looking like ordinary teenagers. Rin had packed them lunches, and now she watched them walk side by side, back into the circus's mess of tents and train cars. Charles held his shoes in his hand, Kell held Charles's shoulders in his arms. Josephine walked beside them, holding the basket Rin had given them. They were trying to laugh, trying to forget they grew up too fast.

Ringmaster passed them on her lone walk through the circus lot. Ringmaster tousled Jo's hair and said, "Get some sleep tonight and don't miss breakfast."

"We going out on the road soon?" Charles asked, as Kell watched him with a big grin.

Ringmaster nodded. "Soon," she said.

They waved their goodbyes, and as she turned from them, her face fell. It all rolled back in, Ringmaster disappearing and Rin returning, tired and old and done.

The problem with Odette and Mauve's plan is that Rin *wanted* to forget who she was.

She wanted to forget, just for a minute, that Bernard was dead and that her mother was dead and that it was her fault. She wanted to just for one day forget about the blue light in the future, a ticking clock to the end when everyone would hurt, everyone would be erased.

She wanted to hurt herself so much she couldn't think of anything else. Maybe she could disappear for good. Her plan sat in her gut like a thick round black stone.

She made sure the kids weren't watching as her shoulders slumped and she continued on through the Florida grass. It was a thick, unbearable tropical summer. She crossed their winter quarters campus. It looked like any other time they parked in a town, except there was no midway. No audience, so no need. Just the Big Top and Back Yard. But that's not where she was going. She made her way through the minefield of hellos and waving hands. The Ringmaster would appear on her face, give a comforting nod, a wave.

"How are you doing, Mrs. Davidson?" she asked. Mrs. Davidson nodded, not finding the words, but some color had come back to her face.

"Maynard headed out, by the way, Ringmaster," Agnes shouted from her stall where she was doing drills. "Just left for the West on the nine o'clock train. He said he'll send a telegram if it ain't safe, but so far no one's heard a thing about the black tents."

Ringmaster nodded. "Good," she said. "How are you holding up?"

Agnes lifted her barbells. Like that was an answer. "Brain can't scream if my body's screaming."

"That's a truth," Ringmaster agreed.

She saw Mauve, sitting with Mr. Weathers at the box office, going through Bernard's old papers by the lone electric light above them in the small stall. Although their hands were holding the papers, their eyes were looking to one another and their mouths spoke in hushed tones. Mauve had red eyes; she'd been crying again. Mr. Weathers looked old.

They looked like they were having the sort of conversation that didn't want a third person. Ringmaster pulled a small tangerine from her pocket that she'd gotten from the cookhouse, walked to the booth's small counter, set it down for Mauve, and kept walking. Mauve liked tangerines; whenever they went down to Florida she ate as many as she could stuff in her skirts. There had been no tangerine hunting this time down here. But Cherry had found some, and Mauve hadn't been at dinner.

Rin left all the others behind her as she left the lights of the main area, sneaking back to the train. They weren't ghosts yet, but someday they could be. She'd seen it. And Bernard was already gone. The Circus King was coming. The war was coming. How was one mind supposed to mourn, be afraid, rage, do anything when there were so many fires burning all at once? How could the world balance more than one tragedy without just falling over dead? How was any of this fair, or even fixable? Were they expected to be able to keep taking it?

Eventually, no one could see Rin as she ducked into the shadows of the flatcars.

She jumped onto the side stairs of the flatcar holding the wagons. She boosted her old body onto the wooden platform, her arms and chest and hips all protesting. She found the green wagon where the duck game was usually housed. She threw her worse leg, the right one, straight out as she used her sturdier leg to lower herself to the ground and get on her stomach. Underneath was the compartment she was looking for, like a wooden cigar box cut into the ornate detailing of the wagon. She pulled on it. It gave.

There was a bottle.

The bottle was old and had a nondescript label on it, from the beginning of Prohibition when companies sold booze and called it house cleaner to skirt the Feds. It was for an emergency.

Feeling the glass on her skin was a comfort. It was an option. She held that option in her hand. She stuck it into her pocket.

She methodically popped the cigar box back into place in the gold-painted wagon atop the flatcar. She told her mind, *Take me away and wake me up when you get there.* But she knew where the perfect spot would be. The sharp dark silhouette of a mountain at the end of their plot of land. The Big Top.

Her creaking limbs moved to get up carefully, her spine popped, her ankles and arches figured out where the ground was. She then walked far enough away not to get caught but not far enough away to be eaten by the plethora of hellbeasts Florida provided. She slunk in the shadows, slowly finding herself at the foot of the Big Top. And then she entered.

She stood in the ghost light, looking up the length of the titan king pole. Their names were no longer carved in it, but hastily painted. The day she brought it back, she made certain everyone took some paint and got to work marking this pole as their tradition. The only paint available was purple, and some of the brushes were too big to be John Hancock-ing with. It was awkward, it was pathetic, but the deed was done and all their names still stood in bright color on the heart of their home.

It was important to have traditions. Rin had realized this when she brought all the strangers together under one roof. Traditions meant history, and history meant stability, and stability meant safety.

The tent was empty. It had been empty for days and nights, as they sat stagnant in the field between a swamp and an ocean. The bulbs above had their light gels left in from when they were all the way in Missouri Valley. The blue ones to her left were still burned out, curling in the middle with a big black hole. Maynard hadn't had time to change them, not even when he loaded in and reset the rigging here at winter quarters.

She sat down on the ring curb, her legs tired and spent. She took the bottle in her hand. She felt so small here, a little girl standing on an empty stage for the first time.

She opened the bottle. She threw it back.

Booze brought a good sort of untethering. No vertigo, no headache, at least not right away. Just floating.

There was something ghostly and sacred about a place where performers play, the echoes of the things that have been here. Theatre was some of the strongest magic, conjuring tears and laughter, flying hundreds of strangers from their seats to another world far away to imagine together. Imagine the days that will hurt the most, imagine the best of all chances, and everything in between.

When it had come her turn to change the world, she believed she could do it with magic.

But so had he.

She felt her ripped shirt collar. A surge of fear and pain and guilt and grief rushed through the tense muscles in her neck.

She took another drink.

✳

After so much noise, the world was finally quiet. She closed her eyes, she swayed back and forth like she was underwater. There, in the dark, she pretended she was no one. She let go of all the kite strings she had wrapped around her fingers that led to all the hearts who loved her, who forced her to love them, who she genuinely loved. She was just Rin, no future or past, and only present and maybe not even that.

This didn't last long. She felt her body grow hot, reattaching to all the worries like they were lightning bolts hitting her all at once. She gave a small sob.

You were always pathetic, the low voice growled inside her rib cage, between her ears, high up into the roots of her hair. *If anyone came in here and saw how useless you really are . . .*

She let the voice envelop her, shake her deep, almost as deep as where she first felt time yield to her fingertips. Her whole body vibrated. She was no one but a stupid Sparkie who had been chewed up and spit out and now spent so much time trying to futilely smooth out her old sun-bleached creases. If they knew who she was, all the things she'd done, all the weight she carried in her shoulder blades . . . she wasn't any ringmaster. She was a fraud.

There was a soft flutter as someone walked through the vinyl entrance. Then there was Odette.

Odette stepped into the tent, her hair wild and without curlers. She was dressed in her favorite pink robe, with her feet stuffed into her big work boots, and looking as if she'd been woken up by a nightmare.

For anyone else, Rin would have stood up, pretended she was grounded and had a strong spine to keep her on her feet. But for Odette, Rin stayed on the floor. She didn't even hide the bottle between her knees, where she ran her thumbs along the mouth's edges.

Odette stopped in the dirt, not saying anything. Waiting. Rin didn't look up. She knew what sort of look she would see on Odette's face. Or maybe she didn't want to know. Was Odette angry, was she disappointed, was she hurt? Maybe Odette still thought Rin was fixable. There was no fixing Rin. But in her drink, her mind was calm, she could breathe, and she didn't need to count her heartbeats in her throat and behind her eyes.

If she let go of her body, if she pretended she was floating away—

Odette was sitting in front of her now, crouched down on her knees.

Odette took Rin's hand, the soft silk of the gloves on Rin's rough wrinkling skin. "Hey," Odette said. "Stop sinking. Look at me."

Rin forced her eyes to Odette's face, but her mind refused to focus. "He's going to kill you," Rin choked.

"He's trying to scare you," Odette said.

"It's my fault. He's gotten stronger," Rin said. "I know he has."

"And like you said, we know that because *we've* gotten stronger," Odette said.

"I can't . . . I can't let him touch the circus," Rin said. "He's going to kill you. I can't take him. I can't go back. I can't lose you. I can't, I can't—"

"Shh," Odette said, reaching out her hand. Rin jolted back.

He used to touch her. He used to make her think things. Odette could do the same. Rin didn't say anything. She just felt cold. She felt as if she sank back behind her skull and floated in something without eyes, something without time.

"Stay with me," Odette said. "Don't go away. Please, Rin."

Rin burst into tears. "He told me once I didn't have a heart," Rin said. She touched her own chest. There was bone there, there were ribs and she could feel the blood pulsing but . . . "I can't feel my heart. It's calcified. He turned it to stone. Or maybe it was stone to begin with."

"You have a heart," Odette said. "How can you even think that?"

Rin struggled to breathe. "I wanted to die. But if I died and he lived, then the world would be his. And I was given this stupid Spark, and I don't know why but . . . if I died, it would die, too, and then there's one less person to make it all better. But I'm so tired. I'm so fucking tired."

"Do you have anything else on you?" Odette said. Rin could see Odette eye Rin's jacket, looking for bulges. "Are you safe?"

Rin burst into tears. "You think I've got a heart, Odette. I don't. I don't." She pounded her chest, her fingers still wrapped around her bottle.

Odette pulled the bottle away. Then she laid her gloved hand on Rin's ripped shirt collar, right on the cold buttons down her front. Rin shivered. But she let her.

Odette said softly, "You have one of the biggest hearts I've ever had the honor to see."

"No. That's not true," Rin said.

"And it hurts that you can't see," Odette said.

"I'm just like him. We did all the terrible things together. The Circus King's circus was mine, too. *I gave him the idea, Odette. He made it because I wanted it.*"

Rin let herself cry. She didn't know how long. Odette sat with her. That's all. And Rin didn't want her to, Rin knew she'd hurt her deep with the bottle. But she didn't know how she would get through the next minute, or the next hour, or the next day or summer or decade without being able to breathe, drink in a silence, and pray it would last long enough for her to stop *hearing his fucking voice in hers.*

"Is this why you won't let me give you your youth back?" Odette said quietly.

Rin stared at the floor.

I deserve to die.

It was my fault, what he did. What we did.

"Where did you get the bottle?" Odette said.

"I hid it in a wagon," Rin muttered.

"Wait . . . what?"

There had once been a Spark that Rin heard of from a couple of towns over. Their Spark was unparalleled; able to communicate with people who had died. They claimed they could talk through the veil, find the essence of the deceased, and channel ghosts. Mauve had thought it was a bunch of hooey. Odette said it was possible but not probable. But Rin had believed it could be real.

"Rin, do you have any hidden anywhere else?" Odette said. "Rin, answer me."

She chickened out the night she and the girls were supposed to travel to see the Spark.

She told them it was because it was a waste of money.

But inside, in that place deep down that even Rin couldn't always rightly see, she knew the real reason. Because if it *was* real, then she would have to face her mother. And how would Rin ever be able to face her?

How do you say you're sorry when it's your fault she's dead?

When it will be your fault that Odette has died?

"Rin, you look at me right now. Look at me and focus."

She'll leave you, the voice hissed from inside her. *You are unwanted.*

The voice was so quiet when the circus was loud. When she wore her velvet coat, when they all called her Ringmaster, when she was swimming in the hurly-burly of the train tracks and the adventure and the magic . . . he wasn't even a dull throb.

But now in this night, she heard him, loud and clear from somewhere inside her. She knew it wasn't really him; that wasn't his Spark. It was something worse; it was a part of her.

If she had just seen him for what he was, if she'd not tangled her life with his, then no one would have gotten hurt.

She'll leave you, he said. *And I'll find you.*

"No," she mumbled to herself. "I'm still here. You don't get to win."

"What?" Odette said. But Rin's world spun.

Rin thought, *I can still change things. I'm still here, and if I'm going through the trouble of being here, I can still fix it.*

Odette screwed the cap back onto the bottle. She stood up and she walked to the trash bin at the entrance. Rin clamored to her feet.

"We tried to finish it by going to the very beginning." Rin stumbled over her words, so much that Odette looked back at her, past the point of anger and more worried than anything else. Rin tried to ignore it. "What if we went to the very end?"

"That makes no sense, Rin."

"No, no, how does the whole thing end?" Rin swayed backward, because the world was an ocean and the future and past were waves that lapped against her thighs, like when she was little and tried to stand straight in the shallow beaches of home. "I can . . . I can go to the end."

What did it even look like? She tried to pinpoint the thread that was the war, all the blood dripping from its golden twine, the screams and stench of death that vibrated around it. She saw it, leading somewhere to the other side of the earth. She couldn't be sure, Mauve wasn't there to navigate her. The end was so far away and yet it felt like she could reach out and choke it in her hands.

A siren sounded. Something red.

Why was everything red?

"Rin?" Odette said, walking toward her.

"I won't loop again, I promise," Rin slurred out.

"Loop again," Odette muttered, "Loop again?" she said louder, a realization clicking. "Rin, what do you mean again?"

Rin felt a dopey grin splash her hot face, and she stepped toward Odette, to reach out her hand and hold her, but Rin

38

THE RINGMASTER, 1945

landed on concrete.

She felt her body splayed out like a dead fish on the sidewalk. People around her gasped and shouted and screamed in surprise. She had just appeared on a sidewalk looking like death, a woman in trousers and a bright red coat smelling of booze. *Slick,* she thought.

She could hear people speaking to her in another language. She couldn't see straight. She crawled to the edge of the sidewalk and up onto a railing and looked over to see a river cutting through whatever city she'd landed in. She felt like she was going to vomit.

She looked around, her head swimming. Where the hell was she?

A city with a river that ran through it. Birds flew above her, singing. Some people behind her kept walking, while others shouted like they were hailing a carriage . . . or a cop. Or no, a soldier. A screaming automobile that was definitely not from 1926 screeched to a stop near her.

She looked at the crowd gathering, the language she heard, the buildings around them. She couldn't focus, because of the liquor, or the sudden jump, or both.

She shouldn't be here. She should go h—FLASH.

WHITE.

SILENT.

She saw the insides of the bodies around her, like an X-ray machine at a carnival.

The sun exploded, the world ended.

No birds. No voices. No anything.

Then a wave of sound and smoke and heat, like a ghost on fire pressing through her skin and vessels and bones and out the other side.

Rin's entire body burned and it felt unraveled like a frayed garment. Something was wrong. She couldn't see, she couldn't hear. Everything was on fire, like every nerve was raw, everything was exposed. She was slowly turning to ash.

It felt like she had swallowed a supernova.

The threads of her life slowly snapped, breaking away, flying into the dark holes of nowhere. She could feel it, like everything was pulling away from her. She was losing her life, and she reached out and grasped for just one string: the thread that led to Odette.

✳

39

THE RINGMASTER, 1926

Dying hurts, and then it doesn't. The first part of death is the body trying to stay alive, swimming against the current, flailing one last time. But then the pain, the loss, gets so great it's like sailing over a breaker wave, out beyond the reef. Eventually, the body stops fighting the end, and that's when it's not so bad. Less like screaming, more like falling asleep after a long day.

Rin had lived a lot. Rin had lived more than most people ever would. She'd seen so many films, she'd swum in the ocean, she'd stood in a spotlight, she'd sung songs and eaten foods all over the world. She had never died.

Her body now turned to the opposite of what she'd always known. Her lungs weren't working, even though she howled. Her eyes wouldn't work, although she could see blinding light. Everything was shutting down.

She didn't think about all the things she could have done or all the things she had left to do. She only thought one thing. *Odette.*

That's what saved her. That's how her Spark got her home.

She could barely feel that the air had changed around her. Her body fell over something: furniture? She couldn't see; there was a wetness from her eyes, but as what had felt like tears flowing suddenly gushed, she realized with numb horror that her eyes had melted. She screamed and screamed and couldn't hear anything. Someone wrapped her in their arms. She knew this because her body became pure agony every time their skin touched the raw nerves left on her bones, until it became so numb and she may have passed out.

She wondered if her mother would be there when she crossed over.

She should have been there for Odette. She should have held Odette for the rest of their lives and their lives should have been a lot better. They'd tried to make meaning out of shadows and they had been so close, *so close—*

But then it started to subside. Like a wave pulling out from the sand, or a terrible crushing pressure released. She was no longer dying. She could feel. She could think. She could hear her own voice, moaning and begging without lips, and then she could feel her lips return. Someone was re-creating her.

A light hit her brain through healed eyes, and she saw Odette. Rin realized they were in the caboose, and she was lying on the ground wrapped in Odette's arms, on her lap. Rin's skin was raw and red and rapidly clearing itself of wounds as the burns and scrapes and chunks of missing flesh slipped onto Odette instead. Odette's arm looked as if the sun itself had scraped her skin and kept driving. Pieces looked as if they were about to slip off, like a glove.

Rin tried to pull away. "No. You can't take this."

"Neither can you." Odette held her firm.

"I won't—"

"You've done your job," Odette said. "Now let me do mine, damn it!"

Odette gripped Rin's arm harder with her bare hand, and Rin watched Odette writhe. Like something beat against Odette, inside Odette's skin. Odette shot back, holding her own arm. Something choked her. Her eyes melted down her cheeks. Rin couldn't look away. Rin reached out to hold her, but she was radiating with heat, and Odette shoved herself back out of Rin's arms. "I'll have to heal you again!" she snapped as Rin ran to hold her. And then Odette screamed and screamed. It would be over soon, but this was a pain that would never fully leave. This was the closest Odette had ever come to death, and it was almost too much for her to hold in her Spark. Everything Rin had felt, Odette now took.

She wouldn't die, but she was dying. The pain without relief.

Rin wanted to take it back, stuff it back inside her. Her chest was tight, her heart ready to drop to the floor. The world felt like it stopped around them, the only thing that mattered was hearing Odette's ragged breathing.

Please no no no, Odette, please hold on—

And then it stopped. Odette's arms healed. Her eyes returned. Rin's arms were whole, her eyes back in her own head. But Rin's beautiful velvet coat was still torn. A big rip in the red. And Odette was sobbing. Rin's hands shook, trying to touch her now.

"Odette—"

"Don't you dare," Odette sobbed. "Don't you touch me." She finally burst into tears, curling into herself. This beautiful song of a person was cracking, hurting with the heat of something hotter than the core of the Earth. She should have healed by now, her skin was clear, her eyes were back. But not everything can be healed, can it?

When we hurt ourselves, we hurt those around us.

Rin somehow found her legs. The toxins were gone, and the caboose held a heavy sobriety. Rin reached for the pitcher of water and a glass, because that's all she could think to do. Odette swatted it away. The water splashed all over. Odette spun around and faced Rin.

"What the hell did you do?" she demanded.

"I . . . I went to the end—the end of the war," Rin said, her throat dry and her words cracked. "I was in a city with a river, and there was a flash of light, and then I was dying. Somehow I . . . I . . . what are we doing in the caboose?"

"When you get lost in the future, you follow the path back to the train," Odette said.

"I . . ." Rin said. "I followed the . . . the path back to you."

"Well, maybe you should do that more often!" Odette said desperately, the dam breaking completely at last. She held her stomach, heaving deep, deep breaths between sobs. Rin set the glass down. She offered her a handkerchief. Odette took it. "I don't know what the hell you've . . ." She trailed into no words, just tears.

Rin tried again, "Can I . . ." hold you, Rin wanted to say, but knew neither of them deserved that. "Can I help you to the bed?" she said instead.

"Fuck you," Odette shot. And she grabbed Rin hard and held her hard, as if Rin was going to slip again back beyond the veil and be gone for good. Rin pulled Odette even closer, and she held her head to her shoulder as Odette cried.

"I'm so sorry," Rin said quietly.

"You think this is a mitzvah!" Odette roared. "How is it good to hurt yourself? You literally were wasting away, dripping apart, and then there is no more you! No more Ringmaster, no more of *my wife*. No mitzvah would *ever* ask you to—"

The door swung open, as if someone kicked it. Mauve entered with a lantern. "What the hell is going on? Is he back?"

Odette and Rin said nothing. They just held each other. Rin looked up to Mauve, her eyes glassy and wide and sunken. It was like Mauve could see the reflection of what had happened in Rin's expression.

"Oh my God," she said. "No."

And then the door kicked in again. A scrawny scarecrow burst in, her eyes big and her hair wild like she'd just been roused to action. She had her hands out, ready to fight. She was a child. "Where is he? What happened? Who's screaming?" Jo said.

Rin felt all the color drain from her face. She knew Jo's eyes had found her, looking disheveled and panicked, her coat torn and blood everywhere.

"What are you doing in here?" Rin demanded. Her voice was anything other than the calm, all knowing teacher Jo knew. Jo stepped back, unsure of what to say. Jo's face was sheet white, like Rin was a ghost. She clenched her jaw and tightened her fists, like she was trying not to shake. This night wasn't Jo's to bear; she didn't have to be a part of this.

"She needs to leave." Ringmaster turned away. For some reason, that pissed Jo off.

"You can't go screaming into the night like y'all are dying and then tell me to leave. I showed you everything about me," Jo said, her fists balled up and angry. "I'm not leaving. You're not okay. None of you are okay."

"But, we're fine now, lovely." Odette stepped forward, but Jo pulled away.

"I know your Spark," Jo said. "I don't need you to calm me down or heal me. I don't want to be calm. I don't want to be healed. I want to know what happened."

Odette rested her hands on her bloody and pink robe, her face sinking in all corners. She sat on the bed, not looking at anything, not all there.

Rin tried to find the courage to turn back to face Jo. But she couldn't. Her shoulders hunched in that torn velvet coat, ruined, her lion hair giving her cover as she stared, haunted, out the back of the train car.

Mauve slammed the lantern down on a counter with the restraint of a fury that couldn't be completely let loose in front of a fifteen-year-old.

"It was the end of the war," Mauve said in a solid tone. "It was a flash bigger than anything blue, bigger than anything in the Great War. It was a nightmare."

"Was it one of us?" Rin asked quietly. Jo still hadn't left. *Please leave, Jo.*

"No," Mauve said. "It wasn't a Spark. It was man-made from a laboratory or a . . . a desert practice field. A bomb."

"That was no bomb," Rin said.

"It was," Mauve said.

"They are so afraid of us," Odette whispered. "And this whole time, they're more than capable of being the monsters."

Rin saw Odette in the moonlight, unscarred, her perfectly smooth skin glistening without a scratch. But the pain was still in her eyes. Rin didn't know if it would ever go away.

"They dropped it on a city in Japan," Mauve said. "They knew what they were doing. It was planned."

"Who would do that on purpose?" Odette said, barely audible. So small, so beaten. Rin was going to vomit. The smell of flesh burning was still in this room. She could taste it. "Oh my God. . . ."

"What the hell is going on," Jo said, but the way she said it sounded like she didn't want to actually know. Rin couldn't look at her.

"We should tell people now," Mauve said softly to Ringmaster. "You said when the time came . . . when we knew we couldn't . . . that we would tell them all. And Jo is here, and Jo should know. Then we'll tell everyone else."

Ringmaster winced, and she touched her healed arm. "All right," she said quietly. But the agreement wasn't as small as two words; something had shifted in Rin's life. She'd failed them all.

She slowly turned around. She saw this little girl looking up at her like Rin could hold all the weight in the world for her. And Rin wished more than anything she could.

"We can't stop the war," Rin said.

"I know," Jo said. "But it's okay. It's over. It's like you said, Ringmaster, we're making sure people are better and smarter and see the good in . . . Ringmaster?"

"No." Rin sagged. Jo wasn't stupid, she could, of course, hear these sharp, jagged tears cutting her voice. "We can't stop the *next* war."

Jo didn't say anything.

"I can see the future, I look ahead to where we're going," Mauve said. "And usually, Ringmaster takes us there. Odette keeps us safe. And tonight, Rin . . . she went to somewhere and sometime very far away. She saw the future is full of ash."

Jo still didn't say anything. Rin watched Jo's face as her brow wrinkled. Rin tensed. The three of them, hopping around and trying to change things, grant wishes, make people better and heal and . . . it didn't matter.

Ringmaster picked at the window's wooden frame, paint flecking off in her hands. There was no bracelet on her thick wrist. She'd not put it on. There hadn't been time. It had been a drunken mistake, Rin's mistake, and Odette had gotten hurt. Rin had chosen to pick up that bottle, had pretended she might find relief where she knew only pain waited. Rin was hurting Odette, hurting them all, with her incessant need to keep picking at the wound of the future.

"Ringmaster?" Jo finally said weakly. Her voice was so young, so little.

"I'm sorry," the Ringmaster said quietly. But that wasn't enough. "What happened when you were a kid, Jo," she continued, "it wasn't the war to end all wars. It was a prologue. We're sitting in the eye of the storm."

Jo finally said, "What year is this?"

"The flash cloud?" Mauve said. "I think around twenty years from now. But people start disappearing in eleven years. There are so many who disappear . . . who are eradicated from the Earth . . . before the cloud." Mauve looked up into the air, reading the stars no one but her could see.

"In three years, the country will collapse," Mauve said. "Everything we own, everything we know, it's going to crumble. Then everything you see outside, dust will cover it all. Big dust storms taking over all the crops. People will starve. In eleven years, many people will disappear, and even more than that will be murdered. There's fighting everywhere, so many countries, people running away in France, and marching on muddy roads in the Philippines, and . . . " Mauve said. "And they will recruit us for this war."

What was the point of moving forward if they knew all this was coming? No, no, Rin could not think like that.

"Us?" Jo said.

"Not tonight," Rin stopped Mauve. "Jo, please go."

"I'm not going," Jo said.

"You are shaking and you look sick," Rin said. "I will take care of it, go."

"I'm not fucking going," Jo said. "I'm a part of this circus. It's my future, too. What do you mean they recruit us, Mauve?"

Mauve looked to Jo, and then to Rin. "The Prince Act," she said. "Our armistice with the not-Sparks. It's because the Act says we'll come to their aid if they need it. We're going to be drafted." Mauve's eyes now darted to Odette and Jo and Rin like they were all already in a trench and filling up with gas. "We'll all go to war."

The words were like a fever breaking, a cold chill and gush of sweat, a final understanding, a conclusive decree. Something Rin had not fixed.

Their future was still death.

They would see war. The families in their crowds would see war, Sparks and non-Sparks. The whole circus would be in uniform. The bodies she saw both in the bleachers and in the rings would be drafted and sent places where they would turn red and raw and slip from their bones. Or no, that's wrong. Those who saw what Rin just saw? Who would feel like she and Odette just felt? They wouldn't be soldiers. They'd be children and women and all the people in their homes who got thrown into blue lights and black trucks, and those who survived longer would die of bombings on London and exploding stars in Japan and . . .

To be buried in a trench ten years ago seemed like a courtesy.

"So what are we gonna do?" Jo demanded.

The Ringmaster fixed the tails of her torn coat. She cleared her throat. She turned around, slowly bracing herself to look like the woman Jo saw in the center ring each night: strong, stalwart, able to carry anything.

But now Rin knew that Jo saw that the Ringmaster didn't really exist. It was another part of the show.

"We keep on with the circus," Ringmaster said. Odette looked at her, incredulous. Surprised? Something softened.

Odette nodded. "We'll prepare from this end and do what we can for who we can. But we've put in years, we . . . you can't go to the future again."

"But the cloud! The ash!" Jo said. "You're just going to give up?!"

"No," Ringmaster shot back. "No, I am not going to give up. None of us are. It can feel like we're hanging by a thread, but every day we can make choices to be kind, to influence from where we are and with what we have to offer. We can't stop the cloud, but here at the circus, we can combat it in the small ways. And the small choices are the—"

"That's horseshit!" Jo flew forward. "It's a fucking circus! The end of the world is coming, and you're telling me some random Tom, Dick, and Harrys in Denver seeing butterflies and a clown is going to do *anything*?!"

"Josephine, stop," Odette said. "You don't know what you're talking about."

But Jo plowed on, "We need to be out there, fighting! Call the president! Call the queen or the . . . the fucking pope, I don't know!"

"That won't do anything," Mauve muttered. Like she knew. Just like she knew they couldn't save Bernard. "We travel through the whole story. Sometimes, we've tried to shift the big things, and worse things happen. You succeed in killing a man high in the ranks of one of the armies, and a worse man takes his place. The gun won't stop shooting, it just maybe shoots somewhere else, or they find another gun. It's an unstoppable force. Butterflies are easier to move than tanks."

"It's not our place to change the entire course of the river," Odette whispered.

"But it *is* your job to fix things, if you have the ability to do it," Jo retorted.

The whole train felt stuck. It sat dead on the tracks like a normal train. There was no magic here. Ringmaster's face was stone.

"Please," the Ringmaster said, "please Jo, we need to sleep. We'll talk about this in the morning."

Jo had hot tears behind her eyes. "I'm not going to let you give up."

"Then trust me and do what I say!" Ringmaster barked.

That was enough. Jo looked like a charge of electricity shot up her neck, into her heart, her shoulders tensed.

"If we're drafted," Jo said, stolid, "who dies?"

Mauve was quiet. Too quiet.

They all would lose someone.

"But Charles doesn't die," Jo said. "Charles can't die."

But Mauve didn't say anything.

Brothers. Fathers. Sisters. Mothers. They'd all been lost before, they could be lost again.

"Mauve, Charles is safe, right?"

Mauve was still silent. Finally, she said, "The boy can be set on fire, but he can't eat fire. He can't go into battle thinking he's immortal. Everyone's thread ends someday, Jo. Even Odette's. Even Charles's."

"She doesn't need to hear that," Odette said.

"I'm sorry," Mauve said. "We said we'd give them a warning."

"So he dies?" Jo said. "From what, a disease? How can he? He didn't get the flu."

"Then he lucked out," Mauve said. "Out on a farm is safer than in the city during a plague."

"You seem to know a hell of a lot about Charles's mortality," Jo said. "So he dies, doesn't he?"

Mauve didn't say anything. Which sometimes can be the loudest yes of all.

"But it's okay, because you all try to change the future," Jo said. "You do it every day. We can change the future!"

"Jo," the Ringmaster said, "you're not listening."

But Jo ran.

Jo burst out the caboose door.

Without thinking, Rin ran after her.

She followed her between the cars, out into the dirt field, past the tent, until there was only swampy grass and stars above.

"Don't go any further," Rin warned her, her knees aching. She held her chest as Jo came to a stop. "There's gators and G-d knows what else."

The eye of the storm, Ringmaster had said.

Jo closed her eyes, trying to see the future; maybe *she* could see something . . . but nothing seemed to come, and Jo gave out a scream. Rin saw the images of Odette's eyes rolling down her cheeks, back in her own skull.

And something churned up from Jo, a black smoke illuminated by a hateful, painful blue lightning. She let it out of her body like her scream, loud and unbridled and painful.

"*Jo, stop!*" Rin said, but her words were swept away by the very real wind that had manifested with the image Jo was unleashing, a large beast erupting from the air, something made of shadows and fractured glass and twisted trees.

Jo's face looked too much like the monsters in her illusion.

But the Ringmaster didn't freeze. She pushed forward and through the false image and grabbed Jo around the shoulders, holding her tight.

Rin wished to no longer be here. She wished Jo would come with her. She wished Jo didn't have this monster inside of her, didn't feel like she needed to become a monster to survive.

She breathed in. She breathed out. Rin's Spark cracked the world like a sharp whip, spreading out like warm, solid ground as their heads tried to stop spinning. The world would end, and she couldn't even think about what that would mean. Right now, she held this little girl in her strong arms and her embrace.

Then there was silence except for Jo's sobbing and Rin's breathing and sniffling.

Florida had gone still, which was not like Florida. There were no sounds of the night, no trees moving, no winds, nothing.

All was still. Everything around them was frozen, completely frozen. She'd frozen time.

So Rin had been right . . . in the Chandelier . . . something was growing, changing in her.

There was still something left of her *to* change.

Jo was in her arms, shaking as they took in a world that looked like statues in Medusa's garden. Jo wheezed, her sweat-drenched hair flipping as she craned to look at the tableau around them. Rin just held on tighter.

She would not let go.

Jo dug her nails into Rin's coat. And Rin buried Jo's head in her shoulder. Jo sobbed, small high-pitched cries like a lost cub. Rin rubbed Jo's arms, hugging her closer.

"Come on," Rin said. "Let's get out of here."

✳

40

EDWARD, 1917

Edward watched Ruth pack her things in a rucksack. The last thing she put in was a necklace from her mother. His heart sank. He knew where she was going. Why she was going.

She opened the door to their train car to . . .

"Stop," he said.

She had to stop, because he'd said so.

"You love me," he said.

She said nothing. She stood in the door, staring at the steel steps leading to the ground. Something was battling inside her.

He just had to keep talking.

"You can't throw away everything we have," he said. "We're going to take on the world, you and me."

"Stop." She stared him down, her big black eyes locking in and daring him. Good, she was looking at him.

He said quietly. "You love me."

"Yes," she gasped.

"You don't want to leave," he said.

"I don't want to leave," she cried.

But something trembled in her words.

Let her tremble. Soon, she would remember how much they had between them. So he coaxed her to their bed, and they quietly wrapped into each other.

"I forgive you," he said.

"I'm sorry," she said.

"Your nerves are getting worse," he said. "You have got to calm down."

"I know," she said. She held him closer. The rucksack was forgotten.

Until he woke the next morning, and he saw the rucksack was still there. But she was gone.

Traitor.

He shot out of bed. He angrily grabbed that rucksack, held it in his hand like he was choking it. His bare feet hit the wood floor, then the steel stairs, then the soft mud. He shoved his body down the midway, screaming, "*Tell me where she went!*" to anyone who could hear. And the whole circus, like ghosts, pointed the way, lighting his hunting path.

When he caught up with her, when he was done with her, she would understand what her role was.

He had tried to trust her. He had tried to be kind to her. He had *tried* to do it the way he had been told to, playing the game by the rules, but the rules were nothing but a leash around his neck. He was no ordinary man, he was a man with the world on the tip of his tongue.

They were bound, Edward and Ruth, destined. If it took his Spark to show her that, then so be it.

So be it.

He always got what he wanted. He would not settle for anything less, because he was not a small man.

The world would burn between his lips. He would raze it to the ground and she would be his. He would tie her to his waist like she was his own shadow. He would take her wings and break them until her flight was nothing but a memory.

No woman would ever dare break his heart again.

No man would ever send him to another trench.

He was unbridled, running through the town, gaining on her.

So be it. This is who he was? So be it. He threw the rucksack on the ground. He came down hard on it with his heel, like he could grind it into dust. She had vanished. So he charged forward; all her favorite things would also be lost forever.

But even under that rage, a small flicker of hope licked the insides of his ribs. If he could find her, if he could love her, maybe he could be human again.

Maybe this could still be a happy ending for them.

✳

41

THE RINGMASTER, 1926

Rin remembered a Yom Kippur from when she was very small, when instead of fasting, her mother had eaten lunch while the rest of the congregation waited to break fast at dinner. Rin didn't think this was fair, because Rin was fasting and so was everyone else. Instead of being embarrassed or telling her to hush up during service, her mother explained.

"When I was younger," she said, "I would starve myself so I could be thinner, so I could feel beautiful. I got very sick. I almost wasn't able to carry you. So when it comes to Yom Kippur, I don't fast."

"And that's okay?" Rin said.

"G-d will never ask us to hurt ourselves," her mother said. "To hurt ourselves is not a mitzvah."

"What's a mitzvah?" Rin had asked. And so her mother had told her that night, over their fast breaking, as Rin shoved challah and donuts into her mouth ravenously.

"A mitzvah is the work we are responsible for, as long as we are part of the living world," her mother said. "We are here to bring light to the dark. And it's not a charity, and it's not a special congratulations. It's just the right thing to do."

Then the Spark came.

Now, she stood beside Mauve and Odette, facing their entire circus company at the cookhouse. Everyone sat on those long benches, looking up to the three women with absolute silence. The sort of silence where people waited for more instructions, because they didn't know what to do next. Rin listened, tired, hopeless, useless, as Mauve explained what the future would look like.

Odette's neck looked strained, like she was trying not to breathe too heavily.

Rin couldn't feel her own hands. But the three of them stood sentinel like statues at the foot of Pompeii.

"Well," Mr. Weathers said. "That's a lot."

"But," Kell said, "it's a long time away. We have time on our side."

Mr. Weathers looked tired. But Kell was young, and he had to contend with this, didn't he?

Agnes sniffed, then cracked her back. "We got into all of this together, didn't we?" Agnes said. "If they're gonna try to scatter us to the whims o' war, we go into it together."

Maynard, just one lone Maynard, nodded, his arms crossed and his body slouched with his left leg over the other. He stared at the grass in the middle of the circle.

"We go in together," Ming-Huá said, her words steady, "we go out together."

Rin looked to Jo, who held her brother's hand so very tight. Mrs. Davidson sat shaking, Mr. Davidson beside her with a sallow face. Bernard not here at all.

"Ringmaster, are you alright?" Maynard asked suddenly.

Rin forced the mask into place, over all the dark circles and headaches and tears she'd allowed herself. The Ringmaster stood straight and nodded. "I am," she said. "I'm thinking through logistics. I want to make sure each of you know you don't have to do this."

"We'll take care of you financially," Mauve said. "We have enough savings."

"Right," Rin said. "So there's no pressure to—"

"It's not about that," Boom Boom grunted.

Rin wasn't sure what that meant, but it seemed everyone was hell-bent on going forward. And she needed to be ready to protect them.

"And even if you stay," Rin said, "the Circus King—"

"This ain't about the Circus King," Agnes said. "This isn't his circus. This isn't his story. We keep going. Am I right, fellas?"

"We worked too hard for him to dictate where we go and what we do," Kell said. "And there are people who need us out there."

Ford nodded. Wally, Jess, and Tina all muttered an agreement. And Maynard cleared his throat.

"So." He leaned forward. "I think we're all waiting to hear the Ringmaster, the Trapeze Swinger, and the Nightingale tell us where we go next."

✳

Colorado.

Odette, Mauve, and Ringmaster decided it was time to get back to work. They gave the circus one last warning, and no one but a couple of ballet dancers and Paulie McKinley resigned. Paulie packed his things, and he said on his last day, "I feel like I should apologize, but I can't. I'm not a coward. I just know what I'm not willing to go back to if we get caught by him."

War was enough on its own. The Circus King was enough on his own. The two looming would be enough for anyone to hightail it. So Rin stood in the entrance of the dressing tent as he put the last lock on his trunk. She nodded, understanding.

"It's been a pleasure working with you," Paulie said. "Really, if you ever find yourself out East, let me know."

They embraced one last time. Then Paulie and his trunk were gone.

✳

They would do a soft open in Estes Park, Colorado. It was a safe haven, more fortified than Missouri Valley. While Mo Valley had been inconspicuous, Estes's valley was high up in the mountains and not easily accessible by anyone who couldn't jump a train to anywhere in the world. The people of Estes were always grateful to have them, because they never got circuses that far up in the mountains. For the most part, they were friendly to Sparks, especially Sparks who brought them cotton candy and cheeseburgers.

They packed everything up at winter quarters. Maynard practiced his sharpshooting with pleasure. Rin had given him another raise for another job. Rin had approached him with her rifle (she'd found a pistol for herself) and said, "You wanna kill a vermin?"

Maynard had looked a little too gleeful about his new post. He bought a couple more weapons. He plotted where the parts of him would stand along the perimeter of the circus, keeping a watchful eye out for *him*.

It wasn't a foolproof plan; there were ways the Circus King could still nab them. There were ways he could bring in a mole. But it was something. Between the mountains and Maynard, maybe they would be okay.

Rin jumped the train from Florida to Colorado later that evening, as the sun went down on the palm trees and then went down over the crest of Longs Peak.

✳

She got up early. There were gels to fix. There was rehearsal to schedule. She sat at her desk, scribbling through agendas and making call lists for the next week. She compiled all the billings, all the dates they'd reserved, reworked the tour track, reworked all the different tracks of each of the performers. She grabbed the needed gels, some gloves, a screwdriver and a wrench, threw it all in a utility belt around her hips, and transported herself up to the scaffolding in the newly raised tent.

When the cookhouse opened, she transported to the line, picked up all of Odette's favorites, and jumped to the caboose with the flapjacks in hand. Odette was in her silk robe, sitting on the bed, looking out the window. She jumped. Rin handed her the food.

"Make sure to take a bath," Rin gently reminded her.

"What are you doing?" Odette said.

Rin handed her the new rehearsal schedule. "We have a lot of work to do if we're going to reopen this week."

Odette looked at the paper. "We don't have a lot of time at night. How will we—"

"We aren't," Rin said. "Not right now."

She kissed Odette on the forehead. Odette looked to the rehearsal schedule. Her eyebrow raised. "It's a half day," Odette said.

"So we can stay sharp, but . . ." Rin said. "But I thought maybe we could have some time tonight. I didn't get back in time when I went out with Jo that day of her first rehearsal."

"Oh, Rin, that was a while ago."

"And you didn't hold it against me," Rin said. "So . . . if you want to spend the day sleeping, please sleep. I'll close the curtains for you. You want to go to the lake, alone or with someone, I . . ."

Odette put her hand on Rin's clenched fist. Rin hesitated. And Odette slowly pulled Rin's fingers apart, massaging her palm to relax.

"Sit with me," she said.

*

Day ran its course outside their window. Evening somersaulted into a late night full of cicadas and fireflies. Then the dawn returned.

Odette and Rin sat on the bed, their backs to the wall, their knees against their chests and their arms wrapped around their own legs, two little girls paired like a painting, sitting silent in the dark that feels so thick, right before the sun peeks through. They'd stayed up all night.

"The way you can pull berries off the bushes when you take a walk in the country, just pop them in your mouth," Odette said softly.

Rin stared at the wall ahead. She tried to think of something, something worth moving forward to see, to hear, to touch. Something that wasn't a smoke cloud, that made this all worth it. Finally, she offered, "Music."

"More specific," Odette instructed.

"I like violins," Rin mumbled.

"Me, too," Odette said. "How about talkies? They're in a few years. We like talkies."

"Yeah," Rin said. "Talkies are something to look forward to." The sentiment felt like a deflated balloon. "I'm sorry," she said quietly.

She expected Odette to sit for a minute, say nothing, and then whisper something very meaningful. She was so good at that. Rin would say something, throwing out her jumbled thoughts onto the table and say *I have no idea in hell how to make sense of this.* And then like a master puzzle constructor, Odette would put her finger up to her mouth, cock her head, look at it from an angle Rin couldn't see, and then in a record-breaking instant, she'd put all the pieces together and say *Here.*

But tonight, Odette let out a small sob. It sounded like she was coughing out a gasp of tears. And then she put her head down on her knees and cried. She was the most beautiful thing in the world, the most brilliant human who could say the world was worth continuing and fighting for if they could pick berries off bushes, and she was crying into her lap with no answers.

Rin let go of her own hands clasped around her knees. She scooted closer. She took Odette by the shoulders with a "shhh," and laid her on her lap. "You're okay," Rin said. "It's over. You're okay. You're okay."

Odette kept crying. Rin stroked her soft blond hair from her cheek, tucking it behind her round pink ears. She kept pulling it back, kept touching her cheek, trying to collect all the tears and take them from her.

But Rin had already hurt her. Rin remembered the burns sifting from her own skin and grafting onto Odette's, slipping between them like a plague, like a disease.

Once, the Circus King had said, *You leave a trail of blood behind you, expecting me to pick it all up for you.*

She was like toxic fumes, curling inside Odette, just like the Circus King had done to so many, had done to Rin.

No, Rin said. *Stop it. Not now. Not him, not here. Not you, not this. Hold her. Love her.*

Odette grabbed Rin's legs and held her as she buried her face in Rin. Rin felt her stomach jump in her throat. There was no way to take the burns away from Odette's memory. G-d, she'd suck it all back into her own body if it meant Odette could smile right now.

"Why did you have the bottle hidden?" Odette suddenly asked.

Rin swallowed. The bottle seemed so small compared to the end of the world, but Odette said it as if they were one and the same. "You know why," Rin said. "And I'm sorry."

When we hurt ourselves, we hurt those around us.

Odette sat up and looked at Rin hard. "For someone who thinks a lot about erasing herself," she said, "you sure don't realize the reality of your death."

"I don't think that's fair," Rin said. "It's a dark place when I feel like that. It doesn't make any sense, you—"

"You always talk about everyone else we saw that night the blue light killed them, in the future, in the war. But you never talk about yourself."

"I wasn't there," Rin said.

"You weren't," Odette said. "And you never wondered why everyone was surprised to see you?"

Rin felt frozen in place. She felt sick. No, she hadn't. But Odette had. Odette had held on to that for weeks.

"No one was surprised to see me," Odette said. "You don't make it to the war, Rin. And I do. So I don't just see the end of the world. For me? My world ends much earlier."

Rin looked to Odette. With Odette, there had been nothing but love, love that grounded Rin's bones and filled her with warmth. And now there was this sadness all over Odette, and Odette let it hang between them, that Rin would die before her.

The sun eventually filtered into the room through the small holes in their cloth curtains. Rin watched the small spots move like fireflies from the wall to the chest of drawers to the ground as the dawn bloomed. Neither of them moved.

Odette held her close. Rin let her. Rin wrapped her own arms around Odette. They lay in bed, pulling their orbits together, trying to hold each other for the rest of time. They'd done more improbable things together, hadn't they?

Decades between them, a thousand performances of the small trapeze swinger flying above a Ringmaster in red, wedding dresses and flower crowns . . . these powerful things cut through her ghosts.

"Us," Rin said.

"What?" Odette said.

"Something good in this world," Rin said. "Us."

42

THE RINGMASTER, 1926

The valley of Estes Park was magic on earth. Of all the places and times Rin had visited, this was her favorite. After washing her face in the basin, she quietly stepped out onto the caboose's vestibule and sat on her small iron seat. The sun's show was beginning.

Estes Park was a sleepy village in a valley with a rocky river cutting through its green hills, dotted with the orange glow of the cozy windows of cabins and shops, surrounded on all sides by large gray and green mountains. The new day rose like a curtain behind their black silhouettes, then slowly the light cascaded down the faces of the western peaks, transforming from dark to purple, pink, orange, yellow.

The colors reminded her of Jo's Spark.

She remembered the first time she saw this place. She'd been a child. She'd heard of misty mountains, solid gray titans standing sentinel. She'd seen them in illustrations of kingdoms that did not exist and never would. Snow caps froze on rock in the deep heat of summer. Peaks that pierced and played along untouchable clouds.

She had not believed such beauty existed with no chains. But here it was, and it asked nothing in return.

The sound of a shofar *roooo*ed out from a large antlered elk below, and she watched it hoof the ground as if it was the spirit of this place. The world was bigger than she had understood then. Everything was grander than her life, or any one being's life. So whatever happened on this planet, there were still the colors on those mountains every morning, without fail.

She stepped gingerly off the vestibule into the dirt. Small pebbles crunched beneath her boots as she walked down the side of the train. A few cars down, a girl stood dumbfounded on her own vestibule of the LQ, looking out at the landscape. Rin looked up to her, stuffing her hands deep in her pockets and nodding out to the mountains.

"Pretty, huh?" she said.

"Yeah," Jo said in awe behind her. Then, "Heeyyyy," she rumbled. "Don't you start that, I'm still angry at you!"

"Oho," Ringmaster said. "Well, we reopen in about four hours, so we should chat about that."

"Oho to you!" Jo retorted. "We're heading toward the end of times and you're worried about tonight's circus?"

"The show must go on," Ringmaster said. "We have years until the war, Jo. But we have hours until Bruce Sikora comes to our tent and needs to see something beautiful."

"I don't care if it's years!" Jo said. "It's my brother."

"I know," Rin said. "I know it is. But you have to keep control of your Spark and we need to—"

"I have my Spark under control!"

"You didn't back in Florida, when we told you," Rin said. "You allowed your emotions to take your Spark, and it was engulfing you. You can't be out of control of your catharsis, Jo. It might feel good at the time, but it'll swallow you up."

"Okay, well, *catharsis* doesn't help protect anyone from anything. I don't give a shit about whatever catharsis is!"

"Catharsis is what we do here in the circus, Jo," Ringmaster said, trying to stay sturdy and steady like a tree with deep roots that Jo could lean on to find her balance. But she heard her voice tremble now. Because in her gut, Ringmaster was afraid. Not *of* Jo, but *for* Jo. "It's all the human connections we make with an audience *and ourselves* when we create something. We hold it, then feel it, then let it go and do better. It's taking a bunch of smoking kindle and igniting it into a fire so we—"

"This is the last thing on Earth I should worry about when there's an unhinged whozits chasing after us and we're running headfirst into another war."

Ringmaster felt the outline of her teeth with her tongue. "Catharsis can do damage and it can heal," she tried, but Jo wasn't done.

"You left Missouri Valley in the hands of the Circus King after he just killed someone," Jo said. "You told everyone in the circus about what's happening but what about everyone else? And what are we doing to save them, to save Charles? We can't give up!"

Rin felt less like a graying lion in that moment and more like the lost, charred, dying body in the train car late at night. The façade was gone and instead stood an old woman.

"You are not the first child," Rin said, "to think you can fix the shadows of dark places. But sometimes shadows swallow children." Rin slowly fixed her sleeves. They didn't need fixing. But she did it anyway. "We have a Spark, but we . . ." She opened her mouth to speak, but she couldn't finish. There was a grief to come, and it felt so heavy.

"You lost yourself in Florida," Rin said. "Through everything life is gonna throw at you, if you lose yourself, you're never going to find your way back."

"Well, if I'm such a loose cannon and everyone is gonna die and the world's ending in big sun explosions, maybe getting lost isn't the worst thing!"

Ringmaster stared at her for a moment. But Jo didn't move. Jo didn't break away.

"Is that what you really think?" Rin said.

Jo's lip trembled.

So Rin put her own hand on Jo's shoulder. "It's okay to be scared," Rin said. "I'm scared, too."

Jo turned away. But she let Rin pull her into a hug.

"Hey." Rin rubbed her back. "Look out there, kiddo. See the Rockies? These mountains have been here for millions of years. Nothing we do is going to take them away. And I take solace in that." She held Jo tighter. "And no matter what happens, we were here. We exist. *No one* can change that."

Jo watched them, still pressed into Rin's torn-up coat. She sniffed, her glassy eyes watching the dawn paint the faces of snowy giants.

How did snow exist in the land of green trees and warm winds? How did the trees stop growing after a certain point? How could the land reach higher than anything else, defying life? Defying rules?

Rin supposed this is what Sparks were; mountains too magical for the mortal realm; solitary, feared, and yet the most powerful beauty. The hope there was more to this life than she'd planned. And maybe, if they kept that standing strong, they could survive, too.

"You see that one little hill right there?" Rin said. "That one, it's got a whole flock of raccoons on the top of it. And chipmunks. You can climb all the way up there, you gotta take some peanuts. There was an old woman who used to work up there taking care of the animals and she made the best hot chocolate."

"It's your Marceline," Jo said. And Rin was caught by that. Jo crossed her arms and surveyed the mountains. "Who showed you this place?"

Rin looked to Jo, and then back to the mountains. "My mother," she said quietly. "We came here once, right when I got my Spark. I used to have all these places I wanted to see, explore the world. So she held on tight, told me to choose one of the postcards I'd collected, and I jumped us here." It was one of the last times they'd spent together.

Jo pulled away, but stood beside Rin. "I didn't know you had a ma. I mean, everyone has a ma. But you just seem like you've been perpetually old."

Rin laughed. "My mother and I stayed at that little white hotel over there, at the edge of the village in the valley? The one that's all lit up."

"Oo, fancy."

Rin elbowed her. "Yes, fancy. I wore a dress and everything. We all gussied up, listened to brilliant virtuosos in the concert hall, climbed the mountains, steered clear of the elk." She smiled warmly. "It was a good string of days. We went hiking, sometimes straight up a cliffside in the canyon. Then at night, we sat out on the front porch of the hotel and pointed up at the way the mountains burst out of the clouds after a rainstorm."

"She knew about your Spark, and she loved you anyway," Jo said.

"Yes," Rin said. "She . . . was a Spark, too. And everyone still loved her."

There was a beat. A bleat from the elk. Way over on the horizon, the hotel. A small connector between the Ringmaster's past and the Ringmaster's present. Some places were just magic like that.

"There's this thing we believe in called teshuvah," Rin said. "It's a sort of repentance, or a redemption. But teshuvah literally means 'to return.' To go home. My mother always said . . . it's not about who you are becoming, but returning to who you once were."

"Who we once were?" Jo said dubiously, with a crinkle of her nose. "What about growing? What about learning? We're supposed to get smarter and better, aren't we?"

"Well, yes," Rin said. "But I *understood* it to mean that . . ." She paused. "Teshuvah means that the person we truly were all along, they were enough. We get tangled along the way, we make mistakes, but we never need to run from ourselves. We just need to remember who we are."

She let the thought hang in the air, and it caused discomfort. She wanted to pull those words back into her mouth, swallow them down, berate herself for sharing so much with someone who needed her to be a pillar. But she didn't. She let her words hang there.

"Not lose yourself," Jo said quietly.

"Exactly," Rin nodded, then gave a chortle. "She does listen sometimes."

Jo let a small smile escape. Rin pulled her in again, patting her arm with her warm hand.

The mountains are safe, Jo, she thought. *They'll always be here. Even after all the wars have ended and everyone is forgotten, there will still be mountains.*

"I'm not giving up," Ringmaster said out loud. "*We* haven't given up. We're going to set everything right."

"Will you let me help, or am I too much of a loose firecracker?" Jo asked.

Ringmaster breathed, and Jo could probably feel her heart pound in her chest.

"I can help," Jo said, breaking away, looking straight at her. "I can. Please, trust me to help."

Rin slowly nodded.

"I trust you," Rin said. "Of course you can help."

Jo nodded vigorously. "Thank you, thank you," she said.

"Let's start small. I'll trust you to take over the illusions at night," Rin said. "I'll give you the person in need that we're targeting, this Sikora fella, and you start working on your skills of deciding what will help someone the most. Yes? More independence?"

Jo nodded again. And then she jumped sideways and gave Rin a gigantic final attack of a hug. "Thank you, thank you! So does this mean that I get to zip through time, too?"

"We're not touching that," Rin said. "You have your hands full with the circus."

The veneer of the lioness had settled across Ringmaster's face again. She took her stance of a teacher. "Now," Ringmaster said, pushing Jo back and looking her in the eye, like checking her face for dirt before school pictures. "Did you eat breakfast?"

"Yes."

"Liar," Ringmaster said. "Go back to camp and get your porridge. Check in with Mauve. I already did earlier, but you go ahead and tell her how this could work from now on. Tell her we talked and I think it's a good idea. Get her opinion and what she's got on Sikora. And eat your damn breakfast!" She playfully swatted Jo's shoulder.

"Okay, Mother." Jo laughed as she jumped back up the incline of their little path.

Rin was hit between the eyes with that laugh, those words. She watched Jo disappear back to camp. They were fragile, even with their Sparks. Two girls who had been beaten and left behind, and they'd both found a seat on the hill watching mountains.

In trying to conquer Rin, the Circus King had made one mistake: he never took her memory away. So her bones were still made of mountains and mothers and the joy of sharing sunrises and sunsets with family. She was bruised, she was cracked around the edges, but she was not broken.

And neither was her circus.

43

THE RINGMASTER, 1926

The sun was low in the sky when Rin finally returned from a long hike. Her body ached, but fresh crisp mountain air rejuvenated her like some sort of mikvah.

The circus sparkled with red and blue and green and yellow. The midway with its brilliant lights, like a starry sky coming to life with rainbows; a fairy glow in the valley against the orange lights of the village beside it. Two hours until curtain, they ate dinner together in the cookhouse. The jittering feeling of an opening night after a long hiatus made this place buzz with energy like an electric bulb. The Big Top was going live again, even after everything.

"It's been a summer," Mauve said, looking around the cookhouse as she and Rin and Odette took a seat on one of the benches with their grub. She rubbed her face, tired. "I hope he would be proud of us. We're still here, after all."

After dinner, the three ladies made their way to the dressing tents with the rest of the company. Rin leaned over her vanity, trying to put on the little bit of makeup over her freckles. Everyone had to wear makeup under those lights, or else they'd all look like ghosts. Rin included, even though it made her feel like a turkey with lipstick on.

"Rin?" Odette said behind her.

Rin turned around. Odette stood there, beside Mauve, against the backdrop of the dressing tent and surrounded by their trunks sitting heavily on the grass under their bare feet. They held up something between them, their four hands clasping a gift: her velvet coat, cleaned and stitched and with a couple of patches, but still her coat.

Rin audibly gasped. "What, how—"

"You've never done a show without it," Mauve said. "Now put it on."

The patches of fabric were from Odette's long silk robe and Mauve's purple shawl. They stood out against the red in a beautiful hodgepodge of stitches. Rin could tell Mauve had chosen purple thread, Odette had chosen red. Their hands had put this together for her.

She felt her lip tremble. "I . . . thank you."

Then it was showtime.

Rin settled into her jacket, her hat, her smile. It was going to be a good show, she could feel it. Mr. Calliope's music struck an opening fortissimo. The spotlights clacked on.

Ringmaster marched into the sight lines of their palace. She took her place in the center. She raised her hands. The nerves of real life fell off her like a cloak as she fell into the rhythm of a performance. In her opening monologue, she relied on the normal pacing instead of experimenting with the delivery. The spec parade surrounded her like a ring of fire. Then the parade left. It was Odette's turn. As the spotlight passed to Odette, Ringmaster took a moment to breathe.

Then the spotlight passed back to her as Mrs. Davidson pressed the interlude, and Mr. Davidson made his return. Things were going to be okay.

Mauve's turn, flanked by dancers. Then Boom Boom and the jugglers, then Yvanna and Charles.

Odette usually made it down to backstage by the time Charles was set on fire. Tonight, Odette rushed to Ringmaster off to the side and rubbed her back.

"How are you?" Odette asked, her voice energized with the sweat of being in the middle of a show.

Ringmaster nodded. "It's a good show. Five-star night."

She had but a moment to go backstage, to see Jo in her Oracle outfit. Jo looked nervous.

"Are you ready?" Rin said.

Jo nodded. "Yeah, I got this. Absolutely." She jumped up and down, from foot to foot, like she was about to run a race.

Rin put a hand on her shoulder. "Just remember," she said, "don't ever imagine anyone in their underwear. It's distracting and an old wives' tale and no one does that."

"Get off, I've been out here all summer," Jo said.

"Okay, all right, big-timer, headliner," Rin said, throwing her hands up in surrender. "Best go make introductions for the great Oracle of Delphi Josephine Persephone."

A short introduction for the Dreamweaver and Ringmaster stepped to the side. Tonight she would stay close, right off to the side of the ring, and watch Jo from the dark. She was the Ringmaster, it would make sense dramatically for her to be watching so closely.

The spotlight turned from Ringmaster, spun to the ring, where the confident girl had already hit her mark.

Jo had grown so much, even since the beginning of summer. And for a moment, Ringmaster smiled.

Jo reached into the air and pulled out colors. She spun them around, painting the peanut-dusted air.

It came too fast.

The colors conglomerated together, reds and yellows and oranges, and then formed a small speck. Could the audience make out what was happening, Rin wondered? This wasn't like anything she and Jo had rehearsed previously. Then Jo raised the red speck high above her head, past the bleachers, up to the high crow's nest of the tent where Kell was in place. The audience's eyes followed excitedly. She'd conjured a sun.

Then she dropped the sun down, down, down.

An explosion.

It tore into a thousand pieces.

Something unearthly, something cruel and evil, flew out in a shock wave that rippled the air.

Ringmaster lost her breath.

No. No. No.

The light erupted upward.

A mushroom cloud, filling the tent.

The ripple slowly rushing the audience.

Their skin was gone.

They all looked down to see their organs, their bones, their eyes melting onto their laps.

Ringmaster looked at herself.

The velvet coat ripped apart beyond the seams.

Her hands slipped off like gloves.

Her white bones dissolved to ash.

She disappeared.

She was dead.

Rin saw Odette. Odette's eyes melted, disappearing, too. Nothing left.

The crowd. Everyone was dead.

The tent disappeared, blown over in ash and dust. Odette erased.

No, it was an illusion. It wasn't real.

Ringmaster tried to scream. But a rancid, burning smell choked her, clogged her throat like a hot fist.

She heard something that sounded like her voice beating back against the wind of Jo's clouds.

She heard the terror-stricken screams of the audience. People thinking they were burned alive. People watching visions of their children charred into skeletons.

Ringmaster shoved forward, jumping over the curb, stumbling, her knee stabbing in pain, but she just closed her eyes and ran to Jo. She opened her eyes and tackled Jo to the ground.

Jo's hands lost the painting. The cloud dissipated. The skin of the audience returned. The skeletons and ashes disappeared as quick as they'd come.

Ringmaster's heart and head pounded as the audience stood in shock and silent screams. She felt like lead as she lay sprawled on the dirt floor of the ring, Jo underneath her.

"What . . . why . . ." Jo started. "But I didn't get to the catharsis!" Ringmaster grabbed her by the arm and, using all the energy she had left to find her footing, she stood. She had to stand for the audience.

"Ah, autumn is close enough to show you a preview of our Hallow's Eve show!" the Ringmaster tried to smile, tried to laugh. "But now we'll show you something more family friendly . . ."

But the connection was broken.

Parents grabbed their children and ran screaming out of the tent. Others shouted obscenities from their seats as they backed away. They wanted to fight, but they did not dare get close.

They'd just survived the unsurvivable. And they didn't know it wasn't real.

Fear throbbed through the tent as it cleared.

There was now something more horrific than the disaster march squawking from the tin man; the absence of Mr. Calliope's music cut Ringmaster's ears like a switchblade.

Odette rushed onstage, trying to touch as many of the crew as she could, but touching was not the right thing to do right now.

Kell stayed above.

Maynard tried to control the crowd as they escaped.

Ringmaster did not let go of Jo's arm.

She marched her back to the dressing tent.

"Is this some sort of wiseass trick?" Ringmaster demanded. "You think this is a game?"

"No," Jo said. "I did what you told me to do. I showed them what they needed to see, and you told me enough the night it happened that I was able to do it! Why didn't you let me finish?!"

"What the hell was the finale going to be?!" Ringmaster said. "What the *fuck* were you thinking!"

"I was showing them what was going to happen, so it didn't happen!"

"That's not what we do! We don't manipulate with fear!"

"So we manipulate with cotton candy and teddy bears?!" Jo said. "It hasn't worked so far! This is war, we can't just paint a bunch of pretty pictures, that does *nothing*."

"You are so wrong, where the hell did this stupid-ass idea come from?! Are you stupid, Josephine?!" Her voice did not sound like hers, and she knew that. She felt the fire roar up in a way it had not in years. In a way she thought she'd forgotten, but the fire, the fire and the explosions and the bodies—

"You said you trusted me!"

"And what a mistake that was!" Ringmaster snapped. Jo slunk back. "You idiot girl! What the hell sort of damage have you done?"

The ashes. The small skeletons. All of the circus had blown away. Her eyes had melted, she could still feel them, oozing a hot trail down her cheeks. Odette was gone, just fucking gone.

Ringmaster whipped away and tried to concentrate, tried to breathe. It wasn't real.

"I was in control!" Jo barged onward.

"You will never be on that stage alone again," Ringmaster said. "You will do exactly what I say from now on."

"I'm not a child!"

"You are!" Ringmaster tore her own hat off and threw it against the mirror. The mirror clattered. Jo jumped. "And you are going to get us all killed! You're lucky I don't throw you out of the show!"

The words were out. She couldn't stuff them back in. They hit Jo hard, like Rin had smacked her across the face.

No, no no no no.

Jo stared at the hat, and then her blue eyes shot to Ringmaster. Ringmaster wanted to take it back.

But Ringmaster couldn't hear anymore.

She could only feel her hands slipping off like gloves.

The burns on her body, as if too much sun had gotten under her skin and now it erupted and boiled out. It popped, it burned, it . . .

Odette held her in a tight embrace. The pain disappeared.

"Shh, dearest," Odette whispered in her ear. "Shh, it wasn't real. It's over."

But Jo was gone.

✳

44

THE CIRCUS KING, 1926

The Circus King's Midnight Illusionatories always arrived in the black of night. It plunged its roots into the land near the tracks, usually in the heart of town. Its wagons and Model Ts were black and red, ghosts amidst the gnarled fingers of Midwestern trees tangled in shadows. Some thought it was beautiful. Others thought it was a nightmare. All were afraid.

The townspeople would learn of the Midnight Illusionatories' arrival from the bills they'd wake up to find pasted to all the farmhouses and city halls and schoolhouses. Even if no one had booked him, the Midnight circus would come. Its three black tents were denser than the night sky, like black holes among the stars. Lanterns lit high on poles bathed the midway in bloodred light, like skeletons of starved prisoners dangling from the air. Drums would pound, coaxing the locals to the spiked gates, like a spider weaving a dangerous web. It was magic.

No, it was Sparks.

When the townsfolk rubes walked down the rows of lanterns, they would be bathed in red light. Everything was red except for the stars above, but most people forgot about anything other than the circus by the time they'd stepped onto the midway.

Music blasted, loud drumbeats leading an army of violins and woodwinds. It sounded like the heartbeat of an army. Like something otherworldly was about to happen. Every single rube would feel powerful, the sort of power that comes with being in the right place at the right time and being in charge of everything in their lives. They were in charge of nothing now, it was too late for them, but they all seemed to grin in their drunkenness. A musical stupor.

Hooded figures stalked the grounds, four spidery legs slinking from shadows and approaching patrons. Once they got close, the hoods came down. Stolen faces of those who had died, people they knew. Torsos would sit on the spider legs, as if someone had dug the corpses up and sewn them on this insect, and then the bodies would move like finger puppets. They were all dead, blue and bloated skin with pus for eyes.

The power the rubes felt would turn to something more potent than fear: guilt.

It's your fault I'm dead, the spider-corpses whispered.

Because this circus was no spectacle. It was no haunted house. It was a haunting.

Shadows swirled around the rubes, following them, shaking hands with other shadows, and the real world was no longer here. Barkers shouted from their boxes: "Come one, come all, see the truth! See the innards under the flesh! See what your world has become and will become!"

Dogs passed the rubes on a long, sewn-together leash. Their faces were pulled back, their ears missing, their fur covered in mange. They screamed in pain as their leash shocked them, making them claw and bite and fight each other.

"See the suffering under a world gilded by President Harding, the apathy of President Coolidge! See the pus and welts behind the merriment the papers sell you! Do not be dulled by the lies! Know what you are standing in!"

This is when the black tents would come into focus. To the left, a dark green light burrowed out of the open flap-doors. Screams and howls came from there. To the right, a bright eerie light strobed on and off. And in the middle, there was a circus with the house lights readied for an audience.

Inside the tent were dark shades of red and blue, white and black. Ushers dressed in dark hoods led rubes to black bleachers, like they were being ushered to an execution. The programs handed out were not programs at all, but obituaries tailored to each and every person who accepted one and took it in their clammy hands. Theirs or that of someone they loved, whichever evoked more fear, guilt, anger. For an example, just an example, one of the obituaries tonight read:

> Charles Reed
> 1911—1943
> Charles Reed was born in Marceline, Missouri, to
> estranged parents. He was reported dead by illness
> on November 8, 1943, while serving in the Pacific
> Theater—

The crowd filed into the tent, where it felt like the heavy canvas curled around them with thick, long fingers, locking them in place. They wouldn't be able to find their way out.

The drums got louder. Darkness. The sound of a radio slowly sliding between channels, never settling on music, just static. The drums roared.

Boom. Boom boom. Boom boom.

Everything shook.

Boom. Boom boom. Boom boom.

The bleachers vibrated. Their bones shook. Their neck hairs stood on end.

A thin blue light spread through the dark, crawling up the inside of the black tent like corpses' fingers digging out of a grave.

Then the sound of ghosts.

A woman's scream. A baby's cry. The howl of a dying animal. Then, a scream from something no one could identify; something with horns that lived deep in cornfields at two in the morning.

A streak of red cut across the blue, like someone had slashed a throat open.

Even if the rubes wanted to leave, they couldn't. They sat on the bleachers, unable to see the stairs or the exits through the dark. Their feet were like lead. They always had been. Was there ever a time they could move their feet? They must have been here before. It seemed so familiar, a circus they'd always known existed and now had come home to.

"Ladies and gentlemen," a low, handsome voice growled through their ears, enhanced surely by some acoustic trick. "You have waited your entire life to find this tent. You feel the anticipation rushing through your bloodstream, the need to see fear, the need to see the truth. You have been asleep in a false comfort when you know your bodies are capable of being splattered open like a sack of meat."

A body fell from the king pole. It splattered in an explosion of guts and bones.

"You like the violence," the voice hissed to the audience. "And that is why it keeps going. That is why we are here, isn't it?"

The audience felt an excitement inside them. The show had been carefully tailored so they would. Something curled through their hearts, down through their insides, into their toes. Whole bodies throbbed, like a deep, guttural need, desire, primal urge. This circus had them.

"You will see beyond the veil," the voice purred. "You will face terrible feats, great destruction, but you will leave stronger. Wiser. You will leave as one of mine."

And the lights blasted white.

Wolves in spiked collars and muzzles marched in time to the center ring, shoulder to shoulder, in one long line.

Stroboscopes flashed in all directions, the lights clicking on and off, and the performance before them felt like a demented dream.

Gorillas and elephants roared in, unaccompanied by handlers, trampling each other. The audience screamed in delight.

"You are in my world," the voice came again from all sides, maybe even inside their ears. "You are in the *real* world. You have waited your whole life to see the beasts. Monsters. You say you don't want to, but you do. You do. Everyone has a dark fascination, don't they?"

The audience had indeed wanted to see monsters, because they were monsters. And it was fun to be a monster once in a while, wasn't it?

Men with broken airplane wings soared over their heads, spilling neon radium in the air, drafting lines of skulls and gravestones. The radio static fl-fl-flipped like a piece of paper stuck on a bicycle spoke, erupting into a euphoric smash of Charleston rhythms, cadences, and chords. This world was nothing more than the world they'd all created together outside of this tent. Now look at it.

Clowns with no mouths, clowns with only mouths that licked their lips, lions with skulls for heads and their veins throbbing, exposed—they all came in on the spec parade. And the audience felt something crawl up their spines.

And then, behind the parade, came the man in a black coat and a bloodred top hat.

The Circus King.

He wasn't a monster. In fact, he was a handsome man. He carried himself on a sturdy frame, his straight shoulders back and poised. He marched high in his black boots. His hair was peppered with a distinguished gray. He moved like a dancer in one of those silent movies with the ballrooms. He looked like a barbarian with the grace of the Queen. He looked however he needed to.

He took off his bloodred hat and rolled it down his muscular arm. He shuffled his feet, giddily. He grinned to the audience. It was a good grin. A grin only seen in dark, lustful fantasies. This man was a star, this man was everyone's best friend, this man had all their eyes in his fist.

"I am your Circus King," he boomed, the voice the audience had heard behind their skulls. "And you are my audience. You and I are bound in this fantastical horror, and you have come to bear witness. For who among us has not sinned? What man does not lie in bed after the lights have been doused—"

The lights smoked out, like he'd blown out a candle.

The music was silent.

"—and the man thinks to himself"—he was a showman, every single word enunciated, dripping with timbre, the "ks" in "thinks" crisp and sharp like a snake—"'what good have I done? What monster am I?' Who looks to his wife and does not think, 'Someday she will die, or someday I may kill her. How would it be to wrap my fingers around her neck?' Ah, you thought you were the only one."

One bloodred spotlight followed a woman who moved like clockwork high above the crowd to the ribbon act. The ribbons were bloodred. The spotlight turned white.

The woman, pale, rolled through the ribbons as if they were shackles.

Then she fell.

She fell.

And she was hanged.

The ribbon curled around her neck, and she struggled, and she kicked her legs until she fell silent. And there was peace.

"Ah," the Circus King's voice came again. "What a terrible thing. And yet all of you sit enraptured in your seats, doing nothing. You watched her die, and you didn't move a finger. Who else did you let die?"

The woman's head popped off, and her spine elongated like a fireman's ladder. Her body crashed to the ground. Her head still stared out to the audience from twenty feet above.

The body at the end of the broken neck's ladder ran along the outside of the ring, her spine working as part of the ribbon now. She twirled around and around, as if on a swing in perpetual motion.

The spine snapped.

Her body grew limp.

Then another head grew.

The first spine fluttered on the ribbon in the wind like a lost feather.

And then it disintegrated.

"Or perhaps you've thought of such things for yourself," he said.

He kept speaking, but the audience felt something deep crack open inside them, and they fell deeper, deeper, down. They remembered dark moments where it felt like there was nothing left to give. Their young boys, brothers, sons, fathers were dead. Soon everyone they loved would die and they'd all be grainy, forgotten photographs in attics. Why keep going if there's no reason to?

Maybe there was no reason.

A gun went off.

In the circle, the carpet turned into trenches.

As the sounds of guns came from everywhere.

And half of the audience saw *X*'s painted on them with red paint by an invisible hand.

"War"—the word repeated over and over again until it just sounded like the cranking gears of tanks, the whistling of cannons, the *rt-t-t-t-t-t* of gatling guns.

"Your worst fears." The hissing voice finally overlapped with war, and the audience shot back in their seats as somewhere in the middle of the center ring, mirrors rose up from the ground and they saw their parents, ex-lovers, old teachers laughing and jeering at them.

They looked like ghouls.

They then melted into the shadows, and a silhouette whispered into view. Now every single person saw themselves as an old, decrepit, helpless corpse strapped to their death-bed.

The mirrors shattered, but the image still stuck in their eyes like shards. The lights blared.

More acts came. They blended together in a hypnotic terror the audience couldn't turn away from.

Animals slaughtered. People beating each other until their bones splintered and their bare bodies were spattered with thick, juicy black bruises. Gangsters holding each other down with knives. Lanky, leering men stalking the gazes of women in the audience, slowly working their way closer and closer like a flickering light that kept changing positions. Shadows with no owner. Firing squads. Bodies eaten by maggots until there was nothing left but a skull and a neck and the heads bobbed unnaturally. An illusion of falling thousands of feet. The blackness of space. The whispering sounds of anxious thoughts from all corners.

And then the finale.

A dance. All the creatures returned to the ring, and the music began again, and all the audience began to feel the pulse in the bleachers, in their feet.

The audience felt their bodies move. They felt the music. A purging of all the terrible bile they'd cooped up in their ugly hearts. This was a place of nightmares, and they were now a part of it. Maybe they always had been.

They stood, their bodies feeling drunk, feeling light.

They pounded their feet, they flailed their arms, they rolled their heads, they screamed, they roared.

The world had betrayed all of them. Their loved ones had broken their hearts. The truth was this darkness, and it was going to devour them all.

It could not be stopped.

They would all die in the end.

It was inevitable after the day, the dark would come again.

So it did not matter how they broke the rules. The rules were there to keep them complacent, to dope them up to do whatever someone else wanted them to do until they finally died. No, they danced tonight. They would take what they want tonight. Fuck the world.

And just as they each felt as if their pulsing bodies would explode in a mind-bursting orgasm, the lights blinked out.

Replaced by house lights.

The high feeling of being invincible . . . of being genuine . . . it dropped out from under them like a trapdoor.

The circus was gone. Only the dark black tent was left.

The audience was abandoned. The work lights clicked on.

There was no conclusion, no ending. Just a longing that would never be fulfilled, never satiated by a proper finale. And the realization that out of all the things they'd seen in that tent . . . the most lingering horror was that they'd enjoyed watching it.

The Circus King watched this from the center ring, invisible to the audience, the entire tent bare without his words. He and his monstrous performers were visible now only to each other, his menagerie of horrific Sparks. He waved a hand lazily to them, and they filed out of the tent to the Back Yard, silent, in a straight line.

The audience couldn't see any of this. Even as he stood there in front of them, they couldn't see him. They wailed, or cried quietly, realizing they had to live the rest of their lives with what they'd just seen. What had just happened to them? It was delicious and he devoured their fear.

"Go," he whispered to the crowd. They all rose at once and turned to leave, like it was their idea.

They wouldn't know they'd heard everything he'd whispered. He'd been there every step of the way, every single moment they felt was not theirs to orchestrate, but he, the conductor, got to see every single moment they thought they were in control.

They didn't have shit.

What a beautiful meltdown.

"Except for you two," the Circus King whispered to two children in the front row. They were his special guests tonight.

He watched them snap out of it.

"Where . . . what happened? Where did it all go?" the boy said, disheveled.

The girl desperately looked around for the man in the bloodred hat. He wasn't there. Not until he was ready to show himself, on cue.

"We have to find him," she said. "Now."

They jumped off the bleachers, clawing and shoving people out of the way. The two children rushed out of the tent, looking for the backstage entrance. The Circus King followed. And there it was, between the tents. He stepped in front of her and allowed her to see him.

"You see me now?" the Circus King said.

The girl jumped. "It's you!"

"You want to talk to me?" His voice was soft and beautiful.

The girl nodded. "Yes," she said. "Please."

"You want it more than anything?" he said.

"Yes."

The Circus King looked past her to the boy, as if the boy was a rather disgusting fly. "Go home."

"Wait," the girl said as the boy nodded slowly and turned his back to walk away. "No wait, no you—"

"Let him go," the Circus King said. And the girl stopped. Together, the two of them watched him leave. Then the girl grinned, her eyes glass. She turned back to the handsome man in the bloodred hat.

"Jo," the Circus King said. "It's wonderful to finally meet you. Welcome to my circus."

✳

45

THE CIRCUS KING, 1926

The Circus King said to the girl: "Come into my office."

He led her through the Big Top's portal into his Back Yard. As they crossed the threshold, he said, "It's sparse, but gets the job done. Four walls, a desk, and a nice kettle steaming with two cups on the desk. Two seats. You can take the one over there."

So this is what Jo saw. And this is what Jo did.

The Circus King stood in front of her, knowing she saw him sitting, pouring tea. "I'll pour you some tea. You like my office?"

"Yes," Jo said, looking around the room that was only there in her mind.

"So you want to join the circus," the Circus King said.

"I've already joined the circus," Jo said.

"Of course!" the Circus King chuckled. It was a kind chuckle, not a jeer or a jest. It was important to be kind. That's why they trusted him. "And I've got a lot of respect for you and your Spark. I've heard a lot about you. I meant to say, you want to join *my* circus."

And she did. She really did. He knew she did. His circus was magnificent. It wasn't afraid to be sad, it wasn't afraid to stray off the tracks. This was home, she could feel it in her numb fingers. And the Circus King would give her something she needed: freedom to touch the world however she wanted.

"So why is it that you've come tonight?" the Circus King asked. He didn't need his Spark to get a response. A simple question would suffice. This was a child. He'd put up enough posters she could find her way. Some of the strongest convincing he ever did had nothing to do with his Spark, but just waiting for someone to make the decision they'd wanted to all along.

Jo took a drink of nothing. "There's a war coming," she said. "My brother is going to die. Everyone I love is going to die. I need to stop it, and I hear you scare people into doing what you want. So I asked around and I found you. Closer than she thought you'd be, huh? You like to keep close if you can find us. So here I am. You found me."

A war? The Circus King narrowed his eye. "A war, you say?"

"Yes," Jo said, as if this wasn't surprising at all. "Mauve saw another Great War coming, years from now. I need to stop it."

The Circus King felt his heart stop for a moment. Was it possible, he thought, that after all these years, under all this muscle he was still afraid?

But he had assumed war would return. War always returned. These idiots who thought it was the war to end all wars weren't there *in* the war; they were hopeful and naïve and that's why it was always going to return. No war could hurt him now, he reminded himself. He wasn't the boy he was when the first one took him. No one could take him. So it was of no consequence, was it.

"I look worried," he told Jo. "You relate to my worry." Then in words that weren't stage directions, he said his line: "There are some performers out there who would wish the world to be full of glitter and sequins, but playing make-believe doesn't keep people from starvation, from illness, from death. While they hop around their Neverland, some of us know that the crowds don't deal in metaphors. They must see it for what it is."

"And you really care about making a difference, huh?" she said. "Not just in it for the easy scares?"

He grinned. "It is a beautiful production."

"Yes," she said. "Yes, it is."

"Well, you know, we'd love to have you," he said. "And you could show off anything you wanted. I'm guessing Miss Ringmaster has you on a tight leash, from what I've heard."

"I could show anything?" Jo asked.

"Yes, of course," he said. "You've got more tea in your cup now, go ahead and drink it before it gets cold."

She did. "How did you do that? You didn't even touch the kettle."

"We are Sparks at our full potential. We shouldn't hold ourselves back because the world is afraid," the Circus King said. "We were given these gifts to reach the stars, Jo." Then he said, "Take a drink. It's delicious, warm, just the way you like it." She did so. He continued.

"But what about your circus family?" he said. "Do you know it's not easy to jump wagons? I suppose they'll live without you."

"Yeah, they'll live," Jo said.

"Got any family?"

"I've got a brother," Jo said. "But he'll be happy with the other circus. And I'll be happy protecting him from what's to come."

"You're a callous person, Jo," he said, chuckling less. "You know what you want."

"I know what I want," she agreed.

"I respect that. You should respect that as well," the Circus King said, his brows raising like a teacher who saw something in a student no one else had caught. "I didn't have an older sister to protect me," he said, in a small piece of honesty. He gritted his teeth. "But we here are unable to be touched. We are strong. We are capable of so much." Well, he was. This girl had a good Spark perhaps, but he saw she was too soft. He could feel her neediness, her want to be loved and belong. It radiated off her like she was a furnace. She was too easy.

Oh well. Everyone, even Josephine, had their purpose.

"I want to be here, Mr. King," Jo said. "I want to be a part of your circus. It was beautiful. And you . . ." She trailed off. He let her.

"You know me," he said. "I'm familiar. I'm family. We are the same, aren't we?"

"I'm starting to think that," Jo said.

He nodded, looking down to his boots and giving a big breath out as he slapped his knees and stood up. Except he'd never been sitting. "All right then. Let's shake on it."

She finished her tea in one slurp and stood as well. The cup would have fallen to the ground if it had been real, but instead she'd forgotten it like she was doing a shitty pantomime, and it had disappeared from her fingers. That part of the scene was over.

He held out his hand. She took it, and he knew her entire body felt the heat of his palm.

"You'll stay here for as long as I'll have you," he said.

"Yes," she said.

"You'll show me what you can do, before I welcome you into my circus." His strong grip tightened on her small hand's joints. He could crush them if he wanted to. But he didn't.

"Right now?" Jo said.

"Yes," the Circus King said. "Right now. Fill up my office with what you have. Whatever you want. The things you have been scared to make. Don't hold back, just let it roll out. Make the entire county see it. Reach the stars." Then, in his parenthesis, his italicized directions in his script, he said, "There is a surge of excitement, unbridled power rushing through your body. Show me the worst things you can."

She jumped, her mouth curling into a grin. She wasted no time pushing back from the Circus King's grip, raising her empty hands, and shoving them down in a hard push, to the carpet that did not exist.

The world exploded. Or at least it seemed to. Out of her fingertips came blood, sharp razors, bodies ripped apart, in a full tidal wave of gore and pain. It cascaded down around their feet, then up the canvas of the tent behind them and the trees and the dirt and the boxes, staining it all. It bled out into the night, the red shrieking light of horrors glowing, shooting up high, high into the sky, a tornado of carnage, a choir of banshees.

This is what the world would look like. This is what had taken her older brother, what tried to take Ringmaster, what would take Charles, and so it was what she would paint the world with. It was what it deserved. And the Circus King could feel it all, my God, he could feel it all!

It was that fear he'd known when he was her age. It was primitive, it was weak. This would be too easy, to hold her in his grip. And he loved that.

"Stop," the Circus King said.

Jo stopped. The illusion immediately wiped away. It was night once more.

She stared at Mr. King, and goodly Mr. King said, "I look afraid. You have scared me. You are powerful. The Ringmaster may have told you that you were wonderful. Well, that's not the same thing as being full of fright. You can't control people with wonder, can you?"

"You can't," Jo said.

Mr. King cleared his throat, fixed his collar, and looked to the little scrawny girl she was. "You have a lot pent up in that head of yours."

Jo nodded, still in her stance, as if she was going to fight the whole of humanity.

"Did that feel good?" Mr. King said.

"It didn't," Jo said honestly. "It was scary."

"That's surprising," Mr. King said, sitting down and waving for Jo to do the same. She did. "I believe it would feel magnificent. Invigorating. Exciting. Stimulating." His eyes flicked dangerously at hers like the light on a wick that hadn't been cut short enough. "You found it stimulating. Didn't you? Under all that anger, there is power. Everyone is afraid of you? Well, let them be afraid." Then he popped into a grin. "Great. Go ahead and finish your tea then, and I'll have one of my Brides show you to your tent. They run this joint like a smooth machine, the things I don't do myself."

"A whole tent?"

"Of course," he said. "I've never seen a Spark like yours. Really, I haven't. I've seen many a person who have the Spark of beauty, of healing, and they're a dime a dozen. But yours . . . it's adaptable and flexible and so rare. You're the greatest part of our greatest show. Go on then."

He watched her grasp at a teacup she'd forgotten about. He watched her finish her tea. Then she stared at the Circus King as he cleared the table with one wave of his arm.

"And see? It's now gone." He laughed. "Tell me, isn't that something?"

"It really is something," she said.

He was handsome. His black hair was peppered with gray, his eyes were kind. He smiled back at her. His jawline was perfect from this angle, he knew. He peppered his own hair with the distinguished look of a gentleman. He'd straightened his teeth. He made himself smell like peppermint. But to his own eyes, he still looked like that boy. That damned boy.

This girl could make illusions, where he could only speak them. He'd never seen his own circus, he'd never seen his own office. He'd never seen his own face the way he wanted it to be. Not in their entirety. He could fool the world, but he couldn't fool himself. With Jo, he could make it all real.

But. He had never been a man who wanted the world. His eyes were set on something—someone—smaller but a lot more important.

"You're excited to be here, Josephine?" he asked.

She shook her head. "It's like . . . my whole life is starting over and I have a chance."

"You do have a chance," he said. He smiled, like St. Nicholas. He winked, and he said, "You don't have to be the Ringmaster's pet anymore. You're free. Now then, you can no longer see me. You will now walk out of my office and wait in the Back Yard for her. Wait. Do not leave. And when she tries to take you, do not let her. Don't let anyone touch you."

It did not take long. Of course it didn't.

The girl stood like a mouse in an open field, waiting for a hawk.

And the hawk came.

Lion hair. Freckled face. Black hat. Red velvet coat.

"You can't see me," the Circus King whispered from the shadows where he waited. Just to be safe, he stepped behind a flat, peering around the edge to see the scene of a ringmaster and a runaway.

"Jo," the newly arrived woman breathed, rushing to her little girl. "Jo, we need to leave here right now." She reached out to grab Jo's wrist.

Jo pulled away, panic rising.

"Jo." The Ringmaster slid down on her boot-laced knees into the mud, trying to embrace her as fast as she could. She grabbed Jo's arms and tried to hold her, but Jo pulled away. "Jo, stop!" The Ringmaster grabbed for air. "Jo, we need to leave, please take my hand—"

"Now it is time to see me," the Circus King said. "Look at me, the both of you."

Only Jo turned her head to hear him. The Circus King narrowed his eyes. He waited for the Ringmaster to follow where Jo looked to see him and his shadow splayed across the rocks and dirt. The Ringmaster could see him now. And then he put his hand to his ear and pretended to pull something out. An instruction.

The Ringmaster pulled the wax from her ears. She withered in front of him, like a bird losing all her feathers. Good. She now knew his powers had grown. She hadn't known his Spark was so much more than verbal now. As usual, he was a step ahead of her.

"Josephine," Mr. King said quietly. "Relax. No one use their Spark while we chat."

Jo's eyes found the firelight in the office's gas lamp that did not exist. Mr. King's voice had been steady. It wrapped around her, fuzzy and safe. She felt her body float.

The Ringmaster stepped in front of her to face the Circus King.

The Ringmaster was murderous. "Let her go," she growled. She to some might have been frightening, a viper ready to strike. Her back arched, her fists like rocks, her boots grinding into the ground.

But he was not afraid. He was relieved.

That smile came again, from his perfect jaw. He had waited so long. "Hello, Ruth," he said.

✳

46

RUTH, 1917

Once he became the Circus King, Edward stopped pretending to be kind. She stopped pretending she didn't see.

"You like it," he told her.

And she did. She liked not having to think all the time. He would make difficult decisions, and she was numb. If she allowed herself to be numb, then she wouldn't be sad.

Once she had fought back, said she didn't want to be with him anymore.

"Oh, is that so?" he said. "Then take your grief back!"

It flooded through her. The years she had lost, her mother gone, and it swallowed her whole. "Please no, please don't," she begged him. And it was gone again. She wasn't happy, but she was content. Calm.

He told her she liked this life, and so she kept on with the circus, she kept on for him.

When he got into her head, she felt herself float away. Detached, as if her soul hung on by a thread and she flew above it all like a kite. It was a good feeling, one that meant that she could put off being human for just a little longer. She didn't have to be a lost daughter, she didn't have to think about her mother or her father or the G-d she couldn't remember how to speak to. She wasn't anyone but a body this man used to navigate his way through his tricks.

The night when she'd finally seen her mother after so many years, the night he told her the truth, it was like seeing her best friend and loving husband slowly melt into a monster right in front of her.

"You remember this is your fault."

"We could have been happy."

"All the things I did, you did them, too! It was both of us! Get off your high horse, Ruth!"

That final night, he screamed at her. "Is this what you want?" And he seemed to fill their sleeping quarters. He grew so big, a dark black hole of a shadow, suffocating her and swallowing the room, until there was nothing but nothing. He reached out his hand, and it felt like he dug into her, nails piercing her skin, ribs, heart, spirit. He breathed in and suddenly she had no air.

She was dying.

Who would she be when he had taken all her breaths? Or worse, who would she be when he used up all her soul?

But it wasn't real. He had one Spark, and he'd made the mistake of telling her what it was.

So that night, she took her grief back.

She packed a rucksack, but he pulled her back into bed with his coaxing words. He held her tight. The night was still as they lay there. The most violent things are sometimes the most silent.

Halfway through the night, long after she'd thought he'd fallen asleep, he had hissed, "You love me."

She did.

"You believe I can be better, and you're going to help me," he said.

She was going to.

"If you leave me," he said, "no one will have the pity that I have for you. They don't know you. They won't give a shit about you. You will be alone. You are unwanted, uncared for, a stupid little thing." Then more silence, nearly as suffocating as his angry words. Eventually though, she could tell he really had fallen asleep. She listened to his heavy, steady breathing.

But there was something else she heard. It was outside the window. Just a small thing.

A busker. Playing the violin. Music.

She realized *he* didn't listen to music. She realized he didn't play. And for the first time in a long time, she realized the absence of music.

Her mother sang prayers, her mother had a beautiful voice. It was something deeper than anything that *he* could touch.

In that moment, music sparked to life inside her.

And she finally disappeared from the place beside him.

47

THE RINGMASTER, 1926

She saw that he still had that boyish smile. He'd somehow made himself look more distinguished, but it was him. He still knew how to turn his head against the current of his shoulders, raise his brow, grin in the creases of his cheeks, and set his eyes on her like she was the only person who mattered in the world.

And maybe that was true, for him. Maybe in his mind, he did love her. She used to get caught up in a web of trying to figure out what he was thinking, or maybe what thoughts were hers and what were his. But not tonight. She wasn't a girl anymore, and she knew it didn't matter what he thought. Only what he said.

Only what he says and what he motions, she thought, a chill running through her gut.

She had promised Odette she would come back. She had to come back.

She closed her eyes. She imagined a string between her and Odette, her and home, far away down the road in Fort Collins where she'd jumped the circus. It had been from down there in Fort Collins she'd seen Jo's fiery pillar illuminate the mountains.

Going back in time to stop things hadn't helped Bernard or stopped the war, and coming face-to-face with the Circus King would be a war of its own. If she couldn't save the people she loved by changing the past or jumping to the future, she would do her damned best here in the present. So she would be strong enough for this moment as she stood here without her bracelet. She wasn't leaving without Jo.

But the Circus King was here. He was here, and he was handsome, and he was grinning at her like he knew she had already lost.

She thought again of Odette and reinforced that glowing string in her mind. Then she stepped forward, wearing all her courage.

"Let her go," she said again.

Now both of his brows raised high, as if surprised, he said, "I wasn't aware she was mine to let go. She requested to be a part of my show, Ruth."

"Don't bullshit me," she said. "You got me here. I see you, you see me. Now she and I are leaving."

"I'm not leaving," Jo said.

"Jo, it's going to be okay," Ringmaster said.

"Jo, we're discussing things," the Circus King said, not taking his eyes off Ringmaster. "Let's all go into my office and have a talk about this. Shall we?"

Around him was his office, and it made no sense, like it was tangled together with dream logic. An office with no walls but with white walls, no door but clearly there.

A part of Ringmaster knew that if she entered, she might not ever leave. But Jo had already stepped inside. And she wasn't letting Jo walk into his jaws alone.

Ringmaster stayed at the entrance, her feet on a threshold she knew didn't exist. Edward stood lazily behind his elaborate, ornate desk. He said, "Give us a moment, Jo. Sit still."

Jo did so. Ringmaster saw her sit on the ground, unmoving, eyes forward, completely disassociated. Floating, like Rin used to float.

She had to get her out of here.

"What do you want?" Ringmaster said.

"Why the accusatory tone?" He sat down in a chair behind the mirage of his desk. He motioned to the chair opposite him. When had that gotten there? "Always a fight with you. Go on then, make yourself at home."

Ringmaster looked to the chair. She looked to Edward. Why did it feel like she still belonged here? It'd been years, and yet here was her other half.

But him being her other half meant she knew him inside and out.

She'd play his game. She would win this time.

She took a seat.

"Unload and drop the gun," Edward said. "I know you must have brought one."

Caught, Ringmaster slowly pulled the pistol from her waist, let the bullets out, and threw it on the floor. It felt like the right thing to do. It was the wrong thing to do. But guns caused so much trouble to begin with. Bernard had been killed with a gun. The war was fought with guns. If something happened to her, Odette . . . if she didn't get home . . . she had to get home.

"There we are. No more weapons between us. So tell me," Edward said, taking out a teacup from his sleeve. It had tea already in it. It wasn't real. It couldn't be real. "Does your saccharine woman husband know where you are?"

"Yes," she said quietly. There was no point in lying to him.

"And the rest of your freak cult," Edward said. "Do they know?"

"Mauve knows."

"Why are they not here with you?" Edward said, offering her the tea. It felt real in her cold hands. The steam was real. It was a perfect illusion in her brain and her eyes.

"Because I didn't want them getting hurt," she said. "But they're waiting at the edge of our camp for me, if I don't return." They'd had a plan. A plan that had already gone wrong.

"Grab her," Odette had said, when she finally caved. "Jump back immediately."

"Don't let go of her," Mauve had said, her voice shaking.

But Rin hadn't been able to touch Jo.

Edward watched her face, trying to read her. He never could, he thought he could, he'd told her he could, maybe he could.

He was her childhood. He held chapters she hadn't seen for years and now saw right in front of her. Like an old song she'd fallen in love with and then forgotten, lost the record to, only to find in an attic decades later.

But there are reasons why people let things be lost.

"You saw her Spark shoot up into the sky over my circus in the mountains, did you?" Edward said. "So how long did it take for you to put it together?"

"Not long," Ringmaster said.

Edward chuckled, as if he was clever.

This was the man who had taught her to hate herself. He knew the truth about her, better than anyone else did, better than she knew herself. If the world spoke about her and everyone else agreed, "The Ringmaster is a good person," Edward King would laugh and say, "You're wrong. She's not." And he would be the right one.

It made no sense. But he'd branded himself in her head. And now that she could see him, see he wasn't a monster but a man she once knew, she remembered he was human.

The lines were getting muddy in her mind. She had to keep her head above his waters. She had to try.

"I never took you for a career circus man," she said, trying to take back the conversation. The more questions he asked, the more she would answer, the deeper she would fall. "I thought you would have found yourself a part of the world to carve out."

"I didn't want the world," the Circus King said, his eyes flicking to her. "I want you."

Rin felt that cold chill in her spine, deep in her bones like a horrible winter in Chicago.

"I made this circus for you," Edward said. "Unlike you, I meant my word when I said I was devoted to us. I kept the circus in your spirit, even after I lost you in Chicago. What did your gravestone say . . . 1918? How's being dead working out for you, Ruth?"

"You know, not all monsters go for the world, because they know they'd fail," Ruth cut him. "So they make their own worlds, ones they can control. You never did this circus for anyone but yourself."

Edward's eyes narrowed. "You are the heart of this circus."

"This circus has no heart," Ringmaster said. "You like seeing the world burn. No one can be happy if Edward King isn't happy."

Edward gave a boyish laugh and tossed his hair. It was nearly endearing. "I haven't heard my full name for a very long time. But I'm sure you haven't either, Mrs. King." He grinned again, raising his left hand for her to see his ring. It was the same ring. Hers was different, one Odette had picked out. "I hear you just go by Ringmaster. That's stupid."

Maybe it was. Maybe it all had been a silly farce.

"You're older than you should be?" he said. She slowly nodded. The Circus King nodded as well, mocking her like a marionette player. "How many years have you aged with all that jumping from time to time?" How did he know? She'd only been able to jump places when they last knew one another. What else did he know? This whole time, she'd thought he was two steps behind her but he'd been running ahead, setting this scene. There was too much she didn't . . . don't lose your head, Rin. "Oh, you didn't know I knew about your Spark growing?" He enjoyed this. "I know you can go to time and space now. Have been able to for a while. Good to see I'm not the only one who's grown with my gifts. And looks like you've been frittering your life away in the tomorrows and not so much in the todays. Good God, you could be your mother's age." He looked down to her velvet coat. "I see you two reunited at some point since we last spoke."

"I reunited with her," she said, her teeth gritting. "She never reunited with me. Then she passed away. And I buried her."

"Ah." Edward clapped his hands together. "That was *her* grave with *your* name. Poor, poor Catherine Dover."

"Shut up," Rin said. "Keep my mother's name off your tongue."

"I refuse to take full blame for what happened," Edward said, maybe the most genuine he'd been since she'd arrived. "She was a selfish charlatan who wanted to keep us apart. *You* wanted *me* to take you away. Don't you use my Spark as an excuse to assuage your own guilt!"

Ringmaster abruptly stood and turned away from Edward, toward Jo. But she couldn't touch her. Edward had said so. No. She reached her hand out, her legs made of lead. "Jo, we are leaving now."

"Oh, you're not," Edward said, standing as well. Ringmaster stared at him, ready to fight. "Well, not both of you." He sat down again and crossed his leg over his knee, like he was getting comfortable. Like he enjoyed this. "A few months ago, you had a loose lip in your clown alley, *Ringmaster*. Davidson, right? I asked him what the weakest point of the Big Top was. He said the king pole. I asked him who the king pole was of not your circus, but your *life*." He raised a brow, quite proud. And he waved a hand at Jo. "So here we are."

Rin narrowed her eyes. Her jaw grinding.

"I've been watching you at every port, ever since I discovered you were alive. The lot managers, telegramming me when your company would show up." Edward was so proud of himself.

"And that oversized perverse homosexual you had working for you?" Edward laughed. Bernard's face flashed before Rin. The love in his eyes even as he'd known he was about to die. "He fought back. Got a lick in for sure. But I could tell in his eyes, even if he wasn't answering my questions, where your heart was." Rin's heart raced. She saw red. "I thought about taking your whore, but this child is under your guardianship, isn't she? Something special about the children we love, it really drives us to do stupid things. Like Catherine Dover, she did many stupid things."

The next second happened as fast as fire shooting through an open door. Rin shot forward, fist first, but Edward barked, "Stop and sit."

She stopped. She couldn't do it. He was a battle of wits, and nothing she could do with her hands would be enough to stop him. It wouldn't win anything. She sat.

"So let's talk about this child, shall we?" Edward said. "I'd love to let Jo go. I know she's a great star of your Windy van Hootenanny. But see, it's that she's joined *my* circus. Entered into a deal, you know? Dumb kids, making rash decisions. But can't break a business deal, Ruth. Just can't. Unless there's an even exchange." This was not said in a mocking tone; it was a confused look with a soft voice. He was but a victim in all this muddle. "I want you. I want you and me, the way it was supposed to be. But I am tired of you pretending you had no hand in any of this. You loved m—" He stopped himself. "I . . . *believe* you loved me. I want you of your own free will."

"Well, good luck with that one, I'd rather die."

"Why do you always have to make things into such a dramatic spectacle?" Edward said, wiping the teacups away. They disappeared into nothing. "This isn't your circus, Ruth. This is me, and I know your nonsense. There are no spotlights here to make you sparkle, there is no orchestration for your little opera. Did you ever think perhaps it was *you* who was poisonous and weak? Perhaps the fault didn't sit with everyone else but you? Or is that too hard for you to face? *You* asked me to take you from New York. You asked to be with me. You asked to marry me. You used to light up, and now I don't know what those freaks have done to you, but obviously something has gone terribly wrong in the time we've spent away from each other. Together, I believe we can fix it—"

"I know you're right," Ruth said quietly. "Because you've made me believe you're right. But that's how I know you're very wrong." She didn't know he was wrong. Every night away from him, she'd lost sleep sitting still in her bed and staring at the ceiling. Sometimes she'd talk out loud to Odette. *Tell me I'm not crazy, tell me he was wrong, please.* Odette always would. However many times she needed her to say it, she'd say it. But it never rang true. Ruth could only keep running away.

Odette was a thousand miles from here. That was another life.

This life was delicate nights in hotels, sitting on pins and needles to find out if he would stroke her silk gown and kiss her or if he would throw a vase at the wall. This life was the electric static of sitting beside him on a train, bowing her head so he would ignore her for just one more second. Once, one morning, when he was very angry, she'd lost her voice altogether. He must have told her she didn't exist anymore, because she just sat in a chair, frozen, waiting for him to bring her back to life.

If he spun her back into this web, she might not die. But she would disappear.

Edward nodded, understanding. His fingers graced his table. He looked to Jo. "Then if you won't stay, there's nothing I can do. She's mine. Completely smitten. Aren't you, darling?"

Jo smiled dumbly. As if she was drunk. She nodded.

"Tell her what you said to me earlier, about joining my circus," Edward said.

"I have a chance now, my life is starting over." Jo giggled. "I'm no one's pet anymore." Ringmaster's stomach dropped.

"Somehow you're even more of a disgusting monster now than you were," Rin spat.

"You find me handsome, Jo?"

"Say one more word to her," Ringmaster dared him.

"Oh, Ruth, I would like to point out something about your little urchin," Edward said. "Happy duo, Charlie Chaplin and Jackie Coogan, are you? Then why, *Ringmaster,* did she leave your circus?"

Ringmaster stopped. This dragged her like a chain around the neck. She balled her fists. Nothing to say.

"And this, you'll love this," Edward said. "She came, of her own accord, seeking *me* out."

Something inside Rin, something sacred and deep and beautiful, was crushed in these words. Snuffed out, like dying kindling. Jo came here of her own accord. Rin had already failed her.

"There's only so much we ringmasters can do," Edward said, still drawing circles with his fingertips on his desk. Rin tried to stay standing strong, but the way he looked at her, she knew. He could tell she was losing. "We can set the stage. We can strike the music. We can hit our marks and say our lines. But the audience must decide to arrive on their own. My posters are not magic. They are simple billings, one of which was picked up by a young girl as she rushed out of a circus that shunned her for telling the truth."

Ruth stared at Jo. Jo stared back at her, dead behind those eyes. Rin saw him slowly erasing Jo, her face getting more slack-jawed, her expression fading away.

"Not a monster," Edward said, folding his hands. "Just honest." He looked to Ruth. "Which is more than you were, waiting until I was asleep to slip out and break my heart. So you could go fuck some carnie whore. I loved you, Ruth."

She supposed that was true. At one point. At some moment, she had loved him, too. There had been train rides, dancing, all the places they'd explored together. That night, outside the tents when he told her what he'd done to her mother, she couldn't kill him.

But she couldn't have killed anyone.

"I want you to love me," Edward said. "But I will not tell you to love me."

"Then what will you do?"

"*We* could make a deal," Edward said. "You could, if you wish, perform in my circus. Be the transporter that you were back when. It was your idea, a circus completely made of Sparks. I built one for you."

"I built one for myself," Ruth said.

Edward wasn't listening. "If you wish to enter into this contract, we would be husband and wife once more. We're still married, you know." The shiver down her spine came back. "I would ask that you never leave my side, until death becomes inevitable."

"Gee," Ruth said. "What a deal."

"You're not in a position to cheek back," Edward said, his eyes widening with hurt. "Always acting as if I was some dirt on your shoe. The poor English boy who couldn't afford anything, who broke his back to give you a life you wanted, even if it meant it was miserable for me. I hate circuses! Ugh. A monster. Is that what you told everyone? You were so pained, you were so scared . . . Well, Jo doesn't think I'm a monster. Jo?" Jo blinked, standing straight at rapt attention. "You'd like to stay, wouldn't you?"

"Yes," Jo trembled. "Please."

"Stop." Ruth stepped in front of her. "Stop it. You know I'm going to take her place. She hasn't done anything. You are not in her story."

They both knew it.

Somehow, even through the visceral vitriol between them, they both understood.

"I would like to hear you say it," Edward said.

"I'll stay with you," Ruth said.

Edward smiled a large, relieved smile. He rushed from behind the desk. He embraced her. Every part of her wanted to die. Every nerve in her skin wanted to shrivel up and scream out in protest at the same time. "Thank you," he whispered.

"*If* you leave the rest of Windy's alone. You and I never hurt anyone. And you never go near Jo again." She narrowed her eyes. "And you ask each and every one of your own cast and crew if they want to be here, and if they don't, you let them go free. You can have me, if you leave the rest of the world alone."

"I could agree to that," Edward said, taking her hat off, wrapping his fingers in her hair.

She shoved him off. "How do I know you're not lying?"

"I don't give a flying shit about your stupid circus," Edward said. "I need *you*."

Maybe she could trust him to keep his word. He really didn't care about the circus, only her. This was always only about her.

Ruth stared at him. "I am falling for this because you're telling me to."

"It is so remarkable how you can never take responsibility for anything, you're always one to blame me," Edward said. His eye narrowed. "I am . . ." He paused, and thought for a second. "I would like to believe that I am telling you the truth." He worded it more carefully. "I want to have a life with you," he said. "I want to leave everything behind and hold you in my arms and have you hold me. Ruth, you were the one place I felt like I belonged. You are my home." He thought for a second, as if he was a lawyer adding footnotes, "And I'll add you are free to believe me or not believe me on that. See?"

There was an honesty in his voice. He was trying.

She was falling into his trap. But it meant the others could get away.

The others had never known the Circus King. They could only imagine dangers where they could follow her. But she'd known in her heart all along, that in the end, she would have to go alone.

The others couldn't have come with her. They all would be trapped.

She'd done what she could. She'd tried. But she'd made her bed when she was fifteen and picked him out of a trench.

"Ruth," Edward soothed, coming closer. Something felt good in her stomach. "I want you. I don't want anyone else. I would kill them all to get to you. But now I have you. That's all I want. You're a pain in the ass, but you're *my* pain in the ass. So let me love you, please? It's your decision. Walk out of here right now if you want."

A faraway thread in her mind tugged at her. Odette. It was familiar but so faint, like a child's chalk drawing washing away with the rain.

She gathered up everything she had left. The Ringmaster swallowed. "One more condition: you give me a half an hour to take Jo safely down the mountain and back to the circus. We've moved to Fort Collins for the night. I won't speak to anyone else. No one will follow me back. I only want to make sure she gets home safe."

She would speak to others. That was a lie. Because any conversation between her and Edward was a game of chess on a board only they could see. Only he could see. And she had to learn to protect herself where she could.

Edward looked skeptical. But he let go of her hair. He muttered something she couldn't hear. Then the office disappeared. It shattered into reality; his muddy Back Yard full of people who were walking around with dead eyes, not speaking to one another, just going from place to place. There was no glamour. There were only boxes and wagons and bare minimal pieces as if he painted over the models with his words.

It was haunted.

He waved to Jo. "She's yours. For five minutes."

"That's not what I—"

"You don't need a half an hour, I'm not that gullible. And if you don't return, Jo will return. If you go anywhere other than your grounds in Fort Collins, Jo will return. If you leave this timeline and pop back or forth, Jo will return. If you spend more than a minute speaking to anyone who isn't Jo, tell anyone else where you're going or come up with some cockamamie scheme with them to try to go back on our deal, you will kill whoever you spoke to, and then Jo will return. And if you don't return, Jo will murder the entire Windy Van Hooten's circus with her own hands. And you wouldn't want to have to hurt your little sorcerer's apprentice." He grinned. Because he had her. "Is that right, Jo?"

Jo nodded calmly from her spot.

Ringmaster felt something stir. A physical aching in her heart. A need to envelop this child and never let the world touch her. To carry her out of this no matter the cost.

She was responsible for her.

And she knew that; she'd always known this, but now that truth burrowed into her chest with the warmth of the sun.

It was joy, in this cold, joyless place.

"It is my opinion that you are doing the right thing," Edward offered as Ringmaster went to Jo's side. "Finally. How many women have suffered because you ran from me? All my ballet girls, I call them the Brides. They all wear your old clothes, Ruth. But now that you've come home, they can be free."

"I am not responsible for what you have done," Ruth breathed quietly. "You might be able to lie to everyone else, but you can't lie to yourself. You know what you are."

Edward could have said more, and she braced herself for the commands to come. But Edward had won. Edward stepped back to watch her pick up the pieces of Josephine Reed.

She put a hand on Jo's shoulder.

"Let's go home."

48

THE RINGMASTER, 1926

One moment, they were in a nightmare. The next moment, they were in the place where she'd built her dreams. She shed the name Ruth, and took up Rin one last time.

It was a quick trip, but it would be the longest night of her life.

She swallowed hard, leading a quiet and entranced Jo down the sleeping midway. Jo would be all right, as soon as Ruth returned to Edward. Rin gently held her hand, guiding her through a dream.

The stars were out tonight.

Whenever she was in the future and looked up at the sky, she couldn't see the stars. The world would keep evolving into a more electric spectacle, and it would wipe the skies clean of constellations.

Without dark, nothing could really shine.

They passed the tents, the food stands, the beautiful signs, the train cars. She remembered Odette and Mauve painting the cars. She remembered renting the engine, meeting the Weathers family. She'd built most of the stands herself, even if Maynard could do it all. She'd set up her room in the caboose, just the way she wanted it and not the way anyone else told her to have it. It was the first thing that was really hers. It was where she and Mauve had grown older and closer and braver. It was where she'd loved Odette.

But it was a home she was no longer allowed. It was already gone. She was already dead.

"You found her!"

Rin startled. Jo did not. Jo was barely breathing, a raspy thing reserved for bodies on their deathbeds. She was a machine, breathing in and out, on hold, the real spirit of the sardonic, whip-smart little girl hidden and buried somewhere else.

Rin turned around, and she saw Odette Paris and Mauve DesChamps standing in the dirt path of the midway, bright smiles with worried eyes.

"Why didn't you meet us at the entrance of our midway?" Mauve said. "Are you all right?"

She only had a minute to speak to anyone. She had to be so careful.

"Jo," Rin said calmly, "can you sit for a second? I'll be right back, I just need to tell Odette and Mauve something. I have to make sure they won't follow me and they won't worry. Don't do anything, please."

Jo didn't say anything. She only stared at Rin. Paused. But still counting seconds in her head, like a bomb.

"It'll be over soon," Rin assured her. She led her to the closest bench. She carefully sat her down, and she slowly walked to Odette and Mauve. Her legs were heavy. The Circus King had thought through every loophole of her Spark. His guidelines were rigid barbed wire around her arms and legs and shoved into her mouth and down her throat. She had only minutes, unable to leave, unable to stay, unable to turn the clock forward or backward, only able to say goodbye and only goodbye for less than a minute.

But Edward had missed one thing.

It might not work, but she reached out her hands to touch Odette and Mauve's shoulders, and they

did not leave the midway. Instead, the midway stayed rooted in that single moment. The night crickets muted. The stars stopped blinking in the sky. The ocean of time stopped still, like ice crawling outward throughout the entire circus, the town, the mountain range, maybe the moon. She didn't know how it worked, but she knew it wouldn't last forever. She could already feel the whole of reality pushing back on her, like she was standing in an ocean that shoved waves onto her tiny body. It wanted to throw her off her feet, under its current. But she held her stance. She held the three of them in place.

Odette blinked, then looked around. "R-Rin?"

"I suspected my Spark grew again," Rin said.

"You look like it hurts," Mauve said.

"It's like someone's pushing a door open and I'm holding it," Rin said. "I can't hold it forever but . . ."

"Why are you doing this?" Odette said.

Because, Rin wanted to say. *You deserve a moment.* The three of them deserved all the time in the universe. But this is all Rin could give.

Mauve's expression fell. "You didn't get out, did you."

Odette studied her, her pixie nose wrinkling. The little things Rin would need to remember for the rest of her life alone. Small things were big things, weren't they?

"No," Odette said. "How do we fight this? What do we do?"

Then came the scene where they were supposed to rally, outsmart the Circus King. There was supposed to be something more than a quiet goodbye. But that's all there was. A vacuous, hurried goodbye. It was another failed attempt to change fate, just like the rest of the summer.

"I have strict rules on me," Rin said. "Or bad things happen. We can't do anything."

"What the hell does that mean?" Mauve said.

Rin swallowed, a lump in her throat. "I am going to hold this moment for as long as I can, but then I have to go back."

"No," Odette said again. "No. No."

"I love you," Rin said to them both. It was said when mediums tried to reach out to the dead, the spirits always desperately screamed out *I love you I love you,* because nothing else may penetrate the veil between them. *I love you.*

"Mauve," Rin said. "you are brilliant and you are the mind of this circus. Please keep it going, please."

"Of course, I'm going to keep it going. And you're going to keep it going, too!" Mauve said. "What about—"

"No, please." Rin gritted her teeth. "Please stop. We agreed, if he ever . . . we all three agreed. We cannot put anyone else in danger. He doesn't want any of you, he wants me. I can't . . . say anything else. Please, please Mauve."

Mauve looked at the ground. Her mouth formed a frown. "I love you," she surrendered.

"There's something we can do," Odette said. "I'm not letting you go."

"I can't say anything else or you're going to get hurt," Rin said again. Because it's all she could say. "Don't come after me. Let me go, Odette."

"We have to," Mauve said.

"I'm tired of you two telling me what can and can't happen," Odette snapped. And then she turned on Rin. "If you had just listened to me! I told you not to go without me!"

"So you could be dead now?" Rin said. "Odette, I can't hold this moment forever. I love you. I'm so sorry. I'm sorry about the pain, I'm sorry about the lunches I forgot about, I'm sorry I couldn't stay longer. I'm so sorry."

"I love you," Odette said, bewildered.

The three of them stood amid the midway, the banners, the Big Top, the memories of a decade of hot summer days and squealing kids and the smell of sweat and sugar. Her life here had been a love letter.

The circus trembled around them, like a breath that needed to be taken. Like Rin was under the water and wanted to stay there forever, but couldn't, because she needed oxygen. Her lungs would burst. Her Spark would collapse like a sprained ankle, dragged into the undertow, and then the moment would be gone.

No matter what would happen from this point on, they had been strong enough to have made their own home. These three girls had turned into women when they found home within, and within each other.

Rin would have to let go soon. Her back ached, her head pounded.

"He won't bother anyone anymore," Rin said.

Odette and Mauve did not let go of Rin's hands.

"It will be all right," Rin said quietly.

And time started again.

Rin pushed Odette's blond hair out of her face.

Mauve wore a frown, a look of thinking about something deep, mathematics and threads already whirring past her eyes. She was trying to find a solution that would never come.

"Don't forget who you are," Mauve said.

But Rin knew she would.

"I only have a couple more seconds," Rin warned them. "Then I have to stop talking."

Odette shook her head, back and forth, like she could change it if she didn't agree. "You know," she said quietly. "No matter what happened, since I met you, I've never been afraid. Because you were here." She squeezed Rin's hand. And her eyes turned red as she tried not to cry. "Now what am I going to do?"

Rin took Odette's gloved hand. She slowly removed the glove. She reached out her hand to Mauve. The three's bare fingers intertwined. Odette broke, her shoulders shaking, deep gasps of grief.

They held each other. All the time in the world would not have been enough.

"I'm not afraid," Rin said. "Because you all are still here."

☀

There was only one thing left to do: make sure Jo was comfortable. Rin helped the husk of Jo up the stairs into the LQ train car. Odette and Mauve waited outside, near the tracks, pretending Rin would come back out when she was done. Odette said, "I'll see you in a minute," and Rin nodded. Her time was up for talking.

Mauve wrapped her arm around Odette. Odette held Mauve. Mauve didn't say anything, but she was looking at Rin like she was formulating a plan. But there was no plan. Rin couldn't allow her heart to hope for a miracle. Rin turned and entered the dark car before she could think about how this was a goodbye.

Rin guided Jo into an empty bunk where Charles already slept above. He had walked calmly into camp. Charles without Jo wasn't the way this was supposed to end. They were a package deal, that's what they'd said.

"Please, lie down and sleep," Rin whispered to the little girl. The girl's hand held Rin's as she steadily climbed into the bunk and lay down. "It's just a dream."

"I'm tired," Jo said quietly.

"I know," Rin said, tucking her in. "But you'll feel better once you sleep."

"Do I need to go back?"

"No," Rin said. "Never. You stay here."

Rin stayed until Jo closed her eyes and quietly fell asleep. Rin held her hand, she memorized her nose and her eyelashes, her black hair and her thin tweedy arms. She wanted to always remember the way Jo filled the room with courage.

Rin had been able to protect her.

And maybe that was enough.

She pushed Jo's hair back out of her eyes, and quietly whispered, "I don't remember much about all the things my mother taught me. But I do know she never let a Shabbat go by without blessing me."

She kissed Jo on one cheek, then the other.

Then she let go.

She fell back, into shadow, as if opening her hand and letting the sand fall between her fingers. Goodbye, midway with the electric lights. Goodbye, the quilt on her bed. Goodbye, painted flowers and dusty spotlights. Goodbye, tangerines and purple shawls. Prairie waves and oceans spilling from girls' palms. Soft bobbed hair with pixie noses and the promise of another dance in Montmartre. Goodbye.

In a small breath of wind, the Ringmaster was gone.

49

THE CIRCUS KING, 1926

It was as if life had come back to him. He stood in his tent with his wife, finally complete. Finally, she was here. It had been such a cold world alone, and he could sense some stirrings of feeling below all the edges and fortresses he'd made within and around himself. She deserved to be dead for all she did, but she was here. She could redeem him. And he could redeem her. This circus could redeem them both.

Ruth always loved this circus. He turned on the ghost light, excited to show off the little he had here. The black Big Top's insides glowed a flaccid, nonmagical yellow. It wasn't showtime, and Ruth had only just joined.

When the audience wasn't here, that's when the real truth of their magical circus would show itself. Only those in control could see the work lights, the stitching on the costumes, all the preparation. Only Edward could see the truth, because only Edward was in control.

"It's large," Edward said, dragging the ghost light to the center ring. Ruth followed, looking around skeptically. It was indeed skepticism, not the fire in her smile he'd seen less than ten years ago.

She'd grown old. He felt like Peter Pan looking at Wendy through the window when he didn't find her in time and she went ahead and grew up.

"You look different than when you left," Edward said. "But I can tell it's still you."

Ruth said nothing. She looked up the king pole, looked to the black bleachers. She was in that bright red coat, and she stood out against his monochromatic world. The world was full of options now, and he smiled to himself. Peace. He did it. He had brought her home, and she would light him up again.

"Well, you can see we have three rings," Edward said. "Arena seating, thrust really. We keep it only on three sides. Grandstand costs extra, reserving ahead of time costs extra. We mostly have Sparks on board. Remember when we used to use the lesser type to do pyrotechnics? Now I can handle it. It's really a wonder; the audience can't tell the difference between us and reality. The demographics we get . . . they're probably not what you're used to." He jumped onto the divider for the center ring and walked alongside her. "Our crowds . . . they like the darker side of things, you know? And they pay well to see that darker side." She didn't look at him, she kept looking all around her.

This should be her palace. But she looked at it like a prison.

"We can sell the whole thing if you aren't keen on circuses anymore," Edward said. "I obviously have enough money that we can do anything you'd like. See the world? Open a candy shop in San Francisco? Hell, we could go to the moon."

Ruth still said nothing.

"Perhaps not the moon," Edward said, still keeping up. "Although that would be quite fantastic. Like that old French nickelodeon. Do you remember? Build a rocket and land in the moon's eye." He touched the edge of the barrier with his toes. "The Earth is a little too complicated for me, sometimes." He looked out to the audience, or where it would be if anyone but the two of them were here. "Sometimes I think about all the men who wanted people like us dead. Even before the Spark, we were all damned in their eyes for whatever reasons: too weak, too poor, too stupid, too different. I remember sitting in that trench, thinking about powerful men and what power meant. When we had the power instead of them, they hated us even more."

Ruth stared at him. Her mouth was a firm line.

"When I heard what you were up to, this other circus," Edward said, staring back down at her. They were so close, and so far away. "I was surprised. With your Spark, you could have done so much more."

"I wish we'd met somewhere nice," Ruth said, her eyes driving through him like a warm knife.

Edward stopped. "Excuse me?"

"Somewhere adventurous and new." Ruth stepped forward. Edward stepped backward. "Like New York City. Sometimes I'd imagine you were an actor like my mother, one of the best. One of the funniest. And we met at rehearsal. And you were happy. It's hard to believe in happiness when darkness is all you've been taught."

He felt something behind his eye, his fists tensed, his lungs wanted to just let go of a breath he'd been holding for so long. But he didn't. Instead, he tweaked his neck. "Don't . . . I would like it if you don't worry about me. *I believe* I'm all right. Especially now. You're alive! We have forever again, my love."

"I've been granting wishes for years," Ruth said, her voice low and flat. "I've had a lot of time to think about what wishes I would have given you. There have been times I wished the Spark never chose you." So did he. "But really, I wish that you could have done good with your Spark. You could have helped people. You could have persuaded them to do better, to heal each other, fix this world. You had a choice in all you did."

Edward grew dark. "I never had a choice." Ruth blinked. Oh no. "I mean to say, *in my very strong opinion* I never had a choice." He was trying so hard, he was trying, Ruth.

Ruth shook her head. "You did. I've met veterans. I've met people left for dead and run out of town, I've met those who have seen so much more evil than we have. And they were kind. With your power, with your smile, you had a choice, Edward." She didn't look furious. She looked piteous. Why did she pity *him*?

"You could tell me that I never again had to accept what you say," Ruth said. "You could really set me free."

"Just give me this chance," Edward said.

Ruth stepped back, her eyes not leaving his. "You spent so much time getting what you wanted," she said, "you ended up with nothing."

He felt that pressure behind his eye. He felt the tension in his lungs. He felt something stirring beneath his fingernails. A memory so far away, the scratchy bedsheets gripped in his fists as he pulled the covers up over his head, the vast prairies that had met him and his new wife, and he didn't know where to even start or what to do, the sounds of insects in the silent rooms when he was alone with himself. But none of that was him. That was someone he once was, someone he might have been if he'd been weak.

The person saying these things to him? This was not Ruth. This was a wretch who had been taken advantage of, assimilated into the gutter rats. He would set them both back on a good path. Everything would be okay.

"You don't talk to . . ." He stopped. He took a breath. "I would rather, if you don't mind, completely up to you, if you refrained from hurting me. It's your choice to give, but a little respect and love may go a long way."

"I do mind." Ruth turned on him, stepping forward, closer and closer. Edward turned and walked away. She followed him, went on with her list of grievances—of course she had kept a list—names of people who didn't matter anymore, and he felt a tug of boredom inside. He turned back around, looked to her poor warped sense of cross-dressing fashion; he needed to get her new clothes. She wore trousers. It would need to change. And how could she march this close to him? She stood right in his face. "Why did we leave New York, Edward?"

Edward didn't know what to say to this. This nagging old maid was a stranger. She had allowed herself to be nothing more than a cross-dressing Jewess, not who she should have become if she had been thriving. His wife! Where was his wife? They'd said vows to each other. He'd promised her the world and he would have given her anything. Who would she have been now if she had never left?

"The day I found your grave," he tried to explain, "was the day my own life ended. It hurt, and then to find out that years had passed and all that time you *wanted* me to hurt. You did it all to me, on purpose, and you were fucking some trapeze swinger? You've committed infidelity, you've lied to me—"

"What happened the night we left New York." It was not a question. Ruth grabbed his collar, and he realized how much stronger she now was. He opened his mouth, but then he closed it. He couldn't trust himself. There had been a near hiccup during negotiations, he had been tempted, but no, he would do this correctly. "Speak!"

"From my perspective," he said, "you said you wanted to marry me. From my perspective, it was your own choice to say that, it wasn't me."

"Liar."

"It was, at least that's what I thought! I had been careful. I remember trying to be careful for you. You have the freedom to have your own opinion, but I can't say I'll agree with it!"

Ruth's glare faltered, for a second. "The way you worded that, I don't know if you're telling the truth. This is another trick."

"I am trying with all my might to be very honest with you, Ruth." He took her hands in his. "We were in love. We married."

"It wasn't my fault," Ruth said, like a heavy cloak slipped from her shoulders, like she would fly away. "Did I help kill those people in Maryville? Did I hurt you? Did I hurt my mother? Did she die because of me? *Why did we leave New York?*"

"Ruth—"

"We left because *you* took us away." Her hair was wild, unkempt. She'd gained weight. She was dressed as a man. She'd been twisted by the world, not him. He'd done nothing to turn her into this beastly hag. He'd tried to save her, tried to give her the world, and she'd left him. She'd pulled away when they were meant to—"You were afraid my mother had figured you out and you would be alone."

Something flared in him, hotter than anything Ruth could feel inside her flimsy heart. Mrs. Dover, watching him from the hearth that night in New York. Ruth looked just like her now.

She wouldn't listen? Fine.

Edward pushed her off. He was still the bigger one. He was still the stronger one.

"This circus is *yours,* Ruth," Edward said. "*You created this one before you ran off with Odette.* That's right, I know her name. You loved *me.* You saved *me!* You took *me* in! I protected you! I gave you everything, you stupid girl! You've ruined me! Now you stand here shoving me away when I'm the only one on this fucking planet who actually gives a shit about you! Where are all those people? Odette, Mauve, this brat Jo, whoever the hell?! They're not here, Ruth!" Ruth looked scared now. Good. She stepped backward. He shoved her back farther. "It's only you and me and what we started to build together!" She tried to cover her ears. He grabbed her arms and forced them to her side. She twisted her wrists to get free, but Edward held her hands down. "Your little friends down there in Fort Collins? Where are they? They're drunks, like you. They're queers, like you." She struggled. She was still a scared little girl. He'd remind her of that. How dare she try him? The panic he used to feel, that she would leave him, like a kite blown out of reach—he knew how to tether her. He knew. "Listen to me! They're hypocrites and self-aggrandizing martyrs, just like you." He would never be alone again. "You surrounded yourself with people who would say yes yes yes! So how are you any better than what you think I am? How have you gotten any better as a person when no one around you cares enough to tell you to even brush your hair?"

It had all come out like a machine gun, spattering her with chains. Ruth stared at him, her eyes narrowed, her body rigid, like his words twisted around her bones and replaced her marrow. Good, let her shake. There she was, the girl he knew was still there, the girl she used to be. They could heal now.

Edward let go. She didn't pull away. He found a breath. He found his heartbeat. He was no longer standing on a precipice lashing out of control, falling falling. He had his grip on the story. And he could fix it.

"I can help you, Ruth," Edward said. "I love you."

Ruth's face cracked. She gave a small sob. Finally, she was listening.

"I . . ." she said. "I didn't know you really loved me."

"And I am sorry about your mother," Edward said. "But she wanted to stop us. She was a terrible, cruel lady. She hurt you, she hurt me. We had to leave." He touched the velvet coat. "Now she can't hurt us. She's gone. They're all gone. It's just you and me now. Ruth and Edward."

He took her coat slowly off, his hands hot against her cold, shivering, blubbering body. Her suspenders underneath looked ridiculous. She stood there, staring at him, waiting for what he would say next.

She said he only knew darkness. But here he was, doing for her what had never been done for him. He'd crossed the universe to find her, to bring her home.

"We'll go to the moon, Ruthie," Edward said. "You and me, just you and me."

50

RUTH, 1926

A lie can only last so long.

She'd been in the dirty dregs of society, and now, like Persephone, she rose back up to spring. Spring was cold and full of rain, but she was alive, and this place was where she was supposed to be. She was good here. In the underworld, there was pain. There were demons who swore they loved and adored her. It reminded her of stories where someone had been lured by sirens into the ocean and spent a feast in a mythical kingdom only to return a hundred years later with long white beards.

She had wasted her entire life away, and yet Edward still wanted her.

She had run away from her responsibilities, but Edward forgave her. Edward had held the brunt of all this on his own for so many years. Now that she was back in the land of the living, the real world and not the sideshow illusion she'd cocooned herself in, she saw the chipping paint, her lecherous infidelious desires, all the narratives she'd braided in her hair like rotting daisy chains. Now that she was back home, it all flooded back like it was yesterday. The bodies she'd seen bury themselves in the dirt, the image of the old ringmaster's bloated body, all the people who went missing, all the scratches on Edward's sobbing face. All along, it had been her hurting *him*. It was for the best the rest of the world forgot her.

Her mother had whispered, in those last days on her deathbed, "I had such hopes for her, why did she let him do this?"

Years later, Odette had said her mother was feverish, that sometimes we get frustrated with those we love when they hurt themselves.

Odette had let her get away with anything, all for a warm bed at night. Or maybe Odette hated herself more than Ruth hated herself. Maybe Odette thought she deserved the treatment of being drained down to her tendons, her melting eyes, the screaming from Japan.

"You must hate me," Ruth sobbed. She collapsed in Edward's arms.

Ruth had slowly suffocated Odette, used Odette, and what a coward Odette was for allowing her to do such a thing.

Edward was no coward. Edward told her the truth, shouted back at her when her fury rose up. They could meet one another on the same plane.

Edward touched her hair, just the way her mother used to. He smelled like her wedding day; dusty pine trees, expensive cologne, and a hint of smoked meats. She'd forgotten his favorite food was ham. She used to make ham sandwiches for him all the time. She'd forgotten that.

"I don't hate you," Edward said. "You are tiring, you drain people, but I am the one you are allowed to drain. Trust me, Ruth."

"Thank you, Edward," Ruth said. His name in her mouth was like cotton candy.

"Now," Edward said. "We do have an agreement, if you remember. You can leave if you'd like. Go back to the gutter. Or you can stay here. Have you come to your senses yet? Will you stay?"

Ruth nodded. "Please don't send me back. Please, I'm so sorry."

Edward smiled. "I got you a gift." He waved his hand. There, in the middle of the center ring, was an entire bar full of glass bottles. "I made it myself. I remembered all your favorites."

Ruth dumbly looked to it, her stomach leaping with excitement. Things were going to be okay. "But," she said, "I'm not supposed to—"

"It's okay," Edward said. "You are okay. Trust me."

That's when the gun fired.

Ruth screamed and jumped back. She watched Edward start, stumbling away from her and screaming. She wanted to go to him, he looked so afraid and so young, but she didn't know where the shooter had been. She felt her heart race. She had to help him, she was a coward.

But Edward wasn't hit. There was a hole in the tent's wall behind him, but he was unscathed somehow.

Then she saw the assassin. Mauve DesChamps stormed in from the shadows, a rifle aimed at Edward. Edward made that pulling motion on his ears. Mauve slowly pulled the wax out of her ears. He said, "Don't kill me! Don't shoot me, don't maim me, don't stab me!" as if he'd said all this before, as if this wasn't the first assassin. Poor Edward, he'd done all this by himself for so long.

Mauve couldn't pull the trigger. They were safe. Mauve knew that. She looked murderous. "You're scared," Mauve said. "Good."

"No, stop," Ruth tried to squeak out, but she was so small.

Edward smirked at Mauve. "Oh, I see," he said. "It's the—" But then a hand clamped down over his mouth out of thin air. A thin, bare white hand, tearing out from behind an illusion of invisibility in the air right behind him. Through the tear in reality was Odette Paris. Beside her, Josephine Reed rolled up the illusion like a cloak, sucking the colors of the surrounding environment back into her palms.

But Edward pointed at Mauve and gestured for the ground. Mauve dropped the rifle, gasping as she stared at her hands.

Kell Weathers jumped from behind Jo and grabbed Edward's shoulders. Odette was too weak to hold the Circus King alone; he was writhing and trying to buck her off, but Kell grabbed Edward's arms and pinned him, pulling him to the ground and knocking the air out of him. Odette knelt, going down with them like Edward was a wayward showhorse and she was safely dancing to the ground. Her hand did not move from Edward's mouth. "No gestures for you, fella," Kell growled, his wings curling around them. "Mauve, you're okay. Odette, take care of him."

Odette closed her eyes. Ruth knew what that meant. She knew Odette had done it to an archduke. Odette, who said she hated being evil, was being evil.

"Breathe," Odette whispered, calm. "Relax."

Edward's muscles relaxed. His shoulders fell, like he'd been carrying the world and had set it down.

Edward grew still. Ruth was defenseless.

And then all eyes turned to Ruth. She was next. She screamed again.

"Darling, it's all right," Odette said, not moving from Edward. "We're going home. Run."

They were letting her go? No. Ruth didn't run. She had left Edward once before, and now she would not be a coward. No, worse than a coward. Who would she be without him? He looked so lifeless lying there under them. They didn't know what they were doing, separating them. She didn't even know how to ride a bicycle. She was so useless, an empty puppet, and she had always needed him—

"Rin?" Odette said weakly.

Ruth burst into tears. "Stop hurting him."

Odette looked stunned.

"You're hurting him," Ruth begged her. "Please, please don't. I need him. *I need him.*"

She couldn't find her feet. She was frozen on the ground.

"Someone grab her," Mauve ordered. "We need to leave."

"Don't you touch me!" Ruth screamed. "I'll fight back! Don't you come near me!"

The tent was still. It smelled like blood and sweat and too-sweet cologne. She was alone.

A scared, shriveled girl trapped behind the face and clothing of an old woman. What had she done to her life? She'd led these people to Edward with her choices, collecting their enemies unwittingly. She'd thought she was searching for love when she'd had it the whole time. She and Ed could have been happy, they could have run away together and never been found.

"Ringmaster?" Jo started forward. Odette said, "Jo, no, stay back." Mauve ran to Jo, jumping over the barrier. Ruth scrambled back.

"No, she's not snapping out of it, no no . . ." Jo stepped forward. Ruth felt her own pulse in her chest. "Hey, Ringmaster, it's us. We got here. Let's go home. We . . . we gotta go."

They still didn't have the gun. Edward had cleverly made them put it down. Maybe she could save Ed. She readied herself. "I know what you're doing to him, Odette," Ruth said. "The same thing you told me he did. You two are no different, no matter what you say."

"How much longer can you hold him?" Kell asked. Odette's eyes were glued on Ruth, like Ruth had already shot her.

Jo stepped forward, standing on the curb of the center ring. "Hey, Ringmaster! Look at me! We're running out of time. Look, I'm not making any illusions. This is all real. And I'm telling you we gotta go home. This is *not* where you belong. This place is cold and scary, and your circus is bright and beautiful and it's everything I've ever wanted, do you get that? We gotta go."

The circus was a lie. This little girl could kill her in an instant. Then she saw Ed, just lying there, sleepily staring at the ceiling of the tent he'd built for her. She had to find the strength to get to that gun. "Oh God, Edward."

"Don't look at him, he's an asshole," Jo said. "I know you wanna, but you can't. Look at me. You had no reason to come up here and save my stupid ass, but you did. Because you know what it really means to love someone. That's right, huh? You're never gonna say it to me, but I know you're a big lug."

"Please let me go," Ruth begged.

"Nope," Jo said. "I'm not gonna do that."

"Jo," Odette said. "He's going to wake up. Get back. I can't hold it forever. . . ."

Ed gave out a moan. Jo's fingers twitched. Ruth felt something caught in her throat. Jo did not move. Ed would come back to her, Ed would be okay.

"You might have to subdue Ringmaster long enough for us to get her out of here," Kell said.

A chill grabbed Ruth's ribs and her spine and split her brain into an ache. No. Never.

The gun was on the ground to their right. Edward was ahead of them. She didn't need the gun, did she? If she used her own body as a shield and she kept Ed close to her, they wouldn't shoot. She just needed to reach him, and she could get him out of here.

Ruth would not leave Edward alone this time. Not again.

Ruth charged forward. Mauve and Odette and Kell braced, their eyes closing.

But Jo slammed between Ruth and the others. She raised her hands. Colors spilled out. In one swift movement, the little girl opened her palms.

Out from her fingers came paints.

They spiraled in the air.

Iridescent blue, sparkling like stars. Rising up to the highest point of the tent. The black and washed-out grays floated away, and instead came galaxies, deep oceans of purple and pink, and the sound of violins and deep cellos and the music from a carousel.

The smell of fresh summer mornings, the sound of birds flying over a lake with the morning mist still floating above, the sunrises over mountains, the peace of a cornfield, the vast blue Kansas sky.

Then came the circus.

A brilliant light of a woman, surrounded by warmth and shining with joy, standing in the center of the ring. She laughed, her voice booming, her hair flying out from under her black hat. The spec parade surrounding her, marching and enveloping her. Jo painted this woman with freckles, half smiles, bright black eyes reflecting all those around her.

This ringmaster made the stars in the sky dance.

"I see you," Jo said. "We all see you."

Somewhere in her, she remembered watching Josephine show her visions to the audience as their eyes lit up. She remembered the heat of the lights on her cheeks as Odette flew above her and Mauve sang her song.

There had been no music with Edward.

But with Mauve, there had always been music, a song floating through the courtyard the night she wanted to end it all. There was always a lilt of a note in her soft, confident voice. There were always open, welcome arms, a grit that couldn't be snuffed out.

And with Odette.

She saw Odette watching with pleading eyes and a breaking heart. Odette held Edward down with Kell, her hands over Edward's mouth and her head and back raised at attention. She hurt, but she was still looking at Rin.

Dancing along cobblestone French streets, holding one another under old bedsheets they'd gotten secondhand but were still the first thing they bought with their own money . . . small moments that worked like notes on a five-string staff, weaving their fingers together and tying their threads into one.

You are my music, Odette.

The colors flew around the old woman, embracing her, filling her up with a warm light. A key change. A bridge in a beautiful, perfect song that hit her in the heart. Unconditional, forgiving strength, full of some sort of hope that the whole of history had not yet erased from humans. Love.

There was love.

Then the colors were gone.

They were all back in a black, empty tent.

Edward still lay stirring under Odette. His eyes fluttered. But there was still time for them to get away with it. Odette looked to her, eyes full of exhausted and frightened tears.

Her own hand shook. She tried to find her center, tried to feel her body and her gut and her heart. Then she saw things even the Dreamweaver couldn't see. Her mother, lighting candles. Her plaid pleated dress, her proud straight back as she folded her hands on her stomach, beamed down to see her little girl. Her daughter.

A memory of that little girl on the beach, running barefoot with the sand between her toes as she pressed forward, kicking up her path faster than the waves could take it away. She felt the wind on her cheeks, her hair blown past her ears and trailing behind like a train. Someday, she thought, she would run so fast, she would fly around the world. Beyond New York, beyond the sea, she would throw herself into the wind and into an adventure. She laughed, because she was brave. She laughed, because she was joy.

And she had jumped into the air, squealing, knowing the world would catch her.

She now stood on the tarp ground of a paint-chipped tent. She held her stomach. She tried to steady her hand.

Jo stepped forward, cautiously. "Rin?" she asked.

Rin pulled Jo into her arms. Jo's fists gripped Rin's shirt, tugging her closer. Rin took a deep breath, oxygen back in this place.

"Let's go home," Rin said softly.

But then hands shoved Odette away. Edward, screaming his way out of Odette's spell, rushed to Rin, snatched Jo and twisted her arm back, his hair spitting into his face with sweat, his eyes bloodshot. Odette rushed forward. Edward spun. "You stupid bitch, I have a Spark that is in the mind, too! Odette, freeze right there and don't you dare move!"

Odette froze like a living statue. Jo tried to struggle. Panic rose as Edward's mouth turned back to her.

"You all failed." He grinned. "You know what I'm gonna do to her, Ruth? Fuck the niceties. I'm selling this snot-nosed spawn to the asylum, and I'll make you forget her with just one word. You'll never see her again, but you'll miss someone and you won't know why! At least your mother knew who you were! That was the mistake I made."

"Edward, stop!" Rin pleaded.

"Touch me, Ruth!" Edward laughed. His eyes were large, his mind seemed to be dissipating in his skull, as if he knew he finally won but he was slipping on thin ice. "Touch me! You can go through time? Then take me!" He twisted Jo closer and Jo screamed. "Jo, stop screaming! And the rest of you, back off now!"

Mauve pushed herself away like the wrong side of a magnet, her face twisted and tears catching in her eyes. Kell walked out of the ring, also caught in a silent cry. Edward's grin fed on the sight of all their tears, and his laugh turned into a lost, mania-fueled chitter.

And Rin touched him.

"Ruth," he said, "I know you trusted me. I know there was a time when you loved me. We're going back there, wherever it is, to the last moment you genuinely thought I had any fucking worth!"

"No." Rin tried to keep her eyes on Odette, frozen Odette, Odette who still had tears rolling down her paralyzed face. But Rin already was thinking it would be a good idea to listen to Edward. She already was looking through time, the threads showing through the cracks.

"*Take us back to the last time you trusted me. Now!*" Edward roared, throwing Jo to the side and grabbing Rin's arm.

The threads spread. The timeline opened. They fell back into space.

But she saw Jo charge forward.

"No, Jo!" Rin begged her.

Jo jumped. Jo reached out. Her fingertips grazed Rin.

The Ringmaster disappeared, along with the Circus King and the Dream-weaver.

51

THE RINGMASTER, 1916

No one knows why the Spark came. But it came during the war.

The trench's walls were drenched with mud, constantly sliding down to their feet and drowning their boots in standing water and grime. There were tanks, far off. Planes above. This was unnatural. The ground wasn't supposed to be dug up like this.

Something broke with the world when it was cut into trenches.

Something had been let loose. A great good. A great evil. No, a greatness left to them to define.

Rin stood still, petrified, watching the boys ahead of her down the trench. They'd soon notice a gaggle of circus performers in bright costumes among the muck.

But they didn't.

Edward held on to her, frozen, shell-shocked. He didn't move. He barely breathed. Rin's own heart beat so hard she thought she could die. And Jo . . .

Jo?

Rin looked to Jo, who held one hand outward with paints covering them like a shield between the past and the present.

Jo stared at the soldiers. Then at Rin.

"When are we?" she said. "Is this the future?"

"No," Rin said solemnly. "It's the past." She squeezed Jo's hand.

Edward screamed, a silent horror becoming real. He fell, dragging her and Jo down into the flooded dirt.

Rin shoved him off with her boot.

Edward shook his head, over and over, slipping in the mud and shit. "No," he said. "No. Ruthie."

Rin said nothing. She stepped back, pulling Jo with her.

"Please," he said over and over again, crumpling to the ground. "No, don't be cruel. Please."

"I'm sorry," she said. She meant it. And it was a kindness, to be sorry.

A canister fell behind Edward. Smoke erupted.

Rin held Jo tight as Jo's colors faded from around them. Jo was too afraid now; she couldn't concentrate. Neither could Rin. Rin tried to keep her wits, she tried to find the thread, split the veil of reality so she could see the way home. But she was frozen. She, too, remembered this hell.

The smoke hit Edward first. Edward coughed, his voice gone, screeching out commands the gas wouldn't allow him to finish. He clawed for them through the smoke, his gestures useless.

The smoke was coming closer.

But then to their left, Rin saw a flash. She heard a pop.

She turned her head.

She saw a little girl full of life who had appeared among the dying men. A little girl with pink cheeks, braids, and a perfectly pressed dress. This girl, this young Ruth Dover, stared at everything around her in shock. Rin saw a young soldier rushing at her, screaming for help. She knew underneath that boy's gas mask there was a handsome face, a clear voice imbued with the blessing of a Spark. And he was getting closer and closer to her—

This girl, this person who had once been her, did not belong here. This was not her story. She had come from New York. She was young. She should have been with her mother. But she had a Spark. She would find a boy just as terrible as this place. And he would follow her, choke her, try to destroy her.

Rin did not feel a fraying thread. She could see her so clearly, no vertigo. Maybe . . . yes, the Ringmaster *could* grab this little girl. The Spark allowed it. She could save her. Perhaps, women grow up to become the person they needed when they were alone.

She could grant her own wish. Like a dream finally realized, she could run and reach her, shield her, change it all.

To change it all, Rin thought. She could change it all. Without the dark of the past, the future—

But Jo struggled to breathe, trying to scream for help as she slowly slid into the mud and lost her grip on Rin. Rin held on to her tighter, pulling her up into her arms, her own eyes starting to water.

The future had already happened. And it was lit up by a circus. She had to get them home.

Edward shoved himself off the shit-ridden ground one more time, one last attempt. He reached out his arms for them, his eyes on fire.

Rin shoved her light out from her heart, a deep force from somewhere further inward than her ribs. It was like music, it was like joy. It was life and love and all the dances in the world, and it came from a small girl who once drew the candlelight to her, beside Catherine Dover. And that light flew out around her and Josephine like a shock wave.

Time stopped.

The Circus King's body froze. Straight in front of her. Only inches away.

Rin leaned back. Behind Rin, time opened for her and Josephine.

The last thing she saw before they disappeared was not Edward dying in the trench in his black suit, his mouth screaming without words.

She couldn't watch that.

She looked to Jo, clinging to her shoulders. She saw Jo's small face, her stringy black hair, her shaking, shuddering body. She was going to be okay.

As softly as she had once touched that boy's hand, she let go of the trench. She let go of the thread between her and the boy. She let go of the smoke and the smell of fear and the sounds of the planes above. Edward was left where he was to have ended. A loop closed.

Her Spark cracked like a whip of white light around them. She reached her hand out to find her own time, held tight to Jo, and jumped forward. They left the past. They went home.

52

THE RINGMASTER, 1926

Summer always seemed to turn to fall so rapidly, without any warning. And this year was no different, despite all that had taken place that summer. One day, it was scalding hot with green grass and lush trees, the next there was a smell of bonfires and the sound of crunching leaves as the heartland turned red and orange.

It meant another season finished, another glowing stream of firefly nights wrapped up for another year. Winter was cold and unforgiving, and that's one reason why circuses hid in places like Florida and Texas during the off months. It would be time to fold everything up, leave the routine of train yards near factories and down the street from town halls and rows of restaurants that started to blend together, and instead get back into a routine of rehearsals and budgeting and conceptualizing new shows. It was an end. It was a death.

But this year, Rin welcomed September. It wasn't too cold, and she had a nice thick scarf Jess had knitted her to keep the sickness out of her lungs. The colors of southern Wisconsin burned bright like a warm fire kindling their tour's finish line.

The rest of Colorado had been good sales, all things considered. At first, people came to see horrors and got butterflies instead. The way the darkness slipped from their local reputation farther down the tracks, even with the new Spark performers who had joined Windy Van Hooten's from the nightmare circus: ensemble members, a woman who could grow her limbs and neck, so many clowns. Wisconsin welcomed them with the changing trees, large smashable piles of leaves, hills that rolled from one fence to the other and over the horizon, and Lake Michigan that looked like an ocean in the middle of the heartland.

This September morning, Rin felt the sun hit her cheeks as she stood next to Mauve and Odette in the mouth of the midway. They watched the Big Top raise high like a slow yawn, and the booths and wagons and sideshows found their marks. The circus settling into a small suburb outside of Milwaukee.

Autumn meant a death, so things could grow back new. Even after she'd returned without him, she could still hear him like a haunt in the quiet hours, in the unfilled minutes. Sometimes she wondered when his voice, all those things she'd learned to think, when would they go away? She didn't have any answers. But every day, she tried again. And in that way, she survived him.

Someday, she hoped . . . no, she *knew* . . . the days without him would out-number the days weighed down by him. Because her story was not his.

"I wonder who we would be," Odette suddenly said, "if we weren't given a Spark. Maybe someone else. Not us. What would that life look like?"

Odette's and Mauve's bare fingers curled with Rin's. They grounded each other. "I like this one," Rin said.

Mauve nodded. "The light hits the trees in a nice way," she agreed. "And the food is always good. And we're all here. Even the ones who . . . well, even Dad, I like to think." Mauve pulled out a bracelet. She looked at it. She screwed up her mouth. "I've been holding on to this," she said.

Rin took the bracelet; *not today,* it read. She'd forgotten all about it amid the hullaboo at the end of this summer. She felt a deep weight pull her down as it sat in her hand now, light as a feather. Grounding her back into this world.

Rin put it in her pocket. "We don't give up on the future," she said, looking out to the galaxy of colors in the trees. "But we can't give up on all this, either."

✳

There was much to do on that last show day. Breakfast, books to balance, winter quarters to prep, rehearsal, the final show itself, and well, Jo. Soon breakfast would be done, and Rin would be off to meet with their Dream-weaver.

But first, she sat with Odette, side by side on their old quilt, Odette's legs crossed and Rin leaning against the wall.

Odette had been very quiet since coming back from the black tents. Rin had never wanted Odette to know what it felt like to have the Circus King in her skull. But Odette had told her it wasn't the Circus King that had scared her.

Rin held her hand now. And Rin said, "I've been thinking. My love, you can take my age down—"

"What?" Odette said.

"A couple of decades, that's it," Rin said. "But that means you gotta meet me in the middle. We'll live a life, a real life, but no more pretending we aren't old. No more pretending we aren't young. We are who we are."

So Odette touched Rin. Rin's face grew young again. Her hair grew brown and auburn, full of bouncy curls. Her wrinkles smoothed, her body straightened, and there in her old same worn clothes sat a younger ringmaster, still old enough to have a few gray hairs but young enough to gain a few thousand tomorrows. She had forgotten how it felt to be right on the top of the mountain of her life.

"Will you still love me when I've got the wrinkles?" Odette asked.

Rin kissed her. "Always," she said.

Odette laughed. "And we're getting a dog."

"No," Rin said.

"A dog, Rin!" Odette said. "A big one."

"You're allergic."

"I'll use my Spark."

"To constantly fix your sinuses?"

"If it means I get a dog." Odette grinned mischievously. "I'm naming him Sparky."

Rin snorted and lost it. "Stop it," she said. "Oh my G-d." And they both broke into laughter. The sort of laughter that doesn't stop. And it lasted all the way through to lunchtime.

✳

The Ringmaster and Jo stood in another field, this one golden and red, as if it was on fire. Jo was quiet, and kept stealing looks at Rin, as if trying to see through Rin's skin to her heart, to see if all the wounds had closed up all right.

Rin wished she could see the same in Jo. With every day, the trench was further away from where they stood. But she knew that just because Jo was safe from Edward King, a soul had hurt another soul and healing took time.

Jo had time, now. They both did.

"Do you know what tomorrow is?" Rin asked Jo.

Jo shook her head. "Uh . . . Saturday? September eighteenth? Closing week? Something in retrograde? Your birthday? No, is it Mauve's birthday? Odette's? Whose birthday?!"

"It's a holiday called Yom Kippur," Rin said, shoving her hands into her velvet coat's pockets. Two little patches stood out against the ruby, a perfect mess. "According to Jewish tradition, the Book of Life is opened on Rosh Hashanah, which was last week. Tomorrow, the Book of Life closes for another year. And while that book is open . . . we can change our story. We can let go of the things we don't want, we can forgive ourselves and others and be forgiven for all the things that went wrong. We return to who we wish to be, who we once were."

"Teshuvah," Jo said. Rin looked to her. "What? I listen."

Soon, the long stark miles of prairie tufts would turn brown, because their time was waning. Books close. Finales are struck up, then the work lights pop on as the audience spills out.

But Rin didn't want it to ever end.

"So we have tonight's performance, and that's what we need to focus on," Rin said, not missing another beat. "You have grown a lot this past month."

Jo rubbed her own arm, cocking her head to look at her feet. Rin remembered the first performance after they'd come home from the nightmare that had swallowed Edward King whole, where at preshow she'd found Jo in the LQ car instead of the dressing room or warming up in the Back Yard. She'd asked her what the hell she was doing not in costume and lollygagging with a box of Cracker Jacks and the funny pages. Jo had just stared at her like she was speaking French.

"You . . . you *want* me to go out there again?" she had said incredulously. "After what I did?"

"*You* want to still go out there, after what *I* did?" Rin had asked.

Jo had trusted Rin enough to not try the bomb illusion again. But Rin agreed to let Jo put in a warning about the future; a more veiled fictionalized account of a what-if. That's what catharsis did well, warning, inspiring, without scaring. So Jo had shown a lone soldier, walking in a cloud of dust, tears streaming down his face. Her illusion would then grow around the soldier to show a war-torn, could-be-anywhere village, though with no visible corpses. Let the audience imagine it was somewhere they knew, somewhere they loved. Maybe then they would feel called to try and keep it safe. The scene would flicker in and out of a beautiful mountain Neverland; a what-could-be-instead. Rin scaffolded it with some narrative about the possibilities of tomorrow, and then they would move forward with whatever Mauve had tipped them.

Rin now cleared her throat. "I know you and Mauve have hit a rhythm of discussing things and leaving me out of it," she acknowledged.

"But I guess this morning, you foregoned that," Jo said.

"I don't think that's a word."

"Forgoed?"

"Even less of a word," Rin said. "But yes, I did speak to her. I think we've settled on what we need. It is, of course, still up to you what you will show in the final illusion."

Jo cleared her throat and readied her hands. Rin had wondered, when they got back from leaving awful people in awful pasts, if Jo would ever want to use her Spark again. Jo did. There were still nightmares. But the kid had also learned she could survive fear. She was stronger than anyone who would want to hurt her.

"All right," Jo said. "Give it to me."

Rin stepped back, and she folded her hands across the buttons of her red velvet coat. "Tonight, there is someone who must make a hard decision, and you need to help them see their future. This means, we need you to put together the best future you can think of. What would teshuvah look like? When the Book of Life closes, what should be written there?"

"Weird, but okay," Jo said. She closed her eyes. "Yeah, I know exactly what it would look like."

"Oh?"

"No war. No more Circus Kings. No more nightmares and no more dead people," Jo said, raising her hands.

"Let's not go defensively, with what it's *not*," Rin said. "Positively, what would it include?"

Jo took a breath in. "Peace," she said. "Family."

Then it came. So quickly, the easiest thing for her to create.

Jo conjured an old barn full of their old dogs who had died long ago. Or not long ago, if they took a minute to realize how fast time seemed to have slipped away when everything else was lost. But Rin could feel it had only been a few years, and the relief of seeing it again was a homecoming. She and Charles would sleep in the barn back in Marceline. It was their own little castle. The dogs protected them. The barn owl was their greatest foe. And the snakes. But they wouldn't bother the kids if they stayed out of the hay in the corner.

It was quiet out there. If they snuck outside in the middle of the night, the whole sky belonged to them, stars and all.

"Marceline," Rin said knowingly, walking into the illusion of the barn that felt so real. The sun seeped through the cracks in the wooden doors, illuminating the straw and dust. Like the spotlights during the show.

This place was just as magical.

"This is where Charles and I were happy," Jo said.

"That's the past," Rin said.

"I hope someday it's not," Jo said. "I don't know, I feel like everyone's got that place they're trying to get back to. One could say . . . teshuvahhhh."

Rin tousled Jo's hair. "That's not exactly what teshuvah means, but yes."

"I can be smart, you know," Jo said, sitting down on a hay bale. She *sat on the illusion.*

Rin looked up to the crossbeam, where Jo and Charles had written their names, alongside the names of their lost brother. There was his name: Jacob. Just as real as he once had been.

She touched the letters. And her hand made contact. Real wood, real grooves of the chiseled lines, and splinters brushed against her skin.

"You're getting stronger," Rin said. "I can touch your pictures now."

Jo nodded. "I've had a good teacher, huh?"

Rin smiled, feeling a thousand miles away.

"Hey," Jo said. "Can I ask who the someone is? What exactly is their decision? Because I don't think my barn is gonna help them."

"It will," Rin said, dropping her hand from the beam.

Jo watched her for a second. And Rin tried not to let her face fall, tried not to let on how much this hurt inside. It reminded her of the painting Jo had shown her during their first practice session, of her and Charles watching their brother leave through that door. The inevitability. The pain. No one ever learns how much love can hurt until the door shuts behind someone forever. Jo had loved her brother so much, it made her chest ache.

Rin's chest ached.

"Oh," Jo said, deflated. "I'm the person, aren't I?"

Rin nodded, not looking at her. She touched the beam ahead of her again.

"Well, fuck that." Jo stood up. "I'm not leaving. I just got here. You need me. I pulled my weight back with the black tents and all that."

"We might need you," Rin said, letting go of the carved names. Her hand fell to her side. Her black eyes looked right to Jo's. "But right now, you need to be safe. We've tried everything we can to stop the war. And we couldn't. And we don't."

Jo froze.

"And your brother . . . but you know about that already," Rin said. She looked to the straw at her boots. "I understand why you did what you did that night. It's why I have to do what I do."

"You're giving up after all," Jo said. "You can't give up."

"I'm not giving up," Rin said. "We're going to keep trying, if it kills me. But we're going to try from here, in the present. Try to move the needle in the ways humans and communities always have tried, before the Spark. But that doesn't mean we'll stop it. We may not change enough."

"You don't know that! Things can change!"

"They can," Rin said. "I don't know if I can save the world, but I know for certain that I can save you."

A silence rang through the sunlight of the barn.

But the illusion didn't fade. Jo needed it. Jo needed to feel its warmth, needed to remember what it was like to have a home.

"It's your decision," Rin said softly. Her thunderous roar was gone. Her voice sounded full of so many cracked edges. "If you want to stay with us, you can. But we will gladly transport you and Charles to a time that is safe."

"After the war?" Jo said.

"After this war," Rin said, "there is another war. And another war. And another. But there are . . . times of peace." She looked up to the rafters, looked up to where Jo had placed a bird's nest. "We went back to that city, Hiroshima. Decades after the war. There were buildings. The air was clean again. There were children and families. And we three walked along the river and we ate a nice meal and . . . and all was well." Rin shrugged. "At least in that moment, it was. Sometimes that's all we can look for, those moments, and hope that we have more and more of them as we work forward." Rin gave a sad smile. "I find solace in that. I have to."

Jo gritted her teeth, looking drained and pale green. "So you're gonna stick me in future Japan to sightsee while you and the circus march on?" she said. "You don't want me then, is that it? How about you sell us to the wagons then, at least you'd make a profit!"

"You will never go to the wagons, I promise," Rin said. "In the future, there are no more wagons. They're outlawed. There will be other horrors, but at least there is that. It is a start. All of this is a start."

There was another silence between the girl and the lion woman.

"I don't want you to go," Rin said.

"Then why do I have to go!"

"Because all the years and all the futures we saw with you staying here in the now, Charles never survives and sometimes you don't, either," Rin said. "Before I even met you, I saw you die. Things might heal after wars, but not everyone survives to see it. But more importantly . . . listen to me, please don't interrupt . . . but more importantly, you should go because you want to." She waved her hands to the beautiful barn around them. "Because this is the future you want. And you shouldn't wait for the future you want if you have the power to make it your present." She thought of Odette's soft smile, right when she woke up, in their bed with the worn-out quilt. She thought about her soft bare hands, her bright eyes, and all the joy they'd no longer delay.

Jo furiously shook her head. "No."

"I am not going to make you go," Rin said. "But the longer you stay here, the harder it will be to leave. And this place is a journey for you, it's not where you want to arrive. Look around, Jo, look at what you created."

"I'll never see any of you again."

"You could come back once in a while to do a special show, if you want. And of course I'll come visit you."

"Until one day you don't," Jo said. "Until one day, the war kills you and I wasn't there to stop it."

Rin stepped forward. She lifted her hand, and she placed it on Jo's cheek. Hot tears ran down Jo's face and into the creases of Rin's fingers. And when Jo looked up at Rin, she must have seen even quieter tears slowly streaking down the Ringmaster's face.

Rin wished that it didn't have to hurt to feel this much.

"Your brother will live," Rin said. "And you will live. And in that way, everything will be all right."

She let go of Jo. She unbuttoned her coat. She let her shoulders free, then her arms, then her hands.

Rin held the red velvet in her fingers. And then she said, "Turn around."

Jo did so. Rin's nose was stuffed. Rin's heart was breaking. Just when she thought she didn't have anything left to break.

Slowly, Rin slipped the soft silk of the insulated coat up Jo's wrist, then wrapped it around her body. Almost in a dream, she buttoned the bright black buttons. Rin fixed the sleeves.

Jo turned around, the velvet coat in place.

Rin looked at her like she wore a gown. She gave a smile to Jo, unconditionally proud of her.

"There we are," Rin said, rubbing Jo's shoulders. "It fits well enough. Get some more meat on your bones and you'll grow into it."

The show must go on.

✳

The Dreamweaver's last show was peppered with iridescent blue butterflies. Mauve sang a new song, a beautiful story about meeting an old friend after a long journey. The clowns hit their stride again, and Tina hit all her marks. Jess beamed as they rode Tina along the hippodrome. Agnes's laugh, Yvanna's flames, Ming-Huá's recitation, Boom Boom's gruff jokes, all the ensemble in their leaps and pirouettes . . . it culminated with Mr. Calliope's music and Maynard's tech, and Rin saw a whole soul made of small parts, an orchestra singing with a thousand notes. The circus was all of them together.

Odette the Trapeze Swinger flew through the sky, curling her body and reaching her hands out to the thin air, sparkling in the spotlight.

Rin held her as she descended. And she stroked her cheek as Odette put her arms around her waist. No one in the audience said a word. It was a start, a small act of courage.

Then it was over. The finale came and went in a fever. Big moments sometimes are so big, the brain can't comprehend them. The moment comes and goes, a shock to the system. All the work of the summer now a wrap, now just a memory found on some souvenir bills, dust settling on the ground as the audience slowly left through the midway lights.

Rin watched the crowd dissipate; all those folks, walking into the future. She felt herself want to cry. Life would still go on, a hundred years from now. But not everyone would be there. The shadows of the lost would cover the living, like they always did. There was no sense to how many people were going to get lost.

Then it was just the circus folk, standing in the ring under the cooling lights, the ghost light still burning and no trace of spectators except for the trail of popcorn buckets they left behind.

Mauve was the only one who was smiling, holding a cup of coffee in her hand. "I decided today was the day I was going to try this," she said gleefully. "I was tired of waiting." No one else followed her line of joy. But she gave a sigh. "I like not waiting for joy."

Everyone hugged one another, signing each other's bills and tousling each other's hair. Usually it was a happy day, the closing, the striking of the last show of a season. But this season had been different, and the two kids who had made this place shine would be leaving. For now.

But Charles wasn't having it.

"I've already told you," Charles said to Ringmaster, tears running down his face. "I'm not going. I've come to say goodbye to my sister, but I am not leaving."

Jo stared at him. "Charles, what the hell? We have to. You're gonna die if we don't go."

"Then I die!"

Odette leaned in closer to her and Mauve. "Uh," she muttered out of the corner of her mouth, "maybe you want to spoil your surprise so he'll go?"

Mauve elbowed Odette. "Don't ruin the surprise, I worked hard for that surprise."

"I want a say in what happens to me," Charles said. "I have lived my life for you, Jo. You are my sister. And I will always love you. But I have to live for me." He looked to Kell. He took hold of Kell's arm. "Jo, I'm happy here."

This was a part of growing up, Rin knew. But Rin looked to Mr. Weathers and Mr. Weathers stared at his kid. "Kell?" Like Mr. Weathers hadn't been aware of this boy on Kell's arm until this very second.

Kell shook his head. "No, no no," he said. "I get a say in this, too, don't I? No." He took Charles by the shoulders, and he looked at him, really looked at him. "If you stay, you will die."

"And if you stay, *you* will die," Charles said.

"His death is nowhere written in stone," Mauve said. "Not like yours."

"That's not fair!" Charles said.

"I trust them," Kell said. "And do you trust me?"

Rin looked to Jo. Jo watched her brother carefully, like looking at a picture she'd seen a thousand times but never understood. Charles was stoic. Charles only saw Kell. Nothing else. Charles nodded, his thick hair falling into his eyes. Wasn't he just a kid a few months ago? Now the way he looked at Kell was like he'd grown a thousand years in just a summer.

He wasn't the only one.

"This isn't the end," Kell said. "I'll come back for you. I'll come visit. But I need you alive, Charles."

Maybe Rin should spoil the surprise. But honestly, it wouldn't make any difference. Charles loved Kell. Rin knew nothing could tear him away from where Kell was.

Mr. Weathers watched his son closely. Rin saw Bernard in Mr. Weathers's soft eyes, she saw her mother's pain in the way he wrung his hands.

"Will they be safe, where they're going?" Mr. Weathers asked quietly, his voice sounding like hoarse gravel. "They can all be together and no one will bother them?"

Mauve nodded. "They'll be safe."

"Go with him," Mr. Weathers said. These words came from an open heart. "Go on, son. Go with them."

Kell looked to his father, dumbfounded. "Pops."

"You three," Mr. Weathers said, "will need each other. Go, Kell. Please."

Kell took Charles's hand. His warm eyes beat something back. Tears. Joyful or sad or both, Jo couldn't tell. But Charles would not be alone, and neither would Kell. It was the sacrifice Mr. Weathers would make for them.

The hardest part of loving a kid is when they have to go out on their own. But that was sort of the point all along; to get to the point where they didn't need you anymore.

Charles and Kell held hands. Jo touched them both on the shoulder. Odette and Mauve took Jo's shoulders. And then Odette reached out for Rin.

53

THE RINGMASTER

They stood in a green field, a blue sky above. There was a big lake next to a farmhouse. A barn on the other side of the field on the end of a stone path stood sturdy in front of the sunrise, with sunflowers planted all around its frame.

"Kell," Charles breathed. Rin could hear in his voice that his heart was a little lighter. "I know this place."

Rin didn't like endings.

"Jo," he said, "it looks like Marceline."

There hadn't been enough time with them. Only a few months. It had gone too fast.

"It is Marceline. And it's yours," Mauve said. "We bought the deed to the land."

"Oh my God! This lake is ours!" In awe, Charles stumbled ahead, through the grass, and then he ran to the lake. Kell followed, his wings spreading over the prairie waves of grass.

Jo lingered behind a little. Rin looked down to her. Jo was smiling, but she wasn't moving forward.

"You better come back," Jo said to the woman standing beside her.

"I will," Rin said. "As long as I'm around."

"I'll expect you for breakfast then," she said.

Rin laughed. "You always fight me on breakfast."

"So dinner then," Jo said.

"That's more like it," Rin said. Mauve parted from the cluster, walking along the stone path to explore the barn. Odette squeezed Rin's hand and also stepped away. Jo watched them go. But Rin stepped closer.

"Now," Rin said, as Jo flipped her hair out of her face and locked eyes with the Ringmaster, waiting. Rin wanted to never forget how Jo looked in this moment, a short little girl . . . no, not a girl anymore . . . she was growing up. She was a Dreamweaver. "Now," she tried again, clearing her throat. "I have three questions before I leave."

"Questions? Okay?"

Rin watched Charles jump into the lake. He gave a squeal of joy. "Are you here of your own free will?"

Jo nodded. "Yes."

"Do you understand that this is your life now and it won't always be easy, working on a farm in the Midwest?"

Jo nodded. "Yes."

"All right," Rin said, and her eyes wandered back to Jo. Rin's coat was so big around Jo's shoulders. Jo should have looked silly. But Rin felt so much pride, so much love in the way she wore it well.

"Someday," Rin said, "Mauve, Odette, and I won't be able to lead the circus anymore. And it still might not be safe for everyone. On that day, I'll send them all here. Will you keep them safe for me?"

Jo gave a small laugh. She seemed to be eaten up by the coat now. But the way Rin looked to her, these words weren't a possibility or an estimation. These words would happen for certain.

"You won't be alone," Rin said. "Kell and Charles will be by your side. And you will find others along the way, who need to be found. But—"

"Yes," Jo said. She said it fast and strong; she said it because she meant it.

With that word, Rin felt her edges smooth. She relaxed her shoulders, she unfolded her arms, and there was a small moment of peace in the air between her and Jo.

This moment, where they could just stand here under the sun.

"Keep up your Spark. And never forget how dark it was," Rin said. "Never stop walking toward the light. Never forget we are still fighting. But," she said, "never forget you deserve the happiness and hope you now have."

"And you'll do the same?" Jo said, and she nodded back to Mauve and Odette.

Rin looked to the two women waiting. And she smiled. Really smiled. "I'll see you in a few hours then."

"So that means for you, I'll see you in a few years," Jo said. "This isn't goodbye, though."

"Well, of course it's not goodbye," Rin said. "Circus people never say good-bye."

"Right," Jo said. She paused. "See you on down the road?"

Rin tousled Jo's hair. Jo jumped into her arms for one more hug. Rin's heart melted. She never wanted to let go. She never would.

✳

The morning waned. The sun rose. Odette and Rin stood beside each other, on the edge of the field, watching the kids splash and swim and scream and laugh. They held hands, Odette resting her soft head on Rin's sturdy shoulder.

"Ready to go home?" Rin shouted out to an approaching Mauve.

Mauve, wild mulberries in her hand, sauntered over to Rin and Odette as she popped a couple in her mouth. "I'm glad this is the future we found. I like this one. It's scary, and it's hard. But it's my favorite."

Rin swallowed, bringing in Mauve for a hug with her free arm. There the three stood, a painting of three women side by side, surrounded by sunflowers and lush grass and blue sky. G-d, that sky. It was still a clear blue, like an ocean reaching out to welcome sailboats back to shore.

Rin said, "So this future is happy?"

"I don't know," Mauve said. "But I like that we are trying."

Odette took their hands. "This moment," she said. "This moment is happy. Right now."

Jo wouldn't see them leave. They were quiet about it, coming in and out, to and from a place with discretion like always. One moment, they were there. The next, it was like they'd never been. Rin knew it was natural. They had stood behind Jo, and now Jo stood on her own.

Let her jump from the bank and into the lake, let her lie on her back in the cool water. Let her see the sky and think of all the things she could now do.

Let her paint fireworks in the summers and candlelight in the winters. These things were not glamorous, they were not loud. But they were powerful.

In that space between there and here, then and now, Rin and her family flew through time. One day, Jo would leave the farm. One day, Rin's circus would face terrible times. One day, there would be darker places, fearsome spaces, days where they would feel the weight of the world on their backs, straining their necks to see the light ahead.

As the shadows of a trapeze swinger, a nightingale, and a Ringmaster would pass from the ballyhoo spots, the unkillable devil, the angel man, and the Dreamweaver would enter the ring. Jo would be the one to wear the coat, lead the parade, through the future Rin would not see.

True courage comes when there is nothing we can do to stop the darkness, but we still hold the torch for those who must walk the hardest paths. Ain't that right, Bernard?

But today? When Rin, Odette, and Mauve landed back in the present, the sky's twilight gave way to the stars, constant bright things through the night. The circus below on the ground sounded with the hustle and bustle of its last night of a season.

Joy was here.

"All right," Rin said. "All over and out."

The three Sparks stepped onto the midway, and together, they walked home.

*

ACKNOWLEDGMENTS

This book is made of small acts of love and a million wishes. So my first acknowledgments are going to be longer than the average bear.

First, the reason this book happened in the first place is all J. You are my heart, the once-in-a-thousand-years kind of love. You are the one who believed in me, who found Stonecoast, paid the application fee, proofread all my query letters, held me all the times I sat on my bed staring at my laptop, and told me I could do it. This book, and all the ones that follow, are stories woven with the love you gave me. I hope you like the circus I made for us.

Thank you to the best agent ever, Rena Rossner, who saw this quirky little circus book and believed in it. She is so patient, so kind, and so smart. You taught me so much, and I'm so honored to work with you.

Thank you to Lindsey Hall, who is an amazing editor and a brilliant human being. Our conversations were some of my favorites through the pandemic; we just click in our view of the world, the weird things we think are funny, and this story. Lindsey, you saw what this book could be, and you kept teaching me and pushing me until I saw it, too. I'm forever grateful to you, and I'm so lucky to work with you.

A massive thank you to everyone who worked on this book. Publicists Caro Perny and Jocelyn Bright. Marketing genius Isa Caban. Cover artist and designer with an incredible vision for Rin's magical circus, Katie Klimowicz. Artist Shelby Rodeffer. Production editor Jeff LaSala. Copy editor Ed Chapman. Assistant editor Aislyn Fredsall. Proofreader Mary Louise Mooney. Cold reader Lauren Hougen. The sensitivity readers, including Anah and Ennis. And everyone at Tor who believed in this. To Rachael, for being my writer sister through this project. To Bryanna, my best friend who, when I called to tell you, you said, "Are you pregnant?" and I said, "No, it's the other thing," and then you screamed, "A BOOK! SHUT UP!" To Emlyn, Cy, Peter, Karen,

Erin, AJ, Celeste, Charlotte, and all of Wonder Woman Dumpster Fire and Estes Park Writing Retreat. You all are my family and a home in a tumultuous world. Thank you to Ted and Annie Deppe for their poetry and their genuine kindness. You took an interest in me and treated me like a professional. Thank you to Guy on Bike and the rest of my family at Stonecoast, who picked up this very lost, very broken girl and said, "Come on, we've got you." So that means a deep, *deep* thank you to our professors, especially Nancy Holder and James Patrick Kelly, who gave their time and hearts long after I graduated. Stonecoast was my Windy Van Hooten's.

Thank you, Mom, for buying me that notebook when I was nine and telling me to fill it up with stories. I still have it. It's under my bed. Also, Mom was there for me whenever I had an agrarian Midwestern-related question. Thank you, Dad, for driving me out to Colorado Springs and keeping me in Chicago and showing me Estes Park. Thank you, Gramma; I know from the other side, you're able to see this book and how it's because of you. Thank you, Bob, a real-life Bernard, for literally everything you've given us. Thanks to Dylan and Dominic, for listening to my very first long story night after night. To my cousin Alex, for buying me that *Walking Dead* comic book and being the first person to call me an author. To my oldest friend, Becca Savoie. To Sawyer and Indi, you two are beautiful and I am so proud to be your aunt. To Andy, Lilly, Oliver, Rowan, Asher, Aiden, Nora, and Quentin; my beautiful niblings. And to Jo, who I have not yet met, but honey if you made it, this book was written because I missed you and you had my heart before I even saw you.

To Jen Finstrom, for being a constant when nothing else was constant, who read my shitty shit for ten years, and because I can't structure my emails to her properly, gave me an idea for an important twist. To Heather, Michael, Laura, Patrick, Gabi, Gabby, Dani, Lenya, and all of my Chicago friends. To my college roommates who treated my writing like it was something real, especially Paige, who spent an entire freshman year sitting in coffeehouses and college quads and L trains teaching me how to write a book.

To Wil, for teaching me kindness and courage. You seemed to see everything while the rest of us were very lost, and you stepped into black circus tents so I wouldn't be there alone. A Spark went out in the world when we lost you.

To my high school English teachers, and to Miss Armstrong, who was the first teacher who took me seriously, in seventh grade. To my DePaul professors at The Theatre School and in the English department, especially Dr. Rinehart and Don Ilko. To Matt, Gina, Zedeka, and the Nebraska Writers Collective for being a good deed in a weary world and always believing this book would arrive. To Fran Sillau and the Circle Theatre for supporting and inspiring so many Sparks in so many people. To Tracy Iwersen and the Rose Theater of my childhood for being my safe haven, my own welcoming home of misfit toys like me. And to my students. I hope you understand me a little better from this book. I hope you know I'm so proud of all of you.

To Sarah Pinsker, for believing in me. To Sally Weiner Grotta, for feeling like family from so far away and being willing to chat into the night about religion and life and all the things in between. To John Wiswell, all of the Zoom Players, and everyone in the science fiction and fantasy community who I look up to and who took time to teach me something important. Even if it was small and you don't remember it, I do. Sometimes the smallest things said at a conference or a gesture of kindness means the world.

To Charlie Finlay, who was the first one to take a chance on me.

To K. A. Applegate, for showing me how amazing books can be. To Stephen Chbosky, for taking time to talk to me in 2008 (I did it, Mr. Chbosky!). And to James Horner, who I never got to meet and who I never will get to meet; your music is what I hear when I write. May your memory be a blessing.

Thank you, Crystal, for seeing me.

To the community and clergy of my temple, a congregation I am so proud to be a part of. To Katie, Emmy, Jamie, Bryan, and Dani Howell for opening your home to us (and an extra special thank you to Dani for holding my hand through the last two weeks of the final draft). To my dear friends Ada, Tiffany, Carson, Mardra, Marcus, Cecilia, Joey, Brandi, Jeremy, Isa, Annette, Alan, Beau, Caulene, Hayley, Caitlin, Melissa, and so many others who over the years supported J and me, paid for a meal here and there, covered groceries, and helped us keep things afloat as we dared to try something ridiculous. And so many thanks to Drew Dillon, who helped us get to the circus when it came to town.

Thank you to Mary Fan, for helping me understand aerial arts. Thank you to CY Ballard for your assistance with costuming. Thank you to Alisan Funk from Stockholm University of the Arts and Ken Hill from Omaha Circus Arts who took time to talk to me about circus and its history and culture. Huge thank you to the Watkins History Museum in Lawrence, Kansas, for answering so many circus questions and directing me toward the open field where the circus would have stood. Big shout-out to the Durham Museum in Omaha, Nebraska, for your preservation of the train cars and allowing a five-year-old girl to climb all over the insides of a caboose. Thank you to the Museum of Science and Industry in Chicago for your very *very* old circus exhibit that somehow has not turned to dust. Thank you to Mike Ziemba and the Watson Steam Train and Depot in Missouri Valley, Iowa. A huge thank you to Denise Chapman, who is the best director I had the honor to learn from, and she took a phone call during her commute so I could ask her a question about the energy circle she taught me. A shout-out to Beaufield Berry for her play *Red Summer,* and all the history she writes into her work. And thank you to University of Nebraska Omaha's LGBTQIA+ archives, that preserved an old chandelier that used to hang inside one of the city's first gay bars.

When it came to reading, some of the amazing history books I read included the standouts *Women of the American Circus, 1880–1940* by Katherine H. Adams and Michael L. Keene and *One Summer 1927* by Bill Bryson. Weirdly enough, the research book that hit me the hardest had nothing to do with circuses or the 1920s; Samantha Allen's *Real Queer America* pushed me through my final revision, and it also helped me feel not so alone here in Nebraska.

And finally, thank you to the trapeze artist in Iowa, sometime early in the millennium in the sweltering July heat. It was a dusty little circus in a small red-and-white tent between two roller coasters. The spotlight caught you and the dust as you swung above like something otherworldly. I knew I'd write about you someday, because you were made of magic.